ALL THE
FEELS

OLIVIA DADE

PIATKUS

PIATKUS

First published in the US in 2021 by Avon Books,
An imprint of HarperCollins Publishers
First published in Great Britain in 2021 by Piatkus

1 3 5 7 9 10 8 6 4 2

Copyright © 2021 by Olivia Dade

The moral right of the author has been asserted.

A CIP catalogue record for this book
is available from the British Library.

ISBN 978-0-349-42798-0

Printed and bound in Great Britain by Clays Ltd, Elcograf S.p.A.

Papers used by Piatkus are from well-managed forests
and other responsible sources.

Piatkus
An imprint of
Little, Brown Book Group
Carmelite House
50 Victoria Embankment
London EC4Y 0DZ

An Hachette UK Company
www.hachette.co.uk

www.littlebrown.co.uk

To all the little girls who learned to stay quiet and not take up space in the world. May you find your inner harpies and demand your due, at long last.

ALL THE
FEELS

1

"NEXT TIME YOU GET IN A BAR FIGHT, DON'T BOTHER COM-
ing back to the set, asshole," Ron shouted. "Do you even *realize*
what you've done? That kind of juvenile—"

By this point, the rant had entered—Alex craned his neck to
catch a glimpse of Ron's Rolex—its tenth minute. And counting.
The amount of blustering tedium the *Gods of the Gates* showrunner
could pack into such a short span of time was impressive, truly.

Alex would applaud if he weren't too busy fighting both a yawn
and his desire to nut-punch his boss.

Ron's nostrils flared with each harsh exhalation, but he made
an attempt to lower his voice. "You're lucky we only assigned you
a minder. Legally, given the amount of negative publicity you've
generated with your drunken stupidity, we had several avenues of
financial and professional recourse available to us, including . . ."

The showrunner was still speaking, but Alex had stopped listening. Instead, he was studying the woman sitting approximately
five feet to Ron's left.

Sharp features, including a beaky, crooked nose. Bright eyes.
Very round body, with comparatively skinny limbs. Short as hell.

His new nanny looked like a bird.

A silent one, though. Not a chirp to be heard, despite the advent
of dawn.

As soon as Ron got word of the events that had transpired overnight, he'd demanded a meeting first thing in the morning. Even though Alex had left the *Gates* set near midnight, and departed the local jail's holding cell maybe an hour ago. He'd barely had time to take a shower and grab an apple by the hotel's front desk before returning to work.

The three of them could have met in a private trailer, but the showrunner preferred public humiliation. So they'd gathered outdoors, near a ragged stockade, where hundreds of Alex's coworkers could conceivably overhear his disgrace, and so could she.

This pale-cheeked stranger. Whoever she was. *What*ever she was.

His eyes were bloodshot, his right eyelid swollen, his vision blurry. If he squinted in the early-morning fog, that lank, ash-brown hair ruffling around the woman's soft jaw might as well be feathers.

Yes, definitely a bird. But what kind, what kind . . .

Maybe an albatross? It certainly worked on a metaphorical level.

No, albatrosses were too long and narrow for the likes of her.

Once Ron had begun his lecture, she'd perched on a makeshift bench several feet away from both men. Quiet and still, she sat silhouetted before the chaos of their battlefield set as it sprawled along the Spanish shore. Yet somehow, even amid the large-scale staged destruction and ceaseless bustle of extras and crew members, she stood out in sharp relief. Incongruously small in stature, if not circumference. Calm. Avian.

Ron was still railing at him—something about *contractual obligations* and *my cousin Lauren Clegg* and *unacceptable conduct for an actor on my show* and *bond company will pull our insurance*, blah blah blah—and, sure, Alex was furious at the reprimand and his allotted punishment and the way no one had asked him what actually happened in that bar, not a single soul, but—

His paid minder, evidently an unfortunate relative of Ron's, looked like a fucking *bird*.

This whole discussion wasn't merely enraging. It was—

"Ridiculous." Alex snorted, sweeping his arm to indicate the woman on the bench. "This bird-woman barely comes up to my chest. How is she supposed to stop me from doing whatever I damn well please? Do you intend for her to cling to my ankle like an oversized bracelet?"

He considered the matter. It would make his workouts challenging, but not impossible.

Ron smirked briefly. "She may be ridiculous, but she's in charge." After casting a sidelong look at his cousin, he turned his attention back to Alex. "You'll do what Lauren says until the series finale airs. Until then, she'll accompany you wherever you—"

Wait. Alex hadn't meant to call *her* ridiculous. More the idea she could effectively keep him out of trouble for months on end.

Ron was talking, talking, talking. "—any time you leave the set or your home. Is that clear?"

Well, no. In his preoccupation with . . . Lauren, was it? . . . Alex hadn't paid much attention to Ron's various pronouncements and edicts.

In theory, a working actor who intended to remain working should hang on his showrunner's every word. But why change his modus operandi after over seven years of continuous, lucrative, once-happy-now-torturous employment?

Even if Ron weren't one of the most tiresome and off-putting humans in the television industry—which was saying something—Alex might still have trouble following along. His brain was a radio that either switched channels frequently or remained set on the same one for far too long, regardless of what he wanted, and the frequency it chose wasn't always the frequency he was supposed to be tuned in to.

That said, Ron and his fellow showrunner, R.J., *were* tiresome pricks, which meant their spots on Alex's dial were particularly patchy and problematic. Over the years, Alex had grown very skilled at hiding any lapses in attention as they spoke.

Today, he wasn't bothering.

"Nope. It's not clear at all," Alex told Ron with a grin that stretched his face painfully. "To my absolute despair, I missed most of what you just said. My heartfelt apologies."

As the syrupy sarcasm of Alex's faux regret registered, Ron's jaw worked. Lauren merely continued to watch them both, her odd, asymmetrical face expressionless.

Marcus, Alex's best friend, would call this *pushing the damn limits* and tell him to bite his tongue and consider the consequences of further insubordination.

Play the film to the end, he'd urge. *What happens if you don't change the script?*

They'd reached the final week of shooting for their series, which meant it was too late to fire Alex, but there could be other consequences. Fines. A smear campaign that would make future jobs hard to find. Even retaliation in the editing room, although Alex couldn't imagine how his character's arc could be more comprehensively ruined than it already was.

He should behave. He would.

Mostly.

"Perhaps you could sum up the situation with greater brevity?" He bent down and produced his phone from its hidden pocket in the quiver at his feet. "I'll take notes this time."

Ron's face turned vaguely purplish, but that was it. The best Alex could do, given the mingled rage and despair and exhaustion incinerating his impulse control. Even Marcus's admonitions couldn't save him, not entirely.

Which was, again, why this whole plan—what he'd heard of it, anyway—was ridiculous. If his best friend's urgings and his own self-interest couldn't keep him out of trouble, how could one improbably short, round woman accomplish the task?

Besides, if they'd actually *asked* him what happened in that bar fight, they would know why he'd brawled and why he'd do the exact same thing under similar circumstances, consequences and minders be damned. Also why he hadn't regretted his black eye or his torn knuckles for a single second.

Good thing his character, Cupid, was supposed to be injured during the climactic battle sequence anyway.

"Go on," he said cheerily. "I'm listening now."

Ron managed not to lose his shit again. Instead, a vein throbbing hard at his left temple, he took a minute to calm himself before speaking.

"From now until the show airs its final episode, Lauren will accompany you anytime you either leave the set or your home," he finally gritted out. "If she can't hack it, you'll immediately receive another minder instead, so don't bother trying to get her to quit. Lauren may be ridiculous, as you say, not to mention joyless, but you won't like her replacement, I can guarantee that."

Alex tilted his head.

That was intriguing. Was his Understudy Nanny particularly vicious? Or odiferous? Or maybe—

"No more bad publicity." The showrunner's pale eyes speared into his, commanding his attention. "Or you'll suffer the full legal and professional consequences outlined in your contract. Do you understand now? Or shall I involve our lawyers in the explanation?"

Alex tapped out a note to himself on his phone. *Choice of joyless*

*bird-woman or smelly murderer as babysitter, now until show finishes
airing. More trouble => lawyers. Ron = serial killer eyes.*

"Is anyone staying in your guesthouse right now?" the showrunner asked.

Looking up, Alex found that disconcerting stare still fixed on
him and answered without thinking. "No. My friend Faroukh
booked a series, so he left last—"

Oh. Oh, fucking hell.

"Then Lauren will move in as soon as you two return to L.A.
The show will pay you fair market value for the rental on a monthly
basis." Ron's smile was smug. "Very convenient for everyone involved."

Alex's jaw hurt, and he flexed it. "And you expect this arrange-
ment to last nine months?"

"Hard to say. But if it doesn't, R.J. and I have already chosen
our course of action." With an impatient flap of his hand, Ron
gestured for his relative to stand. "Do what my cousin tells you, or
else. Lauren, go shake his hand."

Up close, Alex could estimate her height more accurately.
Around five feet, give or take an inch. And at this distance, her
eyes were even more arresting. A clear, soft green with the slightest
hint of blue, they were her only feature an honest observer could
call pretty.

Her palm was ludicrously small, her grip firm as they shook
hands. If she'd taken offense at her cousin's blunt order or his description of her as ridiculous and joyless, she didn't show it.

Because Ron didn't seem inclined to do the job, Alex completed the social ritual.

"Please let me introduce myself." After he let go of her hand,
he swept her a mocking bow. "Alexander Woodroe, at your service.
Or, rather, at your command. For the next nine months, evidently."

"I know who you are," she said without a hint of a smile.

Her voice was unexpectedly low and rich, and he straightened abruptly at the sound of it.

I know who you are.

It was a simple statement.

It was also a condemnation.

No doubt Ron had told her plenty. But she didn't know Alex. She didn't know the first fucking thing about him, and neither did her asshole cousin. Yet there they stood, allied in their judgment of him and what he'd done.

Impotent fury crashed over him, and his self-control disappeared in the churn.

"So you do." As he looked into those clear, calm eyes, his lip curled in disdain. "Shall I call you Mistress Lauren, do you think? Or will Nanny Clegg do?"

THAT COULD HAVE *gone better*, Lauren thought, keeping her arms loose by her sides, her hands unclenched, her posture open.

She'd assumed Ron would speak to his star privately first and allow the actor's anger to dissipate before she met him, but no. Such consideration and discretion were beyond her cousin.

In retrospect, then, she should have skipped what she'd intended to be a simple acknowledgment of his fame and just claimed it was lovely to meet him. Which it wasn't, but he was hardly the first furious person she'd ever encountered, and she usually knew how to handle this sort of situation more skillfully.

After over a decade as an emergency services clinician, she'd better know.

"Please call me Lauren." In hopes of defusing the situation, she made certain her tone was calm and pleasant. "What would you prefer I call you? Mr. Woodroe? Alexander?"

Compared to evaluating incoming ER patients, ones who arrived amid mental health crises and often departed without necessary resources in place to help them survive, this job—this fraught moment—should be a cakewalk. It was both temporary and unlikely to result in trays flung at her head while security guards came rushing into the fray.

It was even less likely to leave her brokenhearted and dangerously close to the end of her mental and physical rope.

"Alex, I suppose." He cast a critical eye over her. "Is this your first day on set? Because I would have remembered seeing you before."

That was likely a veiled insult, one she didn't need to acknowledge. "I arrived over the weekend, so this is my third day on set. We must have been in different areas of filming before now, because I don't remember seeing you either."

And she would have, even hazy with jet lag on her first full day in Spain.

He was memorable. In a much better way than she was.

So was the entire, enormous set. As her exhaustion had eased and she was able to grapple with her surroundings more coherently, the network's brazen, high-stakes gamble on Ron and R.J. had left her increasingly agog. The head of an actual network had given men like *them* control over thousands of people and millions of dollars? Really?

Carry yourself with the confidence of a mediocre white man. Whenever she heard that phrase, she always, always thought of Ron.

No wonder the show went off the rails as soon as E. Wade's existing books had all been adapted. Once the showrunners had to forge ahead using their own ideas, everyone involved was screwed. Inevitably.

Still, the scope of the enterprise and the expertise of the actors and crew impressed the hell out of her. She wasn't a fan of the show or her cousin, but she'd readily admit that.

Alex drummed his fingers against his tunic-covered thigh, his quiver of arrows at his feet. "So tell me, Lauren, what would you do if—"

"I have to go," Ron interrupted. "I'll leave you two to get acquainted. Lauren, you'll stay in his trailer while he's working, and I reserved you the room connected to his at the hotel. Anywhere else he goes, you're with him, and you eat all meals together. Understood?"

As this was the fourth time she'd heard Ron's plan, she didn't especially need the peremptory reminder. He'd been a spoiled brat of a boy, convinced of his own genius and prone to teasing the most vulnerable children—including her—until they cried, and he evidently hadn't changed much.

"Yes," she said. "I understand."

Telling her parents about Cousin Ron's cruelty had only upset them and caused her mother to argue with Aunt Kathleen on the phone. Eventually, she'd spared everyone the distress and begun pretending she enjoyed her cousin's company, and now she was paying the price for her dishonesty.

While you're between jobs, you should go visit your cousin in Spain, her mother had said last month. *You and Ron used to get along so well, and you haven't seen him in years. Aunt Kathleen and I always hoped you two would be closer. She'll be hurt if you don't make the effort. Anyway, you could use a vacation, sweetheart.*

A vast understatement. Lauren had been desperate to get her sleep schedule back in order, and even more desperate to bask in the sun and simply *relax*. And after endless years of overtime— the ER was perennially understaffed when it came to therapists, especially for the overnight shift—she had plenty of savings. Enough to buy her a few weeks before she had to decide where to work next.

Enough to take a vacation. A long one.

During that much-needed vacation, she'd had zero desire to see Ron. But unless she had no other choice, she didn't disappoint her family. Or anyone, really.

So she'd driven to visit Ron the day she'd arrived in Spain, intending only a brief stop at this remote coastal town before she headed toward Barcelona. And then . . .

Then she was stuck. Because he needed help, and if she didn't provide that help, she'd be hearing about it from her parents and Aunt Kathleen.

Besides, she had her own reasons for taking the job.

"Good." Ron turned to Alex. "Show her where your trailer is before we start filming, and do what she says. The bad publicity ends now."

Her cousin strode away, and a small, irrational part of her wanted to spite him. To call him back and renege on her offer and free both herself and Alex, if only temporarily.

But Ron was offering an eye-popping salary and covering all her expenses—including the rent on her duplex back in North Hollywood—for months. All so she'd watch over one man, who, recent brawl and current fury notwithstanding, had the reputation of being charming enough, if somewhat reckless and overly blunt on occasion.

A delightful asshole, his costar Carah Brown had famously called him.

With the money she'd save watching over him, Lauren could take all the time in the world before she decided whether to return to the ER or join her friend's group practice. And what could be farther from an emergency room than the windswept coast of Spain or a television star's Hollywood Hills guesthouse?

So, yeah, she could handle Mr. Woodroe's anger, and she didn't care if he considered her ridiculous and ugly or thought she had a beaky, birdlike nose. Of course he was angry after being injured, jailed, and then dressed down in front of a stranger by his condescending asshole of a boss. And of course a man that beautiful—with thick hair a rich shade of golden brown, long enough to brush his collar and fall in front of his eyes if he didn't push it back; intense eyes the color of a rain cloud, still gorgeous despite all his bruising; handsome features accented by a neat beard; and an immaculately honed body—would disdain a woman like her.

Her nose *was* beaky. Also crooked from that incident her first month at the ER, when she hadn't ducked a tray quickly enough.

She was fat and short too, and she'd been mocked by people much more vicious than him. He'd called her ridiculous, and the word was apt. She'd certainly experienced plenty of ridicule in her life. She'd grown accustomed to it.

His contempt meant nothing to her. She'd do her damn job, and she'd do it well, no matter what he said.

She swiveled to face him. "You were asking me something when Ron interrupted."

"Um . . ." He was watching a gull pick at props left overnight on the battlefield, his brow creased in seeming concentration. "Oh, yes. Tell me, Lauren, what would you do if I wanted to go to another bar after work tonight?"

He meant to begin their work relationship with a test of her boundaries, then.

Fair enough. They might as well make those boundaries clear from the beginning. "Ron said no more bars, so I'd tell you to go to a sit-down restaurant or your hotel room instead."

"What if I went anyway?"

"I'd call Ron," she said without hesitation.

He barked out a laugh sharp as a scalpel. "You'd tattle on me?"

Nope. She wasn't taking that bait. "I'd do my job."

"What if I went to a club?"

"I'd go with you."

"What if I met a woman and we"—he raised his brows suggestively—"got acquainted in a dark corner?"

"As long as you didn't violate local indecency laws, I'd leave you alone, but keep you in sight."

By that point, he was looking less belligerent and more entertained. "If I did violate public indecency laws, what would you do then? Tackle me around my knees and slap a chastity belt on me?"

"I'd interrupt, and if you continued regardless, I'd call Ron."

At the mention of her cousin, Alex's incipient smile died.

"What if I decided to get rip-roaring drunk in my hotel room?" His chin jutted in her direction, its firmness evident even through his full beard. "What then, Nanny Clegg?"

"As long as you didn't cause a disturbance and weren't in medical danger, it wouldn't be my business. I'd leave you to it."

He paused. "What if I *were* in medical danger? You'd call Ron?"

"First, I'd call an ambulance or drive you to the hospital myself. Then, yes, I'd call Ron, because you'd be unlikely to show up for work the next day, and word of your stay in the ER might spread in the media. I'd also contact anyone who could help you defend yourself against Ron's subsequent retaliation." She frowned. What type of team did stars like him have, anyway? "You have an agent and a lawyer, right? What about a publicist? Or maybe an assistant?"

The sneer had bled away, replaced by a look she couldn't quite interpret.

"Whoever can advocate for you, you should probably give me

their numbers. Just in case." She lifted a shoulder. "Things happen, despite our best intentions."

He moved a step closer to her, his brow furrowed.

Funny. A man who, according to Ron, had been wasted enough to get into a bar fight only a handful of hours ago should still smell like alcohol.

He didn't. He smelled like generic hotel shampoo. And he didn't appear hungover either. Just injured and spent.

"I'll give you their information before we leave the set tonight." He cocked his head and studied her. "So . . . what happens now? Are we supposed to socialize in my trailer or hotel room whenever I'm not working or sleeping?"

"From what I understand—"

"I'll braid your hair if you'll braid mine, Lauren." His gray eyes were sharp on hers in the warm morning light. "We can tell ghost stories by flashlight. Maybe toast a few marshmallows over the hotel room radiators."

He was mocking her.

She shook her head. "I have no intention of socializing with you. I'm not your entertainment."

He swayed back a bit, and if she didn't know better, she would have sworn that look on his face was . . . hurt?

No. That didn't make sense.

"Ah. I see." The cynical twist to his smile had returned. "You've assumed the role of sanctimonious bore instead. No doubt it's the part you were born to play."

That time, there was no hint of humor in the insult. It was a jab meant to wound.

No *delightful*. Just *asshole*.

She gazed into the distance for a moment, allowing the faint sting to fade before she responded.

"I apologize." His words were unexpected and abrupt. Raw with exhaustion. When she looked back at him, he was frowning. "You didn't deserve that. I'm sorry."

He sounded sincere. Surprisingly so.

She nodded in acceptance of his apology, and he let out a slow breath.

"I have no good excuse." His jaw worked. "I'm just . . ."

She waited, but he didn't continue.

Instead, he simply sighed and gestured to their left. "Why don't I show you to my trailer?"

INT. VENUS'S PALACE ON MT. OLYMPUS – DUSK

PSYCHE lies on a low couch, eyes closed and unresponsive, edging closer to death with every hour she sleeps. When CUPID enters and sees his beloved, he rushes toward her, distraught. VENUS raises a commanding hand, and he immediately stops. From behind Venus, JUPITER steps into the room, his expression fierce with rage and determination.

VENUS

I told you not to come.

CUPID

She is my wife, Mother. My heart. Let me wake her. Please.

Venus glides toward him, sneering.

VENUS

Your heart is *mine*. Your loyalty is *mine*. Your eternal existence is *mine*.

She grips his chin in one hand, squeezing until his face twists in pain.

VENUS

The life of a single mortal girl matters not. Your place is at our side, fighting our foes: Juno, that treacherous bitch, and her allies.

CUPID

If I fight alongside you, will you promise to spare
Psyche? To save her?

*Jupiter strides toward Cupid, livid, and backhands
his grandson, who crumples to his knees.*

JUPITER

A puny, mewling demigod does not question the will
of all-powerful Jupiter. Your precious mortal will be
dead before this battle ends, a fitting punishment for
your defiance.

*Cupid weeps. Venus clasps him to her bosom and dries
his tears.*

VENUS

Do you understand, my son? Do you now understand what
obedience means?

CUPID

I do. I will obey.

*Cupid strides from the room without another glance
at Psyche.*

2

THE FIRST TIME ALEX ENCOUNTERED THE CONCEPT OF "extra," he'd related to it immediately, on an almost visceral level. *Oh, yes, that's what I am.* Much like the moment his mother had explained what his diagnosis of ADHD meant.

Not everyone appreciated his personality, but so be it. Not everyone appreciated deep-fried turkey on Thanksgiving either, and that was their loss. If he was congenitally, delightfully "extra," however, the dour woman across the room was the opposite.

Nondescript tee. Cardigan. Dark jeans. No jewelry or makeup, and no natural color in that pallid face. Even her eyebrows were relatively pale. Her avian qualities—her sharp features, her short, round frame—were the only memorable things about her appearance, really, other than those eyes.

It might help if she actually said something. *Anything.*

But she didn't. If at all possible, she didn't even acknowledge him.

"Hey, Lauren, pass me that medicine ball," he called out to her. "The one to your left."

She answered without looking up. "Nope."

An hour ago, she'd settled herself on a weight bench in the hotel's empty fitness room, eyes on her e-reader and not him. Even though he was both sweaty and shirtless, states which—he had been informed by trustworthy sources—showed him to best advantage and reliably drew the attention of anyone attracted to men.

Huh. Maybe—

"Hey, Lauren, are you into dudes? Like, at all?" He raised his arms over his head in a luxuriant stretch, then flexed his biceps appealingly, in hopes the incentive might induce her to raise her head.

Again, not a single glance upward. "Not your business."

Half a dozen lunges. A handful of burpees. All his athletic prowess and his carefully honed body, displayed *right there* in front of her. And . . .

Nothing. Nada.

"Hey, Lauren." This time he waited for a response, banking on her inherent politeness.

She finally raised her gaze from her e-reader, head tilted in inquiry, and he basked in the smug glow of victory.

"I once starred in a movie where my love interest was a mime, and my costar spoke more than you." He did a few jumping jacks, as long as he had her attention. "Just FYI."

Her voice was patently unimpressed. "Because she wasn't really a mime. She was an actor."

He frowned at her. "I meant she spoke more on camera."

"Then she wasn't a very good mime."

She returned her attention to her book, and he huffed in displeasure. Normally, any mention of his most unmitigated disaster of a movie provoked lively discussion. But, of course, even *Mimes and Moonlight* couldn't do the trick this time. Not when the woman at the other end of the conversation was a blank wall in human form.

After some over-the-counter painkillers and a good meal from craft services, he'd gotten over the worst of that morning's rage. At least, the portion of it directed toward her. One good midday nap in his trailer later—while she sat on the too-hard couch, phone in hand, and said not a word—and he was ready to admit that her newfound, near-constant presence in his life wasn't actually her fault. People needed jobs, and he couldn't blame her for accepting her cousin's offer, despite the profound dickishness of said cousin.

To put up with Ron's obvious disdain for her, she must need the money very, very badly.

He frowned again.

"Hey, Lauren, if you ever need a loan or something, let me know," he said as he positioned himself on the thick blue mat for push-ups.

With that, he had her attention entirely. Setting her e-reader on the floor beside her, she stared at him with her brow crinkled.

"You met me this morning." Each word contained an entire universe of precise disapproval. Or . . . maybe not disapproval, but something close to it. Confusion? Suspicion? "This past hour is the lengthiest interaction we've ever had."

He paused with his arms fully extended, bracing his weight. "And?"

"And you just offered to loan me money." She enunciated very clearly. "You don't know me well enough for that, Alex."

He tried to shrug while in push-up stance, with only limited success. "I disagree."

Her reaction that morning, when he'd asked what she would do if he were in medical danger, told him enough about her character. She didn't *want* him to get into trouble. She wasn't rooting for his failure and punishment.

None of this was personal, and she had a sense of honor.

Thus: loan. *Loans*, plural, as necessary.

He began to clap between each push-up, considering the matter. It was possible such situations explained why his savings and retirement accounts weren't quite as robust as they could have been. Or so Marcus regularly informed him. Then there was the money he sent his mom every month, and all the charities that depended on his contributions, and the friends he allowed to stay rent-free in his guesthouse when they were between jobs.

Although he was apparently renting out his guesthouse for the next nine months at *fair market value*, so who was the financial genius now, huh, Marcus?

When he turned his head to glance at Lauren, her mouth was slightly open, and she was gaping at him. Now she looked less avian and more piscine.

Finally, with a shake of her head, she picked up her e-reader and got back to her book.

No more clapping. Time for one-armed push-ups instead.

"Hey, Lauren," he said. "We should go to a club together. I think your presence would be very convenient. You're so short, I could rest my drink on top of your head, no table necessary."

Did she ever dance? Probably not.

Much as he hated to affirm Ron's judgment, she did seem distinctly joyless. Not ridiculous, though. The situation: definitely. Her: no.

She exhaled rather more loudly than usual. "Are you almost done with your workout? I'd like to grab dinner and get to bed soon."

"After I stretch." Which he intended to do at length and within full view of her. Just in case she paid attention this time. "Not too long now."

He let himself drop to the mat and reclined on his side, propping his head on his palm, letting his pulse slow a moment. His head throbbed with every heartbeat, which wasn't an especially pleasant sensation.

Still: He didn't regret what he'd done, and he wouldn't bemoan its physical consequences. His discomfort was just penance, considering his past.

"Hey, Lauren," he said. "Who's your favorite character on *Gods of the Gates*? It's me, isn't it? Cupid? C'mon, you know it's Cupid."

When she didn't answer, he stretched his right quad, his jaw cracking in a magnificent yawn.

"I'll take that as a yes," he told her.

WHEN LAUREN WAS growing up, her family owned a cat.

Or, rather, the cat owned them.

When their feline dictator—originally named Slippers, for the white bottoms of her paws, before the family decided Lucifer suited her better—wanted their attention, she wanted it right away. And she *always* wanted their attention. But sometimes they couldn't immediately gather her into a bridal carry, her preferred cuddling position, and rub her belly or scratch her ears, because they had to—for instance—sleep. Or give attention to one of the non-cat members of the household, despite their lesser importance.

She would perch on the nearest table, look them dead in the eye, and nudge something fragile toward the edge. If they didn't pick her up, she'd nudge again. And if they didn't bend to her will then, over the edge that fragile item would go.

Eventually, the family had packed away any smallish items not made of, say, rubber. Which was when the retaliatory pooping began.

When Lucifer died after a long, extremely spoiled, and intermittently malevolent life, though, they'd all cried. Because that cat might have been a diabolical bitch, but she was gorgeous and sleek and intelligent and entertaining as hell, even while she was frustrating the entire family.

Now that Lauren considered the matter, Lucifer and Alex had probably been separated at birth somehow, genetic incompatibilities notwithstanding. He clearly wanted attention, and he was willing to nudge conversational items off the figurative coffee table whenever she didn't give him enough of it.

Also, he was gorgeous and sleek and intelligent and entertaining as hell. Not that she ever intended to tell him that, or dignify his provocative remarks with answers.

He might have offered to lend her money—which was both flattering and insulting, as well as horrifying—but she didn't trust him.

Maybe all his friendliness was sincere.

Or maybe he was hoping she'd become less vigilant about enforcing Ron's rules, or looking for information to use against her at some future date. It wouldn't be the first time she'd been fooled by faux friendliness. Also, he was her job, not her buddy, and she didn't intend to confuse the two.

Which was why, after he'd had a post-workout shower and they'd been seated in the hotel's near-deserted restaurant for a late dinner, she was using her mouth and tongue for eating. Nothing else, other than giving her order and responding briefly to direct questions.

His response: the human version of yowling.

"C'mon, Lauren." He was slumped in the carved-wood chair, looking extremely put out. "Why *wouldn't* we go tandem skydiving over the Hollywood Hills, once we get back home? Wouldn't that be a priceless bonding experience?"

Her acrophobic butt would be bonded to the airplane seat, she'd give him that much.

"Nope." She finished the final bite of her seafood paella with a sigh of satisfaction, trying not to notice how the rich red of the restaurant's curtains set off his gleaming hair and gray eyes.

He glowered at her. "Spoilsport."

For five entire minutes, as he teased free the last morsels of his grilled whole trout, blessed silence descended over their meal.

Then he leaned forward and peered at her from across the table, his gray eyes sharp. "Is this a Napoleon thing? You're short, so you want control?" He gave a little hitch of his shoulder and grinned. "No, I suppose you're not attempting to conquer continents. Just the concept of joy."

If he intended to hurt her with his mockery, he was failing. But she didn't actually think he *was* trying to hurt her.

Other than that lone angry swipe at their first meeting, his words didn't seem to contain any actual maliciousness. Just sharp-edged humor and boredom and restless intellect and desire for human connection.

She wouldn't venture so far as to call him *delightful*. But if he was an asshole, he certainly wasn't among the worst she'd ever met.

That conclusion reached, she couldn't help herself. She just . . . couldn't.

"Not the concept of joy." She laid her napkin beside her plate, her tone bone dry. "Only your particular expression of it."

"Ahhhhhhh." It was almost a purr, breathy and seductive. He sprawled back in his chair like an indolent prince, lacing his long fingers over his flat belly. "She speaks at last. And while doing so, almost—but not quite—tells a joke. Brava, Nanny Clegg."

His faded blue tee had ridden up with his movement, exposing a sliver of skin above his low-slung jeans. The candlelight gilded that crescent of flesh, drawing her unwilling gaze.

Given its somewhat remote location, the hotel wasn't especially fancy, but she'd changed into a dark green swing dress for dinner anyway. Even in jeans and a T-shirt, though, even with that golden sliver of belly visible, he appeared more put-together than her. Black eye or no black eye.

If she didn't know better, she'd think the two of them were entirely different species.

"She has her moments." Her tongue had become untethered, and she could only blame the glass of excellent red wine she'd consumed with dinner. "That said, she's not certain why you're referring to her in the third person."

Her resolution to remain silent was melting away as fast as the candle wax, evidently.

"We prefer first person plural? Like royalty?" He waved his hand primly, as if greeting his adoring subjects. "Very well. We're willing to acquiesce to Her Highness's demands."

"*We* prefer normal human interaction," she said quellingly. "Second-person singular should suffice."

His hoot of laughter made their server look over from polishing glasses at the bar. "If you prefer normal human interaction, I haven't seen any sign of it yet."

She raised her brows. "And you consider your level of chattiness normal?"

"Yes, yes, I'm clearly the oddity at this table." He rolled his eyes. "As opposed to a woman who's convincingly imitated statuary all day."

Again, she could have sworn there was something more than mere mockery in his voice. Something like . . . loneliness?

She swept a glance around the room, looking for anyone else who might be affiliated with *Gods of the Gates*. But apart from an older couple at the bar speaking rapid Spanish to one another—locals, she presumed—the place was empty. And yes, it was late, but it wasn't *that* late.

"You said most of the cast members are gone already. But what about the crew? Where are they?" During her past three days on the set, she'd spotted hundreds of behind-the-scenes workers, but where they went after hours, she had no clue. "And where are the actors who haven't left yet?"

He made that breathy, smug sound again. *Ahhhhhhh.*

His near-purr raised goose bumps on her arms.

"You asked me a question just now. You realize that, right?" Setting his elbows on the cloth-covered table, he leaned forward and studied her face intently. "Does it hurt anywhere? Do you require medical intervention to fix the damage to your psyche?"

"Yes, I realize I asked a question." Her middle finger was *itching* to make an appearance. "Don't make me regret it."

For once, he decided not to push his luck.

"There were too many of us to stay in one place, so Ron and R.J. split us up. Cast members in this hotel, crew in other hotels a bit farther away from the set," he explained, idly scratching at his beard. "And I'm one of the few actors remaining, like I said. Asha, the woman who plays Psyche, is staying with her pop star boyfriend in a local mansion."

Oh, yeah. Lauren had seen the two canoodling on the front pages of various American tabloids. In those photos, both were generally topless, cavorting aboard a sleek, spacious yacht, and laughing in each other's arms.

Alex continued ticking off the names of the remaining cast. "Mackenzie, the woman who plays Venus, even though she's actually ten years younger than me and immortality can only explain so much—"

"Goddammit, Ron," Lauren muttered beneath her breath.

"—refused to be parted from her cat, and the hotel doesn't

allow pets. So she rented a cottage nearby." His sly smile split his beard. "Whiskers considers the furniture rustic but comfortable and the living space more than adequate."

Lauren blinked at him. "Her cat considers the furniture . . . rustic? How—how does . . ."

"How does Whiskers issue such nuanced statements about interior design? Good question. Gooooood question." He waited a moment before continuing, no doubt to build anticipation. "As you'll learn via an upcoming memoir, *Here and Meow: A Cat's Life*, Mackenzie says they can speak to one another. Telepathically."

Here and Meow: A Cat's Life.

"The memoir isn't hers," Lauren said slowly. "It's the cat's."

"Correct. Written using Mackenzie as his medium." His voice lowered to a conspiratorial whisper. "Over the years, I've found that Whiskers shares essentially all of Mackenzie's opinions, other than those concerning cat food." He paused. "At least, I hope that's an exception."

Alex's upper body had begun to droop down toward the table as he rested more and more weight on his elbows, and no wonder. He'd had an exceedingly long day, and another loomed ahead of him tomorrow.

"The only other main cast member left is Ian, the guy who plays Jupiter. But he's probably off mainlining tuna somewhere. Besides, he's a prick." Alex pointed a forefinger at her. "I'd stay out of his way, if I were you. All that lean protein might have helped his muscles, but it hasn't helped his mood. Or his smell, for that matter."

Unless she was mistaken, that was a warning. Because he—the man who'd called her a ridiculous bird-woman—didn't want either her feelings or her sense of smell to suffer.

Setting her own elbows on the table, she rubbed her forehead and considered what to do. What he and Ron both needed from her, and what they both deserved. What was *right*, not simply what was convenient and safest.

He rapped his knuckles against the tabletop. "Hey, Nanny Clegg. You okay?"

"I'm fine," she told the crimson cloth covering the heavy wood surface. "Thank you."

All day, she'd assumed his quest to fill any possible silences with endless verbiage was a strategic choice. An attempt to drive her to quit, despite Ron's warnings. A ploy to gather information he could later use against her. A tactic to relax her guard.

And maybe it was all those things.

Or maybe it was a genuine attempt to be friendly.

Maybe he really *was* a delightful asshole, one who'd found himself injured and in trouble and virtually without friends in a foreign country. If so, no wonder he wanted her company. Until he returned to California, he didn't have many other options available to him.

She raised her head, lowered her hands, and surrendered to the inevitable. "I propose a truce."

His eyes were half lidded and hazy with exhaustion, the dark shadows under the left nearly a match for the bruises under the right. Still, he managed a cheeky smirk. "If you're proposing a truce, that means I was winning the war, right?"

She nodded gravely. "Your anecdote about Whiskers turned the tide."

"Carah Brown calls me a gossipy bitch." He scrubbed his hands over his face, stifling a yawn. "But this gossipy bitch gets results."

"Evidently." She raised her hand to signal the server. "So here are my peace terms: If I promise to be more chatty, you promise to give me a few minutes of silence when I tell you I need quiet time.

Also, no deliberate attempts to break Ron's rules, because I really, really don't want to call him."

"No desire to talk to your cousin, huh?" When the server laid their check on the table, Alex wrote his room number on the slip and left a substantial tip. "If it's any consolation, any right-thinking human would feel the same way."

The amount of time she'd spent with her relative this week was enough to last her . . .

Well, forever. Longer than that, if possible.

But that wasn't what she'd meant.

"I don't want you to get in trouble," she corrected. "And if you do, please don't make me the means by which it happens."

"Also, you don't want to talk to him." He grinned at her, tired eyes alight. "Admit it, Nanny Clegg. Admit it, and I'll agree to your peace terms."

She shouldn't. Simple family loyalty should prevent her from saying it, and Alex could use the admission against her at some point.

Still, her cousin was such a *dick*.

"Fine." She sighed. "I don't want to talk to him."

"Victory!" Alex crowed, raising both fists in the air.

The couple at the bar turned to glare at them, and the kitchen staff peeked out of their doorway to see what was happening.

Her cheeks went hot, and she cast him a withering glare. "Are we done here?"

"Oh, Lauren, bless your naive little heart," he said pityingly. "We're just getting started."

Gods of the Gates *Actor Goes Wild!*

Star Tracker's international sources are getting word that Spanish authorities detained Alexander Woodroe, the actor currently portraying an oh-so-adult Cupid on *Gods of the Gates,* in conjunction with a late-night bar brawl. He was released hours later without charges filed.

No official word yet from the *Gates* camp, and Woodroe's agent hasn't responded to our inquiries, but looking at that mug shot, he certainly doesn't appear to regret anything he's done.

This isn't the first time Woodroe has found himself in hot water. In 2013, he was famously ejected from Bruno Keene's award-winning ensemble drama *All Good Men* mid-shoot, under unclear circumstances. Woodroe claimed Keene was abusive toward his cast, but Keene dismissed the accusation as the fabrication of an actor out of his depth.

"He couldn't keep up with everyone else," Keene said at the time. "So he lashed out. I feel sorry for him, really. I hope he finds resources to help him control his temper, or I'm afraid he'll have trouble finding future roles in Hollywood."

When asked to comment on the scandal, the remaining *All Good Men* cast members refused. The *Gates* cast hasn't responded to requests for interviews this time either. Coincidence? Perhaps. But actors are famously reluctant to turn on one of their own, despite any bad behavior on or off set.

Star Tracker suggests you make this your last time lashing out, Alex, because you know the old saying: Three strikes, and you're out—of work!

3

ALEX WAS NAPPING IN HIS TRAILER AGAIN, WHICH DIDN'T surprise her.

Since they'd met on Monday, Lauren had seen him work one fourteen-hour-plus day after another, arriving on set at dawn and leaving after sunset. Back at the hotel, he exercised and ate and talked with Marcus and—collapsed, as far as she could tell.

It was only their fifth day together, and she was exhausted just watching him. But he'd evidently been keeping much the same schedule for weeks and weeks now.

"This is it," Alex had explained last night over dinner, his voice gravelly with fatigue. "The climactic battle of the gods. It's meant to rage day and night for weeks, and it's the last piece of filming for the entire series. Ron and R.J. want to make it big and immersive, and they want to make sure they get all the footage they need before we scatter to the ends of the earth, so that means long hours for everyone."

Today was the last day of filming, and thank goodness for that. He seemed on the verge of collapse, despite all the naps he'd taken in his sleeping berth while she sat on his couch and read.

There'd been no drinking. No women. No clubs or bars. No fights.

He also got along well with his colleagues, which she considered a good gauge of character. When she and Alex ate lunch among the crew and various extras, he chatted with them easily. They clapped him on the back and teased him about his shiner, and he rolled his eyes and mocked them in return, and the group hilarity occasionally drew indignant shushing from other parts of the set.

As far as she could tell, he wasn't the man Ron had described to her or the man she'd met on a battlefield at dawn. Disagreeable. Defiant. Careless. Out of control, or nearly so.

She stole a glance at Alex's sleeping form. He was turned on his side and facing her, arms hugging his pillow, making little snuffling sounds and occasionally smacking his lips, and yes. Yes, he was definitely drooling, and that shouldn't be cute. Especially since the authorities might officially deem his trailer a disaster area at any moment, despite its relatively luxurious design.

He'd been unable to locate the television remote all week. Candy wrappers and disposable coffee cups littered the table, the tiny patch of counter in the kitchen, and an unfortunate spot just short of the trash can. Books and piles of discarded clothing lay scattered across the floor. Yesterday, she'd found an abandoned, half-eaten apple on the floor of the tiny shower.

She had no good explanation for that apple.

Well, actually, she did. He openly took medication for ADHD every morning—their first breakfast together, he'd shaken the pill bottle an inch from her nose and bellowed, "I have Attention Deficit Hyperactivity Disorder, Nanny Clegg! Imagine that!"— but it didn't always take full effect before he got to the set, and it wasn't a miracle drug.

In her training, she hadn't specialized in the disorder. Still, she knew the basics. His medicine would help him direct his attention where he wanted it for longer stretches of time, but executive function issues would persist despite the meds. On a daily basis, he likely battled time management difficulties. Disorganization. Impulsivity.

Lack of adequate rest and excessive stress made managing ADHD much, much harder. Under the circumstances, then, it was a wonder he was still making it to work on time and getting through his scenes every day.

The cookbook on the seat beside her featured a gorgeous loaf of bread on its cover. Absently, she ran a fingertip over that golden boule, squinted into the distance, and considered everything she'd observed.

He had a curious mind, as well as a sharp tongue. He was a hard worker. He was friendly to coworkers beneath him in the show hierarchy.

He was—

He was awake. Staring at her from his bed, gray eyes alert and watchful.

When had she turned to face him? And exactly how long had he been watching her watch him without saying a single word?

"I, uh . . ." Flustered, she tented her fingers and tapped them together. "I was just noticing how much your bruises have faded."

He didn't move. "Were you?"

His voice. It was—it was *sinuous*. It could wrap around words, twisting them into a purr or a plea or the crack of a whip, and even though she'd been studying him continually for five days straight, she had no idea *how*.

She swallowed hard, unable to muster any sort of coherent response while those intent eyes remained locked to hers.

The weight of his gaze blanketed her. It dragged at her mouth, parting her lips. It turned her limbs heavy. It transformed her thoughts into a distant hum.

Then he finally glanced away, toward his laptop on the floor.

Her next inhalation audibly shook, and her chest hurt—had she actually stopped breathing at some point? *Wow.*

No wonder the man got a huge freaking trailer. That was raw star power at work.

Thank goodness he'd chosen acting instead of, say, founding a cult.

He sat up, and the fleece blanket covering him fell to his lap. "Fanfiction. Discuss."

Her muscles all seemed to be functional again. Which was convenient, since tilting her head in confusion required their assistance. "Huh?"

"Fanfiction." He spoke slowly, as if to a dunderheaded child. "Fiction written by fans, featuring favorite characters from books and television shows and movies."

"Oh." Her best friend, Sionna, read fanfiction sometimes, if Lauren remembered correctly. "What about it?"

"I wondered whether you'd read any before. What you thought of it. If you subscribed to any specific writers." He heaved a dramatic sigh. "I'd hoped for an intelligent conversation on the topic, but alas."

Brushing the blanket off his lap, he stood. "Someone I know writes fanfic, and he—*they* want me to help proofread and give feedback on their stories. But I can't give useful feedback unless I know what a good story looks like, so I've been reading fics about Cupid. The ones with the most kudos."

She rubbed her forehead, making a mental note to research fanfiction and its related terminology on the plane ride back to L.A. "Kudos?"

"Lord, you're slow." He rolled his eyes. "Kudos are basically a thumbs-up. The more you have, the more people who liked your fic."

Ah. Those sorts of kudos. "And after all your reading, have you figured out what a good story looks like?"

His face split into a self-satisfied smirk. "Maybe not, but I've found out what a *popular* story looks like, at least in the Cupid/Psyche fandom. And I wanted to ask your opinion. When you think of Cupid, do you . . ."

He paused, lips pressed together.

"What?" Absently, she straightened the couch cushions and stacked the paperbacks on the coffee table into a neat pile. "Do I what?"

"No." He gave his head a little shake. "I shouldn't."

Alex had hit some sort of conversational limit? *Alex?*

She had to know. "Tell me."

"I can't." His voice wasn't a purr or a whip crack now. It was a whine. "You're not my employee, but you're still working, and I *can't*."

She studied him. "Is this something sexual?"

It was the obvious conclusion, based on one simple fact: Other than their very first meeting, when he'd sneeringly suggested calling her Mistress Lauren, none of his endless mockery had ever involved sex. Not a single time. Which didn't precisely make him a saint, but it certainly removed him from the circle of hell reserved for sexually predatory men.

Come to think of it, ever since that bird reference during their first, fraught standoff, he hadn't mocked her appearance either, other than her height. Alex Woodroe was damnably hard to pin down sometimes.

Not in this instance, however. He bowed his head, and that was her answer.

"So, yes, it's sexual." She closed her eyes for a moment, already knowing her next words were likely a mistake. "Fine. I won't be offended. Just tell me."

He peeked at her through a dangling lock of his obnoxiously lustrous hair. "Really?"

"Yes, really." When he still hesitated, she spread her hands in exasperation. "Well, I'm not going to *beg* you, Alex."

"All right, then. But let the record show I tried to exercise some self-control. For once." Straightening, he propped his fists on his hips and grinned at her. "Here's what I want to know: Does Cupid seem like a bottom to you?"

"A bottom?" She frowned, lost. "Like an ass, do you mean? Because, sure, the way he treats Psyche sometimes—"

"Sexually," he reminded her impatiently. "*Sexually,* you dense woman."

"Oh." She thought for a moment. *"Oh."*

His uncharacteristic reticence disappeared, possibly never to be seen again.

"Because all the most popular Cupid fics seem to involve Psyche pegging him. Often with dildos described as having the same width as her forearm, which is somewhat alarming." He stared at her arm, clearly doing some mental calculations, then winced. "And within the fandom, popular consensus says my character is clearly a bottom, and I'm not certain I fully understand why."

She understood. Now that she'd grasped the context, she *totally* understood.

"You—" Alex flicked a hand at her. "You know things. Explain it to me."

You know things?

It was perhaps the most dismissive, careless compliment she'd ever received. It was also, however, a correct statement. She *did* know things.

And given her knowing-things pedigree, she was shocked she hadn't considered Cupid's possible bottom status before now.

Dammit, she'd read E. Wade's books multiple times. How had she overlooked the way Cupid's special arrow angled higher whenever Psyche climbed on top? And if the books hadn't given her enough clues, the show should have.

In retrospect, Cupid's expression after Psyche pushed him against the wall and pinned his wrists as she kissed him should have told Lauren everything. *Everything*.

Had Alex not realized what his face was doing in that scene? And how had they all missed the Cupid Is Definitely the Little Spoon implications of it all?

"Are you even paying attention to me?" Alex's perfect nose had lifted high in the air, and he sniffed down at her. "You do realize your inattentiveness is exceedingly rude, correct?"

Ah, but it was too late for insults now. He'd told her she *knew* things.

Why did that make her straighten and puff out her chest a little? And even as she preened, why did she want so very badly to laugh? At him, and at herself too?

She didn't laugh. But she did bask in the moment.

Right now, if only for a fleeting snatch of time, she had the upper hand with Alex. She intended to enjoy it.

"Very well, then." With a sweep of her arm, she gestured to the couch. "Sit down, Alex. Nanny Clegg will explain the birds and the bees and the bottoms to you."

"Fucking hell," he groaned.

But damned if he didn't sit down.

4

"HEY, LAUREN," ALEX SAID, AVIDLY EYEING HER EXPRES-
sion. "If I called you a claggy sponge, what would you say?"

To his disappointment, she didn't visibly react. Instead, she
continued frowning at the wall of windows overlooking one of the
Spanish airport's many runways.

"In response to such a transparent attempt at provocation?"
Her voice was preoccupied. "I'd say nothing."

She gave a decisive little nod, then rose from the very wide, very
heavy armchair she'd chosen in the near-empty business lounge.
Before he could react or do it for her, she hoisted that chair, moved
it closer to the windows, and plopped back into its cushioned
embrace.

Then she got out her e-reader and bent her stupid, boring head
over it again, matching words to deeds.

Goddamn. His appointed jailer was fucking frustrating sometimes.

Not that she'd notice, but he wasn't letting her escape his orbit
that easily. Standing, he shifted his own chair nearer to the windows
and even closer to hers than it was before.

Setting it down with a little grunt, he studied it consideringly
before turning back to her.

"That chair is heavy as shit." He gave it a shove for emphasis, and it didn't move an inch. "Are you bench-pressing cars in your spare time, or what?"

Her brow was still furrowed, and she was once again readjusting her sad little ponytail. As far as he could tell, she hadn't turned to a new page in her book yet.

"I'm strong." She flicked him a brief, abstracted glare. "And don't swear in public. There are children here."

In her new position next to the windows, unforgiving sunlight bathed her profile, and he had it. He finally had it. She didn't just remind him of a bird, she reminded him of—

"A Picasso!" He stabbed a finger in her direction. "You look like a portrait by Picasso!"

He sat back in his chair, crossing an ankle over his knee, entirely triumphant.

"Thank you so much." There was a definite sarcastic edge to her words, a sharpness she usually lacked.

Now he was frowning too.

Picasso was one of his favorite artists. Back home, several coffee table books of Picasso's works sat displayed on the library shelves, and Alex flipped through their pages often.

He'd loved Picasso for . . . decades now. Thirty years.

Without his father in the picture, his mom hadn't had much money when Alex was growing up. During long, sticky summers in Florida, when she'd managed to bank enough vacation time at one of her retail jobs and saved a few precious dollars, they hadn't flown anywhere or taken cruises. Instead, they'd gone on road trips up and down the coast.

Fort Lauderdale. St. Augustine. And one memorable time, Miami.

They'd stayed in a cheap motel on the outskirts of the area to save money, but ventured into the heart of the vibrant city itself during the still, humid mornings, before the inevitable storm clouds rolled in every afternoon.

In an art museum there, they'd chanced upon a special exhibit. One of Picasso's portraits, on loan for a month. At the time, he'd been seven or eight, maybe. Not yet medicated, so he tore through that museum like one of the region's famous, terrifying hurricanes, randomly checking off an item or two on the children's scavenger hunt list he'd been given at the entrance, but mostly just wreaking havoc and screeching.

Until he'd seen the Picasso and stopped dead.

That portrait—it didn't look like any he'd ever seen before. It had mottled colors. Mismatched features. Jutting angles and deliberate, defiant asymmetry.

The woman in that portrait wasn't beautiful. But beauty wasn't the point.

He'd hyperfocused on that painting. When his mom tried to persuade him to move on, he'd whined until she gave up and let him stare at it a little longer.

Lauren's face drew his attention the same way.

But in the mid-morning sunlight, the bags under her eyes were more evident, the lines bracketing her mouth and furrowing her forehead more distinct.

She looked tired and stressed. From lingering jet lag and the prospect of more travel to come? The strain of watching over him?

"I'm getting some food," she said abruptly, and jolted up from her chair.

Before he could follow her, a man in a suit appeared and asked for an autograph. As Alex made the usual casual conversation—yes, he was that actor; thank you so much for your kind words; no, he wasn't able to reveal anything about the last season—he kept track of Lauren in his peripheral vision.

She'd piled cheese and grapes and some sort of potato dish on her plate, and it all looked much better than the apple he'd grabbed on the way to their seats. So as soon as he finished with the fan, he joined her in front of the display of small sandwiches and omelettes, where she'd been standing for at least a couple of minutes.

Her vague gaze didn't waver from the serrano ham and Manchego offering. She didn't pay him a lick of attention.

Finally, he reached past her and selected a sandwich with tongs, placing it on his small, white plate. Then, with a shrug, he grabbed a second one too—because dried ham and cheese and aioli, yum—and turned to her.

"Are you attempting to obtain your sandwich via telekinesis?" He waved a hand in front of her eyes. "Or simply asleep on your feet?"

She started. "Oh. Sorry. Just thinking."

With a quiet sigh, she claimed the tongs from him and got her own sandwich.

The two of them hadn't really stood side by side for any significant amount of time before. They were usually either sitting or in motion or at a distance from one another.

Holy fuck, she was even shorter up close and unmoving.

"Hey, Lauren." He watched as she transferred a small chorizo omelette to her plate. "When we stand next to each other, we look like we're illustrating a nursery rhyme or fairy tale."

She slammed her plate down on the counter with a distinct *crack,* and he jumped a little.

"Is that a Jack Sprat reference?" Her soft jaw was set, those astounding green eyes hot with anger. "If so, I'd really appreciate an attempt to restrain your asshole tendencies, at least until we get back to L.A."

Jack Sprat? What the fuck?

He racked his memory, but—

Jack Sprat could eat no fat. His wife could eat no lean.

"Or am I the troll under the bridge, while you're the golden prince?" Splotchy color bloomed on her cheeks, and she snatched up her plate and marched toward their chairs. "Either way, stow it, Woodroe."

She thought he was making fun of her weight or calling her ugly. And for the first time in their brief acquaintance, she didn't look calm at all. She looked murderous and—edgy. Distressed.

Shit. Now he couldn't even taunt her about using an obscenity in front of children. At least, not until he tried to explain himself better.

In her seat, she'd angled herself away from him and toward the window, and he refused to speak to the back of her head. After a moment of thought, he set his plate on a nearby table and dragged his own chair in front of hers, close enough that their knees almost touched when he sat down again.

He ducked his head to catch her eye, with no success. "Normally, I'm loath to defend myself from charges of assholery, as they're typically well warranted."

"They would be," she muttered.

"I only meant that you seem even shorter up close, when we're both standing. That's all." He waited until her suspicious gaze slowly, slowly rose to meet his. "I swear, Lauren."

At long last, she inclined her head in acknowledgment and let out a slow breath.

When she spoke, her voice was heavy with fatigue. "I'm sorry. I shouldn't have snapped at you."

For once, he didn't leap to fill the silence, and he was rewarded for his restraint.

"I didn't sleep well. I mean, I never sleep well these days, but

I especially didn't sleep well last night." Her small hand swept toward the runway, where a commuter jet was racing down the asphalt and poised to take flight. "I hate flying."

This close to her, he could hear her swallow.

"I know all the science behind it, but when you're actually in the plane, it just seems so *precarious*." Her pale lips pursed. "Plus, I always end up with bruised thighs from the armrests. And sometimes they have trouble finding a seat belt extender, or my seatmates complain I'm taking up too much room. It's not fun."

At the thought of a stranger insulting her, his skin prickled beneath his soft tee. "If anyone is rude to you, I can handle it."

"No." When he started to protest, she spoke over him. "*No.* I don't trust you not to escalate things, and I told you I didn't want to be the means by which you got into trouble with Ron and R.J. I meant it."

He glowered at her. "You meant you didn't want to have to report on me, not that I couldn't—"

"I'm not entertaining discussion on the matter." She lifted her chin and looked down that crooked nose at him. "Thank you very much."

When he made a sort of growly sound in his chest, she rolled her eyes.

After a moment, though, she spoke again, her voice softer. "I mean that sincerely, by the way. Thank you for the offer."

"Seats in business class are much wider than in coach," he sulkily told her, lower lip still poking out a tad. "That should help with the bruising issue."

"Good to know," she said, then shoved at his chair. "Now move away and let me eat my sandwich in peace, Woodroe."

He left his chair exactly where it was, and it relieved his feelings considerably.

As he munched on his deliciousness-filled baguette, he gave her a few minutes of quiet and studied her. The lines on her face had smoothed somewhat, even if those shadows beneath her eyes hadn't gone anywhere. She wasn't tugging at her ponytail anymore, and she was actually tapping the screen of her e-reader to turn pages at regular intervals.

"Stop staring at me." She didn't look up, which was extremely dissatisfying.

Making his reluctance clear with a heavy, drawn-out exhalation, he turned his attention to the windows, where an enormous plane was taxiing down the runway. It caught flight and winged toward the sun in a graceful swoop.

He barely noticed.

Today was literally the first time he'd ever seen his minder anything less than calm. Even when her cousin had insulted her.

That morning, he'd wondered whether Ron's disdain bothered her at all, because it didn't seem to. Alex had envied that seeming imperviousness, frankly. His skin was always a little thinner than it should be. Maybe too thin for his chosen profession.

He hadn't intended to hurt her feelings today. That he'd done so anyway was just one more misdeed to toss atop his already massive pile of regrets. Still, he now knew she *had* actual feelings, which was comforting. And she might have snapped at him, but he'd always preferred an honest reaction over artifice.

Someone like her wouldn't lose her temper around anyone she didn't trust at least a little, right?

Yes, he was clearly well on his way to charming her completely. Which meant it was time to up his efforts and introduce her to the wonders of soggy bottoms, baps, and claggy sponges.

"You snapped at me for no reason, Nanny Clegg." He chose a

wheedling tone, one guaranteed to grate on her nerves. "Aren't you going to make that up to me somehow?"

"I apologized." Dragging her finger, she highlighted a passage in her e-reader. "That should be sufficient recompense."

"It's not."

She looked up at him, eyes narrowed suspiciously.

Then she sighed and set aside her book. "What do you want, Alex?"

Ten minutes later, they were huddled around his laptop and streaming Nadiya's season—the *best* season—of *The Great British Bake Off*. Lauren had reluctantly agreed to watch the first several episodes with him. In return, he'd promised to let her sleep peacefully the entire plane ride, although he'd also crossed his fingers behind his back while making that promise, so he couldn't be held responsible for his actions high above the Atlantic.

As they watched, her posture loosened minute by minute, until her shoulders no longer hovered near her ears. Her thighs, covered in stretchy leggings for the long trip, spread farther apart as she leaned closer to the monitor.

And just now, as she'd shifted in her seat, he'd spotted something very interesting indeed. In her chest region. Not that he'd been looking at her breasts, which weren't especially remarkable. But what lay atop those breasts *was*.

He paused the episode. "Hey, Lauren?"

Squeezing her eyes shut, she exhaled through her nose. "Yes, Alex?"

"What's Big Harpy Energy?" He flicked a finger at her T-shirt. "And where can I get some?"

BHE: BIG HARPY ENERGY, the shirt declared in large, bold letters. In smaller text beneath, there was a hashtag: #CRONEGOALS.

"I've heard of Big Dick Energy," he noted with a smirk, "and from all accounts, I'm a prime exemplar of that particular—"

"Can it, Woodroe." She looked down at her chest, then gave a little shrug. "My best friend Sionna lost her husband about five years ago. A few months later, she announced she was founding the Harpy Institute for Crone Sciences. She asked if I wanted to join her and make it a two-person institution, and again, she's my best friend, so . . ."

Another tiny shrug, as if to say, *Really, what else could I do?*

He tilted his head. "The Harpy Institute. For—"

"Crone Sciences," she confirmed. "Sionna came up with the CroneGoals hashtag. I designed the T-shirts. We meet twice monthly to drink wine, binge-watch TV shows, and go over our progress in the Shrew Arts."

She glanced toward his laptop screen, clearly impatient for him to restart the show, but nope. Not after that bombshell.

If he didn't know better, he'd think Nanny Clegg occasionally had . . . fun?

No, that couldn't be right.

But how could anyone who designed and wore a Big Harpy Energy tee be entirely devoid of humor?

"You designed the T-shirts," he said slowly. "Plural."

"Yes."

He raised his brows. "Can I see the others?"

"Not right now, you can't. They're at my duplex." She gestured impatiently at the screen. "Can we keep watching? I don't think all the contestants will be done on time."

Leaning back in his chair, he stacked his hands behind his head and smirked at her. "You realize a killjoy isn't quite the same thing as a harpy, correct?"

Her fingertips massaged her temples. "I would imagine they're somewhere along the same Crone Continuum."

"Not necessarily. For instance, some killjoys are polite and restrained and rule-bound." He raised his eyebrows meaningfully and stared hard at her. "While Big Harpy Energy implies a certain amount of freedom, yes? From rules and guilt and expectations?"

"I seem to recall *someone* in this room playing upon a killjoy's guilt mere minutes ago." She glared at him. "I didn't hear any complaints then."

"Oh, I'm not complaining," he said airily. "Merely pointing out that the acquisition of BHE will require effort on your part. You have some latent harpy tendencies, true. You demonstrated that over by the sandwiches." He nodded toward the buffet. "But it's certainly not *Big* Harpy Energy. Not yet. We can work on that."

He wanted to see it. Nanny Clegg unbound and unrestrained.

If she acted like a harpy, at least she would be *present* with him, not tangled in her own thoughts. A participant, not an observer.

Sure, she'd been civil and professional and upheld her end of their various bargains all week. But for the most part, having her as a companion had been like sharing a room with a ghost. He might be able to interact with her, but she was fundamentally untouchable.

Not that he intended to touch Lauren, a woman who was—in essence—his coworker. But he did intend to see her smile. Laugh, even.

He could make her do both.

He *would* make her do both.

"Whatever." Stretching out her arm, she tapped the touchpad to unpause the show. "Time to find out who proofed their dough long enough."

"You love the series already!" Oh, he adored being right. Gloating always felt *amazing*. "I knew it!"

Her expression remained serene. "It's okay."

He gaped at her, aghast. *"Blasphemy."*

"Shhhh." She raised an admonishing index finger to her lips. "I'm trying to listen."

Despite the severity of her tone, the corners of her mouth had tucked inward again, just a tiny bit, and he narrowed his eyes at her.

Was she winding him up on purpose? Was she . . . was she playing with him?

Still pondering the matter, he settled down to watch the first round of judging. Only to stir some undetermined amount of time later, roused by gentle fingertips tapping his upper arm.

He blinked awake to find—Lauren. Bent over him, those incongruously beautiful eyes of hers kind and patient.

She spoke softly. "It's time to get to our gate, Alex. I waited as long as I could."

When he shifted, her cardigan fell to his lap. She'd covered him?

"Groggy, huh? Naps can do that to you." Before he quite registered her words, her small, warm hand slid into his, and she was helping him to his feet. "All right. Up you go."

Stupidly, all he could do was stare at her and think, *This is the first time we've touched since we shook hands the day we met.*

"Steady now?" When he nodded, unable to find words, her fingers slipped away.

Then they were gathering their belongings and walking down the long hall toward their gate, their luggage rolling along at their sides. About halfway there, he managed to find his wits and his tongue once more.

"I'd thank you for your help," he said, "if I weren't so disappointed by your insufficient harpy energy as you woke me."

He could practically hear her eyes roll. "Next time, I'll kick you awake."

Her words were as dry as the air in the terminal, and he grinned.

"Much better." He dipped his head in approval. "That would constitute Middling Harpy Energy, at the very least. Maybe even Substantial Harpy Energy."

"How wonderful." That deadpan tone was glorious, really. "I look forward to causing you pain in the future, then."

He snorted at the sally, but not because he believed her. By now, even a man as self-absorbed and unobservant as him knew the truth.

She wouldn't hurt him, even if he deserved it.

And at some point, he definitely would. He knew that too.

Casting a sidelong glance at her, he snapped the fingers of his free hand. "Try to get those Smurf legs of yours moving faster, Nanny Clegg. You're going to make us late for our flight."

As she stared at him in disbelief, he smiled back at her contentedly.

DAMN, IT FELT good to be home.

Alex's virtual PA had arranged for car service from LAX, and after a horrifically long day of travel, the sleek sedan was finally pulling up to his house in Beachwood Canyon.

Lauren raised her head from the plushly cushioned back seat, and her bleary eyes widened. "Is that . . ."

As soon as the car stopped, she climbed out and stood on his circular driveway, hands fisted on her ample hips.

"You—you have a mini-castle." Her voice wavered. "With turrets. And a moat."

Then she threw back her head and laughed.

The joyful sound floated through the evening sky, rich and warm, bright as the smile transforming her features into near-beauty, and—

And he couldn't seem to look away.

Fuck, he couldn't seem to look away.

Texts with Marcus: Sunday Afternoon

Alex: Thank fuck, we're finally at cruising altitude

Alex: So BORED

Alex: Nanny Clegg is sleeping and made me promise not to wake her up except for meals, because she's cruel and wants me to suffer

Marcus: Maybe she's just tired?

Alex: SHE'S TIRED ON PURPOSE, TO THWART ME

Marcus: Apart from her malicious napping, how are things going with Lauren?

Alex: . . .

Marcus: Alex?

Alex: She says GBBO is "okay"

Alex: NADIYA'S SEASON, MARCUS

Alex: How am I supposed to put up with such

Alex: I don't even know the right word for it, nothing suffices

Marcus: Wrongheadedness?

Alex: Maybe she truly is a harpy

Marcus: A harpy???

Marcus: That's mean. Do better, man.

Alex: FML

Alex: NO ONE UNDERSTANDS ME

Alex: You know what? I wasn't going to tell you, but now I am

Alex: I just found a treasure trove of smutty Aeneas/Cupid fics

Marcus: Nope, don't want to know

Alex: Apparently our shipping portmanteau is Aeneid

Marcus: Clever, but still NO

Alex: Just wanted to thank you for all that very tender lovemaking

Marcus: OH MY GOD STOP

Alex: Your stamina was truly impressive

Alex: Also your girth

Marcus: AGGGGGGH

Alex: Good luck forgetting this conversation, my stern but loving daddy

Marcus: I HATE YOU SO MUCH

Alex: Off to take a nap now, byeeeeeeeee

Alex: 😘

Marcus: 🖕

Alex: ☺

5

ALEX WAS LOOKING AT HER WITH THE ODDEST EXPRESSION on his fatigue-creased face.

After one last snort, Lauren managed to contain her punch-drunk hilarity. Using the neckline of her tee, she wiped away the wetness under her eyes.

"What?" He braced himself against the door of the sedan, seemingly unaware that their driver had efficiently hoisted all their luggage from the car's trunk and was awaiting his attention. "What's so funny?"

The unaccustomed laughter had hurt her throat a little, and she reached inside the back seat for her forgotten bottle of water. After a swig, she shut the door and flicked a dismissive hand.

"You'll find out soon enough." She tilted her head toward their patient driver. "Let's allow this poor woman to get on with her evening."

"Oh." In a startled rush of movement, he turned toward the uniformed driver, pressed what appeared to be a substantial tip in her hand, and waved her off.

The sedan completed the driveway's circle and disappeared down the narrow, twisty Beachwood Canyon road as Lauren took stock of her surroundings.

If she had a dog named Toto, she'd inform him they weren't in

NoHo anymore. They were, in fact, right below the Hollywood sign, perched high on a mountainside, in a neighborhood where wealthy and famous people lived, rather than middle-class non-entities like her.

On the way to his house, driving up and up again on those tiny roads, they'd passed countless enormous, impeccably maintained houses. No, *estates*. Ones with an eye-popping array of architectural styles ranging from Spanish Colonial to—well, Turreted German Mini-Castle.

A mini-castle with a narrow, shallow moat filled with succulents, which visitors crossed via a tiny drawbridge, because of course. Of course Alex had a castle and a moat and a drawbridge. And what appeared to be stables off to one side. Did he have freaking *horses*?

What was the name of that magazine feature? Oh, right: *Stars—they're just like us!*

Nooooope,

If she turned one way, the lights of downtown L.A. glittered below. A half-turn, and the mountain stretched still higher, those iconic letters startlingly close.

Suddenly, he was startlingly close too. Not touching her, but near enough to exude noticeable heat.

"I could give you a tour of the main house and grounds tonight, if you want." His hands shoved in his jeans pockets, he looked down at her. "Or I can just find us food, show you the guesthouse, and save everything else for tomorrow."

Since she was starving, sticky with travel, and nearly listing in exhaustion, the answer was clear. "The second option, please."

Before she could stop him, he somehow managed to wrangle all their luggage and drag it with him across the drawbridge and up to the huge, dark-wood front door with a lion's head knocker.

All along the way, discreetly positioned outside lights blinked to life and illuminated their path.

At the entrance, he set down the bags while he fumbled for his keys. "Dammit, they're somewhere . . . around . . . here . . ."

A quick glance at the property didn't reveal any other outbuildings. She had to assume she was sleeping in the stables. Which seemed appropriate, as she was most definitely a peasant compared to his handsome prince.

"Aha!" He brandished the keys in triumph. "I win again!"

She kept her voice dry as those beds of succulents. "You had a wily opponent."

With a quick beep of a small remote on his key chain, he deactivated his house alarm.

"You have no idea, Nanny Clegg." Waving her ahead, he stood in front of their bags. "After you."

The air within his home was cool and not as stale as she'd have expected after his lengthy absence. Inside, the castle theme was pronounced but not tacky. Someone—maybe Alex, maybe the owners before him—had left enough touches for character, but nothing more.

The tiled foyer led into a large open area with a soaring, dark-beamed ceiling, the white walls illuminated by warm lamplight. A huge slab of yet more dark wood crowned an enormous stone fireplace, its interior filled with yet more succulents. The furniture—a couple of long, low couches facing a huge television; a marble-topped coffee table; several smaller seating arrangements punctuated by cleverly designed open shelving—looked stylish but comfortable, substantial enough to fill but not crowd the space.

"There's a guest bathroom down that hall"—he pointed toward a shadowy corridor—"if you want to freshen up before eating. I'll see what Dina left in the fridge for dinner."

As she ventured down the dimly lit hall, located the impeccably outfitted guest bathroom, and closed the door behind her, her head began to ache—dehydration again—and she wondered who Dina might be. A girlfriend he somehow hadn't mentioned before now, despite all his incessant rambling?

That seemed unlikely. Dina was probably a housekeeper or his cook.

Lauren's shoulders loosened. Only because it might have been awkward to reconcile her need to watch over Alex with the demands of a girlfriend, who might understandably want privacy for a long-awaited reunion.

Otherwise, his having a girlfriend wouldn't bother her at all.

After relieving her bladder and washing her hands, she splashed more water on her face. Only to discover that his hand towel was made from some form of cotton she'd never encountered before, one presumably blessed by angels during the manufacturing process. The towel simultaneously dried her face and caressed it, and if she weren't a pathologically honest person, she'd have slipped it in her purse.

Once she'd dried the marble-topped vanity with another one of those miraculous hand towels, she contemplated herself in the mirror. Rumpled, water-splotched tee. Under-eye circles fully as dark as Alex's fading shiner. Limp hair falling from a haphazard ponytail.

Still, she'd never emerged from a plane this unscathed before. After a single business-class flight, she was likely to weep in despair the next time she sat in coach.

Faced with Alex's inimitable charm and gimlet eye and expensive tickets, no one had blinked at either her size or her need for a seat belt extender. As he'd promised, the wider seat gave her just enough room to sit comfortably. More than that, its various controls allowed her to lie almost flat after a three-course dinner, a quilted blanket on top of her as she resisted removing her complimentary eye mask and glancing to her left, where Alex was seated by the window in their two-person row.

She hadn't slept much, but she'd had substantial time to herself in the dim cabin. He'd even kept his promise, despite those inadequately hidden fingers he'd crossed behind his back, and let her rest without bothering her. Probably because he'd done some napping himself. At mealtimes, he'd picked at her in his usual way, but—

He hadn't complained that she took up more than her share of the wide armrest between them. He hadn't remarked on how the tray table sat at a wonky angle as she ate because of her belly. And when they'd lifted off and landed, he'd somehow reached new heights of ridiculousness, his whispered asides so outrageous, she ended up paying more attention to him than the thud of gears or the sight of land either dropping away from them or zooming closer with dizzying speed.

She blinked at the mirror, then realized she'd been staring blankly at her own reflection for minutes now.

Exhaustion. That was all her current stage of confusion indicated. Travel fatigue.

When she came back to the great room, she saw a newly lit area off to the side. A casual dining nook, the table now carelessly set with a couple of mismatched napkins and two plates and a jumbled pile of silverware in the middle.

"Grab your own drink from the fridge," she heard from around a corner, and she followed his voice to a gorgeous, white-tile-and-marble kitchen with gold accents.

After plucking a sleekly curved bottle of grapefruit soda from the refrigerator's gleaming depths, she closed the heavy door and turned back to him.

Alex stood bent in front of a built-in microwave, his elbows resting on the marble countertop as he watched a glass container spin inside.

"Hope you like chicken enchiladas. If you don't, you're objectively wrong, because chicken enchiladas are fucking delicious. Especially Dina's." He pursed his lips. "Still, there might be a couple other prepared meals in the fridge, if you're determined to be contrary and incorrect. Shit, I should have put a top over this. It's popping now, and—"

He opened the microwave door and touched the side of the glass container with his fingertip. "They'll still be lukewarm in the middle, but let's throw caution to the wind and eat them anyway. Apologies for my culinary laxity, Nanny Clegg. I know you must be scandalized."

She leaned against a counter and crossed her arms over her chest. "Do you ever run out of words?"

"Nope." He popped the *p* in emphasis. "I remain consistently delightful at all times."

Once he grabbed a marble trivet to put beneath the dish, she followed him into the dining nook. And despite what he'd just told her, he hardly said a word after serving up enchiladas onto both plates. Too hungry to waste time speaking, she supposed. Or maybe he was simply as tired as she was, because he was slumping a bit now, his elbows again propped before him.

The semi-heated enchiladas were as delicious as advertised, spicy and saucy and full of tender meat and beans, but the continuing silence nagged at her, for some reason.

Not that she missed hearing him talk. But—

"Is Dina your housekeeper?" Two forkfuls left of this tortilla. She was already eyeing a second helping. "Or your cook?"

"Both. Also a fucking godsend. I'd be lost and living in squalor without her." He put down his utensils and scrubbed a hand over his face. "Weekdays, she fixes breakfast and dinner, and I usually have a sandwich or leftovers for lunch. She leaves me meals to reheat over the weekends, as you can see."

"So she works Monday through Friday?"

He nodded. "She'll arrive bright and early tomorrow morning. I emailed her a couple of days ago, and since the production would pay her handsomely for the extra work, she's happy to keep the guesthouse clean and prepare food for you too, but that's your choice. Your quarters have a small kitchen if you'd rather cook instead, and there are basic cleaning supplies under the bathroom sink. I'm supposed to let Dina know what you decide as soon as possible."

No housework. No cooking, unless she wanted to do it. How would that even feel?

"Oh, wow. I would love for someone else to cook and dust and . . ." Tiredly, she rubbed her temples. "No. No, I shouldn't have her take over tasks I can do myself." Dammit. "Please tell her thank you for the offer, but—"

"I changed my mind." Without even looking at her, Alex served himself another enchilada. "Her sister just had a baby, and Dina wants to start a college fund for her new niece. She jumped at the prospect of additional pay. Whether you want her help or not, you have it."

The right thing. She needed to do the right thing, but the right thing was so hard to determine when she was so *tired*.

"Okay." She tapped her fork against her plate. "In that case, I'll still clean up after myself, but she can tell the production she's doing the extra work and get the money."

He frowned, looking . . . upset. At her. But why?

"If you said that to Dina, she'd be offended, and I wouldn't blame her. Why are you assuming she'd lie about her work for more money?" Exhaling through his nose, he sat back. "Do you think I'm browbeating her into this? Or that I don't pay her sufficiently for her time and labor? Because I can assure you, Lauren, I'm not, and I do. My mom cleaned hotel rooms for a few years, and I know how hard the work is."

Hey, Lauren, if you ever need a loan or something, let me know. Those generous tips at the hotel restaurant. The wad of bills he'd pressed into their driver's hand.

No, he wasn't miserly with his money.

"You can talk to her yourself tomorrow. Make sure she's not overworked and underpaid. She likes what she does, and she's well compensated for it. She had a real choice in the matter, and she *wanted* to take care of the guesthouse and cook for you." Beneath that beard, his jaw was jutting forward. "Maybe you'll believe her, even if you don't believe me."

"It's not—" How the hell had she messed this up so badly? "Alex, wait."

With a loud scrape of his chair against the gleaming hardwood floor, Alex had hurdled to his feet and was stomping into the kitchen, his plate in his fist.

She jumped to her feet too, sick to her stomach. "Alex. *Alex.* Listen to me. That's not it."

Even when she followed him into the kitchen, he ignored her and continued scraping his half-eaten enchilada down the garbage disposal. His shoulders had become hard bunches of affronted muscle under the thin cotton of his tee, and that only made her stomach churn harder.

Tentatively, she laid her hand on that rock-solid shoulder, desperate to get his attention.

He was warm under her fingertips. He didn't shrug her away, but he didn't turn around either.

"Alex, I'm sorry. I didn't mean to insult either you or her. I just . . ." Crap on a cracker, this day needed to end *soon*. She was so tired, her eyes were prickling and watery. "I hate cleaning and cooking. It's hard for me to imagine anyone doing it voluntarily if they had another choice."

At that, he swiveled to face her, and her hand dropped to her side.

"But you *do* have another choice," he said. "Are you not *anyone*?"

She opened her mouth to answer, then shut it again.

"I don't know" was all she could say in response.

"I see." The angry flush on his cheekbones faded as he looked down at her. "What would the Harpy Institute for Crone Sciences say about that?"

She closed her eyes in relief. That sly sarcasm meant he'd understood. Understood and forgiven her for the inadvertent slight.

Her lips quirked. "That I possess insufficient harpy energy and should retake Harpies 101: An Introduction to the Virago Arts?"

"Ahhhhh." There it was. His purr, its low breathiness a slow trickle down her spine. "Was that your feeble attempt at a joke, Nanny Clegg?"

"Maybe." When she opened her eyes, he was only inches away, head ducked low, eyes alive with alert intelligence despite his fatigue. "I suppose you'll never know."

The air between them abruptly went hypoxic, and his stare mired her in place.

"I'm sorry too." The words were abrupt, his mouth tight. "I can be a bit oversensitive. Maybe I would have been that way no matter what, but it's . . . uh, pretty common with ADHD. I get more upset than I should whenever I think someone is criticizing me."

Her mouth opened, and he held up a hand. "Even when that's not actually what they're doing. I've worked on getting thicker skin, but . . ."

He lifted a shoulder, but the gesture didn't seem casual. Not at all.

In fact, none of this seemed casual, and she didn't understand what was happening.

Clearing his throat, he turned back to the sink. The bubble popped, and she could breathe again. Hear something over her own heartbeat again. See something other than his face again.

"Tomorrow morning, you can either bring food back to the stables or eat here with me. Same for all the other meals." He turned on the faucet, then the garbage disposal, and waited to speak again until he flipped the switch and the buzzing went silent once more. "Unless I go out to a restaurant, of course, because then you won't have a choice. You'll need to be my ball and chain, as per Ron's instructions."

The sudden shift in their situation's dynamics belatedly struck her.

Alex was done filming in an isolated section of Spanish shoreline. He was home, and as far as she knew, he didn't have to report to another job right away. He could go anywhere at any time with anyone, and she'd have to go with him.

Shit.

"Correct. Any time you leave your property, I'll accompany you." Given what a restless person he was, that would probably mean constant activity on her part. A groan rose from deep in her beleaguered soul, but she didn't let it loose. "Do you have plans for tomorrow?"

"Nope." He snorted. "I'm fucking exhausted. I intend to sleep and eat Dina's cooking and talk to Marcus, and that's about it."

"You can't leave without me." It was an order, but also a plea. "Not even once."

He eyed her balefully. "You said that already, Nanny Clegg."

Propping her fists on her hips, she stared up at him. "Promise me you won't."

"Would you believe me?"

He'd tilted his head, watchful. Wary.

She thought for a moment, just to be sure.

Then she told him the truth. "Yes."

With his long exhalation, he bowed his head. And when he lifted his face to hers again, there was no hint of levity in his features.

"I promise," he said.

Time had slowed to syrup once more. Her legs were quivering with tension, her parched lips begging for her to lick them.

He gave his head a little shake. "You're tired. Let me get your keys, teach you how to deal with the alarm system, and show you the guesthouse."

A quick tutorial on his alarm panel later, they were out his door. He didn't let her near her own luggage, instead hauling the bags to the faux stables himself.

At the guesthouse entrance, he passed her a key chain with two keys and another little remote. "These are yours. One key and alarm remote for the stables, one key for the main house."

She studied the remote, whose buttons seemed relatively self-explanatory.

"My first public event is Tuesday night. A charity auction. I'm hosting." His smile turned a tiny bit evil. "There will be a red carpet. Which means you'll have to walk it with me, Nanny Clegg. Cocktail attire required."

She rubbed her temples again. "I'll need clothing. You'll have to accompany me when I get it."

"We'll deal with all that tomorrow. Come on. Let me show you around and tell you how everything works so you can go to bed." With a feather-light touch to the small of her back, he nudged her toward the door. "Even harpies and harridans need to rest sometimes. Otherwise, they're too sleepy for optimal shrewage."

"*Shrewage* isn't a word."

"It is now."

After disarming the alarm and unlocking the door, she stepped inside the stables and found . . . what might possibly be the perfect apartment for her.

The downstairs was one large open area, with comfortable-looking seating, a widescreen television, a small kitchen and dining area, and a bathroom tucked to one side. Not a speck of dust to be seen anywhere, no doubt because of Dina's hard work.

More white marble countertops. Stainless appliances. Shining wooden floors. Even another small fireplace bursting with waxy-leaved plants.

The narrow set of stairs at the other end of the room must lead to—

"The bedroom is upstairs. There's a private balcony, one that overlooks the Hills. If you keep that door cracked, you'll get a nice breeze at night. There's a way to work it out with the alarm. I'll show you." He stood inside the entryway with his arms akimbo. "I think everything is pretty easy to figure out, but why don't you take a look around before I leave?"

She kicked off her shoes and went exploring. All the appliances seemed both expensive and easy to use, and so did the television.

The bathroom . . .

Well, she might never leave the bathroom. It was a much larger version of the powder room in the main house, all marble and gold fixtures, complete with the most glorious hand towels in existence, not to mention *entire bath towels* made from the material. On the back of the door, there was even a robe in that same fabric hanging from an elegant hook. It wouldn't fit her, of course, but she appreciated the gesture.

There was a walk-in shower and a large soaking tub and a generous sink and vanity, and she wanted inside that shower right this second. Instead, she reluctantly left the bathroom and climbed the near-spiral stairs to a high-ceilinged bedroom, dominated by a king bed with a fluffy aqua duvet and gracefully curving headboard. The rug under her feet was turquoise and white and pale yellow, and from all signs, the product of sheep who spent their lives deep-conditioning their wool for optimal softness.

When she came back downstairs, she didn't know whether to kiss him or cry at the prospect of someday leaving the Stable of Dreams.

He was sagging against the door, but straightened when she appeared. "Everything look okay?"

She merely nodded, overcome by the very-much-more-than-okayness of it all.

"The entire property might have basic security features, but make sure to flip the deadbolt when I leave and keep it locked whenever you're in here. Activate the alarm system too. Understood?" There was no trace of amusement anywhere in his features or voice. "I've been lucky to this point, but people know my name, and they can figure out where I live. Be smart, and keep yourself safe."

He headed for the door. "You have my number. Call me if you need me, and I'll be here in less than a minute. See you tomorrow."

She blinked at his back, startled by the sincerity and simplicity of his parting words.

No sarcasm? No parting shots about—

"As always, watch for signs of frivolity and eliminate them with extreme prejudice." He spoke over his shoulder. "Joy and pleasure could be lurking anywhere, at any time. Stay vigilant, Nanny Clegg."

Then the door was closing behind him, and he was gone, leaving her somehow both aggrieved and relieved. But he didn't move far, as she soon discovered.

"I'm waiting!" he shouted from the other side of the door a moment later, his voice muffled. "Can't you follow simple instructions, you dolt of a woman?"

Once she'd clicked the deadbolt into place, he strode toward the main house. One after another, lights illuminated above him, as if spotlighting his progress on a stage, and she watched that progress from the window nearest the door.

His pace rapid, he moved along the wide stone path bordered by pebbles and various drought-resistant plants. Once he disappeared through the front door to the castle, she set the alarm, stepped back from the window, and pulled the curtains shut against the darkness outside.

She should take a shower, unpack, and get to bed, but instead she wandered the house again, uncharacteristically restless. Even rubbing her cheek against the best toweling in the universe couldn't ease that weird, empty pit in her stomach.

It was an odd feeling, to have Alex so far away at night.

A relief, obviously. Dealing with him took a lot of energy.

But the little guesthouse was very, very quiet without his oversized presence, or even his half-shouted, half-laughing conversations with Marcus on the other side of a thin wall.

She must simply be lonely for human contact, however aggravating. After her shower, she'd call Sionna.

Then this niggling feeling—like she'd forgotten something important, or left it somewhere it didn't belong—would disappear. For good, she hoped.

MIMES AND MOONLIGHT

INT. ELEGANT PARISIAN RESTAURANT - EVENING

*JOHNNY and ESMÉE are sitting across an intimate,
candlelit table from one another, virtually alone
in the restaurant. She looks distraught. Concerned,
Johnny reaches for her hand.*

JOHNNY

What's wrong, Esmée?

   *Esmée pulls free from his grip and walks an
imaginary dog. She points to the dog, then herself.*

JOHNNY

I make you feel leashed? Like some kind of pet? But
my darling, if you'd ever *told* me—

   *She shakes her head sadly and pulls an imaginary
rope, hand over hand, then cups her belly.*

JOHNNY

No! Not our instructor from that ropes course! You
can't be having his baby!

   *She stands and bends backward, arms flailing, as if
beset by a strong wind.*

JOHNNY

Of course you're off-balance right now! Let me help
you, Esmée!

   *Esmée makes several indistinct movements. Johnny
shakes his head in bewilderment. She becomes*

*frustrated by her inability to find gestures to
communicate what she wants to say. After a few more
waves of her arms, she gives up with a shrug and
speaks.*

ESMÉE

With you, I'm trapped, Johnny. Like I'm in a box. And
I could never find a way to tell you.

6

"THE GROUNDS ARE ALL YOURS, AND YOU CAN EXPLORE AT will." Squinting against the bright morning light, Alex donned his sunglasses and continued speaking, despite Lauren's complete lack of response. "Other seating areas have spectacular views of downtown L.A., the Hills, and the Reservoir. On a really clear day, you can even see the Pacific."

After downing his ADHD medication with a gulp of coffee, he set his mug on the teakwood table, poked a finger at his remaining cherry-cheese Danish, and grimaced.

Why did he sound like a real estate agent trying to unload a property on an unwilling buyer? This was way too undignified, dammit, even for a man who'd never considered dignity a particularly valuable commodity.

But he couldn't seem to stop himself.

He pointed to a tree-studded area of his grounds. "You can pick your own oranges, Meyer lemons, and grapefruits. Avocados too."

When he glanced at Lauren, her face was pointed in the direction he'd indicated, but her expression was as difficult to read as ever. More so, even, since she wore her own oversized sunglasses.

Before answering, she finished chewing a bite of her apple Danish, because *of course* she'd chosen the most boring breakfast option Dina had supplied.

"Convenient," she said in her imperturbable, irritating-as-hell way.

She probably didn't even like oranges or avocados, because she was the *worst*.

"After you finish eating your apple-filled disappointment of a pastry, why don't you say hello to Dina and work out a good schedule with her? Then we'll head out."

"First of all . . ." She shoved the last bite of her Danish in her mouth, chewing thoroughly and swallowing before speaking again, because she was Nanny Clegg, the world's most rule-bound human. "My pastry was exceptional. Flaky and buttery, and the apples still had a bit of texture. Second of all, where are we going?"

He looked at her with pity. "It didn't even have icing on it. You're a barbarian."

"I repeat." She finished her fresh-squeezed orange juice and put down her glass. "Where are we going?"

"We're getting you a dress. Time to *Pretty Woman* this shit." He cracked his knuckles with relish. "I can't wait until someone refuses to wait on you because you're so obviously an unsophisticated oaf from Kansas or wherever—"

"North Hollywood. Basically just down this hill and over the next one."

"—and then you can leave, brokenhearted and ashamed, only to return hours later, carrying thousands of dollars of haute couture to rub in how much commission money they lost."

She was massaging her temples again.

"Petty revenge is the most satisfying, always." With his forefinger, he pushed her phone closer to her on the table. "You should write that down somewhere. Consider it a free preview of my TED Talk."

For a long, satisfying moment, she appeared entirely speechless. Then she spoke, each word slow and precise.

"Okay, first thing." She paused again, and yet more temple-rubbing occurred. "Why do I need to keep making lists with you?"

"That's your first thing?" He furrowed his brow at her. "It's a weird first thing."

"It's not my first thing. It's an addendum, jackass."

He gasped, loudly enough that a nearby bird flapped away in alarm. "Such language! Why, my delicate ears!"

Her breaths seemed to dramatically lengthen at that point, and he figured she was counting to herself.

After several vastly entertaining and very deep inhalations, she got a hold of her temper. "First thing: I am not a sex worker, and you are not my client. Thus, we cannot, as you so eloquently put it, '*Pretty Woman* this shit.' Second: As you are neither my john nor my sugar daddy of any sort, you will not be paying for these garments, and I can't afford thousands of dollars' worth of clothing I'll never wear again. Third—"

"The production would pay for a red-carpet-appropriate dress," he interrupted.

"Third," she repeated with steely determination, "cocktail dresses don't come in my size, at least not ones you'd find in standard L.A. stores. For something beautiful that truly fit me, you'd need to employ Christian Siriano—"

"I knew you liked reality television! Ha!"

He'd figured her indifference to *GBBO* was an act. It *had* to be. Who could resist Nadiya's sweet, emotional ascent to baking triumph? Also the hilarious duo of Sue and Mel?

"—or, more likely, go online and order something a lot less pretty but also a lot less expensive. Then get it hemmed. Which we, fourth, do not have time to do, since the event is tomorrow night. So, fifth, we need to drive to my duplex and decide which of the few dresses I already own might suffice."

Oooh. He was going to see his stern minder's inner sanctum? Her Fortress of Stultifying Solitude? He couldn't wait.

"You're bringing me home?" He widened his eyes. "But you haven't even taken me out on a real date yet. I don't want you to think I'm cheap."

"For the love of . . ." Now she was rubbing her forehead as well as her temples, and he would feel worse if a tiny little smile weren't also curving the corners of that wide mouth. "I'd planned to visit my apartment soon anyway, since the clothing I packed for a Spanish vacation isn't the same clothing I want to wear here. So we might as well take care of everything today. I'll drive."

He sprang to his feet. "Let's do this, Thelma."

"Sit down, Louise." She pointed a commanding finger at his chair. "You've barely had anything but coffee. Last week, you repeatedly complained about stomach pain because of your medicine, and you told me the best way to prevent that pain was eating more breakfast. So let's make sure you do that."

He hadn't realized she'd been listening to him. If he had, he might not have mentioned—

Oh, who was he trying to fool? *Of course* he'd have mentioned the issue. *Not* saying things was unnatural, which he'd also explained to Lauren multiple times.

She was still talking, so apparently she'd listened to him then too.

"—the label on your pill bottle, you should be taking your medication with plenty of water," she told him. "We'll bring a bottle in my car, and you can drink it along the way."

What he ate or drank wasn't in her realm of professional authority over him. Then again, the concern in her voice didn't sound professional either.

It was personal. It was *present*.

He couldn't see her glorious green eyes, but he knew they'd be warm. Worried.

So he sat his ass back down and ate his remaining Danish without argument before they headed back to the house. Which made her lips quirk that tiny bit again.

He liked it.

He wanted more of it.

LAUREN'S FUCKING DUPLEX. It had a steeply pitched roof and cream stucco siding, and for the entrance—

It had a goddamn *turret*. A small one, but definitely, positively, a *turret*.

If Alex lived in a mini-castle, she lived in a mini-mini-castle.

No wonder she'd lost her shit at the sight of his house yesterday. Hell, he was losing his shit now, because what were the odds?

"Keep breathing." She parked inside the detached two-car garage and thumped him on the back. "I told you not to take a sip of water before we turned onto my street."

Once he stopped cough-laughing and finally caught his breath again, he needed more details. "What's that architectural style called?"

"Dilapidated." Dry as the Santa Ana winds. "Also, according to the real estate agent, storybook. Or Hansel and Gretel."

"Did you know—" He had to stop for another fit of laughter. "Did you know that Ian has a castle too? And it's the tackiest fucking place you've ever seen? He got it a month after I moved into my house, so I think he bought it as some sort of weird dick-measuring thing."

She choked a little too, seemingly on thin air. "Like, my turrets are taller and more upright than yours?"

"There are made-up coats of arms and long axes on the walls inside." Ah, happy memories. "The one time I visited there for a cast thing, I told him straight-faced that my castle had a long axe too, and it was longer than any of his. The next time we were filming together, he showed me a photo of his brand-new custom axe. The shaft was twelve goddamn feet long, Lauren, no lie."

And there he had it. She was actively laughing again, her eyes bright, her smile wide.

"Now, then," he said with satisfaction, "let's go inside and survey the lackluster contents of your wardrobe. We don't have all day for your chitchat, Nanny Clegg. Chop-chop."

She stopped laughing and glared at him, then sighed and got out of her hybrid.

The turret was fun, but the interior of her duplex—which she apparently shared with her best friend, Sionna, who was at work and thus not available for his interrogation—wasn't especially prepossessing. The apartment had decent enough wooden floors and casement windows, but also a tiny, tiny bedroom and an equally tiny kitchen that had, at some point in its lamented past, undergone disastrous updating.

He recognized the IKEA furniture from his lean years in Hollywood, pre-*Gates*.

"Hey, Billy!" he greeted the bookshelves as he moved past them. "Long time no see!"

She just rolled her eyes and waved him into her bedroom, which was disappointingly neat and free from clutter. Any personality she had here, she kept locked away, apparently. He really needed to get a closer look at those bookshelves, or possibly her nightstand.

Women kept all sorts of fun stuff in their nightstands. He knew that for a fucking fact.

Like her kitchen, her wardrobe was outdated and disastrous. At least, assuming she wanted to wear anything other than tees, jeans, leggings, black pants, or neutral button-downs for the rest of her benighted, boring-ass life. Which she apparently didn't, since the clothes she kept packing in a suitcase were from those groups.

"You have a suck-ass wardrobe, Nanny Clegg," he told her.

She blew out an exasperated breath. "My nicer clothes, I brought with me to Spain. They're already in the guesthouse."

He tried to think back. "I don't remember any nice clothes."

"I wore a dress to dinner that first night!" She threw up her hands. "A swing dress! It's dark green and pretty!"

He'd like to see her in it again. At the time, he hadn't paid sufficient attention, clearly.

"Maybe so, but it's not a cocktail dress either." He perched on the end of her bed, and holy Jesus, the woman needed a better mattress, stat. "What do you have that's sparkly?"

Another withering look. "I don't do sparkly."

When she produced a black dress, he nodded. "I see. You do funereal instead."

"It's *lace*." She shook the hanger in his face. "It's a lovely dress, and I feel good in it."

That brought him up short. If her depressing black dress and unmemorable green swing dress helped her feel comfortable in her own skin, he'd have to be a real asshole to insult them.

He frequently was an asshole, of course. But maybe not so much today.

"Let's see it on," he said.

"What?" Her face scrunched up in confusion, and honestly, it was kind of adorable.

"Try it on." His flick of the hand directed her toward the bathroom. "If it's not appropriate for the red carpet, we'll figure something else out. I can call in some favors, or there's always *Gates's* wardrobe department. They'd probably be able to whip up a suitable dress in time."

"I'm not playing dress-up with you," she said dampeningly.

"Why not?"

She didn't have a good answer to that, apparently, because she bustled into her bathroom with the dress. Or, more accurately, stomped, which was a different sort of victory.

After several minutes, she poked her head around the door.

"This has to be good enough, Alex." Her mouth was pale and tight with tension. "I don't want you to call in favors, and I don't want your costume department to do extra work for me."

From what he could tell, she didn't like anyone doing much of anything for her. Ever.

"Okay." He reclined back on the bed, bracing himself on his elbows. "Look, here's the deal. When we walk the red carpet, all the photographers will just tell you to move anyway. They'll want you out of their shots, because I'm the dude their audience pays to look at. Not a random woman they've never seen before and may never see again. So as long as your dress isn't actively embarrassing, it doesn't really matter what you wear."

"Then why all this talk about couture?" Her voice contained entire worlds of strained patience.

He shrugged. "I like sparkly shit."

"Of course you do," she said in that dry Santa Ana voice.

When she stepped out from behind the bathroom door, he had

to smile. Genuinely smile, because yes, that dress was clearly not couture or even high-end, but it *was* lovely on her. It might have been black, black, black, but the floaty knee-length skirt and peeks of pale skin beneath the lace were pretty.

"The dress is fine. You'll be fine." He collapsed down onto the bed and waved her away. "I may not be, however. I need to work on my speech for the auction and get it approved by Ron before tomorrow."

The bathroom door shut again, and she called out from behind it. "What's the charity?"

"A local organization that works to prevent domestic violence and provides shelters for abused women and children." He scratched absently at his beard. "I've been involved with them for a few years. Hopefully my exceedingly handsome face will bring in some high bids, because my speech is currently as heinous and inadequate as your daily wardrobe."

He needed to script a better speech, and he would. It might be especially hard to bear down and finish projects when he was tired, but he'd had years of specialized therapy to help him through situations just like this.

"Are there any other big names coming?" she asked, her voice still muffled.

He closed his eyes, suddenly tired again. "Asha had planned to attend, but she's evidently on a quest to make out with her pop star boyfriend in every Mediterranean port. She sent a big honking donation in apology."

He had to admit, he was a bit jealous. Not of Asha or her ginger boy toy, but of what they were experiencing right now. That all-consuming *need* to be with another person. The sort of raging desire and attraction that meant you couldn't—wouldn't—be parted for long.

He hadn't felt that for years. Maybe for more than a decade now.

"Otherwise, the big names are my cast friends who live in the area. Carah Brown. Maria Ivarsson. Peter Reedton." He hadn't bothered issuing an invitation to Ian, and Mackenzie had already given money on Whiskers's behalf. "I don't think you've met any of them. They'd all finished filming before you arrived."

Marcus would have come too, but he was currently in San Francisco and utterly preoccupied with a geologist named April, and Alex wouldn't get in the way of that.

He'd just make sure Marcus sent the charity a healthy donation later.

Lauren's voice came from near the bed, and he startled.

"Let's get you home," she said quietly. "We both need lunch and a nap, and you need to work on your speech."

She was back in a nondescript tee and jeans, lovely eyes sympathetic as she surveyed his limp, supine form. Her beaky, crooked nose caught the light from one of the casement windows, and he stared.

Maybe she was right after all.

Maybe flashier clothing would only compete with her distinctive features and frame. Maybe they'd distract from what made her interesting and unique.

Not that he'd ever tell her that.

When she held out her hand, he took it. She helped him off the bed, and he gave her fingers a little squeeze before letting go.

"Don't think I missed the wedge heels you packed into your suitcase." He sniffed in judgment, hoisted her luggage, and swept out her bedroom door. "Hasn't the Killjoy Guild of America discussed the dangers of such sartorial folly and extravagance?"

She snorted, and he smiled, content.

Lauren's Email

From: l.c.clegg@umail.com
To: KingRon@godsofthegates.com
Subject: Weekly report and tomorrow's event

Dear Ron—

As promised, here's my first weekly report as to Alex's behavior. I know you didn't want to tell him I was sending you regular updates, but as you may recall, I ~~deliberately remained silent and didn't argue, but also~~ did not agree to that stricture. Thus, I informed him on our first day together that I would be writing you every week, and reminded him of that again today. He said to send ~~"regards so warm they might as well be afire, which, now that I consider the matter, may help prepare him for the afterlife"~~ his regards.

Thus far, his behavior has been ~~irritating as hell, but essentially~~ unobjectionable. On set, as you know, he was hardworking and professional. Whenever and wherever we have encountered fans, he has been kind and charming and patient about selfies. He has also been very welcoming in his home.

Finally, despite your concerns, he has not shared any confidential or damaging information about the production or the final season's scripts, and he has not consumed alcohol to excess on any occasion. ~~Are you entirely certain he was drunk the night of the bar fight?~~

If you desire other information from me, please let me know, and ~~I will consider whether your requests constitute an invasion of Alex's privacy~~ we can discuss the matter.

I know that I am supposed to accompany him to his red-carpet charity auction tomorrow, but I'm unclear as far as what is expected of me at the event. Do you intend for me to walk the red carpet by his side? He has indicated that he expects that, but ~~surely he should~~

~~have someone better suited to such events accompanying him~~ I wasn't certain.

Also, what explanation do you wish me to give for my presence? Alex has indicated that he wouldn't mind my telling everyone ~~"this is Nanny Clegg, the perplexingly short albatross I must carry in penance for my previous misdeeds"~~ the truth, but I don't think that reflects well on either him or your production. If you can, please advise me before tomorrow night.

My mother sends her regards~~, which, unlike Alex's, would be genuinely warm, because she doesn't know you very well~~.

Sincerely,

Lauren

7

LATER THAT EVENING, AFTER ALEX HAD LUNCHED, NAPPED, wrestled his speech into something workable, received Ron's approval, and eaten supper with Lauren in his dining nook, he thumped down into his office chair and made two calls he'd been avoiding.

First, his agent. In theory, that could be a video call, but nah. As was his right as an American, Alex reserved the option to make faces at his phone when displeased by the conversation.

"Alex, *finally*," Zach answered, and fortunately could not see the eye roll he received in response. "Stop dodging my damn emails. We have things we need to discuss."

"Unfair, dude." Alex leaned back in his office chair and swiveled it from side to side. "I didn't dodge your emails. After reading them with laudable—nay, *remarkable*—speed and attention, I simply determined that they didn't require any immediate response."

From the other end of the line, there was an odd sound. Teeth-grinding?

Zach enunciated each word very carefully. "In recent weeks, I've received multiple messages from the producers of your upcoming projects asking about your current behavior. They're all checking in to discover whether you're, as they put it, 'still spiraling out of control.'"

Alex and Zach had discussed the very same topic at least half a dozen times since the incident in Spain, and not once—not a single time—had Zach actually asked him what happened. Even though they'd been working together since the beginning of Alex's career, both Hollywood hopefuls fresh out of high school and waiting tables to fill empty bank accounts.

It was a simple question, and one Alex had deserved after so many years.

"You said all this in your emails." A better person would mute the phone as he yawned, but Alex didn't bother. "Was there anything else?"

A heavy sigh. "In my emails, I also asked whether that woman Ron assigned you is keeping you contained, because another major scandal, and you'll run afoul of the good-behavior clauses in the contracts you signed. You've failed to answer the question. Multiple times."

Keeping you contained. As if he were a zoo animal. A lion, perhaps?

If so, something about Zach's tone in reference to Lauren had rubbed Alex's lush, gloriously abundant mane the wrong way.

He sat up straight. "'That woman' is Lauren Clegg. Or, rather, Ms. Clegg. And she is doing an exemplary job of stamping out all stray sparks of joy and exhilaration I might happen to experience on a daily basis, rest assured."

"Fine. Good." The edge in Zach's tone matched Alex's own. "*Ms. Clegg* better continue to do her damn job, because we can't afford another screwup."

"Whatever her job description might be, *I* am responsible for my own behavior. Not her. No matter what happens, she's not at fault. I want that absolutely clear." The fucking *nerve.* "Is that all? Because I have better things to do. I haven't flossed for several hours, and I hear my future producers are also considering whether my plaque levels are within contractual bounds."

A long silence stretched over the line, and Alex half wondered whether this was it. The moment, the conversation, that would sever their partnership at long last.

The prospect should probably frighten him, and maybe it would later, but it didn't now. Either Zach showed Lauren respect, or he could fuck off to somewhere else in Hollywood.

"I hope you know what you're doing." Zach's voice was tight.

"As much as I ever did," Alex said, then ended the call.

To cool his temper afterward, he read a Cupid/Psyche fic where Psyche was a small village's intended human sacrifice to a clan of werewolves headed by Jupiter—at least until Cupid, Jupiter's grandson, fell in love with her and spirited her away from danger.

After that, matters got rather heated, and it was all *extremely* delightful.

Spirits restored, he then FaceTimed his mother. Complete with video, this time and every time. Without fail. Because he needed to see her expression, her body language, for himself.

Linda answered after two rings, her gray-streaked brown hair gathered into a messy ponytail atop her head, her face lit in a happy beam.

The sun was just setting in Florida, and the warm golden glow bathed her perch on the back porch swing. She set it to rocking, and her tidy yard whooshed back and forth while her face remained steady and centered on the screen.

"Sweetheart!" Her eyes, the same gray as his, creased at the corners with her smile. "I didn't know you were calling today."

She looked good. She sounded good too, and something wound tight within him released. At least, until the next phone call.

He wished he could recapture the joy, the unalloyed comfort, her voice used to give him. That sense of homecoming and acceptance, despite all his grievous flaws.

Her voice hadn't changed. Her love for him hadn't changed.

He'd changed, just over eleven years ago.

And it was for the better, it really was. He should know how he'd wronged someone he loved as dearly as he loved her, so he could do his damnedest never to make the same mistake again. But the guilt, the self-directed anger, had stripped away the simple solace her presence, her loving words, used to provide. Now when he talked to her, he wasn't simply talking to his mom anymore. He was talking to someone he'd harmed, and he couldn't forget it. Wouldn't forget it.

"I wanted to check in and see how you're doing," he said, and it was the simple truth.

No hesitation. "I'm doing great. How about you?"

As usual, she fiddled with the cheap locket around her neck as she spoke. He'd given it to her . . . what? Twenty years ago? Not long after he'd left for L.A., anyway.

She still wore it every day, because she loved the pair of tiny photos inside. On the left: the two of them, mother and child, from when he was a toddler. On the right: the two of them fifteen years later, posed exactly the same way as in the earlier shot.

He'd even managed to find reasonably similar clothing for the second photo, although his mom had insisted he leave out the pacifier for the department-store shoot. If memory served, he'd called her a spoilsport and produced a beanie with a propeller on top instead.

At some point, he'd have to introduce Lauren to his mom. He suspected they'd discover a great deal of common ground when it came to him.

"I'm an exemplar of good health, good looks, and good choices, as usual." He smirked at his mother, who merely rolled her eyes in response. "What's happening for you this week?"

"Not much." She tilted her head in thought. "They finally have the new kid fully trained, so I can take an extra day off. I'm going to set up my big umbrella, put some paperbacks I don't mind getting sandy in my bag, and relax by the water on Thursday."

Alex sent enough money for her not to work, but she preferred to keep busy. Her part-time job at a seaside used bookstore kept her happy and well supplied with reading material.

At least she'd finally accepted a new home by the beach a few years back. She deserved the world, and that would be true even if he weren't roiling with guilt.

"Umbrella or no umbrella, put on your sunscreen," he reminded her. "You remember what your dermatologist said."

"Nag." It was a cheerful accusation, and an ironic one, given his complaints about Lauren. And as if she'd read his thoughts, his mom added, "Speaking of wise decision-making, how's it going with Lauren? You're being kind to her, Alex, I know. Aren't you?"

That tone could still make him squirm, even as a man in his late thirties. As could that calm, piercing, *knowing* gaze.

"I, uh . . ." He licked his lips and swiveled his chair some more. "I made sure she had everything she needed in the guesthouse?"

Dammit. That was supposed to be a confident statement, not a question freighted with guilt, but holy shit, his mother had *powers*.

"Hmmmm." She narrowed her eyes at him. "That's not a yes, Alexander Bernard Woodroe."

"She thinks I'm funny. Mostly." He looked somewhere into the middle distance, where he couldn't actually see his mom's chiding expression, then scrambled to change the subject. "Anyway, we have a charity event to attend together tomorrow, which—"

Motherfucker.

He closed his eyes briefly. *Shit. Shit, shit, shit.*

He didn't want to talk about the event with his mom. He *couldn't.*

"What's it for?" She didn't sound entirely appeased, but she'd accepted the change of topic, which was unfortunate. "The environment? Or that UN global poverty initiative we talked about a while ago?"

"Something like that," he mumbled. "Look, Mom, I should probably go. I just got a text from Lauren about, uh"—fuck, why would she be texting him?—"our apple-Danish supplies"—oh, that was *terrible*—"and I don't want to keep her waiting. She's my guest, after all. My *honored* guest, whom I treat with the utmost respect and courtesy at all times."

Another unconvinced hum was her only response to that. But she let him off the hook.

"All right, sweetheart. Thanks for calling." Her suspicious glare softened into a loving, soft smile. "I'll talk to you soon?"

"Yes. Definitely." It was a vow. "If you need anything at all, call me. Immediately."

And that was a demand. A plea.

Her brow furrowed. "Alex, honey—"

No, they weren't having this conversation. "I love you, Mom. Bye."

He barely let her say it back before he cut their connection, all his werewolf-related peace of mind entirely absent once more.

To calm himself, he could read another fic, of course. Earlier that day, a story had appeared in the Cupid/Psyche fandom involving something called . . . consentacles? Whatever that was, it sounded intriguing.

Or . . . or . . .

He could do what he'd been contemplating for days now.

He opened his laptop.

As soon as Marcus had explained the idea of fanfic, Alex had felt drawn to the concept. And after reading Marcus's stories and dozens of Cupid/Psyche fix-it fics in his spare time, he wanted to write his own.

A literary genius, he was not. But bitching to Marcus wasn't enough anymore.

He needed an outlet. To wrestle with Cupid's warped, regressive character arc. To express how redemptive Cupid's story could have been in the hands of virtually anyone other than Ron and R.J. To apologize to the fandom, even in such an inadequate way, for how Cupid's final-season relationship with Venus and Jupiter had become a glorification of abuse, and how it implied violent, manipulative relationships couldn't be ended or escaped.

By acting out his scenes to the best of his abilities, he'd made that message more powerful. More believable.

He should have quit as soon as he saw the scripts for the last season, but he hadn't. The shame of that burned like bile in his throat.

His fanfiction would serve as therapy and penance both.

And as long as he was writing fanfic, he might as well include pegging. He wanted some damn kudos, and dildos the width of a lover's forearm were apparently the best way—other than actual writing skill—to gain an audience.

For his AO3 account, he chose the screen name Cupid-Unleashed. Chortling with glee the entire time, he selected all the most popular tags for his fic: *Porn Without Plot. Smuttity Smut Smut. Half-Human Disaster Cupid. Bottoms Up. The Peg That Was Promised.*

On the verge of designating Cupid/Psyche as the relationship, he paused.

Asha portrayed Psyche on-screen, and she was his friend and colleague. He didn't want to involve her, even tangentially, in a story about the character he played having sex with hers, because that would be fucking creepy.

Although it would definitely limit his audience, he'd have to write about Cupid and an original character instead. But what to call her?

He scratched at his beard. What . . . to . . . call . . . her?

When inspiration struck, he sat bolt upright.

Why the name was so perfect, he couldn't explain. But somehow he knew, *he knew,* it was what Cupid's lover should be called.

With that piece of information in place, the first line emerged effortlessly from his keyboard, and he beamed at his monitor.

The day Cupid met Robin, he said goodbye to his family for good.

Rating: Explicit

Fandoms: Gods of the Gates – E. Wade, Gods of the Gates (TV)

Relationships: Cupid/Original Character

Additional Tags: Alternate Universe – Modern, Porn Without Plot, Smuttity Smut Smut, Half-Human Disaster Cupid, Bottoms Up, The Peg That Was Promised

Stats: Words: 2531 Chapters: 1/1 Comments: 102 Kudos: 411 Bookmarks: 27

Square Peg
CupidUnleashed

Summary:

Cupid wants to free himself from his unhealthy relationship with his family. And he's about to get help from the most unlikely woman of all—a harpy with a dildo the size of her fucking forearm.

Notes:

Thanks to AeneasLovesLavinia. You rock as a beta, dude. Also, please consider this a fix-it fic for the show, despite my inclusion of an original character.

Fuck knows it needs fixing. Badly.

———————————————————

. . . The harpy pinned him against the marble slab. She was stronger than she looked, and that only made him hotter. More eager for her to lube him up, strap on her harness, and peg his fucking brains out with that alarmingly large dildo she owned.

"Robin," he sighed contentedly. "After tonight, after you've claimed me, I'll be done with my mother forever. Venus will no longer have any hold on me."

"I know," she said. "Once you're mine, you'll never follow her cruel commands again, or even Jupiter's. He may be CEO of your family company, but he's not your boss anymore."

"I think . . ." He hesitated.

She sat back on her heels, her eyes surprisingly pretty and patient. "What is it, Cupid? You can tell me anything, you know."

"I know." He smiled up at her, grateful. "I want to be yours, Robin, so very much. But I was just thinking—even if you left me, I still wouldn't return to them. No matter what."

She nodded. "You couldn't. You've changed too much for that. I'm glad you realize it."

"Freeing myself has been such a slow process, but after five years, there's no logical way I could ever go back to Venus and Jupiter. That anyone would think otherwise baffles and offends me, frankly." He scowled fiercely. "If the two of them ever ordered me to leave you unconscious and dying so I could fight one of their corporate battles, for instance, I'd simply tell them to go fuck themselves. I definitely wouldn't obey."

"So true," she agreed. "You wouldn't ever abandon anyone you truly loved, and after tonight, I promise you: You'll more than love me. You'll *worship* me."

"Ahhhh," he sighed. "I can't wait. Take me, harpy. Take me now."

"You don't give the orders here," she retorted, a predatory gleam in her eyes. "I do."

"And thank the gods for that," he said, turning onto his belly.

Then she got out the lube and the harness, and he took it back. He took it all back.

The size of that dildo was *just right.*

8

"I'M TRYING TO FIGURE OUT HOW I SHOULD INTRODUCE YOU on the red carpet. 'Lauren Clegg, Freelance Foe of Fun'?" Alex stroked his bristly chin in faux thought. "Or perhaps 'Nanny Clegg: Like Mary Poppins, Minus the Umbrella and Any Sense of Whimsy'?"

One of these days, Lauren's middle finger was simply going to raise itself.

She shifted in the back of the town car, trying not to nudge Alex's legs with her knee. "If you don't introduce me at all, won't everyone just assume I work for the show or the charity in some capacity? I certainly don't look like a star. Besides, as I was told only yesterday, you're the *dude* their audience wants to watch. No one will really care who I am, correct?"

Whether the argument convinced him or not, it was helping her. The echoing pulse in her ears slowed and grew fainter, and the lace of her dress resumed feeling soft, rather than stifling and scratchy.

She might be walking a red carpet—*her*, Lauren Chandra Clegg—but no one cared except her. Which was true about many things in her life, come to think of it.

Still, she wished she could distract herself by fiddling with her purse, but she'd left it at the guesthouse. *Clutch or nothing*, Alex had said, *them's the rules*, so she'd wordlessly handed him her ID, a credit card, her phone, and some tinted lip balm, all of which he'd secreted somewhere in his not-quite-navy, obscenely formfitting tux.

He looked like a star. Also the night sky surrounding that star, right as blue turned to velvety black. The color, she'd discovered, was much more evocative and dangerous than plain old black or navy could ever be.

"Correct," he conceded with clear reluctance.

She drummed her fingers on the plush leather seat. "Look, if anyone asks about me, just give them my name and tell them I work for the show. Which I do, so you're not lying, but you're also not revealing my specific role in your life."

"I'm not ashamed of you," he said abruptly. "I'm not ashamed of what I did, and I'm not ashamed of you."

"Okay." The gruff, vehement emphasis in his words left her bewildered. "Listen . . . Alex, if you're willing to tell me, what actually—"

Then she cut herself off, because they'd arrived at the mouth of the red carpet, located just outside the swanky Beverly Hills hotel where the charity auction was occurring. A woman wearing a skinny suit and a headset greeted their driver as soon as he braked and rolled down his window.

"That'll be the publicist for the event organizer," Alex told Lauren. "Just do what she says, and don't get offended by all the photographers shouting at you."

She frowned. "Shouting at—"

Before she could say more, the driver opened the door. Alex swung his legs out of the vehicle and onto the pavement, stood, buttoned his suit jacket, and reached a gentlemanly hand back for her.

He helped her out of the car while she straightened her dress and desperately tried not to flash anyone, and then there were flashes blinding her in little bursts all around as she followed the tug of his grip.

The publicist greeted them both, then gestured for them to move toward the hotel. "I'm here to help, Mr. Woodroe. Let me know if you need anything along the way."

Beneath Lauren's uncomfortable wedge heels, red carpet suddenly appeared. The publicist said something Lauren couldn't hear and guided them over to a journalist with a pleasant but firm "Two minutes, Ted."

The man introduced himself and asked about the final season of *Gods of the Gates* while a camerawoman filmed the interview, and Lauren belatedly let Alex go, inching away from his side. But there were flashes behind her too, and, yes, photographers yelling at her.

"Move! *Move!*" they screamed, and she would gladly go down the other side of the red carpet, where more-normal-looking people were hustling toward the hotel ballroom, but she couldn't. It was her job to stay by Alex, no matter what—Ron had sent a peremptory email emphasizing that very fact earlier today—even though she couldn't control what came out of that endlessly moving mouth, no one could.

"Move! *Move, lady, come on!*"

Up ahead of her, talking to another journalist, was Carah Brown. Behind Lauren and Alex, just entering the red carpet, Maria Ivarsson and Peter Reedton strolled arm in arm, as a woman in a skirt suit and yet another headset spoke and pointed them to a specific news outlet.

Oh, shit, this was absolute chaos, and she was sweating now. Even trembling a little.

Before Lauren quite knew it, the publicist was ushering them to the next reporter, who actually glanced at Alex's companion before beginning the interview. Lauren was blinking against the bright spots in her vision when she heard Alex say her name.

"—Lauren Clegg, who works for the production. So, no, she didn't win a fan contest, although she certainly loves my character." Then he was winking at her, the asshole, and drawing her closer to his side with a warm hand on her arm. "Tell him, Ms. Clegg. Tell them how much you adore Cupid. Not to mention the actor who plays him with such glorious talent and commitment."

She was about to answer, about to say heaven only knew what, when she saw it.

Movement, where there shouldn't have been. Acceleration.

After the hurled tray that broke her nose, after all those patients high or angry or hurting and volatile in their pain, her instincts were sound, and they were fast. *She* was fast. And even amid all the flashes and shouts and sparkly cocktail dresses and various celebrity interviews occurring all around her—

When a pale man with dark hair and dark clothing rushed onto the red carpet, accompanied by the sound of dismayed, panicked shouts, and half leaped, half crawled toward Alex, she didn't have to think. She simply used her body as a battering ram, shoving Alex out of the way, and took his place for whatever this intruder intended.

The man slammed into her thighs, and she toppled, doing her best to land on top of him and hoping like hell he didn't have a knife or a gun. People around them were screaming, and so was he, something about men's rights and red pills, and oh, shit, that elbow in her ribs hurt, and he was clawing at her, spitting at her, and Alex was there too, struggling and scrabbling, trying to get between her and the attacker, both men red-faced and shouting words she couldn't make out, but she wasn't going anywhere. Not until she knew everyone was safe.

Then security came rushing onto the scene, just like in the hospital, and she rolled aside as soon as they had the man incapacitated. From her prone position on the red carpet, she watched him get dragged off to goodness knew where while she panted and evaluated all the places she hurt.

No stab wounds. No gunshots. Just a lot of—

"Lauren!" Alex was on his knees beside her, his hand unsteady but firm on her cheek as he tried to get her attention. "Lauren, *answer me.* Where are you hurt?"

"Bruises," she managed to say. "Just bruises. You're okay?"

"Pristine," he said with awful, bitter sarcasm.

Deep breaths, one after the other. No one was bleeding or broken. Not him. Not her.

The excited conversation all around them was a disorienting tide of noise. It rushed through her head, dizzying her.

Flashes of light, so many of them. People were taking photos. Of her. Of Alex.

"If you're not injured, it's through no fault of your own." Whipping off his jacket, he used it to wipe the saliva from her arm, his cheekbones ruddy with high color. "I want you looked at, and I don't want a single fucking argument from you. He took you down like a bowling pin, and he kept swinging his fucking—"

With a violent jerk of his head, he looked around and yelled, "Where's Desiree? I want a medic here right now!"

"I don't need—" she began.

The sound he made in response to that . . .

Undiluted rage. Directed at her. It shocked her into silence.

He leaned his head close and hissed in her ear, and the heat radiating off him scalded her. "You just got between me and a fucking attacker, Lauren, so if I say you're going to see a fucking medic, *you are going to see a fucking medic.* Do you understand me?"

His chest rose and fell in rapid pants, and when he pulled away, his eyes were narrowed, hot slits on hers, and she nodded numbly.

"Good." The word was a snarl.

Alex brushed Lauren's tumbled hair back from her forehead in a surprisingly gentle stroke, then spat out a vicious, abrupt *fuck* and got up on his knees.

"Where the hell is Desiree?" he bellowed, and then the publicist was running toward them both, wide-eyed and frantic. "Lauren needs medical attention. I'll help you take her—"

"No," Lauren said.

He swung on her, jaw jutting and bunched, and again. That *sound.*

"I'll see a medic." She reached for his hand and squeezed it, desperate for him to hear her. "But I'm really fine. You need to stay here and give your interviews."

He dismissed that with a violent shake of his head. "I don't give a *fuck* about interviews."

"Charity." She kept her voice calm and low, her hand tight around his. "This is for charity, Alex. Women and children who need help. You're the host. The big star."

He dropped his chin to his chest, his upper body still heaving with every breath.

"I'll personally take care of her," Desiree assured him. "One of my assistants can guide you to the right media outlets along the carpet and at the step and repeat. And as soon as she's been checked out, Lauren can rejoin you inside the ballroom."

A minute passed, and they waited for him to calm. To decide what to do.

At long last, Alex raised his head and met her gaze. "Lauren? Do you want me with you?"

Yes. Shockingly . . .

Yes.

"No," she said. "I'm fine on my own. You go ahead. Desiree will take good care of me."

With a chiding *tsk tsk,* he bent close to her ear again.

"You're a terrible liar," he breathed, then moved far enough away to help ease her to her feet. His hands on her were firm but gentle, supportive as she locked her shaky knees beneath her and found her balance.

She thanked him with one more squeeze of his hand before letting go. "Don't say anything we'll all regret."

He grunted in response. Then, after a final, stern look at Desiree, its message clear—*do what you said you'd do, or else*—he followed a hovering young man with a headset to the next interviewer.

Desiree guided Lauren down the peon side of the carpet and into the hotel, and Alex disappeared from sight. Her bruises began to throb in time with each heartbeat, each step away from him.

"Do you happen to have any ibuprofen?" she asked the event publicist.

"If I don't, I'll find some." Desiree's lips quirked. "Otherwise, Mr. Woodroe is likely to feed me to the lions as tonight's grand finale."

Dazed and hurting, Lauren didn't respond to the other woman's wry remark.

But she thought about it as the medic examined her. She thought about all of it.

Desiree's words. Alex's volcanic fury at Lauren and for Lauren. Her own response to such fierce protectiveness.

In that moment, in his enraged concern, he'd put her first. Even above his own charity, his own professional obligations.

It felt . . . odd. Disorienting.

No one ever put her first.

Not even her.

Not until now.

9

BY THE TIME LAUREN MADE IT TO THE BALLROOM, HAIR combed, dress straightened, ibuprofen swallowed, the event was well underway, and Alex was nowhere in sight.

Desiree paused and listened to someone speaking through her earpiece, murmuring something in response. Then she turned to Lauren. "I need to go, I'm afraid. Are you okay on your own?"

Lauren nodded. "Thank you for all your help."

"No, thank *you* for making sure our guest of honor remained unscathed." The publicist's smile looked genuine. "Your table is at the front of the room, right in the center. A woman with a clipboard would normally check your name against the list for the VIP section, but I'm sure she knows who you are by now. You're kind of a big deal."

Lauren winced.

Her fame might be fleeting, but it was also unwelcome. She didn't want scrutiny. For her own sake, but also to protect Alex's privacy. No one outside the show needed to know she was serving as his minder.

"According to my assistant, the intruder is now at the police station, and officers there have your information if they need to get your statement. In the meantime, you shouldn't have any more trouble, and if you do, just ask to speak to me." Desiree shook Lauren's hand. "Take care, Ms. Clegg, and I hope the rest of your evening is significantly less eventful."

When the other woman strode away, Lauren followed at a more leisurely pace, allowing herself a moment to study her surroundings. The expansive ballroom was entirely filled with auction attendees, most of them already seated at the round tables dotting the space. Others still clustered near the silent auction pieces displayed at the back of the room, lined up for the open bar, or stood chatting in small, sparkly clumps of humanity. A small army of discreet servers wound between tables, offering hors d'oeuvres to the assembled crowd of people who were—in general—much wealthier and more beautiful than she was.

For a moment, her feet slowed almost to a stop, as her disorientation dizzied her.

Then the chandeliers overhead dimmed, and the chatter began to hush as stragglers returned to their tables and everyone in attendance turned their attention to the stage. Without further delay, Lauren hustled to her assigned spot, locating it without trouble. As promised, the clipboard-wielding woman near the front tables waved her along without a word, and Lauren sank at last into her cushioned seat with a sigh of relief. She'd made it in time, if only by seconds.

The other seats at her table were filled with familiar, famous faces. Carah Brown. Maria Ivarsson. Peter Reedton. A couple of other people she vaguely remembered from movie screens at her favorite local theater.

She didn't pay them a bit of attention beyond a single glance, because she'd finally spotted Alex. He was walking beside Desiree and ascending the steps to the stage. Just a few words from him, and the publicist began laughing as she took her position at the edge of the platform. Because he was a natural-born charmer, that man. The Pied Piper of too-serious women.

He stood behind a lectern on the brilliantly lit dais, the microphone positioned perfectly for his height, his midnight suit sleek, his face and body beautiful enough to make her teeth ache.

He was brighter than any spotlight.

The wattage of his star power left afterimages behind her eyelids, and that was before he even opened his mouth.

"Good evening," he said, voice rich and confident and amused. "I suspect you know who I am already, but if you don't, please let me introduce myself. I'm Alexander Woodroe, and I play Cupid on *Gods of the Gates*. If you haven't seen the show, you likely think I fly around in a diaper for a living, but no. I save that for the weekends."

The guests chuckled, attention rapt on him.

He cleared his throat, and that wicked smile faded. Gripping the edges of the lectern, he looked out over the audience. "I got involved with tonight's charity five years ago, and there's a reason I've put nearly all my efforts and donations into this one organization. They do good work. Real work. I've toured the shelters and offices, I've met their employees and clients, and before I ever joined their cause, my friend Marcus forced me to do my research."

She frowned. Where *was* Marcus?

"With his help, I made certain the organization ran as efficiently as possible, so any money donated could go as far as possible," he told the sea of tables before him. "I also made sure they reached out to LGBTQIA+ women—especially trans women— and women of color, because we all know our most vulnerable communities often find themselves excluded from the support they desperately need and deserve."

At that point, she began to calculate how much of a donation she could realistically afford, because Alex was a damn effective spokesperson for the charity.

He continued, "The workers are kind, and they treat their clients—abused women and children, people with urgent needs on so many levels—with respect. They—" From this close to the stage, she could see his throat bob as he swallowed. "They *listen*. They *pay attention* to what those women and children say, so they know how best to help. How to reach more people in need, and how to support those people in rebuilding lives free from violence."

His knuckles were white with strain as he held on to the lectern.

"In our world, not—not everyone listens." His voice—it cracked a bit. Wavered. "Not everyone pays enough attention."

He looked down at the floor of the stage for a moment, silent, and Lauren couldn't hear a single whisper of sound from the audience either. As a group, they seemed to be holding their breath as they watched him struggle with . . . something.

This was personal. She recognized guilt and grief when she saw it.

She wanted to rush up onstage and comfort him. Protect him, as yet another threat—this one invisible—tried to take him out at the knees tonight. But she was his minder, not his actual date. They'd known each other approximately eight days, and she had no right to demand his story, no right to offer herself as a bulwark against his pain.

He was a distant star in a midnight sky, and she could do nothing.

When he raised his head again, he flashed that sharp-edged, sardonic smile. "I mean, we're Hollywood types, right? We're self-absorbed. At least, I certainly am. I miss things. Even crucial things. Like, say, when I should stop drinking and leave a bar."

He leaned in close to the microphone, speaking in a faux whisper. "Hint: It's *before* the fight breaks out."

A few gasps, and more laughter.

She rubbed her temples. Had Ron approved a reference to Alex's arrest? If not, if that was an ad-lib, she and Alex were sure to hear about it in the near future.

"In just a minute, Mariela Medellín, our local director, will tell you more about what the organization does, whom it helps, and how it works, because that's important information." He inclined his head toward the dark-haired woman standing to the side and slightly behind him on the stage. "But I'm here tonight as a representative of self-absorbed Hollywood. I'm here to tell you what's in it for you if you donate and donate big."

Was Alex self-absorbed?

When they'd first met, she'd have said yes. Without hesitation. Now, she wasn't so sure.

"I've played heroes on television and movie screens. Demigods. Firefighters. Doctors. Spurned lovers of French mimes." More laughter. "But I've never felt more like a hero than the day I associated myself with this organization and handed them my first check. The day I realized more money meant more resources for those suffering abuse. My money—*your* money—ensures local survivors know their options, know how to get help, know they can leave, know how to build a new life, and know they can do so safely and with ample support."

He raised his brows and leaned forward again, and most people she saw at surrounding tables leaned forward too.

"So here's what's in it for you." He flicked a finger, indicating everyone in the room. "With the money you donate tonight, you can feel like a hero too. Even better, you can *be* a hero to someone who desperately needs one."

His next words were slow, paced so every single one of them sank in. "And I may be a self-absorbed Hollywood brat, but even I understand the most important part: With the money you donate tonight, you can help an abused woman be her *own* hero."

He let them sit with that for a few seconds before speaking again.

"Thank you for coming tonight, and remember: I know how much you made on your most recent films, and I know what you spent on those sharp-looking suits and shiny dresses, so I expect some damn big bids tonight. Lookin' at you, Carah Brown. You owe me for that 'delightful asshole' jab." As Carah laughed and the crowd tittered, he turned on his heel to face the charity's director. "Now please welcome Mariela Medellín."

When the audience applauded, Lauren sat back in her chair and stared at him.

She'd thought she'd figured him out. Maybe not all the details, but at least the basic contours of who he was and what she could expect from him.

She hadn't. She didn't know him at all, and he certainly didn't know her.

But that could change, if she wanted.

And she did want. Entirely too much.

10

AFTER THE LIVE AUCTION ENDED, ALEX HAD TO WADE HIS
way through crowds of attendees who wanted to chat, praise his
speech, brag about the size of their donations, and/or take selfies.
In the end, over an hour passed before he could make his way back
to his table.

He'd missed the dinner, but he didn't give a shit about that.
His thudding skull and thundering heart took precedence over
his empty stomach.

Alex greeted his friends with curt apologies and a promise to
chat later in the evening. Then he immediately turned to Lauren,
seated in her upholstered chair and picking at the remains of her
cherry cheesecake as she listened to Carah swear loudly about
something.

He should wait until they got home.

This wasn't the sort of conversation to have in public, but he
couldn't hold it in anymore. Not after hours spent biting back
the words that needed to be said in favor of smiling and making
idiotic small talk and persuading people to empty their wallets.

Once Desiree had assured him that Lauren really was fine, his
fury toward his minder had ballooned, and it hadn't shrunk since.
Instead, it had only expanded as he'd watched her walk into the
ballroom and study her surroundings with that sharp gaze; as

he'd watched her quietly take her seat, black lace teasing the pale skin of her collarbones; and especially as he'd watched her watch *him* during his speech, her attention rapt and . . . proud, almost.

It had caught at his throat, that look. It had made speaking difficult.

At one of his stupid jokes, a rare laugh had turned her beautiful eyes bright, and—

All of that, all of who she was, could have been *gone*, all because she didn't give a damn about herself.

It was intolerable.

Bending at the waist, he spoke into her ear, quietly enough that no one else could hear. "How badly are you injured?"

"I'm fine." She flicked a hand in dismissal, her voice as low as his. "Just a little bruised."

Lauren would say that if someone had lopped off one of her limbs, but since Desiree had told him the same, he chose to believe both of them. "Good."

Without further ado, he gently clasped her arm and raised her to her feet, and guided her out of the ballroom and down a random hall, then another and another, until they were lost somewhere in the depths of the hotel.

Her forehead creased as she looked up at him, but she didn't resist, and she didn't ask where they were going. She trusted him, evidently. Somehow that only stoked his rage further.

In a deserted, dimly lit alcove, long after they'd last seen another human being, he released her arm and his faltering grasp on his temper.

"*Never* do that again." When he rounded on her, her eyes widened, but she didn't shy away. "If some motherfucker comes rushing at me, you get *out of the fucking way*."

Her brow furrowed.

How the fuck was she confused? Hadn't he made himself perfectly fucking clear?

She gave her head a little shake. "But it was your event. You were the host, and all those cameras and journalists were—"

"I don't fucking *care* where we were or what we were doing, Lauren." He flung his hands wide, so frustrated his skull was throbbing in time with each furious heartbeat. "You didn't know if that asshole had a gun or a fucking knife or—"

"But he didn't," she said soothingly. "I'm fine."

He was definitely *not soothed*.

"You didn't know that when you shoved me aside and used yourself as a fucking *shield*, and let me be clear, Lauren. I would rather die than watch you get killed on my behalf, so if you care about what I want at all, you'll keep yourself safe and *run* if this ever happens again." He gripped his hair with both hands, pulling hard enough that his scalp stung. "Jesus Christ, woman. What the fuck were you *thinking*?"

"I . . ." She was still staring at him, apparently dumbfounded by the novel notion that she should care about her own safety. As always, she was the *worst*. "I didn't think, really. I just reacted."

Not good enough. "Well, figure out how to react differently, and do it now. Otherwise, I'm requesting a different minder. I will *not* let you throw your life away for someone like me."

"Someone like you?" Her eyebrows beetled further. "I don't—"

"Don't change the subject," he snarled. "This is about you, not me, and the way you—"

She interrupted him without apology, and if he weren't so fucking pissed, he'd be pleased by the effrontery of it. "My instincts aren't going to change overnight. I worked over a decade in that emergency room, and I can't simply—"

"You worked in an emergency room?" Goddammit, why didn't

he *know* this? Why hadn't he asked? "I thought you were in some dead-end job and desperate, and that's why you were willing to take work from your asshole cousin."

And maybe he hadn't wanted to hear about her dead-end job, because it would make him feel even guiltier for everything he had, especially once she left his side and went back to that job or its equivalent.

Fuck, he was a self-absorbed piece of shit when it came to the important women in his life.

"Yes," she said and didn't elaborate further.

Too bad. He was asking anyway.

"What did you do there?" He took a breath, the worst of his rage extinguished by guilt. "Are you a doctor? A nurse?"

He could see her as either. In fact, he could picture her excelling in any of a million jobs, each of them more important than watching over *him*, of all people.

"I was an emergency services clinician. Basically, a therapist at an ER." Apparently spotting his blank look of incomprehension, she clarified further. "I saw people experiencing mental health crises who either walked into the ER or were brought there by the police or an ambulance. I evaluated their mental status. Some, I sent home with various supports. Others, I sent to an inpatient unit—voluntarily or involuntarily—or substance abuse treatment. Whatever best protected them from harm and served their needs."

Her soft jaw worked. "Although—never mind."

"What?"

"It doesn't matter right now." Her shoulders slumped. "Anyway, people would get agitated sometimes. I learned how to react quickly to potentially dangerous situations."

Agitated wasn't hard to decode.

Enraged. Hurting. Violent.

She lifted a shoulder and fell silent, and that, it appeared, was that.

Now he knew why her instincts for trouble were so honed. He also knew all his anger—at her, at himself—was justified.

Lauren Clegg was a good, good person.

Lauren Clegg was who he'd longed to be for over a decade now. A helper. A protector. Someone who noticed trouble and reacted quickly.

Which meant there was no fucking way she should have risked herself for him. But given those protector instincts, given how little she seemed to value her own comfort and safety, there was also no fucking way she *wouldn't* risk herself for him.

"I talked to my lawyer while you were with the medic. I'm seeking an emergency restraining order against the asswipe who took you down tonight." He leaned back against the wall, suddenly exhausted. "According to her, he'll probably be charged with assault and battery, plead no contest, and end up with community service and mandatory counseling."

It wasn't enough. Not when the sight of that motherfucker slamming into her was still playing on repeat behind his eyelids, and she kept absently rubbing her ribs. But at least they wouldn't have to deal with statements or forms until tomorrow, because she'd already been through too much tonight.

She pursed her lips. "Does he have a history—"

"I'm not done." The hem of her dress was lying crooked, bunched to one side, and he straightened it. "Lauren, listen to me. I'm touched by what you did. Genuinely. Thank you for protecting me."

One corner of that generous mouth indented. "I suspect I'm about to hear a *but.*"

No, he would not make a pegging joke about hearing butts. Dammit.

"But unless the threat is down by my ankles, like it was tonight, you *can't* protect me," he told her. "You're literally half my height, and—"

"That is not true. Literally."

"—if he'd attacked anywhere higher, there's no way you could have stopped him, and—"

"What are you *talking* about? Do you expect attackers to leap over my head?"

"—I don't want you hurt."

She fell silent, and he did too, because there it was again. The sight of a large man ramming into her and knocking her off her feet, spitting and elbowing her, all while Alex tried in vain to get her out of harm's way and prayed desperately that the man didn't have a weapon.

Practicalities noted and summarily dismissed by his infuriating nanny, he went for the jugular. Guilt. He suspected she marinated in the stuff nightly, and he intended to add to the mix.

"I don't want you hurt," he repeated, "because Ron said my replacement minder would be much, much worse than you. Remember? And if your replacement is much, much worse, I don't think I'll be able to stay out of trouble. And if I can't stay out of trouble—"

"Ron and R.J. will invoke your contract terms and get their lawyers involved." She sighed. "I remember."

"So I need you to protect yourself. For my sake. I don't care much about you, but I care very much about myself."

There. That should do it.

She emitted a sort of disgruntled *hmph*.

Then she angled herself toward him, and her shoulder brushed against his arm, and he shouldn't feel it so *precisely*. Every atom of contact sharp and distinct. But he did.

"You don't fool me." Her voice was low and sure, and if she

extended her accusing forefinger another inch, he could bite the tip of it. "I talked to Desiree while the medic treated me. I know what you did to make the auction a success. I know all the auction items you supplied and all the people you personally called. I know you keep the vast majority of your charitable donations quiet, and after talking to Carah, Peter, and Maria during dinner, I know how your friends and colleagues feel about you."

He dismissed that with a snort of contempt. "Of course the charity said nice things about me. I occasionally give them money. And actors don't tend to bad-mouth their colleagues. That's a good way not to find work ever again."

They also stayed silent when fellow actors complained about directors and showrunners, no matter how justified those complaints might be. He knew that for a fact.

He also knew why. If you raised a fuss, you quickly found yourself persona non grata at casting calls. The necessity of that fuss didn't mean a thing to the power brokers in Hollywood. Which explained why, when he somehow landed the role of Cupid despite the *All Good Men* debacle, he'd considered it a stroke of unbelievable good fortune. Then again, he was often an idiot.

Lauren—a fucking therapist, for God's sake—should know that by now.

"I'm a thirty-nine-year-old man who dresses up and plays pretend for a living, and I'm paid an absurd amount of money to do so," he told her. "That's it. That's all there is to know about me. No matter what you believe, I'm not trying to fool you, so don't fool yourself."

And for seven years, he'd dressed up and played pretend on a show that told viewers they couldn't escape from abusive relationships. Not for good. Not even after years of trying.

He was nothing compared to her. She needed to know that, so she never risked her safety for him again.

"I see," she said, her gaze steady on him.

"I hope you do," he told her, and meant it.

Then, without another word, he led her back to the ballroom.

11

RON WAS AN ASS ABOUT THE ENTIRE INCIDENT, OF COURSE.
Alex hadn't expected better, which was fortunate, as he didn't receive it, and neither did Lauren. The email he got early the next morning simply read, *Congrats on effectively distracting the media from your drunken bar brawl.* Ron had included a laughing-to-tears emoji and exactly zero inquiries about his cousin's health or post-attack well-being.

After that message landed in his inbox, Alex stomped to the exercise room and worked out almost to the point of vomiting, because if he didn't, he would write something he'd regret in response to his boss. Although, honestly, he wasn't even sure he *would* regret it, despite the legal and financial ramifications.

For days afterward, he and Lauren mostly hung around the parts of his property hidden from public view, waiting for media interest in the story to die down. With predictable, gag-inducing discipline, she stayed offline and didn't google herself even once, as far as he knew. And apparently, the paparazzi couldn't manage to locate her number or email address, so she wasn't getting phone calls or messages from randos. His lawyer kept him updated on the asshole who'd knocked Lauren down, and that seemed to be proceeding as predicted too.

Everything was calm. There was nothing to do, really, except hang out with his minder. By all rights, he should be bored out of his goddamn skull.

It was fucking awesome.

Months and months ago, dimly aware he was nearing total physical and emotional exhaustion, he'd ignored his agent's hectoring messages and refused to schedule new jobs for this odd stretch of time, the gap between the end of *Gates*'s filming and the press junket that would accompany the airing of the final season. More work awaited him after the series finale had come and gone, but for now: nothing.

He had no call times. No auditions. No need to set three separate alarms.

Mostly, he just slept and read and worked out and browbeat Lauren into binge-watching baking competition shows with him and eating all their meals together.

To his shock, it didn't even take a lot of convincing.

Something had changed between them during that hotel-hallway confrontation. She talked more. Smiled more. Snapped at him more. She seemed *present* more.

And somewhere in that lazy stretch of time after the auction, she started laughing too. Not by accident. Not because the world became a significantly more amusing place over the course of a week or two.

No, she started laughing because he'd formulated a new goal to define his days: He wanted to make her laugh as often as he frustrated her. Which was to say, frequently.

Both outcomes were equally enjoyable. *Very* enjoyable.

When she laughed, it was loud, her face turned pink, and she covered that face with her hands as she made little snorty sounds through her crooked nose, and it was *the best*. Sometimes, watching her laugh made him laugh too, for no fucking reason.

Today, he intended to earn her laughter by showing her Ian's photos. In fact, when he'd first received the pictures, he'd walked halfway to the stables before realizing it was after two in the morning, and Lauren might not appreciate his waking her up for updates on Ian.

She probably looked cute, though, all rumpled in bed.

"Hey, Lauren," he said as she approached their normal breakfast spot outside. "Ian sent the cast all-new pics of his home reno efforts last night."

No doubt spotting the glee in his expression, she plopped down into her usual chair and narrowed her eyes at him. "What did you do, Woodroe?"

"I might have mentioned something about my dungeon."

Her brow crinkled. "You have a dungeon?"

He sent her a chiding look. "If I didn't, how could it have been on the cover of *Modern Dungeons Monthly* for their annual 'Most Beautiful Dungeons' issue? Last year, it was only number thirty-three on their '100 Oubliettes to Watch' list, so this is a real triumph for me. And so I told Ian, shortly before he decided to do some home renovations."

At that point, she bent forward and preemptively covered her face. "Please say he didn't."

He scratched his bearded chin reflectively. "I might or might not have had someone mock up an issue of the magazine. My dungeon had vaulted ceilings."

"*Alex.*"

Over the past couple of weeks, his fondness for that scandalized tone had markedly increased.

"Ian, by sheer coincidence, has recently decided to dig out a dungeon of his own." He produced his cell phone. "You should take a look."

"Oh, jeez," she muttered, but she peeked through her fingers.

Then her mouth dropped open, and she scrolled to the next photo, and yes. Yes, *that*.

Pink cheeks. Hands on her face. Little snorts amid gales of laughter.

His morning was complete.

"Is that—" She giggled more, then tried again. "Does he have a wet bar in his dungeon?"

"Don't forget the gold-plated shackles fastened to the wall of each marble-floored cell." He snickered. "In our cast chat, I called the dungeon his Gilt Room of Pain and asked when Christian Grey planned to pop by for a visit. At that point, Ian had some very unflattering things to say about my character. I was hurt."

She shook her head at him, but she was still smiling. "You're unbelievable."

"You have no idea."

He offered her the serving tray he'd brought out earlier, which he'd used to carry their drinks and two plates of bagels topped with cream cheese, lox, thin slices of red onion, and capers. Her fingers paused over the bagel with the most cream cheese, but she reached for the other plate, leaving him the bagel she'd silently deemed best. He managed not to roll his eyes, but it was a near thing.

He plucked her plate from her hands and claimed it for himself. "This bagel had the most salmon. Don't be so selfish, you absolute shrew of a woman."

The remaining plate, its bagel mounded high with cream cheese, he plopped in front of her, and she stared at it in silence for a minute.

"Thank you," she finally said, very quietly.

"For what?" He scoffed. "Taking the most salmon? You're

welcome. Please feel free to thank me when I claim whatever slice of cake has the most frosting too."

Lauren wasn't really into frosting, he'd learned, which was preposterous. Possibly un-American.

"What are your plans for today, Nanny Clegg? Heading to Griffith Park and breaking up children's birthday parties for unlawful displays of joy and levity?"

At some point in the near future, he intended to find a new nickname for her, although he wouldn't entirely retire Nanny Clegg from circulation. But this version of Lauren, the one that laughed and chatted, deserved a different option.

"I'd thought—" she began, only to be interrupted by the chirp of her phone. "It's Sionna. Give me just a minute to tell her I'll call back after breakfast."

As she got to her feet and moved away, he heard an unfamiliar woman's voice say, "Wren! How are you doing?"

Wren?

How the fuck had he missed that?

All this time, he'd had the niggling sense he *knew* what type of bird she reminded him of, and he hadn't been able to put his finger on it.

But of course she was a wren. Of *course*.

A winter wren, specifically.

While she was still chatting with her friend—and it was oddly pleasing to see her animatedly talking and relaxed with someone other than him—he got out his own phone and did some research to confirm his memories.

Yes. That was it.

Winter wrens were very small: check. So round they looked like little balls: check. Brown and gray feathers: check. Loud and cheerful song: If her joyful, snorting laughter was an equivalent, check. Not particularly fast-moving on their feet: check.

Huh. Nests built by males were called *cock nests*. Better not to speculate about that.

When Lauren returned to their breakfast table, he complained, "You were so incredibly chatty, our bagels aren't even hot anymore."

She dropped into her chair. "Our bagels were never hot, jackass."

"Ahhhhhhh." He sat back and beamed at her. "Good harpy energy, Wren. Maybe even Big Harpy Energy."

"You heard Sionna, huh?" She picked up her bagel and studied it, evidently deciding where to bite first. "Whatever. Feel free to call me Wren. It's certainly better than Nanny Clegg."

"Ice cold," he whined through a mouthful of his own bagel. "Like chewing a glacier."

When she failed to bite back more laughter, he was tempted to record the snorting merriment, just so he could replay it whenever he needed to smile.

He didn't, since that would be creepy. But he tried to memorize the sound anyway, because soon enough, like the winter wren's chirping song, it would be gone too.

LAUREN TRIED TO tell herself she wasn't wearing her BE THE SHREW YOU WISH TO SEE IN THE WORLD tee on purpose, to please Alex. That would be a lie, however, since she definitely was. He just seemed to derive such *joy* from it. Even after three weeks in L.A. together, having seen all her T-shirts repeatedly, he grinned at the shrew tee's appearance each time.

Other than that one evening, the previous week, when his brows had drawn together in thought instead.

"Do you consider yourself a shrew, then?" he'd asked. "Genuinely?"

They'd been watching the sunset from one of his outdoor sitting areas, and he'd been glancing toward her tee every so often, uncharacteristically muted.

She was honest in response. "Not particularly. But I've been called one before."

He'd set his bottle of sparkling limeade down on the low, polished concrete table with extreme care, his jaw jutting beneath that beard. "By men?"

She nodded. "Most times. Usually when I refuse to go along with whatever a patient or coworker wants. I don't tend to budge when I know something is wrong, so they call me a shrew or a bitch."

There was an odd sound emanating from Alex's chair. A rumble.

"It doesn't offend me or hurt my feelings," she added reassuringly. "If I get called a shrew or bitch for following my conscience and my training, so be it."

"Well, that makes everything totally fine, then," he said, his sarcasm thick enough to choke them both.

She needed to explain herself better. "It's not right on a societal level or even a professional level, but it is fine on a personal level. It has to be, because otherwise I'd spend my life angry and sad, and I don't want that for myself."

Not that she'd successfully managed to avoid anger and sadness in her work, but that was a tale for another time, if she ever shared the story at all.

His hands were still curled into fists at his sides, and it was time to change the subject.

"Hey, Alex, I have a question for you. Are *baps* slang for something else in Britain? Because when we watch *The Great British*

Bake Off, it seems like people get smirky when someone uses that term."

Thoroughly distracted, as she'd intended—yes, she already knew *baps* meant breasts, not just hamburger buns—he proceeded to gleefully explain British slang to her, and the serious portion of their conversation ended.

That night, she'd lain awake again, wondering why he kept getting so angry on her behalf. Angrier than she'd ever been for herself.

She didn't get it. But it did make her feel . . . warm.

Speaking of warmth, it was a chilly night in L.A. despite the daytime heat. She was making herself a cup of tea, and maybe Alex might want one too.

The door to the main house was unlocked. The alarm was off too, because obviously it was. Despite all his lectures and concern for her safety, the man refused to protect himself adequately. Since her arrival, she'd harangued him on the topic more than once as he'd rolled those expressive eyes of his.

He wasn't watching a baking show in the great room, and he wasn't working out in the gym, and he wasn't reading in the library. There was no way she was venturing into his bedroom uninvited—or at all, she corrected herself; she wasn't venturing there at all—so he was either somewhere on the grounds or in his personal office.

When she peeked inside the half-open door to that office, she spotted him behind his big desk, in front of his computer, typing away. After knocking lightly on the doorframe, she waited for a response and didn't get one.

"Alex?" she called.

Still no answer.

Sometimes, he hyperfocused on certain activities, to the point where he wouldn't respond to anything but physical contact. Accordingly, she came up behind him and reached out to touch his arm, only to see—

What in the world was he writing?

Because she was almost certain she'd just inadvertently read something about Cupid and lube and harnesses and dildos the width of a woman's forearm, which—

Oh. *Oh.*

Her head gave a warning throb. "Are you writing *fanfic*, Alex? For your own character?"

That got his attention.

"What?" It was an absent question, devoid of his usual sharpness.

His head turned in her direction, his gaze fuzzy with interrupted concentration, and he sort of looked through her. Then his eyes focused and widened as he fully registered the situation. Immediately, he fumbled for the mouse and minimized his word processing screen.

"Oh, fuckballs." He sighed. "How much of that did you see, Nanny Clegg?"

Letting out a breath through her nose, she pursed her lips. "Not much? Enough."

"Hmmm." He eyed her assessingly for a long moment before shrugging. "Eh. Whatever. I suspected you'd find out at some point anyway."

All concern gone from his expression, he maximized the window again. "This is my first fic. I'm just doing final edits before posting. You're welcome to read it if you want, but FYI, there's some graphic content. As in, most of the story involves pegging."

"I shouldn't." Dammit. "Alex, this is the sort of thing I'm supposed to report to—"

"I figured since you won't let me have any fun in real life, I could at least have a good time in fiction." He grinned happily at her. "I've been writing a few words a day. It's been fucking amazing, actually. In the story, I work through a lot of my unhappiness about Cupid's character arc and how Ron and R.J. completely slaughtered—"

She pressed a hand over his mouth, but he continued to speak.

"—Veebus mmmd Jupimmmmr are totmmmf manipumm—"

"Alex," she said, raising her voice over his and doing her best not to notice how surprisingly soft his lips felt against her fingers, "stop talking. Ron and R.J. would want to know about this. The less you say to me, the less I can tell them."

He licked her palm, eyes sparkling wickedly, and she jerked away from him with a glare.

"There. That's better." Turning back to the computer, he frowned for a moment, then changed a word. "Yes, *thrust* instead of *rammed* in that sentence. A vast improvement, if I do say so myself. And now the story is ready to post."

She rubbed her forehead hard enough to hurt. "*Alex*. If Ron or R.J. found out you were publicly criticizing the show, even under a pseudonym and through a fictional story, they'd probably have grounds for legal retaliation. And what would other directors and producers think? Would they still want to hire you if they knew you'd insulted your own production?"

His career. He was jeopardizing his entire *career* for the sake of a story about pegging, and she didn't understand. Maybe she would after she read the entire thing, but not now.

"Look, I'd rather you not report me to Ron, but do what you have to do. You're an honest person, and I don't want to put you in an uncomfortable position." He swiveled to face her. "I'm going to post the story, though, no matter what, so don't bother arguing with me about that. I need to do this, and I will."

This day was always going to come. She'd known it from the beginning.

Her duty had finally collided with her personal loyalty to Alex.

She tried to clear her head. *What is the right thing to do?*

With him so close, storm cloud eyes intent on her, she couldn't corral her thoughts, and she didn't have any idea how a good, honorable person would choose to act in this situation.

"I need to think," she finally told him.

Then she turned on her heel and fled the mini-castle as if the evil undead from Tartarus were chasing her.

LATE THAT NIGHT, she checked AO3 and found his story.

She read it and tried not to wonder which of his exes might have inspired the character of Robin. Then she went back and rewatched scenes from the last several seasons of *Gods of the Gates*. Specifically, the scenes involving Cupid, Venus, and Jupiter.

She bookmarked CupidUnleashed's account on her laptop.

She sent Alex a pissy, one-sentence email: *I hope Cupid's partner uses less lube next time.*

She went to bed, sincerely hoping the next day would be easier.

What she didn't do: write Ron or R.J.

<u>Texts with Marcus: Saturday Night</u>

Alex: Found out tonight that various men have called Lauren a bitch or a shrew

Alex: If I knew who they were, I swear to God, Marcus

Marcus: You'd . . . what? Join them? You call her a shrew all the time. Also a harpy.

Marcus: Also a killjoy.

Marcus: Also your dour jailer.

Marcus: Also a harridan.

Marcus: Also a spoilsport, wet blanket, sourpuss, nemesis of joy, enemy of lightheartedness

Marcus: "Maria from The Sound of Music only terrible and incomprehensibly short and without apparent musical inclinations"

Marcus: "if Jane Eyre had been like Nanny Clegg, Rochester would have thrown her into a river instead of pursuing a bigamous marriage with her whilst keeping his poor wife locked in an attic—never mind, I don't think I want to be Rochester in this scenario"

Marcus: "if this were Les Misérables, I'm totally Valjean, and she's definitely Javert"

Marcus: "I've never related so intensely to Harrison Ford in The Fugitive"

Marcus: "she's essentially the Terminator, pitiless and unstoppable, and I'm Sarah Connor"

Marcus: "someday, epic poems will be written about my sufferings under her despotic rule"

Alex: Well, I don't mean ALL the things I say, you know that

Alex: Besides, she thinks my bon mots are funny

Alex: I can tell, her mouth twitches like a millimeter

Alex: Although that could be a nervous tic she's developed because of me, come to think of it

Alex: Hmmm

Alex: Never mind, it's definitely a smile, I've decided for certain

Alex: And I've never called her a bitch, that'd be rude

Marcus: [sarcastic clapping]

Alex: Traitor

Alex: Go on, leave me to suffer while you indulge in yet another sloppy display of public affection with your April

Marcus: Don't mind if I do

Alex: Marcus?

Alex: MARCUS!!!

Alex: Some best friend you are

Alex: If I'm Julius Caesar, you're 1000% Brutus, dude

12

ALEX'S NORMAL SLEEPING PROBLEMS TOOK TWO WEEKS TO find him in L.A.

His best guess: He was so exhausted when he arrived, even *his* stubborn brain had to give up and let him sleep soundly for six or seven hours at a time.

But then, after two weeks, he began waking up at all hours of the night again, his mind racing. Or he'd take forever to fall asleep in the first place, staring at the ceiling as his damn thoughts refused to stop churning. It was torture. Especially since he couldn't handle it the same way he'd done for years now, not without either disturbing Lauren or breaking a promise to her.

To calm his asshole brain enough for sleep, he tried everything else he could think of, but reading fanfic didn't work. Writing fanfic didn't work. Using his home gym didn't work. Masturbating didn't work. Even watching *GBBO* didn't work, which was genuinely painful to acknowledge.

After another week, he couldn't stand it anymore.

Just after two in the morning, he got up and got dressed. Once downstairs, he deactivated the alarm Lauren had nagged him to set for the night—*Your safety is important too, you know*, blah blah blah—and opened the front door, locking it behind him.

He tried not to make any noise as he walked to the edge of the property, but the damn motion-sensor lights kept illuminating along his path. Stopping for a moment, he squinted in the sudden brightness and waited for his eyes to adjust.

Then the lights above the guesthouse's entrance flickered to life as well, and the door opened, fuck it all, and Lauren poked her head around the wooden slab. "Where in the world are you going at this time of night, Alex? Are you okay?"

He could pinpoint the exact moment worry turned to annoyance.

She stepped onto the stone path in front of her door, her feet bare, her fists on her hips. "For that matter, where are you going without me? Because you promised I would accompany you any time you left the property, and you seem to be headed toward the side gate. I.e., off the property."

Her eyes were puffy with sleep, and she was squinting against the glare too. Her hair was rumpled, one strand sticking straight out above her ear. She wore a nightgown that was essentially an oversized tee, so faded the color was no longer obvious, so big the exact shape of her body was a mystery.

Somewhere over the past three weeks, though, he'd apparently pieced together enough clues to make a good guess. And now he had a much better idea of what her lower thighs looked like, so that was another bit of the mystery unraveled.

Not that he cared about solving that particular case. He was just naturally curious.

Her legs might be comparatively skinny for her frame, but they still looked round and soft. Sticking out from under that inadequate nightgown, they were . . . vulnerable. So were her feet.

"If you're stepping outside, you need to put on some damn shoes, woman." He scowled at her. "Even toddlers know that."

She didn't budge. "Don't change the subject, Woodroe."

"I have trouble sleeping. Long walks help." He jerked his chin toward the guesthouse. "I hereby promise not to participate in any joyful revelry that might occur along my path. Go back to bed."

Her eyes closed, and she took a breath. Two.

"Okay. Okay." She held up her hand to stay him, small palm out. "Just give me a minute to get dressed, and I'll join you."

He glared at her. "That's ridiculous."

"That's my job." She disappeared inside, only to emerge a couple of minutes later, clad in her BIG HARPY ENERGY tee, leggings, and sneakers. "I'm ready. Let's go."

Her soft chin was set, her posture resolute. After almost a month together, he knew she wasn't going to be swayed from her decision, no matter how tired she might be. And while he'd tried his best not to disturb her rest, he couldn't say he didn't welcome her company.

Still, he had to point out the obvious. "With your Smurf legs, I'll have to walk in slo-mo up and down the stairs. They're literally twice your height."

"Without having seen them, I can't say for sure, but I'm guessing that's *literally* not true." Her cheek was still creased from her pillow, and he kind of wanted to trace the lines. "Unless each step is ten feet tall."

He scanned her up and down, then raised a brow. "Ten feet? Really?"

"Fine." Oh, that scowl. It looked good on her. "Nine feet, ten inches."

"That's what I thought," he said smugly.

Heaving a gusty sigh, she locked the door behind her and set the alarm, then handed him her keys, phone, and ID. "I don't have a pocket."

"Is this my life now? Am I a mere pack mule?" Mournfully, he shook his head as he deposited everything in the left pocket of his track pants. "I imagine you'll expect me to carry you up and down the steps too. Which, again, will tower over you like monoliths, but I shall persevere. Perhaps I can rig up a pulley system of some sort."

Her jaw was making an odd, grinding sound. "I don't believe that will be necessary."

"But you don't know, do you?" He grinned at her. "Have you ever seen this set of secret stairs before?"

Her face lit, her irritation temporarily forgotten.

She swiveled her head, scanning his property. "The secret stairs? We're near those?"

The name wasn't entirely accurate, as many people—locals especially—knew about them. But since the century-old sets of narrow, steep, public stairs on the mountainside cut between the private estates of various wealthy and/or famous people, his neighborhood didn't exactly advertise their presence.

"Evidently, you haven't gone out the side gate yet." He waved her ahead. "After you, Smurfette."

Their steps shushed over the pebbled path as they walked, and he shortened his stride, then shortened it again. For all her bustling, she didn't get anywhere quickly. And for all his restlessness, he didn't seem to mind. The steady sway of her ample backside was both calming and oddly mesmerizing.

Wait. Was he watching her ass? What the fuck?

Lengthening his steps, he hustled until they were walking side by side, and he no longer had a rear view. "I'd hoped to reach the stairs before dawn, woman. Channel your shrew nature and scuttle faster."

He'd been gunning for a middle finger, but all he got was an eye roll. Disappointing.

No matter. Perseverance was good for the soul.

They reached the edge of his estate a minute later. A stone wall lined this side of the property, with faux turrets bracketing the lone, heavy door made of dark wood.

She paused to eye those turrets. "Really?"

"If you can't properly commit to a theme, Nanny Clegg, that's a flaw in your design, not my estate's." He stood in front of the gate and fished out his own keys. "Anyway, this set of secret stairs runs alongside my property. There are hiking trails nearby too, but they're not officially open after sunset, and they're not lit. That's when they have the best views of downtown L.A., though, with all the lights."

Her eyes closed for a moment. "Please tell me you don't hike alone at night on unlit paths."

"Well, I don't anymore." He patted her on the shoulder. "I'll have you with me now."

She groaned.

Even through her tee, the warmth of her skin heated his palm and tingled in his fingertips, and it was *absurd*. An overwrought response born from exhaustion, clearly.

"I'm sure the coyotes will be excited to meet my new companion." He removed his hand and beamed at her, determined to ignore his baffling overreaction to such glancing physical contact. "Also the possums, skunks, raccoons, and snakes."

Her skin was going to wear off if she kept rubbing her forehead so hard. "Holy crackers."

"What?" He tilted his head, the picture of innocence. "NoHo doesn't have coyotes?"

"No," she said emphatically.

"NoHo," he corrected, just to earn another glare. Which he did.

He unlocked the door and ushered them both through before shooting the bolt closed again. On his own, he wouldn't have bothered securing the property during a relatively brief, late-night jaunt, but with Lauren living there . . .

Well, it was different.

She stood in silence for a moment and contemplated the stairs, which both ascended and descended into darkness.

He didn't rush her. "When you're ready, we'll head down. That's where my favorite section is."

When she turned to face him again . . .

That smile. Oh, God help him if she ever realized what he'd do to elicit that brightness in her astounding eyes and that sweet curve of her mouth.

"I'm excited to see it." She waved a hand. "Why don't you lead the way, and I'll follow behind?"

The steps were too narrow to walk abreast, and yes, perhaps it was safer not to allow himself the sight of her ass again. But something in him rebelled at the thought of not being able to see her easily and evaluate how she was doing.

"The steps are steep and made of granite, so if you fall, you'll do some damage." He frowned down at her. "Hold on to the rails."

"Yes, Dad." She blinked up at him, eyes wide.

Such sass. If he weren't lecturing her, he'd congratulate her.

"If you get tired or start hurting anywhere, you tell me and we'll stop," he added.

Setting her fists on her hips, she watched him. "I thought you needed exercise to deal with your insomnia."

That's not as important as you.

"I have a gym back at the house. Besides, if you hurt yourself, you won't be able to go anywhere. If you can't go anywhere, I can't go anywhere." He started down the steps, adding over his shoulder, "And as we both know, my self-interest is paramount, always."

She gave a noncommittal hum in response, then followed him.

They descended in silence, but her breathing sounded steady, and the calm rhythm of her footsteps didn't falter.

Beside them, his stone wall turned into a wooden fence, then a chain-link one, then an adobe barrier as they passed property after property. Occasional branches impinged on the path from trees swaying in the mountain breeze, and other garden greenery glowed under the motion-sensor lights that flickered to life as they passed beneath. His neighbors' homes came into view, then disappeared again steps later.

The glittering vista of downtown Hollywood lay at their feet, far below.

He kept his pace slow, allowing her to take her time. "My favorite stretch is called the Saroyan Stairs. One hundred and forty-eight steps. Which sounds like a lot, but—" No spoiling the surprise. "Never mind. You'll see."

When they reached the bottom of the first set of stairs, they walked side by side along neighborhood streets to get to the next. Even at their modest speed, he could feel his restlessness easing, stride by stride.

"How far up can you take the stairs?" She sounded a bit breathless as they descended the next steps, but not too winded. "All the way to the Hollywood Sign?"

"Almost," he told her. "It's a tough climb, though. Sometimes you have to go down some steps before you can keep going up. Let me know if you ever want to do it."

She huffed out a half laugh. "For now, I think this midnight jaunt will suffice."

Then there they were. The Saroyan Stairs.

He halted at their summit, and she joined him. In the semi-darkness, her pallid skin glowed like the moon.

"Oh," she said, voice hushed. "Oh, my."

He forced himself to look down at the steps instead of at her.

It was a double set of stairs, divided in the center by built-in granite planters bristling with cheerful, waxy-leaved succulents and puffs of decorative, drought-resistant grasses. And where there weren't planters, there were small benches.

The design was practical, but beautiful too. A sort of garden oasis amid those unforgiving steps marching up and down the mountainside.

On more nights than he could count, he'd exhausted himself climbing and descending, only to rest on one of those stone slabs and contemplate the undeserved miracle of existing in that moment, in that place, perched high on a mountainside, looking down on the breathtaking sparkle of Hollywood.

The Saroyan Stairs were special. Before leaving for Spain, he hadn't anticipated sharing his late-night pilgrimages there with anyone. Not even Marcus, much as Alex loved his best friend.

Lauren's presence wasn't an intrusion, though. It was a completion.

"This is so lovely." Her voice ached with joy and . . . melancholy? "Thank you for bringing me here, Alex."

I didn't exactly have a choice, he almost said, but that wasn't true. Not really. And this wasn't the right place for lies or sarcasm.

He cleared his throat. "You're, uh, welcome."

"Why don't I take a seat on one of the benches, and you can make a few trips up and down the stairs?" Her smile was so kind and sincere, witnessing it stung. "That way, you can burn off some energy while still keeping me in sight. I want to make sure you can get some sleep once you're back home."

With a jerky nod, he waved her toward the nearest bench, a

few steps down. Once she was settled, he took off at his normal pace, a near-jog, down those 148 steps and then back up.

Once he'd made one lap, she called out as he passed by, "How old is this stretch?"

"The 1920s," he answered without breaking stride.

Her voice floated behind him, pursuing him down the stairs. "You're going so fast. Please be careful, Alex."

After that, she left him alone, but her gaze rested on his skin like an extra layer of clothing. Another lap, and he tossed his shirt at her feet as he raced past.

It helped, but didn't entirely fix the issue. The night must be muggier than normal, even as high up as they were.

Maybe forty minutes later, when he'd emptied most of the detritus from his brain, he registered familiar noises.

The hoot of an owl. The chirp of another bird, one he couldn't identify.

When he passed Lauren the next time, he slowed. "Did you hear that?"

Her brow furrowed. "Did I hear what?"

"Hooting. Chirping. Birds." Panting, he paused a couple steps below her bench, and they were suddenly even in height, eye to eye. "Not a wren, most likely, but I suppose I have one of those anyway, right?"

Reaching out, he gently flicked that distinctive nose, then kept going. Only to discover, the next go-round, that Lauren wasn't looking at him anymore, and she'd hunched her shoulders in a way he hadn't seen in weeks. The serene smile lighting her face for the past hour might never have existed. Her expression had turned as blank as the day they'd first met.

Shit.

Halting at her bench, he used his discarded shirt to swipe at his face, his chest, his arms. He made quite a show of it, in fact, and got nothing in response. Not a glance, not a comment.

Well, fuck. He was going to have to say something, wasn't he?

"I'm an asshole. We both know this." He set his fists on his hips and ducked his head, trying in vain to meet her eyes. "However, in this particular instance, it might be helpful to know the specific way in which I demonstrated said assholery just now, because I truly have no idea."

She exhaled through her nose. "It's okay, Alex. Don't worry about it."

"If I don't know what I did or said, I can't deploy that particular action or phrase when an urgent need for assholery might arise again. As always, preparation is key." No response. Fine, then. He'd be sincere, damn it. "If I don't know, I also can't avoid doing whatever I did again. I don't want to make you angry."

"I'm not angry," she said quietly.

Hurt, then. Fuck. That was *way* worse.

Frustrated and panicky, his pulse pounding in his ears, he climbed to her level and crouched in front of her, until she couldn't avoid looking at him.

"I'm sorry." Reaching out, he covered her hand where it rested in her lap. His palm was sweaty, but she wouldn't mind. For all her austerity, she was surprisingly tolerant. "Whatever I did, I'm sorry, Wren."

There. She'd flinched.

"Wait. Is this about my new nickname for you?" When she slid her hand out from under his, he sat back on his heels and obeyed her silent directive not to touch. "Because Sionna calls you the same thing, and you don't seem bothered at all."

"She calls me Ren. *R-E-N*. Short for Lauren." Her attempt at a smile was short-lived. "As I just discovered, you apparently call me Wren. *W-R-E-N.* Short for 'my minder has a ridiculous beak for a nose.'"

"No. Lauren, no." He kept his voice stern. Firm, because he was serious for once, and she needed to know that. "I call you Wren because, yes, your features and overall appearance may be some-what avian—"

She looked away again, and goddammit, he should have started somewhere else. But he was committed now, so he kept barreling forward, as was his custom.

"—but I *like* that." He paused for emphasis. "I don't find any-thing about you ridiculous."

She shook her head, eyes still on a nearby succulent. "That's not what you said when we met."

He should have known that would come back to bite him in the ass one day.

"I was calling the entire situation ridiculous, not you," he told her. "Ron misinterpreted because he's a dick, and I should have corrected him then. But let me be clear now: I like your nose. I like looking at your face. I like looking at *you.*"

Her gaze flew to his, and he rushed to add, "But more impor-tantly, I like birds. Specifically, I like winter wrens. They're my favorite species."

Caution and hurt still pinched her brow, so he kept talking.

"Early in my career, I was in a found-footage horror film called *Thump in the Woods.* Maybe you've heard of it?" When she shook her head, he continued, "Anyway, I was cast as one of three col-lege kids filming a project about a famously haunted cabin in an isolated Maryland forest, where people theoretically disappeared and died via decapitation by ax. As you might imagine, it didn't end well for us poor students."

When he mimed the swipe of an ax, complete with a whistling

sound and a final *thud,* the corner of her mouth indented slightly. He took that as a promising sign.

"The three of us did our own filming in the woods, and it was a hard, low-budget shoot. The directors progressively restricted the amount of food we got, and they kept waking us up at night with ostensibly scary sounds we'd have to react to on camera. It rained and rained and rained, until our tents flooded." He sighed and scratched his beard. "We were all fighting on camera, which the story called for, but some of that tension bled into off-camera interactions too."

She hadn't even heard the relevant portion of his explanation, and her eyes had already warmed, her posture opening—arms no longer crossed, shoulders relaxing—as she bloomed in sympathy for him, and goddammit, she needed to stop being so fucking *good.*

"I almost lost my shit completely, Lauren. I came very, very close to walking away from that movie a dozen times. The only thing that kept me going, the only thing that made my daily existence bearable, was the local wildlife." He thought back to his favorite animals. "We saw squirrels. Deer. Birds. Especially this one type of bird, which had an incredibly loud, cheerful song."

She nodded, obviously cognizant of where his anecdote was going. But he needed to say it anyway, because he couldn't stand for her to think ill of him.

"It was a wren. A winter wren. Small and round and bright-eyed and . . ."

Wonderful, he almost said. *Amusing. Adorable. Charming.*

Her mouth had turned soft, and her lips parted as she stared at him, her face only inches away. She didn't utter a single word, though. She simply waited for him to finish whatever he had to say.

He lifted a shoulder. "Ever since then, I've liked birds."

Still, she said nothing. Her patience was endless. Endless, and agonizingly sweet. He couldn't comprehend how someone could simply sit and *listen* for so long, without needing to interject her own thoughts, without defending herself or leavening the mood somehow.

He'd bet his mini-castle that she was an exemplary therapist.

He already knew she was an exemplary human.

"If you don't want me to call you Wren, I won't," he said. "But it's not an insult. It never was."

He rose to his full height once more, and she tipped her head back to watch.

When she'd ascertained that he was done speaking, she finally responded, her words simple and ringing with sincerity. "I apologize. I thought the worst of you without asking for an explanation. Again. I'll try to do better. And yes, you can call me Wren."

He couldn't stand the remorse in that low, sweet voice. "Well, it's not as if I've never insulted you. You had cause to be suspicious."

"True. You've insulted me once or twice." Her lips twitched, and his own shoulders relaxed. "Not about that, though."

"Not about that," he agreed.

As he tugged on his damp shirt, she tipped back her chin to stare at the dark sky wheeling above. "Did you work out your restlessness? Or do you want to do more stairs?"

"I'm done with the stairs." For tonight, at least. He couldn't make any promises about tomorrow. "Do you want to head back? Or do you want to sit for a few more minutes?"

After his late-night rambles, that was his custom. His mind finally calm and clear, he could take time to reflect on the beauty around him and be grateful. But she'd been awakened from sleep, and they'd been out for well over an hour now. Any normal person would want to start the hike back to the mini-castle.

"I'd like to sit for a while," she said, to his surprise. "Is that okay?"

"Sure." He perched on a nearby step. "I'm in no hurry. Just let me know when you want to leave."

She gave a little hum of agreement, and they sat in peaceful silence. After a few minutes, the motion-sensor lights from surrounding properties extinguished. Stars seemed to wink into existence then, suddenly much more visible in the velvety darkness. At the foot of their mountain, Hollywood sparkled in the distance.

Stars above, stars below.

"I told you about the job I almost walked away from." Angling his body toward her, he studied her face upturned to the sky. "You owe me, you tight-lipped vault of a woman."

At that, she lowered her chin, meeting his eyes. "What, precisely, do you think I owe you, Woodroe?"

There was tolerant fondness in that gaze, in that voice, and he wanted to wallow in it.

"Tell me why you left the hospital." It was ostensibly an order. A challenge. But even he could hear the hint of a plea beneath the bluster. "Why leave a good job to work for someone like *Ron*?"

He infused her cousin's name with all the loathing it deserved, because he couldn't seem to get over it. The bastard hadn't even asked how Lauren was doing after she got body-slammed by that asshole on the red carpet. Not *once*.

Her hesitation strained his limited patience, but he held steady, stayed silent, and received his just reward after several fraught seconds.

"Well, first of all, I want to be absolutely clear that I didn't leave the hospital in order to work for Ron." Her mouth pursed slightly, as if she'd tasted something sour. "I'd planned a month-long vacation in Spain and Portugal, and my mom convinced me to visit him at the beginning of my trip. I was going to head over to Barcelona that Tuesday, only . . ."

Only then, Alex's bar fight had happened, and she'd been recruited as his minder.

The thought boggled him.

One day. One more day, and she'd have left. One more day, and he'd never have met her.

His shirt was damp, and the night was getting colder, and he shivered.

Her brow pinched as she studied him, and he preempted what she was about to say. "Don't try to get out of this by claiming I'm too cold to keep talking. Pay your debt, Nanny Clegg. Why did you leave the hospital?"

She stretched out those short, cute legs, braced her hands by her hips on the granite bench, and looked up to the sky again.

"I made it thirteen years," she said, her voice so low he could barely hear her. "Longer than any of the other emergency services clinicians who started around the same time as me. I was considered the old lady of my department before I left."

While still in her late thirties? Jesus.

"The schedule was hard. Some weeks, I worked seventy hours, and I was on call a lot. The pay was good, though, especially with all the overtime, and I liked the camaraderie." She lifted a shoulder. "I usually took the overnight shift and worked holidays, because I didn't have a partner or kids to come home to. It was the only fair thing to do."

He couldn't help it. He groaned out loud, because holy fucking Christ, she was the fucking *worst*.

"What?" The heat of her glare was impressive, really, especially for such a self-sacrificing *idiot*.

He sighed dramatically. "Nothing. Go on."

After one more irritated glance, she did. "Anyway, it was tiring. But that wasn't why I left. Not really."

The instincts that had made her shove him aside on the red carpet had been honed in the ER, she'd said. People would get *agitated*, she'd said.

He drew the natural conclusion. "It was the violence?"

In what seemed to be an unconscious gesture, she touched the crooked bridge of her nose, and now he knew. Some asshole in the ER had broken it.

Motherfucker. He needed to climb a thousand more steps. A million, to work off all this rage.

To his surprise, she shook her head. "It wasn't the violence."

He narrowed his eyes at her suspiciously, and she huffed out a little laugh.

"I mean, yes, people could get violent sometimes. Mostly they'd just insult you, but sometimes they'd throw stuff. Once in a while, they'd throw punches too, but security could handle that."

She sounded so damn *calm* about it all. Unruffled, as if that kind of abuse didn't take a toll eventually. As if her safety didn't matter.

"Patients would get angry because I didn't prescribe them meds." She raised an authoritative forefinger. "Which I couldn't do, just to be clear. Or because I was ordering involuntary inpatient hospitalization. Or because they were drunk and impatient, and I couldn't evaluate them until after they sobered up, and they couldn't go home before an evaluation."

When he stretched out his own legs, they brushed against hers, and he let them. In that moment, he needed the contact. "But that wasn't enough to make you quit."

"No." She drew in a slow breath, and blew it out through her nose.

Her eyes were brighter now than the stars above could explain. She blinked hard once, twice, and he wanted to interrupt, to make her laugh, to offer his shirt as a tissue.

He didn't. He waited and kept listening. Which, for someone like him, was harder than any other reaction would have been.

Her mouth worked, and then she kept speaking. "My job involved seeing people at their very lowest. A lot of times, the problems were beyond anything I could possibly fix. People were suicidal because they'd lost their jobs or their housing. Kids wanted to die because they were being bullied. And after the hundredth time I had to add someone to a wait list for transitional housing or shelters, the hundredth time I put a mom and baby back out on the streets because I had no other alternative, the hundredth time I sent a kid back to the same situation that caused them to self-harm in the first place . . ."

No wonder she was crying. Absurdly, he was swallowing back tears too.

"It's hard, Alex." She knuckled away the wetness beneath her eyes. "It's really hard."

He couldn't imagine. Frankly, he didn't *want* to imagine.

"Even inpatient hospitalization . . ." Her hands curled into fists on the stone bench. "There can be ugly power dynamics there. But when you're trying to keep someone alive, inpatient hospitalization might be the only reasonable solution. Too many times, there are just no good options. None."

After that, the silence stretched into minutes, and he realized she was done.

"You burned out," he finally said.

She inclined her head. "I burned out."

"So you took work from your asshat cousin because you had no job and needed money."

"Well . . ." As she considered that, her face scrunched adorably. "Yes and no. I have savings from all my overtime, so no matter what, I could have afforded a few weeks of rest before deciding what to do next. But this job buys me more time. And I figured nothing could be farther from the emergency room than a Hollywood production and a Hollywood star's estate. I needed some distance, and I'm getting it."

He shifted uncomfortably on the steps, shoulders tight with something that, unfortunately, felt very much like guilt. "But you're not resting. You're still working."

Right now, for instance, she should be sleeping, and she wasn't. Because of him.

She huffed out a quiet laugh. "This is as much rest as I've gotten in over a decade."

"You need some time off." He scowled at her. "Actual time to yourself."

But she was supposed to be watching over him all the time, and Lauren never shirked her responsibilities. Short of vowing to stay inside the bounds of his property for several days in a row—something he didn't think he could actually do, which she would know all too well—how could he possibly get her some much-needed time off?

"Ron could assign me a substitute minder for a week or two." However smelly and horrible that Understudy Nanny might be. "We can tell him you're sick or something."

Her voice was resolute. "I'm not lying, and I'm not subjecting you to whatever my cousin's Plan B might be."

The damn woman wouldn't even let him do a favor for her.

Lauren Clegg might well be the most frustrating human being on the face of this planet, and coming from him, that was a fucking *indictment*.

"I could promise to stay inside for a few days." Desperate times, etc. "Six. Or five? Definitely four."

She just rolled her eyes at that, which . . . okay. Fair. "You're not going to let this go, are you?"

"Nope." He drummed his fingers against the steps. "What if I vow on the grave of my imaginary childhood friend, Captain Fluffytail, to immediately crush underfoot every flicker of enjoyment I might exp—"

"Wait," she interrupted. "We're scheduled to visit Marcus and his partner in San Francisco next weekend, right?"

His virtual PA had bought the plane tickets and arranged for the hotel and transportation earlier that day, in fact. He nodded.

"Ron considers Marcus a good influence on you." Her brows were drawn in thought. "If you're absolutely determined to get me a couple of days off, I'll ask him whether I can transfer custody of you over to your BFF for the weekend."

It wasn't a terrible idea, actually. The physical distance it would impose between them, though . . .

Somehow, even when he'd been envisioning time off for her, he'd assumed he'd still see her. Every day.

He wasn't ready to say he'd miss her. He just—wouldn't *not* miss her. That was all.

"Custody?" He frowned at her. "I'm offended by your word choice. Nay, *hurt*."

She chose to ignore that. "I'll send him an email when we get back home."

Speaking of home . . .

"Then we're decided," he said. "C'mon, Wren. Time for you to stop talking, *finally*, and let us both get some sleep."

He got to his feet and held out his hand to help her up. Her grip was firm and warm, the contact a punch of sensation fierce enough to leave him dizzied. Once she was standing, he let go in a hurry.

In silent agreement, they began their slow trek back up the steps, with him leading the way. Because again: no more staring at her ass.

"Why does your imaginary childhood friend have a grave?" she asked after they'd reached the second set of stairs, her voice breathless.

At the sound of it, he slowed even further. "Because vowing over a grave sounds more dramatic than a simple promise." He aimed an unrepentant grin over his shoulder. "Sue me."

The corners of her mouth were indented. "So Captain Fluffytail is still alive?"

"Since I made up Captain Fluffytail approximately five minutes ago, yes, I'd say she's still alive." After a moment's contemplation, he added, "Unless a coyote got to her already. She was very fluffy and delicious. Irresistible coyote chow, really." He shook his head sadly. "Poor Cap. We hardly knew ye."

That inimitable snorting laugh floated through the night, and he grinned up at the stars.

"You're the worst," she declared between fits of giggles. *"The worst."*

It shocked him into laughter too, because Jesus. The *irony*. The irony *killed* him.

"Rest assured, Wren," he gasped. "I was just thinking the same thing about you."

13

EARLY THAT SATURDAY MORNING, LAUREN ESCORTED ALEX
to the airport security check-in, reminded him to behave himself
as he rolled his eyes and complained about how her unwarranted
lack of trust wounded *his very soul,* and—after returning his final,
oddly tentative wave in her direction—watched him disappear
from sight.

Driving back to her duplex was . . . strange.

Their weeks spent almost entirely in each other's company
had connected them somehow. Tethered them together, like it or
not. And with each mile she traveled away from him, that tether
strained at her chest.

When his plane lifted off an hour later, safely and on time—
she checked, because otherwise she'd worry—the tug became an
actual ache. Which was ridiculous, obviously.

The ridiculousness of her reaction didn't make it any less painful.

Upon hearing of Lauren's imminent visit, Sionna had changed
shifts so they could spend most of the weekend together. As soon
as Lauren pulled into their detached garage and walked up to the
turreted entry, her friend burst through the duplex's right door
with a tackle-hug that almost tumbled them both onto the porch
floor.

"Ren!" Sionna shouted. "My favorite hag from another old bag!"

Helplessly laughing, Lauren gave the expected response. "Sionna! My shrewish sister from another mister!"

Then they were staggering into Lauren's half of the duplex, and Sionna plopped down on the couch and eyed her friend speculatively.

"So . . ." Arranging herself more comfortably, she sat cross-legged. "Tell me how the best-paid babysitting job in the world is going."

For some reason, that set Lauren's teeth on edge. Just a little. "Alex is an adult. I'm not babysitting him."

Damn, it was dusty in here. Also overly warm and stale. Striding to the window, Lauren heaved until it unstuck itself and opened a few inches.

"Okaaaay." Her pixie cut rumpled and adorable, as always, Sionna tilted her head. "Then tell me how your non-babysitting job—in which you're paid to accompany a grown man every time he leaves his house in order to ensure he doesn't get into trouble—is going."

Okay, it did sound a bit like babysitting, when she put it that way. But—

"I've come to the conclusion that Ron overreacted." Setting her hands on her hips, Lauren turned to face the couch. "If Alex is somehow careening out of control, I haven't seen any sign of it. And I've spent . . . what? Five weeks with him? I probably would have noticed by now."

Idly, Sionna hugged a throw pillow to her substantial chest. "He's not drinking to excess?"

Lauren directed a pointed glance at the wine bottle and glasses her friend had miraculously produced since entering the apartment, even though it wasn't yet noon.

Sionna only laughed.

Grinning, Lauren dropped down onto the couch too. "Anyway, to answer your question, he hasn't had a single drink since we met."

Sionna's brow pinched. "So what the hell happened in Spain?"

"I have no idea." She angled herself toward her friend. "But I'd bet my savings account he had good reason to take a swing, and it had nothing to do with alcohol."

"That . . . is not what the tabloids reported." In the sunlight glaring through the windows, the silver strands threading through Sionna's deep brown hair glinted like tinsel. "But you're not a betting person, so I believe you."

No, Lauren wasn't a gambler. She trusted her own judgment when it came to evaluating the mental state of others, and Alex was many things—many, *many* things—but not the spiraling near-addict Ron had described.

As if reading Lauren's thoughts, Sionna raised a dark brow. "So if he isn't what Ron and the tabloids told you he was, what *is* he?"

"Ummmm . . ." How to describe him? "He's a smartass, through and through. He likes to annoy everyone, but also make them laugh. He's impulsive, quick-witted, and curious. He can be self-absorbed, but he's a surprisingly good listener when he tries. He's generous and loyal and never shuts up, as far as I can tell." Lauren frowned and considered the issue. "Maybe when he's sleeping? Not that he sleeps much, honestly."

Sionna's brow arched higher. "You know this from firsthand experience?"

"Are you saying—" Lauren stared at her bestie, aghast. "Of course I don't know! We're not—he's not—"

She cut herself off, unsure how to finish her own sentence, cheeks suddenly ablaze.

"He's not your type?" Sionna nodded thoughtfully. "I can see that. Marcus Caster-Rupp—his best friend, right?—is much more handsome."

Oh, Lauren knew what her BFF was doing, and she wouldn't fall for that trick, not in a million years. Only—

"Marcus might be more traditionally handsome," she heard herself declaring fiercely, outrage in every syllable, "but Alex is approximately a million times sexier. Especially with that beard. And those eyes."

Not to mention that *purr* of his, the one that raised every hair on her body and snatched the breath from her lungs.

At this point, both Sionna's brows were practically levitating above her head. "So, in your opinion, the man you've spent over a month in close quarters with is very sexy. And has eyes. Also a beard."

Lauren threw a throw pillow at her best friend's annoying face. "Shut up."

Catching it nimbly, Sionna grinned at her. "Nice aim. I see you've made progress in the Crone Arts while you've been gone."

She would not hide her burning face. She *would not*.

Her best friend's smirk softened. "I mean it, Ren. You seem . . ."

Oh, jeez. Lauren waited for Sionna's verdict, skin prickling with discomfort.

"You seem more comfortable in your own skin," Sionna finally said. "Less like you're watching yourself and everyone else from a safe distance. I don't know whether that's because you left the hospital or because of your million-times-sexier-than-Marcus-Caster-Rupp charge, but either way, I'm happy to see it, babe. I've been worried about you for a long time now."

As Lauren blinked at her best friend, belated revelation rounded her mouth into a silent *oh*.

How had she missed it all these years? In retrospect, it was beyond obvious.

Sionna might have created the Harpy Institute for Crone Sciences out of newly widowed grief and rage, but she'd also created it out of concern for Lauren. Because she wanted Lauren to engage with the world again.

No, more than that. She wanted Lauren to claim her own space in the world and *defend* that space.

And if Sionna was correct, maybe that prickle Lauren felt wasn't entirely discomfort. Maybe it was excitement too. Maybe it was *life*.

Swallowing hard, she looked down at the threadbare edge of the couch cushion.

Either way, it was temporary. Once *Gods of the Gates* aired its final episode, she'd never see Alex again. Better not to dwell on her rioting thoughts, her rioting emotions.

Her rioting body.

Screw it. It was after noon *somewhere*.

Lauren got up from the couch and went looking for a corkscrew. "I'll drink to that."

APPROXIMATELY TWELVE HOURS later, the two of them were still ensconced on Lauren's couch, swaddled in blankets and facing her television.

"I'm so horny," Sionna groaned, and tossed another handful of caramel popcorn toward her mouth with only middling accuracy. "Why does this show have so many sexy actors? Fuck, it's a fucking hotness *cornucopia*."

She thought for a moment. "Not Jupiter, though. It looks like he has tiny biceps on top of his actual biceps, which freaks me out."

Lauren snorted in agreement and continued gnawing on her Twizzler.

She'd intended to suggest a different show, but when her friend had proposed taking another stab at *Gods of the Gates* for their usual Bottom-Top-Switch debate, she hadn't argued.

Her chest still ached a bit. Watching Alex on-screen helped, at least in the moment.

The scene switched to one involving Venus and Jupiter and Cupid, and Lauren chewed fast, swallowed her Twizzler, and paused the show.

"Tiny biceps!" Sionna wailed, flinging a hand over her eyes. "Oh, shit, you paused on a shot showing his tiny-biceps-on-his-biceps!"

"Forget about the tiny-biceps-on-biceps for a second, Sionna." Sitting up straight, Lauren poked her friend. "Since you've actually watched this show in its entirety, unlike me, I want your opinion on something."

Her hair standing up in clumps, Sionna emerged from her blanket burrito. "I am here to tender a professional verdict, as needed. Despite the trauma induced by your screenshot." She pointed at Alex. "Cupid might be a bottom but might also be a switch. I think we'd need to watch his sex scenes with Psyche again to be absolutely sure. Several times, preferably."

That . . . was probably not a good idea. And also—

"That's not the opinion I wanted." Lauren waved a hand at the screen. "I need you to watch this scene and tell me whether Cupid's relationship with Venus and Jupiter is abusive. Because I have my own opinion, but maybe I'm missing some necessary context."

Once she unpaused the second-season episode, they watched the scene in silence.

"Well, Venus and Jupiter are horrible to everyone, but . . ." Sionna frowned. "This is different. More intimate. Cupid is her son and Jupiter's grandson."

Lauren nodded.

"They manipulate and control him, and tell him they love him, even as they use him for their own ends. They order him to do things that make him miserable, like separating Dido from Aeneas." Sionna drummed her fingers against the sofa cushion. "I don't think we've ever seen that particular episode together, but when Cupid tells them he loves Psyche, Venus slaps him across the face."

Lauren winced.

"I don't think there's any question, really. It's abuse." Sionna turned to face her. "When he broke free to be with Psyche, I considered that a huge step forward for his character."

On the way to the airport, Alex had told Lauren entirely too much about the final season, but she didn't want to spoil her friend's future viewing experience.

"So . . ." she said carefully, "if, for instance, the final season showed Cupid abandoning Psyche and assisting his mother and grandfather instead—"

"It would send a definite message that survivors of abuse can't ever truly escape their abusers or form new, healthy relationships." Sionna's scowl pinched her round face. "Plus, it would just be fucking terrible storytelling. I mean, what would be the point of all those years of character development, then? What would be the point of his relationship with Psyche? Why would they show him breaking free, only to put him right back where he started?"

Knowing Ron, Lauren could guess.

"Cynicism about human nature. Shock value. It's possible the writers might not even see the relationship as abusive." Clearing her throat, she added, "Um, if that were to happen in the last season."

Sionna flopped back and gazed up at the ceiling. "Oh, come on, Ren. You don't indulge in random thought experiments, and you live with one of the stars of the show. I suppose I don't need to watch the final season now."

Lauren's shoulders slumped. "I'm sorry."

"It's okay." Sionna twisted her neck to meet Lauren's eyes. "Care to tell me why you wanted my opinion on this?"

Even with her limited viewing of *Gods of the Gates*, Lauren had reached much the same verdict as her friend. And if she and Sionna were right—if Alex was right—

Then no wonder he was so angry at the final season's scripts. No wonder he'd damned the showrunners in his fic on AO3.

She sent her friend an apologetic grimace. "I can't say, and I'm so sorry. Again."

"It's fine." Sionna waved a limp hand. "Can I get back to my ogling and unassuaged horniness now?"

Thanks to her best friend, Lauren had finally decided for certain: She wouldn't belatedly report the fic to Ron, and she wouldn't make Alex take the story down.

It might be a foolish, dangerous choice, but she'd made it, and she'd stand behind it.

"Yup. Ogling time is recommencing, starting . . ." She pressed *play*. ". . . now."

LAUREN ROSE FROM her bench when she spotted Alex striding hurriedly toward her at the airport Sunday evening.

Oddly, it felt like seeing him for the first time. Or maybe . . . seeing him for the first time in color, instead of gray scale.

He wore a slate-blue Henley and slim-fitting, dark-wash jeans, and his golden-brown hair flopped *just so* over his brow. His beard offered grit and depth to his pristine features. His forearms were strong and muscled, his hands broad and capable as they gripped his carry-on and another huge, random bag.

His rapid walk could better be termed a prowl, because he was all animal grace, all fluid motion. When he saw her, his rakish grin creased his cheeks, and . . . oh. Oh.

Forget all those fluorescent bulbs overhead. Alexander Woodroe emitted his own light, and she had to blink against the glare of it.

At the charity event, she'd called it star power. Charisma. But his appeal, his draw, was more personal than that now. Too personal.

Lauren swallowed hard and watched his rapid approach, almost light-headed at the prospect of his nearness.

Only yesterday, mere hours ago, she'd told Sionna he was sexy, and she'd believed it. But today she *felt* it. In the exact spot where her friend had advised pressing her phone when it vibrated for the millionth time from one of Alex's texts.

Dammit. Her libido had chosen a *terrible* time to emerge from hibernation.

A moment later, he was there, halting only inches away, his gray eyes aglow with warmth and crinkled in good humor. He was breathless from his haste in a way that emphasized the rise and fall of that honed chest. The chest she'd spotted damp and shirtless several times, but hadn't appreciated properly. The chest she suspected she'd be seeing in her dreams now.

For a moment, she could have sworn he was going to hug her. If he did, she was relatively certain she'd pass out.

Then the moment was gone, and they were walking toward the exit, and he flashed that infuriating, charming smirk at her. "Miss me, Wren?"

"Terribly," she said dryly, and with more sincerity than she would wish.

"Likewise." He slung an arm around her shoulders, tugging her into his side for a split-second embrace before releasing her.

"In fact, your absence made me philosophical. If a tree misbe-haves in a forest and no one is there to scold it, did the tree really misbehave at all? I say no. Let me explain my reasoning, in scin-tillating and exacting detail."

His monologue lasted for several minutes straight, which was convenient, because the imprint of his body against hers had left her unable to speak.

But the ache in her chest was gone. Completely, utterly gone.

Alex: In an airplane AGAIN

Alex: So BORED

Alex: ENTERTAIN ME, CARAH

Carah: Where's Lauren, you whiny bitch

Alex: I thought I was the designated gossipy bitch, but if I can be two types of bitches, all the better

Alex: I contain bitchy multitudes

Alex: Anyway, Nanny Clegg is off having fun with her friend Sionna for the weekend, which is completely unfair, since she won't let ME have any fun

Carah: I liked Lauren

Carah: I enjoyed meeting her at the auction

Carah: What exactly has she stopped you from doing, may I ask

Alex: SO MUCH, SO SO MUCH

Alex: She nags me to eat enough breakfast when I take my ADHD meds, even when I'd prefer to get going and do other things, which is really annoying

Alex: To be fair, my stomach hurts today because I didn't eat enough breakfast

Alex: Which is really annoying too, because I hate it when she's right

Carah: . . .

Alex: And I should have been having fun with Marcus and April, and I did have fun, but Lauren stopped me from having MORE fun by having her phone on silent and not answering my messages, and then I was checking my phone all the time instead of paying attention to Marcus and April, and that's totally on her

Alex: And THEN, when I should have been binge-watching baking shows with my best friend, instead I had to go out and buy her a present

Alex: I got her a blanket, because she's a wet blanket

Alex: Get it????

Alex: It's really soft and quilted and fluffy

Alex: A pretty green with just a hint of blue

Alex: I think that's my favorite color

Alex: She's a killjoy and the worst but she deserves soft, pretty things, and she doesn't do anything nice for herself ever, which is also extremely annoying, as you might imagine

Alex: As I said: THE ABSOLUTE WORST

Alex: Carah?

Alex: Carah, it'd be nice if you RESPONDED at some point

Carah: Sorry, too busy laughing to type

Carah: Alex, you are a fucking delight

Carah: I have to go film myself eating lutefisk in Maria's honor, so entertain your own whiny ass while I try not to hork on camera

Carah: BYEEEEEE, MOFO

Alex: Carah?

Alex: CARAH, COME BAAAAAAAAAAAAAACK

14

THE NEXT TWO MONTHS DID NOT PASS IN A HAZE. ALEX'S presence wouldn't allow for that, and neither would Lauren's new-found attraction to him.

She might sometimes be tired from late-night walks, frustrated at the intractability and irascibility of her charge, and irritated beyond belief at his continual needling, but she was wholly present. Wholly engaged, body and mind. Wholly *herself* in a way she wasn't with anyone but Sionna.

For years, she'd spent her daily life encased in a bubble of calm and neutrality and observation, but no more.

Alex punctured that bubble daily—hourly—with his sharp gaze, incisive commentary, and biting sarcasm. With his unabashed flaunting of his honed body. With the way he flung himself head-long at her and everything else he cared about in his life, like it or not.

Often, she *didn't* like it. But she liked *him*.

Despite his quick temper and caustic sarcasm, despite the way her skin prickled in his presence, she'd never laughed more in her damn life, and she'd never flipped someone off more either. He loved aggravating her. *Loved* it.

With Dina, though, he was as soft as Captain Fluffytail.

Evidently, he'd first met his housekeeper on a tour of his

charity's shelters, and after hearing her story, immediately offered her work.

Dina was Lauren's age. Beautiful, plainspoken, savvy, and confident. Engaged to a good, kind woman. Her own hero, as Alex might have said. But he'd been a supportive sidekick in her time of need, and Dina adored him for it. Sometimes, when Lauren saw the two of them together, laughing in the kitchen, sunlit and affectionate, the sweetness of the sight stole her breath.

The feel of her gorgeous blanket did the same, as she curled up beneath it every night, encased in soft warmth because of him.

This morning, however, he hadn't stolen her breath. Just her patience.

"Finish your breakfast, Woodroe. We need to get going." She tapped the edge of his plate, still half filled with velvety scrambled eggs and roasted herbed tomatoes. "You've already missed one appointment with your stylist, and from what you've told me, she'll eviscerate you with her trimming shears if you cross her a second time."

Also, he definitely needed a haircut and beard trim, stat. Con of the Gates, the annual fan convention for *Gods of the Gates*, began tomorrow, and at the moment, he resembled a particularly fetching hobo.

"Every time I try to look at you, my neck hurts," he whined in between bites. "How am I supposed to eat under such inhumane conditions? And why are you literally the height of a growth-stunted mouse?"

They'd discussed proper usage of the word *literally* too many times. She wasn't having that particular conversation again.

"Then don't sit next to me on the bench. Take one of the chairs, where you won't have to bend your neck so much to see me." Once he'd scraped up the last of his meal, she removed his plate and stacked it with hers on their tray. "Or better yet, just don't look at me."

"But I like looking at you." He stood with a luxuriant stretch. "And if I sat farther away, I couldn't complain that you're a literal pain in my neck."

Automatically, she said, "That's not what lit—"

Wait a second.

"Oh, I know what it means. I've always known." He smirked down at her. "I just like fucking with you, Nanny Clegg."

I will not toss him down this mountainside, she told herself. *I will not.*

His smile died, and his brows slammed together. "Uh, just to be clear, I meant 'fucking with you' in the sense of teasing you, not, um . . ."

Instead of shoving him over the cliff's edge, as he so richly deserved, she elbowed him in the ribs. "I know what you meant."

He yelped and cast her a wounded look as he clutched his side. Even though she'd put zero force behind the jab.

"Abject cruelty," he complained. "Just for that, I'm not letting you carry the tray back to the kitchen, you vicious virago."

Then he swept off in a dramatic huff, flawlessly balancing the tray on one arm like a seasoned waiter. Which, given his profession, he'd probably been at one point, now that she considered the matter.

Their debate over neck pain continued during the entire car ride to the salon, and even while he gave his keys to the valet.

Yes, curbside valet service. At a hair salon.

She sighed. *Stars. Just like us, my ass.*

As they neared the salon's discreet entrance, bracketed by

ornamental palms, she stopped and made her final stand. "By looking down, you're at least working with gravity, Woodroe. When I look up at you, I have to fight against the laws of nature."

He snorted. Which she could see very clearly at this close distance and from so far below.

Even his nostrils were attractive. It was highly unfair.

Nevertheless, she made her closing statement with what she considered laudable aplomb. "Which means, of course, that my looking at you causes more neck pain than your looking at me. Thus, you are a bigger pain in the neck than I am. QED."

"QED? Really, Wren?" He laughed down at her, and then—oh, *asshole*—casually leaned over and rested his forearm on top of her head, as if she were a console in his damn car, and he was going to *pay*—

"Excuse me," a voice said from behind Lauren. "Are you Alex Woodroe?"

In a doomed attempt to recover her lost dignity, Lauren slid out from beneath Alex's arm and backed several steps away, allowing the fan to greet him without an interloper.

The woman was a pretty redhead, maybe in her early twenties, and the usual conversation occurred. He confirmed his identity, thanked her for her gushing admiration, and agreed to a selfie. And then—

Cell phone held aloft in one hand, the woman nestled close and placed her other hand on the upper swell of his ass. With a strained smile, Alex tried to slide away, but his fan wasn't giving up so easily. She laughed and followed his movement while taking more photos, and no.

No.

"I'm so sorry," Lauren said as politely as possible, "but I'm afraid that will have to be your final photo together."

The fan didn't move an inch, and she didn't acknowledge Lauren's words. Another photo. Another. Then she began filming a video.

Alex's smile didn't reach his eyes, and Lauren could almost see him grasping for his self-control, could almost hear him urging himself to stay calm and out of trouble.

"—and lucky me, here I am with Alex Woodroe," the woman was saying. "You would not *believe* how hot he is in real—"

At that point, Lauren marched behind the pair and physically removed the fan's hand from Alex's ass. The woman gasped. Apparently at Lauren's effrontery, which was rich irony indeed.

The redhead swung around, livid color streaking her cheeks.

"Wait your turn, you ugly bitch," she hissed, and suddenly she wasn't so pretty anymore. "I wasn't done yet."

"Yes," Lauren said simply. "You were."

The other woman took a step toward her, still filming, and Lauren honestly wasn't sure what was going to happen, but she was ready for it. No one was putting unwanted hands on Alex in front of her. *No one.*

Then he was smoothly stepping between the two women, his own cheekbones ruddy, his breath coming hard and fast.

The smile dawning on his face—

Lauren had never seen anything like it before. It was the fevered, gleeful beam of a berserker leaping into battle, wild and sharp and full of rage, and oh shit, she had to—

But he was already speaking, each word suffused with poisonous good cheer. "How grateful I am that you took time out of your busy schedule to grope my ass without my consent and abuse my companion." When the redhead gasped again, Alex's anarchic grin only widened. "She has too much dignity and kindness to say what needs to be said. Namely, that if you have nothing better to do with your free time than insult total strangers, you should occupy said time better. My suggestion?"

The woman was trembling with affront and humiliation, cell phone pointed toward Alex, and Lauren tried to tug his arm and lead him away, but he was a stone statue under her fingers.

Alex leaned in close to the redhead, his tone genial. "Go fuck yourself, lady."

She jerked as if he'd slapped her, before erupting.

"You asshole!" She was shouting at him so loudly, people a full street over were craning their necks to watch the confrontation. "I'm going to tell everyone on social media about this!"

His laughter dripped with mockery. "Please do."

At his total lack of either fear or remorse, she stomped away, already stabbing feverishly at her phone's screen.

His chest still heaved with every breath, and incredible heat radiated from his lean body, even through his tee and jeans. He stared after the woman, and when she turned around to film him again from a distance, he offered a jaunty wave.

Oh, shit. If Ron heard about this—and he would, Lauren was almost certain—he was going to retaliate against Alex somehow.

"Alex." She rubbed her temples. "You can't—"

He turned to face her again, his expression abruptly darkening. "I have an appointment to keep, and if I talk about what happened right now, I'll lose my shit. Let's just go inside."

When she hesitated, he sighed. Not one of his usual, overdramatic gusts of breath, but a genuine sigh.

"Please, Lauren." Waving aside the waiting doorman, who'd watched the entire encounter with barely contained glee, Alex swung open the salon's heavy wooden door and held it for her. "Please. Let it go. Just for now."

Slowly, she nodded.

They went inside, and the waiting area was cool and elegant. The impeccably styled man who greeted them from behind a glass desk asked if they'd care for refreshments, before gliding into a nearby room to gather their chosen drinks.

While they waited for his return, Alex blew out another hard breath and ran his fingertip down her bare forearm. Her skin tingled beneath his touch, the fine hair there standing on end, and she jerked her gaze up to meet his, startled.

"I still can't talk about it." He stared at his fingertip, now skimming over the veins on the back of her hand. "But are you okay?"

She covered his hand with hers. Squeezed it. "I'm fine."

One more deep breath, and Alex dropped his hand and stepped away. "Then let's focus on the matter of greatest importance here: me. Specifically, whether I should cut my hair short and get rid of the beard entirely, or just trim things a bit."

"It's your hair." Confused, she frowned at him. "Why are you asking me?"

"Holy shit, Nanny Clegg." He squeezed his eyes shut, and this time, his sigh was gusty and dramatic and entirely fake. "Why must you make everything so *difficult*? Oh, that's right. Because you're a *millstone* around the neck of *humanity*."

Indignant, she set her hands on her hips. "Look at me, Woodroe. Do I seem like the kind of person who knows how best to cut and style hair?"

His lips twitched, but he opened his eyes and attempted a deadpan stare. "Yes."

"Didn't you once tell me *I* was a terrible liar?" Raising her brows, she flicked the limp ends of her straggly hair. "Pot, meet kettle. I believe you two will have much in common."

He bit his lip and glanced away for a moment, then got himself under control.

"Lauuuuuuuuren." It was an outright whine. "Tell meeeeeeeeeeeee."

Fine. If he really wanted to know what she thought . . .

"The longer hair and beard kind of make you look like a Viking." A stupendously gorgeous one. The whole look was way too enticing, frankly. "So if that's what you're going for, just get a trim."

"Ahhhhhhh." And now he wasn't a Viking anymore. He was a big cat instead, with a shaggy mane and a purr that vibrated through her in that familiar, disconcerting way. "You like my beard, Wren?"

It was a lazy taunt, and she wanted to deny it.

She couldn't. Because she was, in fact, a terrible liar.

He bent close to her ear.

"Admit it," he breathed. "You like my beard. You like my hair."

She clenched her unsteady hands, unable to speak. Unable to think.

Thankfully, a tall, lovely, elegant woman swept through the door to the waiting room then, her impeccable greeter close behind her carrying a tray of drinks.

Alex scowled at both of them for a moment before shrugging and gathering his stylist into an enormous hug, which she returned.

After a few social niceties, the two of them disappeared into the actual salon. Lauren stayed in the waiting room, took a seat on the low-slung, velvet-covered couch, and accepted her iced tea gratefully.

Her ear still tingled from Alex's breath. And for reasons she preferred not to parse, she was way, way too hot.

15

WREN STOOD FROM THE COUCH AS ALEX ENTERED THE room. For a moment, she simply gazed at him, blank-faced.

Then her Santa Ana voice made its dry-as-fuck return. "When you said you were getting your hair cut, I didn't realize you meant that literally. As in, one hair."

"It was more a shaping than a cut, you follicular philistine." He stroked his beard fondly, then ran a caressing hand through his hair. "Now I'm the best-coiffed and -bearded Viking in the village. Peasants will be lining up to be plundered by me."

Her extraordinary eyes flew to his. "Please tell me you didn't make your haircut decisions based on my input."

Having been told mere hours earlier that he too was a terrible liar, he didn't answer. Instead, he merely opened the door and waved her ahead.

Once the valet brought his car around, they climbed inside, and he paused before putting it in drive. "Anywhere else you want to stop?"

"I think we've had enough excitement for the day." Her lips were tight again. Pinched. "Let's go home."

From that expression, he could only assume her patience had run out.

Sure enough, she was silent only a minute before stating firmly,

"I'd like to talk about what happened outside the salon now, if that's acceptable to you."

Fortunately for them both, the scalp massage during the shampoo had lowered his blood pressure to a nearly normal level again.

"If it weren't"—he slipped on sunglasses to combat the glare—"how exactly would I stop you?" When he contemplated the issue, only one good solution came to mind. "By kissing you?"

Her silence seemed to expand, filling the entire car.

When he chanced a glance over, she was staring at him, open-mouthed, cheeks pink.

"You could stop me by *asking me to stop*," she said slowly, pronouncing every word with crystalline clarity.

Oh. Right.

With an especially casual shrug, he turned his eyes back to the traffic. "Fair enough. Anyway, it's fine. Chastise away, Nanny Clegg."

The roads seemed particularly clogged today, even for L.A., and he resigned himself to a long, boring lecture about professional conduct and legal consequences. Nothing he hadn't heard a thousand times before, but for Wren, he'd at least pretend to listen.

She didn't say what he expected, though.

What she said was worse. Much, much worse.

"People say terrible things to me all the time." Her voice was entirely matter-of-fact, free of both anger and self-pity. "They have since I was a child. At some point, I just stopped telling my parents or anyone else, because it upset them so much, and there was no point."

No point to telling her parents she'd been hurt and insulted? *No point?*

Because her feelings were less important than protecting theirs?

She was still talking, even as his pulse rocketed back to near-stroke territory. "It's not right, but it's also not important, as I've told you before. Reacting to insults directed my way isn't worth your time or energy, and it's certainly not worth your job or professional reputation. I appreciate your instinct to defend me, more than you know, but you have to learn to let it go, Alex, the same way I have."

By all rights, the car should be festooned with the exploded remains of his head.

"What?" Somehow, that was all he could articulate. *"What?"*

"Thank you for caring about me." She cleared her throat. "But retaliating against people who insult me isn't necessary or wise, and you shouldn't do it again."

For some reason, his poor, exploded brain filled with her expression the night he'd returned from visiting Marcus and April.

He and Wren had been standing just inside the doorway of the guesthouse, where he'd escorted her after their late dinner together. Before they parted, he'd offered her the huge plastic bag he'd kept protectively tucked in the carry-on bin the entire flight.

For some reason, he was nervous, his hands not entirely steady.

She'd blinked at him, confused, her own small hands motionless at her sides.

"This is for you," he'd finally told her, impatient and uncomfortable. "Take it, you impossible dolt of a woman."

Slowly, her face filled with befuddlement, she'd accepted the bag's handles, then looked inside. Her brow furrowed even further, and she stumbled toward the nearest table.

When she removed the blanket from the bag, those ludicrously short fingers stroked the fabric. Once. Again. Again.

"Is this—" She spread the silk out over the table, still caressing. "Is this a . . . blanket?"

He'd planned to say, *When it gets wet, it's just like you!* Only—

first of all, the phrasing raised images of Wren, uh, wet. In various ways. Which was . . .

Disturbing. Yes, that was the word. *Disturbing.*

Second, this particular blanket was dry-clean only. He'd already taken care of that overnight, in a rush job.

And third, he didn't feel like mocking her anymore.

No, he kind of felt like his sinuses were burning with some odd mixture of rage and pain, because she looked so *stunned* to receive a gift. So *bewildered* at the thought that someone else had thought about her and procured something for her, even as a stupid, stupid joke about how she was a wet blanket, ha ha, so funny.

So instead of making fun of her, Alex simply told her the bare facts. "Yes. It's a blanket. It's made from charmeuse silk. Dry-clean only, but Dina can take care of that periodically, when she brings in some of my clothing for cleaning and pressing."

"It's silk?" She licked her lips and bowed her head, hiding her face from him, her hand still slowly moving over the shiny charmeuse. "I . . . I don't know what to say."

He forced himself to heave an exaggerated sigh, despite those prickling sinuses. "Just say thank you, Wren. Were you raised in a barn? Or is the Killjoy Guild unfamiliar with standard expressions of gratitude upon receiving a gift?"

She'd haltingly thanked him, the blanket clutched close, those beautiful eyes big and confused and . . . lost.

As lost as he'd felt then, and as lost as he felt now too, because what the actual, ever-loving *fuck*?

Stomping on the brakes, he abruptly turned the car into a fast-food parking lot.

"Let me get this straight." Swinging into a space, he brought the car to a jolting halt and cut the engine. "You're not important enough to defend? Even when someone insults you *to your fucking face,* literally two feet away from me? I'm not supposed to react to that in any way?"

"I know how loyal you are, Alex, and I know it goes against your instincts to let those sorts of incidents go," she said soothingly, and once more, he was very definitely *not fucking soothed.* "But they're not worth your career. I'm not worth your career."

If his head had already regrown, it would have detonated a second time.

"That is not—I repeat, *not*"—for emphasis, he stabbed a finger into the air—"your fucking decision, Lauren. I am the only fucking person in this car and on this *planet* who can decide what my career is worth, and it's not worth my fucking *soul.*"

He wished like hell he'd come to the same conclusion a year ago, before the final season's filming began, but it was much too late to right that particular wrong.

"Do you think you're the only one here who wants to act based on what's right, rather than what's convenient?" Behind his eyes, that prickling began again. Hurt and rage. "What exactly do you think of me, Lauren? Just how callous and selfish do you fucking think I am?"

"I don't . . ." She put a hand on his arm, her fingers gentle and trembling. "I don't think you're callous or selfish."

"Then don't ask me to act like I am," he snapped, as pinpoints of heat flashed to life on his skin everywhere she made contact. "I don't know what sort of people you've had in your life before now, but I am *not* them. And if that makes you too uncomfortable, you have your asshole cousin's number. Feel free to fucking use it."

Silence. Then she removed her hand, and he was floating in space, untethered and alone and disoriented.

The haze in his vision, in his head, took a moment to clear, and then—

Aw, fuck.

Closing his eyes, he gripped the steering wheel and rested his forehead against its leather surface, doing his damnedest not to ram his skull into it again and again. As always, his wounded rage had driven him too far, and now she was going to call Ron, and he'd never fucking see her again, ever, not even—

Her cool palm rested lightly on the nape of his neck. She gave him a gentle squeeze there.

"Alex." Her voice was warm. Tender. "Tell me what happened at that Spanish bar. Who were you defending?"

The question took a moment to register.

Then he heaved out a near-sob. Relief. Gratitude.

Because she wasn't leaving him. Because she'd *asked*. She was the only one who'd *asked*, in all this time. Even Marcus, amidst his preoccupation with April, hadn't asked what happened, hadn't questioned the version of events offered by the tabloids and Ron.

Marcus had sympathized and worried for his best friend, but he'd *assumed*. That Alex had been drunk. That Alex, bless his reckless goddamn heart, had made another stupid fucking spur-of-the-moment decision.

And maybe it was spur of the moment, but it wasn't stupid, and he didn't regret it.

"I went to the bar for one drink. A beer, because I—because I was lonely," he told the steering wheel, his voice thick. "It was crowded, and there were no empty stools or tables. So when I got my drink, I propped myself against the wall and started watching people. And after about two sips of my beer, I noticed this beefy, sunburned Brit at a nearby table hitting on a redheaded server. She was almost as short as you, and a few years younger than him. Maybe early twenties. Pretty. Irish accent."

Lauren's fingers on his neck felt like a benediction, and he sighed in appreciation.

"She wasn't into it. She kept edging away from him, and she looked nervous, and when she raised her arm to get someone's attention, maybe a bouncer or the manager, I saw faded bruises around her wrist." In that moment, despite the bar's dimness, those bruises had seemed illuminated by spotlight to him. Unmistakable. Unendurable. "He yanked her arm down and told her he wasn't done talking to her yet, and she yelped in pain."

Lauren's slow exhalation tickled the side of his arm. "So you intervened."

At that point, his blood had been pounding in his temples, and the cacophony in his head had drowned out everything but one imperative: *Fix this. Now.*

"I removed his hand from her arm. Not gently. Then he took a swing at me, and I swung back, and all hell broke loose." He didn't know who'd given him the shiner. Not the Brit, anyway, since that fucker had gone down with the first punch. "Right before the police came, she managed to pull me aside and begged me not to mention or describe her, because she was on the run."

Thus the bruises and the fear in her expression, in her every movement.

"I tried to offer help." In fact, he'd done his own begging, but she'd been terrified out of her fucking mind, too terrified to do anything but flee. "Then the cops arrived, and she sprinted toward the employee area and disappeared into the back, and I never saw her again."

He hoped to fuck she'd found somewhere safe to hole up and gotten help. *Real* help. The sort of help that would let her stop hiding and rebuild a life free from fear and violence.

Lauren made a sort of humming sound. "Then the police questioned you, and you didn't say a word about her."

"I kept my promise," he said simply.

Another squeeze of his nape. "And I take it the Brit didn't mention his own transgressions when describing yours."

"According to him, I punched him unprovoked, in a drunken rage. It was like she'd never existed." Which was what she'd wanted, but horrifying in its own way. "I didn't argue. I just called my lawyer, who called other people. They sprang me from jail and got the charges dropped."

And then, only an hour or so later, a stranger had appeared on a shoreline battlefield.

Lauren Clegg. His nanny. His friend. His obsession. His confessor.

And if she was playing priest to his unrepentant sinner, he might as well scour his soul entirely clean, right?

"Before we end this game of True Confessions, you should know: Bruno Keene is a fucking abusive asshole, and I was telling the truth when I said that. The crew and other actors on the *All Good Men* set didn't want to risk their reputations by backing me up, and I get that"—mostly—"but I was telling the truth."

"Okay," she said quietly. "Okay. I believe you."

She was stroking his neck now, gently playing with the ends of his hair there, and it was so soothing, he wanted to cry. With each moment, his skull's throbbing waned, and his pulse calmed, and his head felt—he didn't know. Lighter?

And then—and then . . .

Those caresses, those slight tugs of his hair, weren't so soothing. His scalp was tingling, afire with the tease of sensation, and he didn't want to cry anymore.

He wanted to kiss her.

Her. Nanny Clegg. Harpy-in-Training. Killjoy Extraordinaire.

His friend, who had the warmest, loveliest eyes he'd ever seen, sharp, fascinating features, and a round, soft body that he sometimes found himself staring at for no good reason.

And she was touching him, stroking his neck, and—

He raised his head and looked down at her.

The concern in her gaze touched his heart, but he didn't want concern right now.

He wanted *heat.*

Her fingers remained threaded through his hair, and the weight of her palm on his nape seemed to drag his head lower, lower, lower. Her soft chin trembled, and her lips parted, and shit, he wanted to taste that mouth and discover if it was exactly as tart-sweet as she was.

But—fucking hell. He *couldn't.*

As far as he could tell, she tolerated him with grudging fondness. He certainly hadn't noticed any signs of attraction. Even if he had, he was her job, and he wasn't fucking *harassing* her at work.

Reluctantly, he shifted away from her. Her hand fell from his nape, and he bit back a needy sound in favor of his usual nonsense. "Now that I've bared my very soul to you, Sister Clegg, stop trying to distract me from the matter at hand."

He shook a chiding finger at her, but she didn't take the bait. Instead, her gaze was still warm and tender on him, and he allowed that look to soak into his heart like rain on parched, cracked earth.

Then he made his position clear. "If you don't want me to defend you because it embarrasses you or makes you uncomfortable, then okay. I won't like it—I'll fucking *hate* it—but I'll accept your decision and try my best to do what you're asking. But if you don't want me to defend you because you don't think you're worth the risk to my career, then that's a different matter entirely, and no. I refuse to abide by your wishes."

Fretfully, she rubbed at her temples, but he didn't let her off the hook.

"So what is it, Wren?" With his forefinger, he tipped up her chin until she met his eyes again. "Do I follow your advice or my own instincts?"

Her face puckered in thought, and it was fucking *adorable,* and he hoped like hell she gave him the answer he wanted. Because a woman who'd spent her life serving and protecting others at the cost of her own safety and emotional well-being deserved a champion.

A better one than him, obviously. But he was what she had right now, poor woman, and he wanted her to accept his entirely inadequate fealty.

He wanted her to accept *him*.

After a long, fraught minute, she exhaled slowly.

"Your instincts," she said. "God help us both."

16

POOR MARCUS. WHEN HE CLIMBED INTO LAUREN'S HYBRID that Friday morning, he had no idea what awaited him. But she did, and she didn't envy the man.

On their way to Marcus's house, Alex had shared his plan with her. "I can't fucking take any more anguished puppy-dog eyes, Wren. And since he wants us to room together at the hotel during Con of the Gates, I'm giving him the Full Alexander Woodroe Treatment."

She made her voice as arid as humanly possible. "I hesitate to ask."

But he knew by now that she'd be curious, no matter how much she might deny it. So instead of badgering her, he merely turned up the Tom Petty song piping through her speakers and shouted along to "You Wreck Me" until she gave in.

She stabbed at the volume controls. "Fine. You've defeated me with your atonal wailing. Tell me what the Full Alexander Woodroe Treatment is."

As obnoxious in victory as always, he pumped both fists in the air—accidentally hitting her roof, to her poorly hidden amusement—before explaining.

"Through my sparkling wit and cunning repartee, I intend to capture his attention and keep it from straying to his lovelorn state." He'd rubbed his hands together, satisfaction with his plan radiating from every perfect pore on his stupidly handsome face. "Essentially, I won't give him the time or mental space to be a wretched, blubbering heap of a human being."

If she didn't know better, she'd have thought him unsympathetic to Marcus, who'd sunk into abject misery after breaking up with his girlfriend. But she'd witnessed Alex rushing to his friend's side at the slightest hint of trouble, and noted how he checked on Marcus's mental state with nigh-alarming frequency via texts and FaceTime calls.

So yes, he was sympathetic. This was his way of helping, but doing so in the most annoying manner possible, because Alex was . . . Alex.

Thus far, he'd followed through on his plan, and it was a novelty not to have his barrage of words entirely directed at her, for once. Certainly, Lauren got her share along the way—as they drove to pick up Marcus at his home, and as the three of them headed to the airport, flew to San Francisco, and rode to the convention hotel—but Marcus received the bulk of the verbiage.

"—really pleased with the reception of my most recent fic," Alex told his friend as they neared the hotel. "The one I wrote with Cupid as an actor, starring in a popular television show. You beta-read it for me a few weeks ago. Remember?"

Oh, crap. He should *not* be talking about this within earshot of a stranger.

From the front passenger seat, Lauren twisted around to tell him so, but Marcus was already on it.

"Alex—" Frantically, he jabbed a finger in the direction of the driver who'd picked them up at the airport. "Of course I remember, but you shouldn't—"

Completely unfazed, Alex waved a hand toward Lauren and

cheerily barreled on. "She probably doesn't know, though. Anyway, Lauren, I made actor!Cupid miserable and angry because of his incompetent, overprivileged showrunners, who completely fucked up the final season of his show and glorified abusive relationships in their scripts. But then he meets a woman named Robin, who—"

"Yes, yes." Lauren massaged her temples. "Pegs him until he's a font of joy and light once more, albeit a font who can't sit comfortably for a day or two. I read it."

After Lauren had finished that fic, she'd found herself unable to stop staring at her own forearm for minutes afterward.

"You did?" He beamed at her. "Oh, good."

Marcus groaned and scrubbed both hands over his face.

"Anyway, I already have over two hundred comments and a thousand kudos." Alex buffed his fingernails against his really soft-looking gray-blue jacket, which he'd layered over a crisp white tee. "All exceedingly well deserved, if I do say so myself."

When Marcus had climbed into her car that morning, his wretched mental state hadn't been hard to spot. He was hollow-eyed and slumped, his mouth downturned despite all his attempts at politeness and good cheer.

Now he appeared slightly less despondent, but significantly more freaked out.

"And you do say so. Much too loudly," he whispered. "Alex, shut the hell up before you get yourself fired, man."

"I felt much better after writing that story." Alex leaned back against his seat, hands folded behind his head, the picture of contentedness. "Now I know why people journal. Only I don't think the writing would be as satisfying without the pegging."

His head tilted as he considered the matter. "Then again, many people's journals probably include pegging, and good for them."

Then, thankfully, they were nearing the circular hotel entrance, and she braced herself. For fans, of course, but also for possible paparazzi. According to Sionna's email that morning, the incident outside the salon yesterday had gone viral, and bloggers and media outlets were likely clamoring for Alex's commentary on the matter.

To Lauren's relief, she wasn't yet part of the public story. *They haven't figured out you're the woman that asshole fan insulted,* Sionna had written, *probably because she didn't include the part of the film where you removed her groping hand. All the better to pretend she was the innocent victim in the confrontation.*

Lauren had gone offline again to protect her own equanimity, but she wasn't a fool. At some point, someone was going to realize that the woman who'd deflected a red-carpet attack on Alex was the same woman he'd defended from insult in the viral video, and then—

Honestly, she had no idea what would happen. But she still didn't want to explain her role in his life. Her job was an insult to him.

He didn't need a keeper. He needed companionship and understanding.

The car was slowing as they neared the drop-off area, and she couldn't pretend she was calm. Not when her palms prickled with sweat and her heart skittered in her chest at the prospect of confronting crowds by Alex's side.

Even without the prospect of paparazzi, she'd be worried. About bloggers and fans and hotel employees and . . . *everyone.*

One derisive sidelong look, one passing comment about her face or her body, and he'd detonate. She knew it.

In his car yesterday, she'd watched hurt and anger—at her, for her—darken those storm cloud eyes and twist his perfect face.

She'd cradled the hot, vulnerable nape of his neck in her hand as he shared stories he'd told no one else, as he shared his pain, as he shared his huge, loving, impulsive, honorable heart.

And she'd told him to follow his instincts, because how could she not? In that moment, how could she spurn his generous emotional response to her?

But even if she'd asked him not to react, she wasn't sure he'd be able to contain himself if someone insulted her.

Because he cared about her more than his career.

It was bizarre. Bizarre and touching and, frankly, terrifying.

Whatever they'd become to one another over the past fraught months had an end date. In less than a year, she'd be gone from his life, while he could have several *decades* left in his career. Rationally, it made absolutely no sense to risk his professional reputation for her sake.

But when it came to anyone he cared about, Alex wasn't rational. At all.

That reckless loyalty caught at her throat and hitched her breath, and it also scared the living hell out of her. As she'd told him so many damn times, she didn't want to be the means by which he destroyed anything precious to him. And he'd clawed his way to professional success over two decades of hard, hard work, despite the complications posed by his ADHD, so his reputation in the entertainment industry wasn't merely precious.

It was irreplaceable.

Whether he agreed or not, it was obviously way more important than whether some random person she didn't give two hoots about thought she was ugly.

She might have protected him from an unexpected attacker on the red carpet, but she didn't know how to protect him from himself.

The driver parked the car at the hotel entrance, and Lauren took a slow, deep breath before opening the passenger door. As the three of them climbed out and gathered their minimal luggage, a crowd of fans descended on both actors.

Those fans paid her no attention. Good.

Even as Marcus and Alex eventually made their way to the reception desk in the airy, sprawling lobby, no one seemed to realize she was accompanying the two men. Or if they did, they didn't care. Which was the correct reaction, because she didn't matter.

Once they'd all checked in—Ron had approved Marcus and Alex staying together in a suite, so she had her own room on another floor—they prepared to go their separate ways.

That tether tugged at her chest again, harder than ever, but she ignored it. It was better for her not to be in his immediate vicinity. Safer.

After pocketing her room key, she gave both men a nod. "I'll see you at your Q-and-A session, Alex. Have a good evening, Marcus."

When they stood so close, it hurt her neck to look up at them.

It hurt her heart too.

They were both tall, both exceedingly beautiful, both stars with their own powerful gravitational pulls. Soon enough, though, she'd have to wrench herself out of Alex's orbit and float out into space, a satellite adrift once more.

He was speaking, gesturing to her, but the buzz of the crowd, of her thoughts, drowned him out. Was he saying something about walking her to her room?

In all honesty, she would love a buffer on the way there, especially since some of the convention's attendees might recognize her from the red-carpet video. She should go on her own, though. That was the right thing to do.

So she pointed apologetically at her ear, mouthed *I can't hear you*, and fled as Alex's grin transformed into a scowl, Marcus watched them with a gaze as sharp as his best friend's tongue, and fans with phones poised for selfies descended on both men.

When she got into the elevator, Alex's aggrieved stare from across the lobby seared the side of her face, and she had to turn away and hide behind the closing door.

Yes, she was doing the right thing.

But leaving Alex felt wrong, wrong, wrong.

OTHER THAN WREN'S abrupt, exceedingly rude departure, everything else was proceeding according to Alex's very wise and well-thought-out plan.

He and Marcus had entered their blue-and-gold suite minutes before, then claimed their chosen bedrooms and unpacked. Or, in Alex's case, opened up his suitcase on the provided luggage rack and called it a day, because he didn't unpack for trips of less than a week.

The rooms were comfortable but generic, and they didn't matter. What did matter: Alex's commitment to continual, provoking conversation. It was a particular skill of his, cultivated over decades, and it proved as effective as always.

Marcus was thoroughly distracted from his lovelorn misery, and would remain so, at least until Alex's upcoming Q&A session. But Alex figured he could guilt his best friend into coming along and staying the whole time, no problem. And after the two of them were done with their con obligations for the night, he'd badger Lauren into joining them for dinner.

A better person would let her have the night off, now that he'd been safely deposited into Marcus's custody. But Alex wasn't a better person, obviously, and he wanted Wren and Marcus to know one another. He wanted them to get along.

Just because it would be awkward if they didn't, what with her babysitting him until the final season finished airing. Since Marcus was back in L.A., the three of them would clearly be spending a lot of time together.

Although, in theory, she wouldn't need to be present if Marcus was.

Whatever. Alex's friends should be friends too. That was only logical.

While Marcus got ice from the nearest machine, Alex sprawled stomach-down on the bed, propped himself up on his elbows, and texted Lauren.

You abandoned meeeeeeeeeeeeeeeeee, you heartless harpy, he tapped out.

One minute passed. Two. No response, and no Marcus with ice.

Both his closest friends were slow as fucking molasses in winter.

You owe me a good dinner in compensation, he added. I'll pay, because I know you hate that, and it'll be just punishment for your various sins. Marcus will come too, because whenever I don't distract him, he looks like an abandoned kitten, and his face may very well freeze that way, and who would cast him then? Besides, he likes you. He said so on the way to our suite. Do you like him?

Nothing. Not even blinking dots.

Fine. He could carry the conversation all on his own, because that was how charming and efficient he was.

Wait, what am I saying? Marcus is the nice one. OF COURSE you like him. He frowned, struck by a sudden thought. But not more than you like me. Right?

He waited, drumming his knuckles against the duvet.

Right, Lauren? he added after another minute.

No answer. No dots.

Alex huffed out an aggrieved breath through his nose and switched to all caps to relieve his feelings. GAH, YOU ARE THE WORST.

Marcus reentered the room then, shoulders slumped, an abandoned kitten once more.

Dammit. Back to the plan. "How long does it take to get ice? Did you personally trek to the arctic tundra and cut the cubes yourself?"

"The machine is on the other side of the . . ." Marcus sighed. "Never mind. I'm sorry I took so long."

A quiet *ding* signaled a new email in Alex's personal account. Maybe Lauren had responded that way instead of texting, for whatever reason?

But no, it was an email from the last person he wanted writing him. Dammit.

"Fuck," Alex groaned, then tapped the email to open it. "I have a new message from Ron and R.J. The subject line is *Inappropriate behavior and possible consequences.* As if I don't know what horrible things they could—"

Wait.

No. No, that couldn't be right. Alex had been skimming and distracted, and he must have read it wrong. Ron was an asshole, sure, but Lauren was his goddamn *cousin.*

A second reading didn't change anything.

After chastising Alex for *unacceptable rudeness* to that terrible fan yesterday, and yammering about how his behavior was *in violation of behavioral expectations and contractual obligations*—nothing Alex hadn't read before, and nothing that bothered him, given the context of said rudeness—Ron had added a postscript.

P.S. I suppose this is our fault, for saddling you with such an ugly minder. Tell Lauren to put a bag over it, if she has to, but stop letting her face get you in trouble. Although that doesn't fix the rest of her, right?

Ron had added a crying-laughter emoji at the end.

He'd also cc'd Lauren.

There was no misinterpreting that.

Alex's skull began pounding, and annihilating rage detonated within him, sweeping unbearable heat over his entire, rigid body.

"Those motherfuckers," he whispered. "Those cruel motherfuckers."

That awful woman from yesterday had deserved what she'd gotten from Alex, but she was just an entitled, pissed-off stranger. Not worth thinking about for longer than it took to verbally smack her down.

This—

This, he couldn't abide. Not for a single minute. Not for a *second*.

That fucking emoji. That careless amusement at Lauren's expense, with Lauren *as the fucking audience*. All that, after Ron dared to call her—Wren, the woman with the most beautiful eyes imaginable, his fucking *cousin*—ugly?

No fucking way Alex was going to stand for that. She'd tell him to let it go, but he couldn't. He couldn't. He *wouldn't*.

No one, fucking *no one*, was going to mistreat a woman he—

Not again. He was not fucking allowing it *again*.

His hard, heaving breaths hurt his chest, and his vision had turned so hazy, he didn't even see his best friend approaching the bed. Marcus removed the phone from Alex's clenched hand and said something, but all that blood pounding in Alex's ears muffled the words, and his brain was pinballing in a million different directions, too many to make sense of anything but the imperative hammering against his cranium.

Fix this. Fix this now.

A walk, he finally managed to decipher. Marcus wanted to go for a walk.

Oh, Alex would walk, all right. Right to a fucking stage, and a fucking microphone.

"No time." Alex's joints ached as if with fever, but he stood and shoved on his shoes, then stalked to the door. "Let's get going. I have a Q-and-A session to attend. You can keep the phone for now."

He could barely hear his own words over his freight-train heartbeat.

Marcus slipped the cell into his front pocket, right next to his crotch, but Alex didn't give a shit. He didn't need a phone to do what was right.

Fix this. Fix this now.

It was a howl in his brain, driving him inexorably onward, and vaguely, he acknowledged Marcus saying things to people, maybe fans, but he couldn't focus on them over all the *noise.*

When the moderator and conference organizers greeted Alex and Marcus at the assigned hall, he grappled for enough self-control to be polite, because none of this was their fault.

Right then, for a fleeting moment, he could hear something else through the cacophony of rage.

It was Marcus. Not the Marcus worriedly standing beside him backstage, but the Marcus of other occasions, other terrible moments.

He pleaded, *Play the film to the end. What happens if you don't change the script?*

But Alex couldn't. The future beyond this moment, this stage, was a wall, unknowable and opaque. He needed to smash through it, and there was only one way. Only one path forward.

Marcus was watching him carefully. "I know you're angry, but—"

"Don't worry," he said, distantly impressed by his own calm voice. "I'll be fine."

He would be. Better than fine. He'd be *free*. Of his own self-loathing, of the show, of the howling fury in his fucking brain.

Then he was striding onstage, and the microphone felt good in his grip. Powerful.

Cameras were aimed his way, and cell phones too, and he offered all of them a feral smile, entirely delighted that his words would be livestreamed for the entire fucking world.

For endless minutes, he answered questions from the moderator and spectators as coherently as he could—because, again, none of this was their fault, and he wouldn't be a dick to them for no reason. All the while, he paced, waiting for his moment.

It would come. Someone would ask. He knew it.

If tasked to identify the moderator in a police lineup, he wouldn't be able to do it. The only person he could see clearly in a huge room packed with people was her.

Wren, wearing an austere blue button-down and dark jeans. In the front row, at the very end, in her reserved spot. Days ago, he'd secretly asked the organizers to bring in a special chair without arms for her, because the seating at cons was fucking unforgiving.

Much like me, he thought. *Very appropriate.*

As unbothered by insults as she claimed to be, that email had to have hurt. Especially coming from a fucking member of her *family*.

If so, it didn't show. She didn't look hurt. She wasn't hunched or flushed or curled in on herself or avoiding his eyes in embarrassment.

No, she was staring up at him, brow furrowed, perched at the edge of her chair. His Wren, poised for flight. His dear friend and protector, ready to leap between him and danger.

Which she, in fact, had already done.

It was his turn to leap for her, because she deserved it. She deserved *everything*.

He gave her a little nod. Appreciation. A vow.

Another question from the audience. Another. They were running out of time, and the session was about to end, and was he *really* going to have to bring this up himself?

But then—

A nervous woman in the third row stood to ask a question. *The* question.

Her voice wavered. "Wh-What can you tell us about the final season?"

Thank fuck. *Finally.*

He bared his teeth in a wide, delighted grin, but she did not appear appreciably comforted. Which was fair. He was a lion with a gazelle in sight, and while she was not the gazelle in question, her instincts for danger were sound.

"Your question is about the final season, correct? You're asking what I can share about it?" When she nodded, he smiled at her one last time, then looked directly into the bank of cameras streaming his every movement, his every word. "Thank you for such a fantastic closing question. I'd be delighted to answer."

Lauren flew to her feet, somehow sensing imminent trouble, and Marcus was already striding toward center stage, but it was too late. They were too late, and Alex was smashing through the goddamn wall, fuck the consequences.

Fix this. Fix this now, his brain howled.

So he did.

17

LAUREN BURST INTO THE DESIGNATED HALL FOR ALEX'S Q&A session, frantic to talk to him. But even as a volunteer ushered Lauren to her assigned seat—a special one without arms, and she'd immediately known who'd arranged *that*—the moderator strode onstage, and the session began.

Shit. *Shit.*

She was too late.

After receiving Ron and R.J.'s email, she'd taken a few minutes to calm herself in her hotel room. The insult itself didn't particularly bother her—if she had a dollar for every time her cousin called her ugly during their childhood, she'd have enough money in her savings account for several Spanish vacations—but having Alex read it . . .

Well, that stung a little, if only because it put their differences in such sharp relief. It wasn't as if he could somehow overlook the fact that he was an unabashedly beautiful human being, and she was not. He didn't require a *reminder*, though, and she didn't either.

But that small sting had faded quickly, entirely subsumed by sheer terror at what might happen next. Because Alex would *not* handle the insult well, and if she looked upset at all, he would go ballistic. So she'd needed to get entirely calm, and then she'd intended to find him before he had the chance to speak to anyone other than her or Marcus.

But he hadn't been in his suite, and he hadn't responded to her frantic texts, and by the time she'd worked her way through the crowds outside the hall, she'd run out of time.

Bowing her head in defeat, she took her seat and sent a plea winging to the heavens. *Please let him not have seen that email. Please.*

After the moderator's introduction, Alex didn't simply walk onstage. He *prowled*, bright streaks of color high on his cheekbones, face split wide with a rage-filled smile, and oh, yes, he'd seen the email.

But as he answered the moderator's questions, he remained polite and jovial, and if his voice had sharper edges than normal, she and Marcus—because surely Marcus was here somewhere?— were probably the only ones who noticed it.

After a few minutes, she exhaled slowly and began to relax.

Despite his ridiculously wide protective streak and volatile temper, he was a professional. He'd survived in a tough industry for almost two decades, and despite a couple of bobbles and challenges along the way, he'd managed to construct a very successful career.

He'd do the right thing, much as it might pain and enrage him. She had to believe that.

Then: disaster.

That poor, scared young woman in the third row asked about the last season of the show, and Alex's *expression*. She'd seen that same expression only yesterday. The beam of a berserker ready to slash and burn, and laugh as he did it.

He hadn't been restraining himself. Not at all.

He'd been lying in wait.

As soon as that expression registered in her brain, she scrambled to her feet, and from the side of the stage, thumping footsteps heralded Marcus's attempt at intervention, but Alex was already speaking. Already offering his knife-edged grin to the cameras filming his every word.

"As you know, cast members aren't allowed to say much about episodes that haven't aired yet." He wasn't pacing anymore. He was entirely still, enunciating clearly and distinctly so his message couldn't be mistaken. "However, if you're interested in my thoughts about our final season, you may want to consult my fanfiction. I write under the name CupidUnleashed. All one word, capital *C*, capital *U*."

Oh, no. *No.*

The stories Alex had written, the comments he'd made . . . Ron wouldn't forgive them, and he wouldn't forget. He'd do his best to drive Alex from the industry in retaliation for how the actor had so scathingly criticized *Gates*'s scripts and showrunners.

She knew her cousin, even if her cousin knew next to nothing about her.

She wrapped her arms around her middle in a futile attempt at self-comfort, even as a hush fell over the enormous, packed hall. Her knees watery, she dropped back into her seat and curled in on herself, hiding the tears that glazed her vision.

Alex had incinerated his career. Because of her.

Two decades of such hard, hard labor and dedication; all those endless days he'd had to show up on set and harness his towering energy in service to work he loved, even if he didn't always love his scripts; the reputation he'd painstakingly built . . . he'd tossed all of it away.

For her.

She didn't think she'd ever felt so small before. So racked

by shame. To have been the means by which Alex got hurt was *unbearable*.

He was done.

And maybe it shouldn't matter, compared to the flaming shreds of Alex's reputation, but *they* were done too, she and Alex and whatever they'd had together. Because there was no way Ron wasn't firing her. Within minutes, most likely.

Alex was still speaking, still setting his professional reputation ablaze, even as she covered her face with both hands, bowed her head, and tried not to let her tears fall.

"Those stories will also give you some insight into my feelings about the show in general," he informed the audience, all razor-edged good cheer. "Also, fair warning: Cupid gets pegged in my fics. Delightedly and often. It's not great literature, but it's still better than some of this season's—"

He didn't finish his sentence. He didn't need to.

Everyone knew what word he'd playfully omitted: *scripts.*

"Well, never mind about that," he said, and she could *hear* the smirk in his voice.

She huddled tighter in her chair, because he'd ensured there was no way to misinterpret what he'd said, no spin that could explain away or disguise his loathing of his employers. The power brokers in Hollywood wouldn't forgive such open disloyalty. She knew almost nothing about the entertainment industry, but even she understood that.

There was a moment of silence, and she was afraid to look.

"No, that's everything." Alex's words were muffled through the ringing in her ears. "I'm done."

Then he was gone. The crowd erupted into scattered applause, then shocked laughter and conversation—*Can you believe what he said about the scripts? I'm looking at his AO3 handle, and holy shit—* as Lauren continued to sit in her special damn chair, motionless.

Minutes later, as a new crowd began to fill the hall, her phone buzzed. Slapping away the wetness on her cheeks, she read her incoming text.

It was from Alex.

Marcus ordered me to go to our suite and call everyone in my camp. Come on up, Wren. It's a party! After a moment, another message appeared. I know you aren't happy with what I did, and I'm sorry for that.

He was sorry for her unhappiness. Not for the damage he'd done to his career.

Then again, he had years ahead to mourn that. Decades. The rest of his life.

Her legs shook as she got to her feet and headed for the exit. She was going to her room, because nothing she could say, nothing she could do, would help Alex now. With one exception.

In the elevator, she texted him back. Promise me you'll listen to what your team and Marcus say. Promise me you'll do your best to salvage this situation.

He wrote back immediately. I promise. Unless they tell me to do something that's wrong. In which case, I won't budge.

It was a deliberate echo of what she'd said about her experiences at the hospital. The times she'd run afoul of her colleagues or patients or supervisors.

She sagged against the elevator wall, bereft.

Another buzz. Where are you, you intolerably plodding harpy?

She didn't answer.

When she got to her room, she let the door slam shut behind her. Her phone buzzed several more times as she emptied the few drawers she'd filled with clothing and other odds and ends, but she ignored the peremptory summons.

Once she was completely packed again, she checked her inbox, just to confirm.

Ron's email had arrived five minutes before.

I should have known you weren't capable of doing such a simple job, he'd written. *You're fired, and we're not fucking paying for your hotel room or the guesthouse anymore. Good riddance.*

She could check out over the phone, so she did. Then she caught a cab to the airport and took the first flight back to L.A. A seat in coach, of course. She couldn't afford more, and it was where she belonged.

By the time the small jet took flight, she'd texted Alex one last time—On the plane; I'm so sorry—and turned off her cell, because he needed to concentrate on salvaging his career, not on her, and his increasingly agitated messages *hurt*.

The bruises forming on her thighs, pressed into her flesh by the armrests, hurt less. Which was saying something.

She'd almost forgotten how it felt to squeeze into a space too cramped to contain her comfortably. She'd almost forgotten the specific pain of attempting to make herself as small as possible, contorting her arms and legs in a way that hurt her joints and made relaxation impossible. She'd almost forgotten the reality of her life.

In the end, despite all her attempts to be small, despite the discomfort of those attempts, she'd still have bruises. Pain following pain. It was unavoidable. Inevitable.

She'd accepted that for herself long ago.

But Alex hadn't been willing to accept it for her.

He'd witnessed her pain, and destroyed himself to avenge it.

For that reason, and for that reason alone, she wished to God she'd never met him.

Gods of the Gates Cast Chat: Friday Night

Ian: I want Alex kicked off this cast chat

Ian: I fucking told you, and so did Bruno Keene: cast poison

Ian: Our future careers may depend on the success of Gates, and he just shit all over it because he thinks he's too good for us, the ungrateful motherfucker

Carah: Oh, give me a fucking break, Ian

Carah: We all know everything Alex said (and wrote) is true

Carah: And yes, maybe making all those things public knowledge wasn't the smartest decision he's ever made, but I've never seen him THAT angry without damn good reason

Asha: I've worked closely with him for years now, and yes, this

Asha: And I've never seen even the slightest hint that he thinks he's too good for us

Mackenzie: Whiskers is very upset and worried about what may happen to Alex

Marcus: I can't share any specifics, but I can definitely tell you he had just cause to be very, very angry at Ron in particular

Carah: I knew it

Carah: We all knew it, except fucking Ian

Maria: As far as our careers depending on the success of Gates: our show has been a blockbuster for years now, and if you haven't already capitalized on its popularity to help your career, that's on you, Ian, not Alex

Peter: The final season of the show can't make or break our careers, and Alex never said one word about our acting

Peter: Just about the scripts and Ron and R.J. as showrunners, and like Carah said: fair enough

Carah: FYI, everyone: I just put out an official statement saying that Alex is not only a good friend, but also a valued, talented colleague who has always behaved with impeccable professionalism on set, and I hope to act alongside him in many future projects

Carah: I didn't even use profanity, because I too am a goddamn PROFESSIONAL

Ian: Another fucking traitor

Carah: I didn't insult the show, I just defended my friend, so fuck you very much, Ian

Summer: Should we all put out the same statement, to show our solidarity?

Maria: YES

Peter: Solidarity. I'll do it right now.

Asha: Same

Mackenzie: Whiskers agrees that solidarity is the way to go here, and we'll match Carah's statement

Marcus: After that Bruno Keene shitshow, this is going to mean the world to him

Marcus: Shit, I can't believe you assholes made me choke up

Marcus: Thank you, everyone

Ian: You're ALL fucking traitors, and I hope your careers tank because of this

Marcus: To quote a great leader, and I think I speak for all of us here: fuck you very much, Ian

Carah: Marcus, please tell Alex I want to talk to him about all the pegging, because I am fucking INTRIGUED by that shit

Mackenzie: Whiskers also has pegging-related questions

Maria: I love all of you SO MUCH

Maria: Except Ian, naturally

18

IT TOOK FIFTEEN MINUTES FOR ALEX'S HAZE OF FURY TO dissipate.

The march back to his room, Marcus at his side, passed in a blur. When his best friend pressed a familiar-looking phone in his hand and told him to call his camp, he did so automatically. The opening conversations with his horrified lawyer, agent, and publicist seemed to happen at a distance, to someone else entirely.

Then, when Lauren still didn't answer his tenth or twentieth text, it hit him.

He knew why she wasn't responding.

The world around him snapped into focus, and he could suddenly hear something other than his own deafening heartbeat. Only then could Alex do what Marcus always advised, and play the film to the end. The advice seemed especially prescient today, because yes: the end. That's what he'd brought upon himself in all his righteous rage.

He'd burst through the wall, all right. Waiting on the other side? Disaster.

He didn't regret what he'd said and written. He didn't even regret the possible consequences for his own career, although he'd devoted his adult life to that career and—with several notable exceptions—loved almost every minute of it.

The camaraderie. The cameras. The way different roles immersed him in different, fascinating cultures and forced him to learn and hone new skills. If he couldn't land another role, he'd miss all of that. Still, his conscience was worth his career.

But he bitterly regretted the consequences for all the people around him.

He'd fucked over nearly everyone in his orbit. His agent, who relied on the income from Alex's work. His castmates, who would rightfully shun him for shit-talking their final season, the project to which they'd devoted so many years of their lives and love and labor. His mom, because after this, he might not land enough work to continue supporting her as he wanted—or he might get sued, and not be able to support her at all. His charities, which also needed the money his work brought in. Abused women and children, who might not have a safe space to rebuild their lives if his savings ran out.

Lauren. Fuck, Lauren. The woman he'd meant to defend and avenge.

He'd fucked her over too, because there was no way Ron and R.J. would keep her on their payroll after this. Not when her entire job description entailed keeping Alex out of trouble, and he was currently in a shit-heap of *that*.

An indeterminate amount of time later, his phone dinged, and there it was. The text he'd been waiting for. Confirmation that his worst fears had been realized.

On the plane; I'm so sorry.

Of course she'd apologized to him. Of course. It'd be funny, if it weren't so awful.

As she'd told him on that set of starlit stairs overlooking downtown L.A., she needed time. She needed a break from the work that had burned her out.

He needed her.

But she was already gone, because of what he'd done on that stage. Already on a plane home. Not the home they'd shared for months, but her little turreted duplex in NoHo. And soon, she'd have to return to work, ready or not, because of his inability to fucking *think ahead*.

No wonder she hadn't returned his earlier texts.

Shit. In the space of five minutes, he'd fucked up everything. *Everything*.

When Marcus entered their shared suite after his fan photo sessions, he found Alex in an armchair, elbows on his knees, face in his hands.

"Well," Marcus said when the door closed behind him, "the good news is that the media is no longer focusing on your fan incident yesterday."

Alex groaned and lifted his head.

Marcus sat on the coffee table facing Alex, his expression sympathetic but matter-of-fact. "I thought you'd be juggling three separate phone conferences right now. What's going on?"

"As a group, my team decided my input was neither necessary nor beneficial as they formulated a response to the situation." Slumping wasn't enough. If he could, Alex would simply dissolve into the seat. "Zach and my lawyer and publicist are all discussing the issue amongst themselves, and they said they'd contact me when they reached a consensus. At that point, I either approve their game plan or not."

"I see." Marcus nodded. "Have you happened to glance at the cast chat recently?"

Alex's hands were a friendly, comforting place, and his face decided to revisit them. "No. Too chickenshit."

Something cool and smooth nudged his arm, and Alex looked up again.

Marcus was holding Alex's cell. "C'mon, man. Don't you trust me?"

Shit. As Marcus very well knew, Alex did trust him, and to prove it, he was going to have to access the cast chat, where everyone now hated him.

You're the worst, dude, he almost said, but that reminded him of Lauren, and if he thought for longer than a few seconds about Lauren, he wouldn't be able to function at even his current, minimal level.

"Fine," he grumbled, eyeing his best friend suspiciously.

As soon as he opened the cast chat, he saw Ian's messages from a couple hours before and cringed. But then . . .

Nothing but love and support.

Back into his hands went his face, this time to disguise his stupid wet eyes.

Marcus chafed his shoulder supportively. "Maybe we should reclassify you as a weepy bitch instead of a gossipy bitch."

Alex raised a trembling middle finger.

"Have you checked your email yet?" Marcus's voice was gentle. "Because I imagine Ron and R.J. had something to say."

"Before I stopped checking my phone, I got a message from them. I forwarded it to my team, but didn't actually read it." He took a shuddering breath. "I wasn't ready."

"Are you ready now?" It was a genuine question, not a demand.

His best friend would give him as long as he needed. Thank fuck for Marcus.

"Yeah. I suppose." Using the backs of his hands, he swiped away his grateful tears, then accessed his inbox. "Here we go."

It was no worse than he'd expected, really.

Too late to remove you from the show, blah blah blah. *Consulting with our lawyers about legal and financial consequences,* blah blah

blah. *As the public now knows, you're an embarrassment to your profession,* blah blah blah. *Not welcome at the convention or future publicity events,* blah blah blah.

It was the last bit that jolted him from the cozy depths of the armchair.

> *As you've defamed us and our show, we are no longer interested in helping you. Thus, Lauren is fired, as she should be after such gross incompetence. Also, we have ceased paying for your virtual PA as of this evening. If you want her continued assistance, you'll have to shoulder her hourly rate yourself.*

The *gross incompetence* part set his teeth on edge, but there was something else niggling in his brain, some sort of idea . . .

Yes. There it was.

For the first time in two hours, the pounding in his skull eased, because he could see a possible path forward again. One he could actually live with.

Surging to his feet, he strode into his bedroom and slammed his still-open suitcase closed again, then zipped it shut. He tossed it onto the bed, then reached for his phone and ordered a ride to the airport. Next step: an airline ticket back to L.A.

When Alex began scrolling through possible flights, Marcus cleared his throat. "Care to tell me what's happening?"

Whatever. The car ride to the airport would give him time to buy a ticket.

"Take a look at my inbox." He tossed his phone to Marcus. "I'm no longer welcome at the convention, and all the relevant conversations with my team are happening over phone and email, so there's no point in staying. I might as well go home."

Using a text-to-speech app, Marcus listened to the showrunners' message.

Once the entire vitriolic email had been read aloud, he glanced up at Alex. "You're going back to L.A. tonight?"

Alex inclined his head. "If I can catch a plane, I'll fly. If not, I'll rent a car."

"You're going after Lauren," Marcus said neutrally.

He managed a hoarse laugh. "Of course I am."

And when he caught up with her, he was going to do his damnedest to convince her to stay with him, because he wasn't ready to say goodbye. Not now.

Recently, he'd begun to wonder whether he'd *ever* want to say goodbye. Whether he'd ever be willing to miss one of her rare, piercing smiles. Whether he could ever happily live without her deadpan comebacks, her gentleness, or the way her snarky tees molded against her small breasts and the curve of her soft belly.

Maybe Lauren still thought they were simply minder-and-charge, or platonic friends, but he knew better now. He'd known better ever since that temptation-soaked near-kiss in his car.

"I have to go," he told Marcus. "My driver should be here in about five minutes, and making my way through the lobby will take a while."

Marcus's sharp stare could have peeled grapes, but Alex didn't flinch.

Finally, his best friend sighed. "I'll run interference. Let's go."

They finally managed to reach the hotel entrance just as the car pulled into the circular drive. Alex half tackled Marcus in a hug, then flung himself inside the SUV, slammed the door, and fastened his seat belt as quickly as possible.

"To the airport?" the driver asked, her gray hair in a coronet of braids.

"To the airport," Alex confirmed. "As quickly as possible. I'll double the fare if you get me there in time for a flight at ten."

"You got it." Her foot stamped on the accelerator, and the SUV jolted around the circle and onto the streets of San Francisco.

He bought his ticket for that late-night flight as they wove through traffic and streaked along straightaways, then managed to send Marcus a quick message of reassurance despite the rough ride.

Going to fix this. Don't worry.

He wasn't talking about his career. But his best friend likely knew that already.

ALEX SHOWED UP at her duplex just before one in the morning. Which was only appropriate, since they'd often gone for their nightly walks around that same time.

It was a sign, he decided. A definite sign.

When she answered his peremptory knock and repeated doorbell-ringing, she didn't look like she'd been sleeping. She did, however, look like she'd been dragged backward through several different circles of hell.

"You look like shit," he told her. "Being away from me doesn't suit you."

She did not seem especially impressed by his opening conversational salvo. Lips in a thin, tight line, she merely stood in her doorway and looked up at him, eyes puffy and red-rimmed from traveling fatigue.

"Such a terrible hostess." Dramatically sagging under the weight of his very light suitcase, he shook his head at her. "But if you require a lesson in appropriate etiquette, I'm here to assist. According to Miss Manners, you should invite me in, lest I collapse on your front porch from exhaustion. It's the only polite thing to do."

On second thought, perhaps that wasn't the best advice, given Lauren's overly generous nature.

Quickly, he clarified, "But if any other dude shows up at this hour of the night, don't invite him in. He could be a miscreant. Or a vampire. Although maybe that's covered under the miscreant umbrella?"

She closed her eyes and took a deep breath, then moved to the side of the doorway and waved him in. "Just shut up and come inside, Alex."

Once he did, he found himself oddly unsure what to do with his hands.

Given his druthers, he'd tug her close. He'd wrap her in his arms and hold her, basking in her proximity, reassuring himself that whatever relationship they'd formed hadn't simply ended.

Wren was absurdly, wonderfully round. Abundant, despite her diminutive height. She'd be soft and warm under his hands and against his body.

He wanted to feel it. He wanted to feel her.

But his proposal would impose the same old barrier between them, so he needed to keep his hands to himself. Accordingly, he set his small suitcase on the wooden floor and lowered the handle, then folded his arms across his chest.

Wren had changed into one of those faded, oversized tees she used as nightgowns, and her bare legs appeared especially pale against the darkness of the living room. The only light filtered in from the bedroom, where she'd apparently turned on a lamp.

They were alone in her house at night. Her bed might be rumpled. Welcoming.

He caught himself studying her legs again, and quickly glanced away.

They stood there in her small, dim apartment, staring at each other for a long minute. He blinked first, because of course he blinked first. Lauren was a fucking machine. A Terminator, as he'd once informed Marcus, albeit a very short one.

Finally, as if on cue, they spoke at the same time.

"I'm sorry," they both said, and frowned at one another.

Then, in unison once more, "*You* shouldn't be sorry."

More frowning.

"You first," they both said, and Alex couldn't help it.

He laughed until his eyes were wet again, and the crushing weight in his chest had lessened enough for him to draw something near a full breath.

When he calmed, there was still no levity in her expression or those lovely eyes. Then again, she hadn't heard either his apology or his plan yet, so he wouldn't count that as defeat.

"Because I'm nothing if not a gentleman"—he polished an imaginary monocle—"please speak first. While keeping in mind that if you apologize for anything, I may have to murder you. Thus proving my point: You shouldn't let strange men into your apartment."

Not even a lip twitch. Dammit.

"Murder me as necessary, but I need to say it." Her voice was gravelly, hoarse, and entirely determined. "I'm so sorry you endangered your career because of an insult to me. As soon as I understood that was even a possibility, I should have resigned and told Ron to find you a new companion."

If she took one of those *Which* Gods of the Gates *Character Are You?* quizzes, she'd definitely be Atlas, the poor bastard. No question about it.

"Jesus Christ, Wren." He heaved a heartfelt sigh. "Why are you so determined to be a martyr? I'm not sorry I caused problems for myself. I'm sorry I caused problems for *you*. Along with a few other people, but they're not my priority right now. You are."

Her brow furrowed even further, which he hadn't thought physically possible. "What do you mean?"

"You needed time before deciding where to work next, and you needed money to buy you that time." He hung his head. "When I lost my temper at Ron, I took away your extra time and income, and I apologize. You have every right to be angry with me."

She held up a palm, her expression twisting in distress. "You were trying to *avenge* me, Alex. Because you were upset on my behalf. How in the world could I be angry at you for that?"

God, he wanted to roll his eyes *so damn much*. But he couldn't, not with her obvious confusion and remorse and . . . whatever else was carving deep lines into those distinctive features.

"Lauren, you're fucking terrible at being angry at other people for mistreating you or overlooking your interests." A home truth, and one he hoped she understood. "Your lack of anger does not reliably indicate a lack of wrong done to you."

She blinked those gorgeous eyes up at him, looking lost.

Whatever. They'd have plenty of time for informational lectures soon enough.

"Anyway, the good news is that I'm here to right this particular wrong." He beamed at her, more certain than ever that he could fix everything. "I have a plan."

"Oh, shit," she muttered.

Ignoring that, he carried on. "The production used to provide a virtual assistant for me, given my organizational issues. In Ron's email, he said—"

"Wait." She held up a hand, somehow looking even guiltier. He could only assume it was a Guinness world record of some sort. "I can't believe I didn't ask this right away. What's happening? What did Ron and R.J. do?"

"According to my agent and lawyer, I should be able to avoid financial retaliation and a lawsuit. That said, I'm disinvited from upcoming publicity events and forbidden to comment on the show, and both you and my virtual PA are fired." The other, non-*Gates*-related consequences didn't need to be discussed now. Or, preferably, ever. "Which brings me to my brilliant pl—"

"Not so fast, Woodroe." Forget about birds. She was a fucking *badger*. "What about the post-finale jobs you had lined up? Have you heard anything about them?"

He stared with great interest at her bookshelf. "Not all of them." Not yet, anyway.

"Oh, Alex." She dropped onto her sofa as if her legs had collapsed beneath her. "I'm so—"

Nooooope. "If you say 'sorry,' I swear to God, Wren, I'll—"

"What?" She raised a challenging brow. "You'll what?"

Okay, perfect lead-in. "I'll remove the gym benefits from your employment package, and you'll have to work out with me in my home gym."

Her mouth opened, then closed.

"Just kidding," Alex said. "You don't have gym benefits, so you actually will have to work out with me at home. Assuming you want to work out, which isn't a requirement or anything. You do you."

That wide mouth had dropped open again, and she looked delightfully fishy.

"I wasn't joking about the employment package, though. My lawyer is still"—amidst much complaint, given her other efforts on Alex's behalf that night—"drawing up the contract, but it should be ready within a day or so. I'm happy to negotiate terms, as necessary."

At first, he'd considered offering Wren work as his continued nanny-slash-companion, but he already knew what her response to that would be. She'd turn down the offer, claiming she'd already proven her inability to keep him out of trouble.

So he'd come up with a different solution. A better one.

"I don't . . ." She licked her pale lips, and his own legs turned a bit weak. "I don't understand."

"Jeez, you're slow." When she merely stared up at him, he heaved an exaggerated sigh and explained, "I'd like you to be my new personal assistant. Not virtual. In-person."

Her nose wrinkled, and it shouldn't be so damn cute. "That makes no sense. Why not rehire your previous PA on your own dime and keep things virtual? She clearly has more experience than I do. Besides, I have several job options in my actual field of work, so my income isn't dependent on your largesse. Hers might be."

Dammit. He'd hoped she wouldn't think of that.

"I'm keeping her on too." He shifted his weight. "Otherwise, I'd feel bad."

How he was going to produce enough work for both women, he hadn't yet determined. He'd burn that bridge when he got to it, as was his custom.

She pointed an accusing finger at him. "You just told me you've lost jobs already—"

"I didn't actually say that. You merely *surmised*."

"—and I already know how generous you are to friends and charities and everyone else on the face of this planet, except maybe Ian and Ron—"

"Like you're one to talk, Lauren Chandra Clegg, aka Ms. I'll-Drop-My-Entire-Fucking-Vacation-the-Moment-My-Dickish-Cousin-Asks."

"—so there's no way you can afford two PAs long-term, and even if you could, I won't accept make-work when I could be doing actual work instead."

At some point during the discussion, she'd risen to her feet again. Right now, she was staring him down with her hands planted on her hips, her chin raised high.

She was so fucking *stubborn*, and he wanted to plant a kiss on that soft, truculent chin as much as he wanted to call her *the absolute worst*. But his entire plan was slipping through his fingers, goddammit. There was no time for kissing or even insults. He needed to find a winning argument, and he needed to find it now.

"But keeping me in good order is a two-person job," he pointed out, desperate.

She held up her forefinger and middle finger. "Yes. You and your PA. Two people."

"But—" Shit. "If you don't come work for me, you won't have as much of a break. You said you needed time to get over your burnout."

At that, she actually smiled. It was small and sad and grateful and terrible.

"I've been able to save money these past few months, so I'll still have time. Not as much as I originally thought, but some. Enough." She audibly swallowed. "Thank you for thinking of that, though. Thank you for thinking of *me*. I appreciate it more than you know."

A very kind and polite goodbye was on its way, he could tell. If he didn't conjure another reason for her to stay by his side within the next five minutes, she was gone from his life for good.

He would come up with that reason. He *would*.

But first, he had to ask. "That email . . . are you okay?"

"I'm fine." Her eyes were earnest on his. "It's nothing I haven't heard before. Ron used to say stuff like that all the time when we were kids."

He closed his eyes and took a long, deep breath.

Upon seeing his expression, she quickly added, "Which doesn't excuse his rudeness, of course, but it's fine. I just wish you hadn't seen that message, because I know it upset you more than it upset me. Obviously."

And that killed him. Absolutely gutted him.

He didn't want her upset, but he did want her angry. Or maybe not even angry, but at least *cognizant* of the wrong done to her. He wanted her absolutely unwilling to accept that kind of cruelty as a normal or acceptable part of her life.

But it wasn't up to him.

"And I know you don't want one, but I do owe you another apology." When he opened his mouth to protest, she raised a hand. "Let me finish, Alex. Please."

Goddammit. When she said *please,* he couldn't do anything but what she wanted.

Glaring at her all the while, he braced himself to listen.

"If you say I shouldn't be sorry for getting you in trouble, I'll try not to be, and I won't apologize for it again." Her mouth turned down at the corners, which he hated. *Hated*. "But I can and will apologize for not being by your side as you dealt with the fallout. You asked me to come to your suite, and I should have done it. I should have supported you."

Her absence had hurt. He couldn't deny that, even as he'd understood her reasons for leaving. Or, at least, he'd thought he understood. But if she hadn't been angry at him—

"I just . . ." She twisted her neck and stared into her lamplit bedroom for a few moments before turning back to him, her eyes glassy, and he hated that *even more*. "I knew it was the end of our time together, and I was"—when she blinked, the tears slipped down her cheeks—"I was really sad, Alex. I didn't want to distract you with my own feelings, though, because you had more important things to deal with."

Again. Gutted. Because *again*, she'd placed herself below everything else, everyone else, in his life, and she didn't even seem to notice. Didn't acknowledge how *wrong* that was.

She tried to smile, and it was wavery and heart-wrenching. "I'll miss you."

Then she was stumbling forward, and her arms wrapped around his waist, and she was leaning into him, just as soft and warm and precious as he'd imagined.

That worn nightie didn't disguise the electric feel of her body against his, or her obvious lack of a bra, and he tried to keep his telltale reaction angled away from her. He didn't want to ruin the moment or cut it short.

Because she was hugging him. Nanny Clegg. Wren. His Wren.

Ducking his head uncomfortably low, he rested his cheek against her hair. It smelled like coconut. He'd had no idea, until just now.

When her arms began to loosen, he bent down and framed her sweet, sharp-featured, tear-stained face in his hands. He pressed a kiss to her forehead.

Her cheeks were wet and cool, and they fit perfectly in his palms.

He gazed into her eyes, and the moment felt as solemn as a ceremony.

Wait.

There it was. At long last, his excuse.

On the plane, he'd checked his email and read a message from his virtual PA. After canceling all his upcoming publicity-related travel arrangements and agreeing to work directly for him, she'd asked for a vacation of at least two weeks before resuming her normal schedule. He'd said yes, of course.

After all, he had nothing to do. Nowhere to be. With one exception, as his PA had reminded him.

One glorious, fortuitous exception.

"You don't have to miss me." The plan spooled out before him, perfect in every possible way. He pressed a fierce kiss to the wispy hair at her temple, triumphant with joy. "I have another brilliant idea, Wren, and I'll take care of everything. All you have to do is say yes."

She blinked up at him. "Oh, Jesus."

Lauren's Email

From: mclegg58@umail.com
To: l.c.clegg@umail.com
Subject: Checking on you

Hey, honey—

After your cousin called Aunt Kathleen this afternoon, she told your father and me what happened at the convention earlier today. I'm so sorry, sweetheart. Are you doing okay?

It all sounds terrible, and it's not fair that you lost your job because Alexander Woodroe couldn't manage to behave himself. I have no idea what Ron wanted you to do, honestly. How could you possibly have guessed what would happen? And even if you'd known, did he expect you to physically tackle Woodroe onstage and muzzle him until he calmed down?

That said, your Aunt Kathleen is very upset, and she keeps calling and saying over and over how you owe Ron an apology for allowing him to be humiliated in that way. Again, I know it's NOT your fault, but could you possibly tell Ron you're sorry in a brief email? If you forwarded the message to me, I could send it to Kathleen, and I think she'd feel better then.

Also, now that you have some free time, your father and I would love your company for a few days! We've been thinking about painting the den a different color. Maybe sage green? Anyway, you know how your father hates doing the corners and edges, and my knees won't let me sit on the floor for hours anymore, so your help would be more than welcome. You're so good at cutting in.

When you visit, I'll do a roast and make Potatoes Anna, your favorite. ☺ Just let us know when you can come.

Love you, sweetheart,

Mom

19

"OH, JESUS," LAUREN SAID WITH FEELING.

Say yes, he'd urged, and God help her, she'd almost agreed to whatever Alex's cockamamie plan might be on the spot.

He'd ruined her. Without him, everything should have been quiet and peaceful since her late-night arrival at her duplex. Instead, everything had been quiet and *boring.* Quiet and boring and—sad. Too sad to sleep, given how she'd wound up sniffling every few minutes.

And now he was touching her, cupping her face with his warm, strong hands, and she couldn't remember why she'd been crying only moments before. If pressed, she wasn't certain she could reliably recall her own name.

"Such suspicion, Wren. I'm terribly offended." He made a *tsk*ing sound. "As an apology, I'll accept your willingness to hear me out before you say no. Agreed?"

His solemn frown had entirely transformed into a grin of smug triumph, glee over his no-doubt-awful idea beaming from his fatigue-creased face. With one last, gentle sweep of his thumbs over her damp cheeks, he dropped his hands and took a half step back, and her skin abruptly prickled with chill.

The handsbreadth of space didn't allow her to regain her equilibrium. Not when he still stood within easy touching distance, close enough that his flagrant appeal, his unabashed sexiness, was an unavoidable taunt.

Another Henley clung to his chest, cream-colored and unbuttoned just enough to show a flash of golden, hair-dusted skin, its pushed-up sleeves framing his thick, corded forearms. Faded jeans hugged those strong thighs close. So close.

She had to drag her gaze away from his thighs and his forearms, but his face wasn't any better. Despite the shadows under his eyes and the lines bracketing his mouth, his smile was the sun. It dazzled her with its brightness. It burned away everything but him.

For a moment, helpless before that face, that voice, that body—all Alex was, and all he'd been to her—she could only blink and stare.

He tilted his head. "Lauren?"

His storm cloud eyes saw her entirely too well. Under their scrutiny, she blinked again and tried to remember what exactly they'd been talking about.

"Sorry." She shook her head, hard, and gathered her scattered wits. "Listen, if this is about working for you—"

"I'm not offering you another job." His face drooped, and damn, she knew it was an act, but it still tugged at her heart. "You're not going to hear me out? Even though I said please?"

She cast her eyes to the ceiling. "First of all, you didn't say please. Second, even if you had, saying please isn't some magical incantation guaranteed to bring you your heart's desire, Alex."

"It's not?" He frowned at her. "Then why have I been bothering all this time?"

When she covered her face with her hands, shoulders shaking, even she didn't know whether she was laughing or crying.

"I don't think you're giving my proposal the solemn consideration it deserves," he complained, but she could hear the smile in his voice. "I'm calling the Humorless Harpies of America hotline to report your various misdeeds. I may file a formal grievance, if matters don't improve."

"Heaven forbid." After wiping away telltale traces of wetness, she dropped onto the sofa. "Go on, then. I'll give your proposal my full, stern, joyless attention, as required by HHA bylaws."

The fondness in his regard tripped her already-racing pulse. "That's all I ask."

Her sofa could accommodate three people, but he settled right next to her and turned until his bent knee nudged her thigh. He didn't apologize for the contact. Didn't move away.

She couldn't breathe.

"Come with me to the wedding next weekend." He held up a hand, as if preempting her refusal. "You were already supposed to accompany me, so I know you don't have other plans."

The . . . wedding?

Oh. Oh, right. His ex's ceremony amongst the redwoods.

Stacia said it was the only setting that could possibly dwarf my towering self-regard, he'd told Lauren weeks ago, rolling his eyes fondly. And when she'd frowned at the injustice of that insult, he'd only waved away her concern. *She was just teasing me. We've been friends for a long time.*

Lauren understood the wedding part now. But without an assigned minder, he could attend the event with anyone he wanted. Why bring *her,* of all people?

Alex was still speaking, even as she attempted to puzzle out his intentions. "—never let me hear the end of it if I arrived alone, and you were already supposed to be my plus-one. Since we both have time right now, and you hate flying, I thought we could do a road trip up the coast. Together."

His words were tumbling over one another, uncharacteristically breathless, and he rubbed his palms along his hard thighs. "Which would be perfect, since I do my best thinking as I drive, and I have decisions to make about my career. Also, my virtual PA needs a couple weeks off, and travel arrangements aren't exactly my strong suit, so . . ."

Okay, that made sense. Kind of.

After a steadying breath, she looked up at him. "You want me to accompany you as your PA on a trip up the coast? I mean, I'm happy to help with the arrangements, but wouldn't you rather bring someone—"

"Not as my PA." His stare pinned her in place. "Not as my paid companion either. I'd cover your travel expenses, because I need your organizational help, but that's all. This wouldn't have anything to do with business."

Her throat prickled anew at the evidence that he truly did value her company. He truly did want to spend time with her, with or without a mandate from Ron.

Still . . . she'd need to start work again soon. Once she did, they might go weeks without seeing one another, or months, or—

She swallowed over a thick throat.

Their lives might never intersect again.

Did she really want such an extended, potent reminder of what she'd soon miss so terribly?

She glanced down at her lap. "I don't know."

"About my paying for the trip?" His hand covered hers, and her bones turned liquid. "We both know I can afford it."

That wasn't her main concern. But still . . . "For now. Maybe not for long."

He didn't argue. No, he did something infinitely worse.

"I need you." Suddenly, their fingers were interlaced on her thigh, and his voice was low and hushed and much too close to her ear. "Wren, please."

They both knew he didn't actually need her. But she couldn't turn him away, not when he spoke to her with such pleading, such . . . intimacy.

Her scattered thoughts buzzed through her head, fuzzy and contradictory, and she tried to gather them into an orderly row.

Under these circumstances, what was the right thing to do?

Because of his loyalty to her, his professional life had just fallen to pieces around him. He could use a friend, and he could use help planning his trip. Spending this time with him might hurt her more in the end, but if he wanted her by his side, she needed to do better than she'd done in that convention hotel.

She owed him.

More than that, she . . . cared about him. Very much. Even though he was a major pain in the ass and a total brat and the sexiest, most bighearted man she'd ever met.

For him, she'd do the right thing. Which, in this case, wasn't the wise thing, but fine. Earlier that night, she'd reminded herself that pain was inevitable no matter what she did. She'd survive.

He lifted their joined hands and rested them against his bristly cheek, and people on other continents must have been able to feel the thud of her rocketing pulse.

"Please," he repeated, and it was a raw whisper, his breath warm against her wrist.

She sucked in a deep breath, but there wasn't enough air. "You're not paying."

It wasn't merely a cease-fire. It was full-on surrender. They both knew it.

"I am." Oh, crap, he was rubbing their hands against his jaw now, and the prickle of it was delicious. "I defended your honor, Lauren. You owe me, and an honorable woman pays her debts."

When she chanced an outraged glance upward, his eyes were alight. Dancing.

He was playing her. He didn't actually think she owed him, but he was more than willing to take advantage of her guilt, and dammit . . .

Dammit. It was working.

"To be specific, you owe me two weeks of good hotels and gas money and fresh seafood and tour tickets and whatever souvenirs I may choose to buy you along the way. And you have to promise not to apologize for any of those expenses. Which will all be covered, to make things absolutely clear, by me." He raised his perfectly arched brows, the cocky bastard. "It's the least you can do, really."

"Two weeks?" She should remove her hand from his. She would, any moment now . . . once he stopped playing with her fingers. "The wedding is next Saturday, so how in the world—"

"We can leave tomorrow. It's not as if you have an extensive wardrobe to pack." He directed a damning glance toward her bedroom closet. "A week up to the redwoods and the wedding, and a week back. Two weeks, Wren. That should cover your balance. For now, at least."

Over her lifetime, she'd had very few male friends. She hadn't realized just how *affectionate* they could be. Because that was definitely Alex pressing a kiss to the back of her hand, the brush of his soft, warm lips a jolt of lightning down her spine, and she couldn't *think*.

Maybe this was what friendship with a man looked like without work involved?

Through the muddle of her clouded thoughts, something was niggling at her.

"Alex, I—" Right. That was it. "I can't leave until Wednesday, at the earliest. When I told Sionna I wasn't working anymore, she took Tuesday off so we could hang out together."

In theory, she could ask Sionna to reschedule, but she wouldn't.

Two weeks of him paying for everything? Nope. Not acceptable.

Then he was letting go of her hand, and she wanted to wail at the loss of contact, only—

Only he was cupping her face again, his thumbs sweeping over her cheeks, and her breath stuttered to a halt. He stared down at her for a minute, unaccountably solemn once more.

His hands slid lower, until he was cradling the nape of her neck with one palm and stroking her back with the other, and—and her face was suddenly nestled against his chest.

"You drive a hard bargain, you intransigent shrew." He spoke against the crown of her head, his lips brushing her hair with every word, even his ostensible insult a caress. "We'll leave first thing Wednesday morning, so be ready. Pack your pretty lace dress and sensible wedges. We're dancing at the wedding."

He smelled like sunlit cotton and starlit nights on a mountainside. Fresh air and warmth. Somehow, her arms found their way around his waist, and she was clutching him too.

Her eyes closed, and her throat was dry as Death Valley. "We are?"

It was a rasp. A trace of sound, and she let her mouth shape the words against the soft fabric over his heart.

He shuddered against her, his hands tightening possessively.

When he spoke, his tone brooked no dissent, and she didn't offer any. Couldn't.

"We are," he said.

ALEX LEFT WITHOUT kissing her on the mouth. Barely.

He'd wanted to. He'd been about to. And then he'd looked

down at her and finally acknowledged just how tired she was. Red-eyed, the thin, soft skin underneath those eyes bruised with fatigue. Uncharacteristically emotional and weepy, her body pliant and trembling with exhaustion against his. Ginger in her movements, as if still stiff and sore from her plane ride.

Their first kiss deserved better, and he refused to take advantage of her lowered defenses. If she chose to kiss him, he wanted her to do so with all her strength and alert intelligence intact.

Still, he'd taken his time before letting her go, and she had to realize how he felt. What he wanted. He hadn't exactly been subtle about it.

He wouldn't push her, but he wouldn't disguise his feelings either. Not anymore. And after the way she'd clung to him, he hoped—

His phone buzzed from the other side of his desk, and he eagerly snatched it up.

Sadly, the message wasn't from Lauren.

Instead, his agent had sent a peremptory text. Block out time to talk Thursday afternoon. We need to be on the same page before Saturday.

Alex's ex, Stacia, was one of Zach's clients too, and the wedding would likely include other Hollywood power brokers as guests. The desire to talk beforehand was reasonable.

The tone wasn't.

Now that Alex was in disgrace, Zach apparently believed his client didn't get a say in when they'd meet. But Zach, sadly for him, was incorrect.

Going on a road trip, Alex wrote back. See you Saturday at the wedding. We'll talk that morning.

Then he temporarily blocked Zach's number, because fuck that dude. Alex had better things to think about right now. Much, much better things.

Namely, his plans for Lauren. His sweet, recalcitrant Wren.

The woman he wanted to make his, somewhere along the coast of California.

As a kid, he'd considered July the best month of the year, because that was the month his mom usually tried to take off for a week. Or better yet, two weeks. Once she got approval, they'd count their available money, determine their loose itinerary and strict budget, and set off in her tiny Chevette hatchback, venturing up and down the Florida coast.

Those days on the road had seemed endless. Sun-drenched and sticky. Literally sticky, since her car's AC didn't work. Even the wind whipping through the windows couldn't cut the humidity, and his lower legs stuck to the textured vinyl seats, leaving a perfect, pebbled pattern on his skin each time they stopped for gas or a fast-food meal.

Every afternoon, they'd watch the thunderheads roll in and either find a motel for the night or veer onto the shoulder for a few minutes. With the windows up, the glass would turn steamy, and he'd draw pictures in the condensation. A dog. A knight. Stars. Together, they'd wait and talk and pass each other Twizzlers or the Pringles can until the torrential downpours ended and she could continue driving once more.

Those weeks were the best of his childhood, bar none, and his mother had worked herself to the bone to give them to him. He wanted to give Lauren something similar, if he could.

There was no way she'd accompany him to Florida anytime soon. But on a road trip up the California coast instead, he could help her relax. Really relax.

No work, no responsibilities. Just exploration and rest and companionship. Constant proximity and privacy and huge beds in cool, dim hotel rooms.

He wasn't a kid anymore. His mother—much as he adored her—was nowhere nearby.

This was going to be the greatest fucking July *ever.*

Texts with Marcus: Saturday Night

Marcus: Sorry, I meant to check in earlier

Marcus: I was busy with normal convention stuff, but also April and I worked things out ☺

Alex: Congrats, dude, I'm happy for you both

Alex: Please give her a hug from me

Alex: Which shouldn't be difficult, since you're no doubt clinging to her like plastic wrap

Marcus: Well, you're not wrong

Marcus: Obnoxious, but not wrong

Marcus: You doing okay? After everything that happened last night?

Alex: Great!

Marcus: . . .

Alex: No lawsuit + no fines + no press junket = ROAD TRIP!!!

Alex: With Wren, obvs

Marcus: Obvs

Marcus: I hope you noted the sarcasm there, because it was distinct

Alex: Nope, I spotted nothing but sincerity

Alex: Anyway, on Wednesday, we're heading up the coast to Stacia's wedding

Alex: I plan to woo her along the way in my own unique, extremely charming way

Marcus: So you've finally realized you're into her?

Marcus: Thank fuck

Marcus: I thought we'd both be sitting in our rockers at a nursing home before you noticed

Alex: Self-reflection is not my strong suit, dickwad

Alex: Also, please note how I didn't make a dirty joke about the "into her" bit

Alex: This is just part of my transformation into a gentleman worthy of Lauren's affection

Marcus: She seems fond of you as you are

Marcus: If I were you, I'd just stay an asshole

Alex: I should probably be offended,
but we both know it's true

Alex: Wish me luck, dude

Marcus: Good luck, drive safely, and let me know how it goes

Alex: It'll be great

Alex: As I always say, CLEAR EYES, SMARTASS, CAN'T LOSE

Marcus: You've literally never said that before

Alex: Let me rephrase

Alex: CLEAR EYES, SMARTASS, FUCK YOU

Marcus: Love you, man

Alex: FINE, I LOVE YOU TOO, ARE YOU HAPPY NOW

Marcus: Yes, very much so

Alex: Good, you deserve it

Alex: Still, fuck you

20

"I'M *EXCELLENT* COMPANY ON ROAD TRIPS." ALEX AIMED A
blinding grin Lauren's way before turning back to the traffic.
"Charming. Witty. A veritable fount of wisdom and knowledge. So
stunningly attractive that I'm essentially my own tourist attraction
and/or scenic overlook. By the time we're amongst the redwoods,
you'll be having such a great time, you'll wonder how you ever traveled without me."

It was just after noon, and they'd only recently hit the road.
Because . . . Alex.

Despite his insistence on an early start time that morning—
"You already made me wait until *Wednesday*, Wren, which is
essentially next year"—he'd had them sit down for one of Dina's
delicious, huge breakfasts before they departed. Because, he claimed,
Lauren *owed* him the consumption of croissant-based French toast
stuffed with a heavenly cream cheese–strawberry mixture, since
he'd defended her.

Then he'd confessed that he hadn't packed yet, and insisted on
modeling way-too-flattering outfit possibilities for her and parad-
ing around shirtless as he changed, and . . .

Well, they'd gotten a late start. But as he'd pointed out, this
was meant to be a vacation, and they had plenty of time and nowhere in particular to be before Saturday.

It was wonderful, frankly. All of it.

The travel plans. The uninterrupted time to talk. The lack of divided loyalties. The car.

The shirtlessness.

"I'm going to have a great time? That's odd." She angled herself toward him. "I seem to recall a brand-new bumper sticker on your very expensive car reading—and I quote—*NO FUN*. In all caps. I assume it was purchased for this trip?"

The sight of it had stopped her dead in her tracks that morning, as she'd approached the mini-castle. Alex had pulled his car up just outside the front door, and she couldn't miss the decorative addition. Not with its bright red letters against a stark white background. And yes, the car itself was that same shade of cherry red, but the sedan was also sleek and pristine and entirely unsuited to smartass bumper stickers.

Upon second thought, maybe the combination of car and sticker *was* perfect for Alex. Slick lines and gorgeousness leavened by a healthy dose of the ridiculous.

"The bumper sticker's an *homage*," he declared loftily, his attention on the road, his eyes hidden by his stylish sunglasses. "A nod to our past as Nanny Clegg and her irascible yet irresistible charge."

"I see," she said dryly. "I didn't realize it was an act of historical commemoration. My mistake."

The sun blazed overhead, and the car's air-conditioning battled valiantly against the July heat. The rolling hills surrounding them were parched and golden, with patches of green from brush, and she couldn't wait to get even closer to the water and the ocean breeze. But to be perfectly honest, she'd barely managed to glance outside the passenger window so far. Because Alex might be aggravating, but he was also right: He *was* irresistible.

He'd modeled countless outfits for her, all of them glorious on him. But in deference to the temperature, he'd chosen to wear a plain white tee today. Or at least, it would have been plain on almost anyone else. On him, it was an artful garnish on a perfectly plated dessert.

Oh, heavens, it was *tight*. It strained against his biceps and lovingly clung to his broad shoulders, and its immaculate whiteness made his skin glow golden in the sun.

The snug fit of his faded jeans showcased the shifting muscles of his strong thighs as he braked and accelerated over and over, the rhythm hypnotizing. And between those thighs—

No, she wouldn't look there. Not again.

Truly, her current preoccupation with his lean, strong body was his fault entirely, and it had started even before the half-naked fashion show. As soon as he'd spotted her standing on his circular drive that morning, he'd come bounding out of the mini-castle, his face creased in a huge, beaming smile, and stridden directly to her.

He hadn't stopped a discreet foot or two away or waved from a distance. Oh, no.

Instead, he'd moved close and punctured the generous, invisible bubble of space that usually surrounded her and opened his arms wide, and what could she do then, really? What else could she do but walk forward into those arms, into his all-encompassing embrace?

He'd bent low to rest his cheek against her hair, and he'd murmured, *Finally, you exasperating shrew, finally*, and he'd wrapped around her like—

Like the blanket he'd given her, maybe. Warm and luxurious. More beautiful than anything she'd ever hoped to have or even dared to want.

But she *did* want him. And she'd had him for endless seconds on that driveway, maybe even a minute or two, because he hadn't given her a quick squeeze and let her go. No, he'd held on tightly, and she hadn't moved away either.

As they'd stood embracing one another, the warmth of his skin soaked through his clothing and heated to scorching against her fingertips on his back, her arms around his waist, her cheek on his chest. His jeans rubbed against the smooth fabric of her leggings, and the friction rippled through her until she swelled and ached between her thighs. Despite the barrier of her cotton bra and T-shirt, she was very much afraid he could feel her nipples harden against his stomach, and if she didn't know better—

Well, surely she'd been mistaken. That was his phone or his wallet, not . . .

At the sense memory of that firm ridge against her upper belly, she reached desperately for her water bottle and took a long, long drink from the condensation-beaded plastic.

She would not look at his zipper placket again. She would *not*.

Even though, when they'd finally stepped apart on his driveway, she could have sworn his jeans fit a bit . . . differently . . . in that region than they usually did. And the kiss he'd pressed to her flushed skin then hadn't landed on her temple or forehead.

He'd kissed her cheek, maybe a bare millimeter from the corner of her mouth.

Friends, she told herself for the millionth time that morning. *He's my all-too-affectionate friend, and he doesn't understand what he's doing to me.*

When he spoke again in the hushed, intimate cocoon of the car, she had to jerk her gaze up from—dammit—where it kept drifting, despite her best intentions.

"That bumper sticker is essentially a monument, Wren." He

glanced behind him before switching lanes. "Also, my car isn't *that* expensive."

He was smiling at the road ahead and the bumper-to-bumper traffic it contained. When a song he especially liked played over the discreetly placed speakers, he hummed along, off-key. His shoulders were loose, his movements easy and fluid.

Despite all his professional woes, she'd never seen him look so relaxed and entirely pleased with himself and the world.

His happiness didn't hinge on her presence, of course, but the sight of his joy still ignited a spark of pleasure inside her. Because he was able to let down his guard in her company. Because he deserved every bit of his seeming delight. Because he wanted her beside him in this car—which was, no matter what he claimed, unmistakably luxe.

"Really? It's not that expensive?" Brows raised high, she traced a fingertip over the pleated interior trim on the passenger door. "Because I don't remember fabric folded to look like origami inside vehicles in my price range. Or massage settings for buttery-soft leather seats."

She did *not* like the speculative glance he darted her way then.

"Don't even think about it, Alex," she said sternly. "If you buy me a damn car, I'll immediately donate it to charity."

"You'd do it too." It was a grumble. "Harpy."

She snuggled deeper into her seat, satisfied. "Correct."

He heaved an aggrieved sigh, despite the smile still creasing his bearded cheeks. "Okay, so this model wasn't cheap, but a bunch of my costars have sports cars instead. Plural."

A sports car couldn't possibly be any more luxurious than this. She caressed the sleek, polished wood on the dash, tracing the herringbone pattern with her fingertips.

They were stopped in traffic for the moment, and he appeared to be staring at the dashboard too, although the sunglasses made it hard to say for sure.

His white teeth sank into his lower lip, and the car ahead of them accelerated.

They didn't. .

"Alex?" Even as she pointed to the now-open road, the SUV behind them honked. "Alex, we need to move."

The next honk was way longer and part of a growing chorus of discontent, and he jumped a little before facing forward again and stomping on his own accelerator.

He cleared his throat and paid careful attention to the road. "Sorry. Lost focus for a minute there."

He jabbed at the control screen to lower the temperature and raise the fan speed for his side of the car, high color burnishing his cheekbones.

Another tap. Another. "It's fucking hot in here. Shit."

Maybe the sun was more intense on the driver's side, because she was pretty comfortable.

She frowned. "Do you need more water?"

"Nope." His tone did not invite further discussion. "Anyway, my mom has the same model as mine, just in a different color. I kind of liked the idea of us driving matching cars."

He'd clearly bought her that car, and the sweetness of the gesture pierced Lauren's heart.

He rarely mentioned his mom, although Lauren knew the two of them talked regularly on the phone. She'd wondered about their relationship, but now she knew: Alex loved his mother. He wasn't a man to love half-heartedly, and their matching cars were further proof.

"Does she live in California?" Lauren asked.

They were nearing Santa Monica. Soon, they'd merge onto the

Pacific Coast Highway and drive right along the water for miles and miles, heading up the coast on that famous ribbon of road sandwiched between the vast, sparkling ocean and steep, rugged mountains. Decades had passed since her last extended trip along the PCH, and she couldn't wait.

Maybe his mom lived somewhere along their route?

He shook his head, his mouth tight. "Florida. Near where I grew up."

What kind of woman had raised the man beside her? And why hadn't Alex—who chatted at frankly ludicrous length about everyone else in his life—discussed her more?

Lauren twisted to face him more directly, readjusting her seat belt so it didn't bite into her neck. "Are you two—"

"I have a favor to ask," he interrupted, the words abrupt. "How do you feel about filming me?"

The images that appeared in her febrile brain should have embarrassed her. But she was too busy wondering why he'd cut off that line of conversation so decisively, and also too busy melting into a puddle of lust all over his lovely leather seats, to feel the appropriate level of shame.

"What, uh . . ." Another long, not-cold-enough sip of water. "What exactly do you want me to film?"

Probably not what she'd just imagined, sadly.

"You're not online much, right?" When she shook her head, he steered them down the California Incline, and then they were on the PCH at last. "Carah—do you remember her? From the charity event?"

Here, next to the Pacific, the temperature wasn't scorching, but pleasantly warm. The blue, blue water stretching into infinity loosened something long-knotted inside her, and the ocean breezes beckoned. Without even bothering to ask first, she turned off the AC and rolled down her window. He shot her a pleased grin, then lowered his too.

The whipping wind roared in her ears, and she raised her voice to be heard. "Carah Brown. Very kind, very funny, uses the word *fuck* more than any other human alive?"

He snorted. "You remember Carah. Anyway, she films herself eating weird foods suggested by viewers and posts the clips all over the internet. When we were texting yesterday, she suggested making my own videos on the trip as a way to connect with my fans outside of *Gates*, and I thought it was a decent idea. But I need a camerawoman."

"Me," she said.

"You," he confirmed. "Assuming you're willing."

In theory, she was, but . . . "I know nothing about filming people."

"Luckily, I know a lot about being filmed." He set his left elbow on the windowsill, and the arm of his T-shirt rippled in the rush of air. "It'll be fine, Wren. It's just an experiment. If it doesn't turn out well, I don't post anything. No problem."

Well, she'd warned him. "Okay. I'll do it. You want me to use your phone?"

"Yup." Leaning back in his seat, he dug out his cell from his jeans pocket and handed it to her. "Why don't we do a test run in Malibu?"

His phone had more features than hers, and she took a few minutes to learn the various options as they passed Pacific Palisades. By the time they neared Malibu and veered inland, she thought she could at least shoot a basic video. Probably.

She turned toward him as far as she could and propped her elbow on the dashboard to steady her camera hand. "Ready for your test run?"

The traffic had turned heavy, and he took advantage of a temporary stop to check himself out in the rearview mirror. As she could have told him, he didn't need any adjustment. He was already the epitome of casual, sun-kissed stardom, his dishevelment only adding to his appeal.

"All right." He let off the brake for a few feet, then had to stop again. "Let's do this, Wren. Three, two, one, and . . . action."

She tapped the red circle on the screen and kept the camera focused on his profile in the driver's seat.

"Hi, everyone. I'm Alex Woodroe"—he shot a brief grin in her direction and winked at his audience—"the beloved and exceedingly attractive star of *Gods of the Gates* and various films, some more low-budget than others. I'm driving up the Pacific Coast Highway on a multiday road trip, and I thought you might like to hear about where I am and where I'm going."

Doing her best to keep the phone still, she nodded encouragingly.

He waved a hand, indicating their surroundings. "Right now, we're in Malibu, where L.A.'s rich and famous come to hunt the Sasquatch of Youth."

At that, she choked on thin air, and tried to cough-laugh as silently as possible.

He frowned. "You okay?"

When she waved him on, he added confidingly, "As everyone in Hollywood knows, if you catch the Sasquatch of Youth, it'll grant you an extra decade of casting viability in exchange for its freedom. For that reason, sasquatch-hunting is the main local industry in Malibu. The city should really advertise it more."

If this was a test run, she could respond without ruining anything, right?

With her free hand, she groped for her water bottle and took yet another huge gulp. "Alex, are you entirely sure these are the sorts of travel insights you want to share?"

"It's the only explanation for Carah Brown, Wren." When the car came to another stop, he turned to look directly into the camera. "Did you know that Carah is ninety-three years old?"

When Lauren laughed out loud, so did Alex, and she couldn't resist engaging with his nonsense. "Maybe she has a *Vanity Fair* cover portrait that's aging for her?"

"Solid literary allusion. Nicely done." When he reached out for a high five, still grinning, she gave it to him. "Anyway, Carah's ancient, and the Sasquatch of Youth lives here. That's really all you need to know about Malibu."

He held up a finger, as if he were a scholar making one final, crucial point. "Oh, and some people in Malibu try to keep their beaches private and only accessible to the super-rich, which is total bullshit. But I suppose they need seclusion for sasquatch-hunting purposes."

Oh, holy crackers.

"I hope you've enjoyed your scintillating view of me and Malibu's delightful stop-and-go traffic." He flashed another bone-melting smile in the camera's direction. "Thanks for watching, and remember to get out there, have fun, and don't let Carah Brown fool you. She's pretty, but she's also old as fuck and mean as hell. Can't say I didn't warn you, people."

Still shaking with suppressed laughter, she tapped the screen to stop filming.

"How'd we do?" When the traffic began to move faster, he returned his full attention to the road. "Never mind, I was obviously brilliant, so let me rephrase: How did *you* do?"

When she played back the video, he remained in focus the entire time, and everything he'd said was clearly audible. Unfortunately, so was everything she'd said, and his theoretical audience could see her arm as he high-fived her.

Dammit, if she'd simply kept out of the conversation and camera view, they could have used that clip, because he'd been . . . himself. Entirely himself. Funny, sharp-edged, intelligent, and ridiculous. Irascible and irresistible, as he'd said earlier.

"I'm sorry." She sighed, placing his phone in the center console. "If I hadn't butted in, that video would have been perfect for uploading."

He lifted a shoulder. "Do you have any objections to being in the video?"

She hadn't said anything embarrassing, and it wasn't as if she'd paraded herself in front of the camera. So after a moment of consideration, she shrugged too. "No. Not really. But as you once told me, you're the one the audience wants to look at and listen to. Not some random woman."

"I don't care about them, Wren. *I* want to look at you. *I* want to listen to you." Before she could do more than blink at him in befuddled pleasure, he added, "But are you sure you won't mind the public visibility? I don't anticipate a huge audience, but what I said at the con is still a big deal in some circles. There's a possibility the clips could get some traction."

"If so, I'll just stay offline for a few days again." Carefully, she smoothed a finger over the folded pleats inside the door and avoided looking at him. "You really want me in the video?"

"Videos. Plural. If you're willing." He reached over and hesitated. "May I touch you?"

When she nodded, he laid a hand on her knee, and she breathed out shakily. "It's more fun with you participating. Please, Wren."

Her leg was on fire. His thumb brushed back and forth over her kneecap, and the thin, stretchy fabric of her leggings offered no protection from his heat, from the electrical current generated by his touch.

She required yet another desperate gulp of her water before she could speak. "Okay. As long as I can stay behind the camera, okay. I'll do it."

He gently squeezed her knee, and she bit back a gasp. She wanted his hand, those agile fingers, higher. If he ever cupped her between her legs and squeezed like that—

"Good." His palm slid slowly up her thigh before returning to the wheel. "Get ready, then. Later today, I intend to tell people about the recent zombie sightings along the coast."

She nearly choked on another sip of water. "Zombies, Alex? Really?"

Surely a grin *that* wicked violated state law?

"Really," he said, and accelerated into the sun-spangled road ahead.

THE PINK-GOLD LIGHT rested warm on his smiling face as Alex wrapped up his fourth and final segment of the day. "Anyway, if you travel to Morro Bay, there are two main things you have to remember. One, there's a rock shaped like a t—uh, breast. Two, protect your braaaaaaains at all costs. That's basically all you need to know."

Although this was definitely *not* a real travel show, she couldn't let such a major oversight stand. "Also, Hearst Castle isn't too far away, and I hear it's well worth a visit."

"You've never been?" He furrowed his brow at her briefly before turning back to the road. "Maybe we should have a castle-off on our way back down the coast. Mano a mano. Or, rather, castle-o a castle-o. Mine against Hearst's. Who do you think would win, Wren?"

She didn't hesitate. "Hearst."

He gasped loudly, outraged. "How dare you?"

"I'm a philistine, clearly." The light was going fast, and she wanted to take a few pictures of the sunset with her own camera before nightfall. "Say goodbye, Alex."

"Goodbye, Alex," he parroted in a sing-song voice.

She shook her head. "Smartass."

When he grinned happily at her, she tapped the screen to stop filming. Only to notice, as she settled back in her seat, a two-lane sea of red brake lights maybe thirty seconds ahead of them, with absolutely no cars coming toward them. Not a good sign.

Alex slowed in preparation for the backup. "What's going on?"

"Is that smoke?" She squinted in the gathering darkness, and yes. That was definitely smoke in the distance. Not an enormous amount, but enough to cast a growing haze. "Let me see if I can figure out what's happening."

The GPS, now that she was paying attention, indicated stopped traffic, but didn't note a reason for it. Luckily, the freeway information number proved more helpful.

After listening to the message, she ended the call and relayed the bad news. "Evidently, there's a brushfire at the side of the road ahead, so we're getting detoured. No estimate about how long the road will be closed."

He groaned. "Shit. This is going to take forever."

The sun had sunk below the oceanic horizon, and he tossed his sunglasses into the center console, his brow furrowed.

"Once we're on the detour, what do you want to do?" she asked.

In her mind, there was only one good choice, but he might not agree.

His fingers drummed against the steering wheel as he braked to a halt. "The detour road will be slower, obviously. And because we'll be heading inland, we'll have to go over the mountains, which means driving on twisty roads that aren't well lit at night. We'd intended to make it farther, but . . ."

"Let's stop for the day and wait until the roads are clear," she finished for him, relieved that they were in agreement.

At his insistence, they hadn't made reservations for particular hotels or tourist sites—he'd wanted to keep their schedule relaxed and spontaneous—so they had nothing to cancel. Stopping early made complete sense.

He nodded decisively. "We have a plan."

Two extremely slow-moving hours later, after Alex had serenaded her with various off-key '90s hits and she'd actively contemplated the merits of hitchhiking, they reached their first decent-looking hotel. Only to find that they couldn't reserve a room, despite the deployment of his most charming smile.

"I'm so sorry, but we're completely full, and so are all the other nearby hotels. I just checked for another couple a few minutes ago." The clerk at the front desk winced in apology. "With the PCH closed, people wanted to stop for the night. And Hearst Castle is having an event, so most places between here and San Simeon are probably booked too."

Shit. They needed someplace to rest. Dark circles had appeared beneath Alex's eyes, and they wouldn't both survive two more hours of his unique vocal stylings.

Who would die, she couldn't say. But definitely one of them.

"Do you have any suggestions?" Alex leaned his elbows on the counter and scrubbed his face with both hands. "Someplace within easy driving distance that might have vacancies?"

"Maybe check around Cambria? There are B and Bs there, and a few motels. Nothing fancy, but . . ." The clerk lifted a shoulder. "I wish I had better news for you, Mr. Woodroe."

So the young woman *had* recognized Alex. Lauren had wondered about that.

At the sound of his name, he straightened and made an obvious effort to perk up. "Thank you for your help . . ." After glancing at her name tag, he smiled. "Carmen."

With laudable patience, he posed for a selfie and autographed one of the hotel's notepads, and then they were back in his car and headed down dark, twisty roads toward Cambria.

No Vacancy. No Vacancy. No Vacancy.

But then—

"There." She pointed to the right. "That looks like a B and B. Want me to run in and check if they have rooms available?"

"Have you never seen *Psycho*, woman?" He turned into the small parking lot. "Of course I'm not sending you in alone. Jesus Christ."

All the official spaces were occupied, so he simply parked on a strip of gravel.

The reception area was small and somewhat dated but appeared clean. The young man behind the counter frowned at their arrival, and she knew what he was going to say before his mouth even opened.

"I'm so sorry. We're full. And from what customers are telling me, so are all the other lodgings in the area." He cast them a look of seemingly sincere apology. "Any other night, we'd have plenty of room, but . . ."

At sunset, the temperature had dropped significantly, and the reception area wasn't particularly well heated. When Lauren shivered, Alex guided her against his side with a warm hand between her shoulder blades, pressing her against his hard furnace of a body, and she shivered again for an entirely different reason.

A hundred-dollar bill suddenly appeared between his fingers. "Are you absolutely *certain* you have nothing available? We need two rooms. Large, small, whatever. We'll take anything you have."

Lauren shifted slightly away to stare up at him, because *really?* People actually did that in real life? And who the hell carried around hundred-dollar bills and produced them that freaking smoothly?

Alexander Woodroe, apparently.

The young man's eyes landed on the bill, and he licked his lips. "Well . . ."

"Yes?" Alex's grin had turned smug, as he sensed imminent bribery victory.

"We actually have one room free," the clerk said, and she could *feel* Alex's chest puff out in triumph. "But we haven't been letting people stay there because the AC won't turn off, and it's freezing. We're getting it fixed tomorrow. That doesn't help you tonight, though."

A flick of Alex's hand dismissed that concern. "We'll just get some extra blankets for the beds. No problem."

"Uh . . ." The young man visibly swallowed and cast a longing glance at Alex's money. "Not beds. Bed. A full."

Her chin dropped to her chest at the prospect of more driving and more high-volume sing-alongs to Def Leppard. She allowed herself one sigh, then slid out from under Alex's arm and prepared to soothe his own disappointment and frustration.

Only to find, instead of a frown or weary resignation, an expression of dawning delight.

"Let me get this straight." He braced his hands on the counter and leaned in closer to the clerk. "There's only . . . one bed?"

The young man blinked at him. "Yes, sir."

When Alex pumped his fists in triumph, punching the air, Lauren and the clerk both jumped.

"This is the best day of my fucking *life*!" he shouted. "Only! One! Bed! My second-favorite trope!"

He swung around to beam at her. "Lauren! Did you hear?"

Oh, she'd heard, all right. His mom back in Florida probably had too.

"What do you say? Can we do this?" He clasped his hands under his chin like an innocent schoolboy, which he most definitely was *not*. "I promise to be good."

He—wanted to share a bed with her? Really?

Dropping her gaze to the scratched wooden floor, she tried to think past her instinctive buzz of excitement and pleasure, the bolt of sensation between her legs when she pictured the two of them in bed together. Intertwined. Naked. His weight on her, his strong, capable hands spreading her wide and—

No. No, she shouldn't sexualize this. That wasn't fair to him *or* their friendship.

But if she shared a room and a bed with him, the memory would haunt her once their road trip ended. She'd dream about it. Mourn what had been and would never be again. The wisest answer, then, given her burgeoning, ill-conceived feelings for him, was a firm *no*.

The *right* answer . . . that was tougher to pin down.

His thumb on her chin gently guided her gaze to his. "Look, Wren, it's okay. If you're not comfortable, we don't take the room. No problem. I mean that."

His gray eyes were warm. Sincere.

He did mean it, she knew. He wouldn't begrudge her a refusal, no matter how disappointed he might be.

But if she agreed, she'd undoubtedly make him very happy. Which would, in turn, make *her* happy, at least in the moment, and also allow her to avoid a repeat of the evening's earlier, extremely unfortunate, "Pour Some Sugar on Me" Incident.

She was tired. She was stiff from a long day in the car. And damn it, she wanted to know how it felt to share a bed with him. Just once.

She let out a slow breath, then turned to the waiting clerk.

"Let's do it," she said, and jumped again at Alex's elated whoop.

Maybe it wasn't the wisest answer, but it was *her* answer. The right answer.

At least for tonight.

21

ALEX EXHALED AS HE PACED, AND HE COULD ACTUALLY SEE the puff of air. Even though it was July. In California.

Well, he couldn't say the kid at the front desk had misled them. The small room contained only one full-size bed and no couch. Its air conditioner chugged away at full blast no matter which setting he chose. And as the clerk had informed them while pressing the key into Wren's hand, the windows were indeed painted shut.

The room felt like the world's smallest hockey rink. Under normal circumstances, he'd be bitching nonstop. But since they were only staying there because of him . . .

Well, he'd only complain *occasionally.*

Behind the room's flimsy bathroom door, Wren was showering. Hopefully under the hottest water she could stand, because those sheets were going to feel like ice.

The sheets they'd soon be under. Together.

Shit, he couldn't keep staring at the door. It was damn creepy. And if he continued imagining rivulets of steamy water running down her lush, wet, naked body, no amount of glacial cold could prevent his own body from visibly responding, and he didn't want to scare her away when she emerged from the bathroom.

She'd trusted him enough to share a bed. He wouldn't violate that trust.

Resolutely turning away from the bathroom door, Alex got out his phone and occupied himself by uploading the day's videos on various platforms, tagging Carah wherever possible.

The sound of running water stopped, and he bit his lip.

The towering pile of extra blankets they'd carried to their room and spread over the bed might keep her warm. But if the blankets weren't enough . . .

No, he wouldn't think about it. He couldn't. Not when she was coming out so soon, her soft skin damp and flushed with heat, almost like they'd just been—

Nope. No. *No.*

When she emerged from the bathroom in a cloud of steam, dragging her suitcase behind her, she was wearing one of her oversized T-shirt nightgowns and a new pair of leggings. Nothing he hadn't seen before, but he suspected she wasn't wearing a bra this time. Maybe not panties either, and *that* was a thought he was going to do his very best to forget.

"Ahhhhhhh." When her eyes flew to his, he grinned at her. "My just-one-bedmate returns."

The edges of her hair had become wet. Random strands were sticking to her rosy cheeks and neck, and within moments, those bits would feel like icicles against her skin. So would the air. So would the wooden floor.

Sure enough, as soon as she registered the absurdly low temperature in the main room, her face immediately pinched into a pained grimace, and she made a sort of gasping squeak.

"Holy crap," she breathed, immediately starting to shiver.

He would not check what the cold had done to her nipples. He would *not.*

She wasn't wearing socks or slippers, and she sort of bounced on her tiptoes to the bed, trying to make as little contact with the floor as possible before hurriedly ripping back the mountain of covers, diving inside, and yanking everything up again.

Covered to just below her eyeballs, she peered at him from her nest, her brows beetled in chilly outrage.

She was fucking adorable, and he couldn't help laughing.

"Stow it, Woodroe," she snapped from beneath a billion blankets.

He held up his hands, palms out. "Hey, now. I merely welcomed your return to Elsa's California retreat. Otherwise, I didn't say a word."

"Whatever." Her muffled voice was grumpy as hell, and that was even *more* adorable. "In my defense, I didn't know I should bring pajamas suitable for company. Or arctic conditions. I think they used a Zamboni on these sheets. Holy crap."

Dammit. She sounded genuinely uncomfortable.

"Do you want us to check out and go somewhere else?" He wanted to stay, wanted to share a bed with her, but his needs weren't as important as hers. Not even close. "If we drive far enough, I'm sure we can find a place with vacancies. One that's not running a cryogenics experiment on the side."

She uncovered her mouth, and he could actually see her teeth chattering. "No. I want you to stop talking, take an uncomfortably scorching shower, and serve as my personal hot water bottle under these covers. Hurry up."

They were going to cuddle for warmth?

Holy shit. All his fanfic and real-life dreams had come true. This really *was* the best day ever.

On top of that, she was being undeniably—if understandably—shrewish and demanding, which was yet *another* dream realized. After all, if she didn't trust him, she wouldn't bitch at him. It was an honor, really, and a genuine pleasure to see her entirely unconstrained by politeness.

"Big Harpy Energy," he said admiringly. "Big. Huge."

She squinted suspiciously at him. "Is that another *Pretty Woman* reference?"

It totally was. "I can neither confirm nor deny that accusation."

"Oh, for the love of . . ." She closed those beautiful eyes for a moment. "Just shut up and get hot for me. Please."

He grinned down at her provokingly.

"You know what I mean," she muttered. "Just do it, Woodroe."

He bowed. "Your wish is my etc., etc."

Rolling his suitcase behind him, he headed for the bathroom, shut the door, and prepared to provide as much body heat as humanly possible. The water in his shower: near-boiling. His imagination: fervid. His dick: in his fist, because if they were cuddling, he was going to get hard unless he'd literally just had an orgasm.

It only took a few strokes. He'd been primed for days and days, and the sight of her in a bed, glaring at him and possibly panty-free, had pushed him to his breaking point.

She'd be so soft under him, around him. Wet and needy. And if she rode him, her weight would hold him firmly in place, no matter how desperately he pleaded and bucked into—

Head thrown back, knees weak, he swallowed down his groan and slapped a hand against the shower wall to brace himself as he came.

"You okay?" he heard her call through the door. "Alex?"

Sometimes, there was such a thing as *too* innocent, really.

He cleared his throat before calling back, "Fine. Just lost my balance for a moment."

Scrubbing everywhere only took a couple of minutes, despite his post-orgasm shakiness. Still, he was nearly sweating from the water's heat by the time he rinsed off. When he emerged from the shower and grabbed a towel, the mirror fogged over and stayed that way.

His suitcase contained very few acceptable clothing options for this momentous occasion. He hadn't packed pajamas, because he didn't wear pajamas. A tee and boxer briefs would have to do, because he was *not* wearing jeans to bed. Not unless she insisted.

The clothing stuck to his damp skin, and he'd much rather be naked, but so be it. Wren's comfort was worth his discomfort.

One good toothbrushing later, he left the bathroom. From what he could tell, she hadn't changed position, and her shivering shook the mountain of covers.

"Good news," she said through all the blankets. "I don't need to visit that ice hotel in Sweden anymore. Just shine your damn flashlight over the ceiling and call it the aurora borealis, and I'm good to go. Life goal achieved."

"Seeing the Northern California Lights is truly an experience to be treasured. Congratulations." Fuck, the room was *frigid*. "Ready for company?"

She tossed back the blankets and waved him forward impatiently. That was answer enough.

Within three quick strides, he was at the bed. Getting under the covers only took a breath, and then there she was, shaking with cold, lying only an inch away.

If she wanted a personal hot water bottle, he would be one. Gladly.

When he spread his arms, she immediately scrambled into them. Gathering her close, he tucked her head beneath his chin and surrounded her with his body as best he could, and shit, she was soft and plentiful and *chilly*.

"Put your feet against my legs," he told her, then bit back a pained gasp when she obeyed. "Hands on my belly or under my arms."

Apparently she now had icebergs for extremities. Jesus.

Slowly, her hands crept from his cotton-covered back toward his abdomen, and he flipped up the edge of his tee for her. "Skin on skin, Wren. Otherwise, this won't work."

He stifled another gasp at the feel of her hands on his bare flesh. How ten points of arctic cold against his goose-bump-prickled stomach could excite him so much mere minutes after his last orgasm, he didn't know. But they did. She did.

He shifted his hips, just in case, and she snuggled closer.

"Oh, wow. You're so warm." All her snappishness had disappeared, and she now sounded . . . dreamy. "So hard."

Dammit. He was almost entirely certain he'd shifted far enough, but maybe she had some sort of preternatural erection detection ability?

She went stiff in his arms, and her face against his neck turned noticeably hot. "I mean, muscled. Strong. Not hard."

He swallowed back a million inappropriate responses, because he wouldn't scare her. Not even for the sake of a good dirty joke.

Time to change the subject.

"So . . ." God, what the fuck was he supposed to say now? "What do you think about the consent issues inherent in sex pollen stories?"

At the sound of his own words, and the absolute silence that followed them, he stifled a groan. Jesus Christ. Why couldn't he have come up with something—anything—else? Holding her might feel like inhaling sex pollen with every labored, lust-stricken breath, but he didn't need to *talk* about it.

"Sex . . . pollen." The words were puffs of warm, moist air against his skin, and he shuddered. Not from cold. "Do I want to know?"

He couldn't help but snicker. "Probably not. But I'll send you links to my favorite sex pollen fics anyway. I have a few book-marked."

"Oh." Her fingers curled against his belly. "I, uh, may not need you to send me the links, then."

When he tried to move far enough away to see her expression, she clung to him like a limpet. "Lauren Chandra Clegg, have you been looking at my bookmarked fics?"

Her entire body seemed to radiate fresh heat, and she didn't need to answer out loud.

"You *have*," he crowed. "You've read about pegging and con-sentacles and—"

As she'd done once before, she plastered her hand over his mouth, and she really should have remembered his previous re-sponse. This go-round, he licked her palm more slowly, swirling his tongue along the way. An enticement, not the trick of a naughty friend.

She didn't move her hand.

Her eyelashes fluttered against his neck, and her thighs shifted. Parted, if only an inch.

She stretched a little. Resettled herself tighter against him with a low hum. Her nipples suddenly made themselves evident against his chest.

Well, then.

He twisted his neck, scraping his beard against her fingers, butting her hand like a cat in need of petting. In a halting move-ment, she stroked his jaw. His cheek. Smoothed her thumb over his eyebrows.

Her breathing had become more rapid. His too.

No part of her felt cold anymore, and fuck knew he was on fire.

When she slowly traced his lips with her forefinger, he opened his mouth and took it inside. Sucked. Held the pad of her finger carefully between his teeth.

She—

Shit. She *moaned*.

He trembled. Then nudged his knee lightly, so lightly, against the seam of her legs. It was the lower-body equivalent of his open arms. Not a demand, but an invitation.

Then she was straddling his thigh, her fingers digging deliciously into his back, the heat of her sex scorching through her thin leggings, and the *sound* she made as she pressed against him, squirming, set him alight. He slid his hands down her back slowly, waiting for her to protest. Waiting for her to stop him.

She didn't, so he cupped her generous, unbelievably plush ass in his hands and hitched her tighter onto his leg. Harder against the muscles there, to give her pressure where she needed it. She inhaled sharply and arched her back in response, and yes, yes, he wanted her to rub against him. He wanted her to *use* him for her pleasure.

It was all delirious heat and joy, all friction and panting.

Until he angled himself in a way he hadn't intended, trying to get closer, as close as he could, and his hard cock—he was thirty-nine fucking years old, so what the fuck? Why had his normal refractory time failed him now?—pressed against her belly.

She gasped again, and her hips stilled. So did her hands.

Disentangling himself from her felt like severing a limb, but he did it anyway. He'd vowed to behave, vowed not to scare her, and like the asshole he was, he'd broken his promises.

"I'm sorry." The words were too loud, too abrupt, but he couldn't seem to control his breathing or his voice or much of anything right now. "I'm sorry, Lauren."

Her bedside lamp was still aglow, and he could clearly see her gorgeous eyes. Her beloved, fascinating face. Her expression, twisted with—

Was that *hurt*?

"Why are you sorry, Alex?" Her chin trembled, and she clenched that soft jaw tight. "Are you sorry because it's me in this bed with you, and not someone else?"

His mouth literally dropped open.

"What—" He gave his head a shake against the too-hard pillow, befuddled and disbelieving. "What the hell does *that* mean?"

Her quivering chin tipped high, and she blinked hard. "Here we are, living out your favorite fics. One bed. Cuddling for warmth. And maybe you got caught up in things and forgot exactly who was in your—"

He laughed. He laughed loudly and uncontrollably, and by the time he calmed himself, Lauren was huddled as far away from him as possible in their bed. Which wasn't far, because she wasn't a small woman, and the bed wasn't particularly large.

"I need to tell Marcus about this," he said, only to realize he'd made things worse, because her already-pained face collapsed in on itself in absolute humiliation and horror. "No, Wren, *no*. Whatever you're thinking, *no*."

Okay. He was doing this.

No more hesitance. No more weighing words and consequences. He should have known better. He wasn't made for restraint.

He was made to love. Loudly and forever.

"I need to tell Marcus, because just this week, he called me an oblivious moron for not realizing I was into you long before now. Weeks ago. Shit, months ago." When she gasped, her mouth gaping in apparent shock, he rolled his eyes, because *really*? She truly hadn't realized? "And you're wondering whether I somehow didn't realize you were the woman in my bed, you were the woman grinding against my goddamn thigh—"

He shook his head, amused and frustrated and horny as hell. "I need to tell him you're just as big an idiot as I am. Maybe bigger."

Her words were so quiet, he could barely hear them over the ceaselessly chugging air conditioner. "You're . . . into me? Are you . . . are you sure?"

The horror twisting her features had vanished, replaced by caution. Watchfulness, even as hope trembled at the corners of that tempting mouth.

Aggravation evident in every word, he laid out the evidence. "Lauren, I've kissed your forehead. I've kissed your cheek. I've hugged you for frankly absurd amounts of time. I've stroked your thigh. I begged you to go on a road trip with me and share my bed. I jerked off in the shower like ten minutes ago thinking of you on top of me, holding me down, and coming on my cock. And despite that, I accidentally stabbed your stomach with my stupid damn dick moments ago, after using your full legal name. How the fuck is my desire for you—specifically *you*—even in question?"

Her eyes were wide. Dazed. "I didn't know you . . . did that . . . in the shower. I thought you'd slipped."

"But you knew about the rest of it. Unless you're having amnesia issues. Which, incidentally, is another of my favorite fic tropes, so if you're an amnesiac or want to pretend to be one, let me know, and we can have some fun with that."

Oh, the role-playing possibilities were *endless*.

"I remember everything, but . . . I had no idea what it meant." She was still blinking at him from across the bed. "None."

Did she think he randomly stroked women's thighs just for the fuck of it?

The more he considered what she'd said, the more upset he got. "No matter what happens or doesn't happen between the two of us, sexually and romantically, I thought we were friends. Real friends. So how the fuck could you think I would use you as a generic body in my bed?"

It *hurt*. That she thought so little of him was an arrow piercing his chest, ripping through muscle and bone, punching a hole in his heart.

It was too hot under the blankets now, and he flung them away and heaved himself out of bed to stand, vibrating with pain, on the freezing fucking floor.

"Alex . . ." she said, but he couldn't look at her. "Alex, I'm— *fuck*."

Then she was right there. Kneeling on the bed in front of him, reaching for him. Her small, strong hand clamped on his neck and yanked him toward her, and she kissed him. Hard.

Her mouth was hot on his, her lips demanding, and when he opened to her, her tongue swept inside his mouth without hesitation and claimed her territory. He sucked on that bold tongue, battled it, stroked it with his, and his stomach swooped in lust and joy.

Distantly, he felt a tug against his scalp. She'd speared her fingers through his shaggy mane, which he'd kept long just for her. Just for this. Just because he'd dreamed about her fist in his hair, directing his head where she wanted it to go.

Of course, he'd also dreamed about doing the same thing to her.

Her other hand was sliding under his tee, up his back, and he was palming her ass once more, plastering her against him until her softness yielded to the contours of his body, and no, he definitely couldn't detect panties underneath those thin, thin leggings.

This was getting out of control quickly. Too quickly.

Before they went further, he had to know.

He ripped his mouth from hers, wild and panting and needy. "Does this mean you want *me*? Not just someone to keep you warm?"

His voice was hoarse. Gravelly with desire and longing.

After sliding her hand out from under his tee, she cupped his face between her small palms tenderly. So tenderly he had to close his eyes against the ache in his chest.

"This means I'm sorry." She kissed his eyelids, her lips warm and gentle. "This means my doubts had more to do with me than you, but they were still unfair to both of us."

Her lips brushed his temples softly. So, so softly.

"This means I want you. Only you." She took his bottom lip between her teeth and nipped, and he shook against her. "And *this* means I've wanted you ever since you walked toward me in LAX looking like a freaking god. That damn Henley should be *outlawed*."

She licked his mouth open and conquered him anew, and he returned the favor. With one arm bracing her shoulders and neck, her skull cradled in his hand, he surged forward, pushing her flat on the bed and crawling over her.

On his hands and knees, her body caged within his, he was supplicant and conqueror both. He dragged his open mouth over her cheek, along her jaw, down her neck. "How far do you want to take this tonight, Wren?"

When he licked a certain spot behind her ear, then blew on her damp skin, her breath hitched, so he did it again.

"I—" Her blunt fingernails bit into his back as he sucked at the shadowy skin of her neck. "Just—just kissing, I think. If that's okay? It's so cold in here, and I don't want our first time together to happen under a pile of blankets. I want to *see* you."

She didn't owe him anything. Everything she'd already offered was more of a gift than he'd ever earned.

"Whatever you want," he vowed. "However you want it. Nothing more, nothing less."

Her smile was tremulous and lovely and wide and entirely his.

He urged her beneath the covers once more, because he didn't want her cold. Not for another moment. Then she was back in his arms, her hair soft against his fingers, her mouth hot and eager on his, and he'd never read a fic this fucking good.

Not one. Not ever.

Rating: Explicit

Fandoms: Gods of the Gates – E. Wade, Gods of the Gates (TV)

Relationships: Cupid/Psyche

Additional Tags: <u>Alternate Universe – Modern</u>, <u>Sex Pollen</u>, <u>explicit consent but when it comes to sex pollen things are always at least a little hinky</u>, <u>truly endless scenes of Cupid going down on Psyche</u>, <u>Venus is awful as always but at least Psyche gets some orgasms out of it yay</u>

Stats: Words: 8249 Chapters: 3/3 Comments: 183 Kudos: 771
Bookmarks: 56

In the Air Tonight
PsycheStan

Summary:

Venus releases pollen from a special flower, one that causes insatiable lust, into Psyche's home—then sends Jupiter for a visit. The goddess hopes her son Cupid will be repulsed by the sight of his would-be lover with his grandfather and spurn Psyche.

Little does Venus know: Psyche expected something like this to happen. She planned ahead.

Notes:

Cupid may only be half a god, but I'm pretty sure that half includes his tongue.☺

The magical webbed shield created by Minerva vibrates once. Twice. Again.

Psyche barely has time to make it to the phone before the fire claims her, body and soul.

"Dido," she pants, one hand already sliding between her legs, into the wetness that has bloomed in the space of a heartbeat. "Venus. Our plan."

"Got it. I know what to do," her best friend says, then hangs up.

Dido, the most loyal and stalwart of BFFs, will find Cupid and explain to him what his mother has done, and what Psyche has already decided is acceptable. If he's willing to provide relief, he'll come.

And if he does, so will she. Around his fingers. On his tongue.

Psyche laughs weakly, hysterically, and convulses in her first orgasm, collapsing onto the floor.

In her last conscious act, she activates the full powers of Minerva's shield. No creature, god or mortal, can enter her house now. With one exception.

The next thing she knows, she's on a bed, not the floor. A pillow cradles her head. Her body is endlessly aflame, her sex aching and swollen. And she's not alone.

Cupid is there, sprawled on his stomach between her splayed thighs.

"There you are," he says, then bends his dark head and sucks her clit until the world explodes into fiery spangles around her.

22

"ANYWAY, I LOVE A GOOD SEX POLLEN STORY." ALEX GRINNED at her, totally unashamed. "They're usually filthy as fuck."

He was pacing the room to keep warm as Lauren checked under the bed and in the covers for more stray items he'd managed to misplace during the chilliest, hottest, most amazing night of her life.

They'd made out for hours, entwined and breathless, their hands roaming over arms and legs and backs and occasionally asses. He'd kept his promise, though. They'd kissed and kissed and kissed and fallen asleep cuddling, but nothing more. He hadn't even copped a feel of her breasts, although she'd allow that tonight. *Demand* that tonight.

She intended to demand a lot more too.

If he still wanted her. Which, from all signs, he appeared to.

When she straightened from one last inspection of the blankets, he was right in front of her.

"Hot as fuck," he repeated. "Much like you."

Bending low, he kissed her lingeringly, sweet and soft and slow. From corner to corner, he sipped at her mouth. Explored, as if he hadn't traversed the same territory repeatedly the night before, as if her lips were endlessly fascinating, endlessly alluring to him.

Her skin bloomed with heat under his attention, despite the cold. Her whole body sensitive and tingling, she wound her arms around his neck and melted against him.

When he lifted his head minutes later, he clapped a hand to his neck, stretched his back, and groaned. "Shit, Wren. Why are you literally the size of a fucking squirrel? Did you choose not to grow out of sheer, stubborn maliciousness? Because honestly, I wouldn't put it past you."

Instead of dignifying such naked provocation with a response, she pulled free and went to check the bathroom one last time. Along the way, she glanced out the room's window and smiled.

"It's lovely here," she said, staring at the ocean in the distance.

Within two strides, he was standing next to her, shoulder to shoulder.

He trailed his knuckles down her cheek. "It is."

She considered herself a logical person. Rational.

Still. Maybe there was something special about this room. About this small town and its worn-down, clean, unpretentious B and B with its malfunctioning air conditioner.

Not sex pollen. But . . . something.

Under other circumstances, without that overactive AC, she didn't think she'd ever have kissed him. But she'd hurt him by wondering whether he might have used her as just a warm body on a cold, lonely night, and she'd been desperate to assuage his distress. Desperate enough to show him how she felt and how much she wanted him. Desperate enough to yank him close and kiss him the way she'd been imagining for weeks.

She needed time to think, time to work through what had happened. But overnight, she'd reached a tentative conclusion: Somehow, at some point, her work in the ER had consumed her so completely that—except with Sionna—she no longer considered herself anything but a therapist and a daughter. Not a potential romantic partner, a sexual being, or even an interesting person.

No wonder she'd burned out. No wonder the thought of going back to the ER still caused a ripple of nausea in her belly. No wonder she'd doubted her appeal to Alex and interpreted all his attention, his inability to keep his hands off her, as friendly rather than romantic.

She'd do better in the future, because they both deserved it.

She didn't doubt his desire for her anymore, and she wasn't denying hers for him.

He was still standing beside her, still gazing down at her with uncharacteristic solemnity and in uncharacteristic silence, and she claimed his hand in both of hers. Raised it to her lips. Kissed his cold knuckles.

His mouth curved into a smile with no sharp edges. "What was that for?"

"Because I like you." She kept her voice matter-of-fact, since it *was* a fact. A basic truth. "Because I'm so happy we're going on this trip together. Because I want to hear what your first-favorite fanfic trope is. Please tell me it's not sex pollen."

He *beamed* at her, and she smiled back.

"I love soulmate AUs." Turning her wrist over in his grasp, he traced something along her forearm with a gentle, shiver-inducing finger. "My favorites are soul mark ones, where your soulmate's first words to you appear somewhere on your body, like a tattoo, in their handwriting."

One of his bookmarked fics had that premise, and despite all her natural skepticism, she too had found the sheer romanticism of the idea seductive. Soulmates. Inseverable bonds. True pairings, designated such by powers beyond human command.

Too bad those didn't exist in real life.

"I read your bookmarked soulmate fic recently. I liked it."
Gently tugging her hand free from his, she turned away and used
the hotel-provided notepad to write a quick thank-you to the poor
housekeeper who'd have to clean the chilly room, then placed the
note beside the generous tip Alex had already left on the nightstand. "All right, I'm ready to go now."

He grabbed both their bags. "*Finally*. Shit, you're like if a tor-
toise took downers."

"One of us scattered his belongings everywhere, and I needed
time to locate everything," she said as she opened the door. "I
won't say who, but his name starts with an *A*, ends with an *X*, and
rhymes with *Schmalex*."

He snorted and followed her out.

As the door began to shut behind them, though, he held up a
hand. "Let me take one last look before we go. I might see something you didn't."

That was . . . surprisingly cautious from a man like him, but
it couldn't hurt to check a final time. So she used her body to
prop open the door and appreciatively watched the play of muscles
along his shoulders and down his back as he glanced inside the
bathroom, ran a hand over the sheets, and fiddled with the dresser
and nightstand.

"Nothing," he finally said, rejoining her. "The Abominable
Snowman's coastal hideaway is pristine once more." When the
door clicked shut, he slung his free arm around her shoulders,
and they headed for reception. "You know, I'll bet there are absolutely *filthy* fics about the Abominable Snowman somewhere
on AO3."

She raised her brows. "Do you plan to write one?"

"After all the subarctic inspiration I got last night?" His grin positively seethed with wicked intent, and he tugged her closer. "I think we both know the answer to that question."

Even though she shook her head at him, she had to laugh. Because yes, *of course* Alex was going to write Abominable Snowman smut. And if her suspicions proved correct—

"Do you think the Abominable Snowman has ever been pegged?" he asked, his brow furrowed in thought.

Yup. There it was.

She only hoped the fandom was ready, because if not: Goodness help them.

SINCE THEY'D GOTTEN a late start and stopped earlier than anticipated yesterday, they had a long haul ahead of them for their second day of travel. Five hours of driving in total, interrupted by various stops for tourism and food.

By the time they reached their hotel in Olema that evening—Lauren had made reservations from the road, unable to resist lodgings built directly atop the San Andreas Fault—she and Alex were both tired and ready to get out of the car. Still cheerful, though, and still chatting easily.

"I take back everything I said about Hearst Castle." After removing both their bags from his trunk, Alex locked the car and followed her to the hotel's entrance. "Due to its critical lack of turrets, I'm afraid it's a zero out of ten. Would not recommend."

"This morning, you told me the grounds and castle were amazing." She raised her brows. "Was that a lie?"

"Why do you listen so closely to everything I say, and then remember it?" He frowned down at her, reaching over to rumple her hair with his free hand. "It's all very unfair."

She batted his hand away. "You're just mad because I said Hearst Castle was more impressive than your castle."

"*Turrets*, Wren," he emphasized. "They had towers, not turrets, which means I win our castle-off. Clearly."

"If that's the only criterion, I too would win a castle-off."

"Not against me," he said smugly as they entered the lovely reception area.

The lighting was pleasantly dim, the scattered couches and chairs overstuffed and upholstered in jewel tones, and the check-in desk marble. The night's stay would be pricey, but he'd insisted they go somewhere as classy as he was.

When she'd suggested a bed of hay in a stable, then, he'd laughed delightedly and kissed her at a stoplight until she'd collapsed against the passenger door, dizzy and tingling.

She wanted more kisses. More everything. As soon as possible.

That morning, on the tram going up to the castle, he'd looped his arm around her shoulders and bent low to rest his cheek on her hair. Over lunch at a café in Carmel, he'd scooted his chair so close, his thigh had pressed against hers the entire meal. When they'd stopped at Big Sur, even Alex had been stunned into silence by the sight of a roiling ocean pummeling the rugged shore, and he'd held her hand tightly as they watched in awe. At Half Moon Bay, he'd dramatically pouted at the attention she paid to the surfers and vowed to parade around in a wetsuit whenever possible, if that was what it took to gain her undivided focus. Then he'd yanked her close on a bench by the shore and claimed her mouth with ferocious intent.

By the time they crossed the Golden Gate Bridge, she was the one resting her hand on his knee and sliding it up his thigh. Not too far, but far enough to tell him what he needed to know.

She was all in. And when they finally reached their hotel room, she'd gladly show him.

The young woman behind the reception desk was friendly,

although she didn't seem to recognize Alex. Not even when he braced his hands on the countertop and leaned forward with that famously charming grin, his voice conspiratorially low. So low Lauren's belly dropped, and she had to rub her thighs together just a bit.

"I know we made reservations for a standard king room, but do you have anything with a big, jetted bathtub? Doesn't matter what it costs." He winked at the woman, who appeared slightly dazed. "We're celebrating."

"There's, uh—" The poor clerk swallowed hard. "There's the honeymoon suite. The private balcony has a large whirlpool tub and a dining nook."

He didn't hesitate. "Sold."

Oh, goodness, she'd seen that suite on the hotel's website, and the *expense*.

"Alex—" she began.

He skated his knuckles over her cheek. "Trust me, Wren."

She did. Heaven help them both.

The clerk changed their reservation, and she smiled at them as she handed over their keycards. "Third floor, all the way at the end of the hall. Please let me know if we can be of further assistance."

"We will. Thank you so much for your help." With one last dazzling smile, Alex straightened and grasped the handle of his suitcase. "Good night."

Lauren offered a polite nod and took hold of her own luggage.

As they walked to the elevator, he reached for her free hand. "How do you feel about ordering room service and eating out on the balcony?"

Unaccountably nervous, she stared at the patterned carpet underfoot. "Sounds good."

As soon as he pushed the call button, the elevator doors opened, and they stepped inside. When the doors slid closed again, he turned to face her, their fingers still intertwined.

"You know," he said conversationally, "if you were to worry—even for one moment—that I'd pressure you to do anything you didn't want, I'm just warning you now that I'd be hurt and angry, and I'd probably compose an epic poem about the wrong done to me. Or at least write a sulky limerick."

She huffed out an amused breath. "You once tried to bully me into a sushi-eating contest, if I remember correctly."

"I was concerned your diet was seaweed deficient." Somehow, he kept a straight face. "That doesn't count."

"Bullshit," she said, and he clutched his chest and gasped in faux shock at her language. "Alex, I know what you're trying to tell me. It's sweet, but it's not necessary. I want to—" The elevator doors opened on their floor, and she lowered her voice to a whisper. "I *want* to do things with you. It's just . . . been a while."

His firm grip on her hand led her out of the elevator and down the hall. "For me too, Wren. But we have all the time in the world."

Anyone who called gray eyes chilly had never seen his.

Right now, she couldn't imagine ever being cold again.

23

"SHIT, WREN," ALEX SAID THROUGH A MOUTHFUL OF THE hotel's signature gourmet pizza, and scrolled down his YouTube page. "I already have over two hundred thousand views and six thousand comments on my first clip, with more coming in all the time. Same with the other videos."

From what he could tell, the views and comments had trickled in slowly at first . . . until Carah responded to his clips on her various social media accounts and threatened to nut-punch him—"Also my main sasquatch-hunting tactic"—the next time he encountered her *geriatric ass*.

Apparently, she'd dedicated her next video to him, and it involved eating testicles. Hopefully not human, but he didn't know for sure.

"The Fans of the Gates blog called your videos 'irresistibly charming.' And I think"—Wren paused and tapped something on her phone—"yes, *Celebrity* magazine picked up the story too. They posted something an hour ago. Apparently, you're 'predictably but delightfully unfiltered, and exactly the blast of effortless cool needed in these hot summer months.'"

She made a gagging sound.

Totally rude. Utterly delightful.

He grinned at her and tickled her ribs until she giggled, the sound ringing through the cool night air. "Incomparable Harpy Energy there, Wren. But I thought you didn't vanity search?"

"Not for myself." With a wave of her short, broad hand, she flicked the notion aside, as if it were *that easy* to resist finding out what everyone thought of you. "I figured you'd want to know how various media sites were reacting, though."

The addendum remained unspoken: *And I wanted to see it before you did, in case it was bad, and I needed to talk you down from doing something dumb.*

Which . . . okay, fair.

"In the YouTube comments, there's a lot of speculation about my talented camerawoman and travel companion." A sidelong glance didn't reveal any signs of tension at that news. No hunched shoulders. No furrowed brow. "Apparently our chemistry is *magical*."

The corners of her mouth tipped upward before she took another bite of her own pizza.

A fourth slice beckoned him, and he answered the summons. "Anyway, they want to know if you're my girlf—"

His phone chimed. A FaceTime call from his mother, which he couldn't ignore.

He put down his pizza. "I'm sorry, Wren, but I need to take this. It'll be five minutes. Ten, tops."

When he got to his feet, she smiled at him, entirely unoffended. To give her a few minutes of peace and quiet while she ate, he headed for the living room, then tapped his screen to answer the call.

"Hey, Mom," he said as he slid open the balcony door. "How are—"

Then he saw her face. Specifically, the dark bruises surrounding her swollen left eye.

Absolute horror staggered him, landing like a punch to the diaphragm. "*Mom*. What—"

"I had a bike accident, Alex. Just a bike accident." She was speaking loudly and clearly and calmly, and he could barely understand a word. "I hit a patch of gravel and went down, but I'm fine. I went to the doctor, and I'm *fine*. But I wanted you to know as soon as possible, so you wouldn't . . ."

Her explanation didn't stop bile from rising up his throat, bitter and corrosive. He bent over at the waist, trying not to retch, and the phone dropped from his nerveless fingers onto the wooden deck.

His chest was a bellows, heaving as he sucked air into his straining lungs.

Then something touched his neck. A cool palm. Wren's hand cupping his nape, gently squeezing.

His mother sighed, and her voice floated through the darkness. "I should have used audio first. Dammit."

She sounded sad. Sadder than she'd been since—

He shuddered.

"Sweetheart," she called. "Sweetheart, please talk to me."

With a shaking hand, he managed to pick up his phone, then straightened. When Wren began to move away, he reached out for her, and she halted, allowing herself to be drawn against his side. She was warm and soft and safe in his embrace, her head against his heart.

He needed her there.

"No one—" Swallowing back more bile, he tried again. "No one hurt you?"

"I wiped out on gravel." His mother's tone was strained but patient. "My neighbor saw everything, so if you don't believe me, you can ask her."

He wouldn't do that. He couldn't, not without humiliating his mom.

"But, sweetheart . . ." Linda tried to smile, blinking back tears. "You need to start believing me."

Wren's hand on his back stroked up and down, up and down, and he could breathe again. He could think again.

"Okay." It was a hoarse thread of sound, and all he could manage.

"Okay." His mom's gaze flicked over to the side. "I'm fine, so why don't you call me later? Your friend is obviously worried about you, and I don't blame her."

Lauren's other hand rose from its perch on his chest, and she gave his mom a little wave. "I'm Lauren Clegg. Lovely to meet you, Ms. Woodroe."

"Ahhhhhh. Lauren. At last." Linda's smile widened, crinkling her unblackened eye. "I'm delighted to meet you. I've heard a lot about you, all of it good."

Wren's Santa Ana voice made its triumphant return. "He must save that for when I'm not around."

Linda laughed outright, and his pulse stopped echoing in his ears. "I'll let you two get on with your evening. My hammock is calling my name. Alex, are you all right?"

He cleared his throat. "If you're all right, I'm all right."

"Then we're good. Love you, sweetheart." Despite the bruising, she seemed calm and content once more. "Talk to you later tonight or tomorrow. Either is fine."

"Love you too," he told her, meaning it with every fiber of his being.

She switched her attention to his companion. "Good night, Lauren. I hope to see more of you soon."

Wren's smile and murmur of thanks were as soft as she was.

A few more pleasantries, and the conversation was over.

At least, *that* conversation. There was no avoiding further discussion with Wren, given how he'd lost his entire fucking mind at the sight of his mother's black eye.

Her arm around his waist guided him inside and to the couch, and he collapsed onto the cushions beside her. She gently removed the phone from his hand, setting it on the coffee table.

Without his conscious volition, his head fell to her shoulder, and when she began carding her fingers through his hair, he closed his eyes.

"I'm sorry." He was so fucking tired suddenly, all that fight-or-flight adrenaline abruptly gone. "I just . . ."

Her voice was quiet. "You don't have to tell me. You have a right to your privacy."

"I want to." He sighed. "It's just hard, because I—I fucked up, Wren. Big-time."

A quiet little hum, and she nestled closer.

He allowed himself a minute to get his shit together, to bask in her silent support, and then forced himself to start talking.

"My dad left when I was a baby, so Mom and I were a team from almost the beginning. She looked after me, and when I got older, I looked after her too. She . . ." God, why were the words so difficult to find? "She's an amazing woman. Smart, funny, kind. She worked so fucking hard to give me everything I needed, even though her pay at all those customer service jobs was absolute shit. She had no time for dating. Hell, she barely had time for friends."

He huffed out a tired laugh. "She says I took all her energy, which I'm certain is a complete exaggeration. Slander, really."

"Oh, don't pretend. We both know the truth." Wren lightly

tugged at his hair. "You're an orchid, Woodroe. Gorgeous but high-maintenance."

An orchid?

Yeah. He liked that. Almost as much as he liked her fingers in his hair. "Gorgeous, huh?"

She snorted. "Holy crackers, Alex. Shut up and keep talking."

"Just FYI, that's a contradiction in—"

"You know what I mean."

He did, so he continued the story, even though remembering *hurt*. "In high school, I mowed lawns for cash during the summer. One of my regulars, Jimmy, seemed like a good guy. Owned an antique store. Paid well. Always friendly. Sometimes my mom would track me down to say hi and bring me lunch before her shift, and I—"

His voice cracked, so he swallowed and tried again.

"I introduced them," he finally managed to say. "She was in a hurry and didn't want to bother, but I pushed her to meet him, because I knew I was leaving right after graduation. Heading to L.A. to be an actor. My mom and I were going to be apart for the first time, and I wanted her to have someone steady to lean on while I was gone. I didn't want her to be lonely."

"You were trying to look out for her." Her voice was gentle. So gentle.

He nodded. "They hit it off right away, but she wasn't sure. After a few months, when she said she might break up with him, I told her she was too used to being alone. That he was a decent man, and she should give him more of a chance." His breath shuddered in his lungs. "And then I left for L.A. I started working at a café and going to auditions and making friends, and I didn't check in with her as often as I should have."

"You were a teenager, in other words." Her fingers in his hair, sifting, stroking, didn't pause. "A normal teenager out on his own and trying to make a life for himself."

His spine was melting under her touch, when he should be tensing instead. Should be vibrating with self-hatred, instead of pleasure.

Still, he couldn't seem to pull away. "They kept dating, then eventually got engaged. I drove back to Florida for their wedding. I walked my mom down the aisle to that man."

"I see," Wren said quietly.

She probably did. At the ER, she'd undoubtedly heard some version of this same story countless times, and he suspected each iteration had broken her heart anew.

"I started landing more parts, better parts, and I got really busy. A lot of times, I just didn't answer her calls, and I never visited. We'd go a week without talking. Two weeks. Eventually, we hardly talked at all, and I barely noticed." Because he was a terrible son, which he'd only realized once it was much too late. "Now, when I think back to the few conversations we did have, I realize she stopped mentioning friends at some point. She stopped talking about Jimmy, except in this careful fucking voice, and even then, she only said he was fine. They were fine. When she told me he'd persuaded her to quit her job, because he could support them both, I thought that was great. A goddamn *blessing*."

Wren's hand stilled. "Because she'd worked so hard while you were growing up, and you wanted her to have time to herself."

Her defense of him was kind but ill-conceived, and he didn't bother responding.

"They were married for nine years. Nine goddamn years. They visited me twice in all that time, and I never visited them at all, and I didn't even think about it, Wren. I didn't even wonder if something was wrong." His throat was thick, and he swallowed hard. "Jimmy died of a heart attack when I was twenty-eight, and I finally came home. For his funeral."

It was a typical Florida afternoon in August, steamy and scorching, the clouds roiling overhead as the thunderstorms began to roll in. He'd looked down at his mother and finally *seen* her. Finally *noticed*, there at his stepfather's graveside.

In the tropical heat, she was wearing long sleeves. A blouse that buttoned to the neck. A thick layer of makeup on one cheek, heavy enough to call attention to itself if anyone studied her carefully. Which he hadn't, until that moment.

Years later, he'd recognize the way she moved that day. Gingerly. Slowly. The same way Marcus had moved when he'd fallen from his Friesian on set and cracked a couple of ribs.

She looked decades older than her actual age, and maybe a casual observer would think that was grief. But those weren't temporary creases on her face. Her gaunt, sunken cheeks weren't the result of a single week of mourning.

"She said she was fine, just sad, but I didn't believe her. That time, I didn't believe her, and I begged her to roll up her sleeves and unbutton the first three buttons of her blouse, and—" His breath was hitching, and his cheeks were wet, and Wren was wiping away his tears with a clean tissue, and he hadn't earned her kindness. Not at all, but he was so fucking *hungry* for it. "Then I drove her to the hospital, because that motherfucker died of a heart attack in the middle of beating the living shit out of my mother, and not for the first time."

"Oh, Alex." She stroked his neck. "I'm so sorry. For her, and for you."

When he eased away and stood to pace, she didn't try to hold on. "I don't fucking deserve your sympathy, Wren. I introduced my own goddamn mother to her abuser, convinced her to stay with him when she wanted to leave, and couldn't be bothered to notice when he isolated and beat her. For years, Lauren. I didn't notice for fucking *years*."

"But . . ." Her brow was furrowed, her expression pained and soft. For him.

What wasn't she getting here? What hadn't he explained clearly?

Ten steps up, ten steps back, as his heart thundered anew. When he passed the couch, he whirled to face her, hands spread in an appeal for her to understand. To finally, finally *get* just how unfit he was to be her lover, and how selfish he was to pursue her anyway.

"I couldn't be bothered," he repeated, his voice ragged. "I couldn't be bothered to ask how she was really doing and press her for more details, or wonder why all her friends seemed to vanish, or check that *she* wanted to quit instead of being pressured into it by her asshole husband so she'd be as isolated and dependent on him as possible."

Lauren shook her head, her mouth firm with determination. "You weren't trained to recognize signs of domestic violence, Alex. You were a normal twenty-something kid who lived across the country and had his own life and concerns, and your mother didn't tell you what was happening. Your stepfather's abuse was not your fault. Not. Your. *Fault*."

What she considered exoneration, he knew was nothing of the sort. If anything, it was further damnation.

"You're right. She didn't tell me." His eyes were blurry, and he squeezed them shut. "Maybe she thought I'd tell her to stay, the same way I did before. Or maybe she thought her self-absorbed asshole of a son just wouldn't care."

"I am entirely certain that is *not* true." She was standing now, arms extended high so she could cradle his face in her warm, tender palms, and he didn't have the strength to move away a second time. "People in abusive relationships are often too ashamed to tell anyone, and scared of what might happen if they *do* tell someone."

She met his eyes, her gaze unwavering. "If you'd known what was happening, would you have helped her?"

"How—" His voice broke anew, and he was crying again. "How can you even ask me that, Wren?"

Her thumbs stroked his wet cheeks. "I'm asking because I know the answer."

"Of course I'd have helped h-her." His chest bucked in a lone sob. "I *l-love* her."

For all the good it had done her when she'd needed him most.

Lauren was insistent. Inexorable. "Have you ever hit your mother? Kicked her? Thrown something at her? Lost control and injured her in any way, or deliberately hurt her?"

He recoiled, aghast, but she didn't let go.

"No! I would *never*—" Desperately, he shook his head. *"No."*

"Then the only person at fault here is the man who abused your mother. Not her. Not you. Him." Wren's eyes were wet too, but clear as the ocean, without a single eddy of doubt. "And if you have trouble believing that, you might want to see someone about it. A counselor."

He swallowed over a sore throat. "Not you?"

"I'm happy to listen, but I can't be your therapist. We're too close." She bit her lower lip. "No wonder you were so upset at this season's scripts. Ron and R.J. had Cupid abandon Psyche and their healthy relationship to return to his abusive family, and you—"

"Acted the whole thing out to the best of my ability, even though I knew it was wrong." His cheeks were tight with salt, his eyes sore. "Even though I knew it would hurt vulnerable viewers who might be struggling to leave violent relationships. I should have walked away from that fucking show, Wren. Walked away and not looked back."

Again, he couldn't spot a single shadow of condemnation in that extraordinary gaze. "So tell me, then. Why didn't you?"

Selfishness, his brain immediately reiterated. *Cowardice.*

But that wasn't the full story, was it?

"If I'd walked away—" He pressed his lips together. "My lawyer said it would be a clear violation of my contract, and I'd owe Ron and R.J. a shitload of money. And I was afraid I'd ruin my reputation in the industry. Which is ironic, given what happened at the convention, but . . ."

She nodded. "You didn't want to bankrupt yourself or break something you'd been building for two decades. That's understandable, Alex."

"No. That's not it. Not entirely." Within the cup of her hands, he shook his head. "I think I'd have paid that price, if I would have been the only one paying it. But without savings, without a paycheck, how could I support my mom? How could I keep funding my charity? How could I afford to pay Dina?"

"Honey . . ." She stroked his cheeks with her thumbs. "Honey, that's not self-absorbed. Not in the slightest."

"I don't . . ." Bending uncomfortably low, he rested his forehead on her soft shoulder again, and she resumed stroking his hair, and oh, fuck, the *relief*. "I don't understand how you can say that, when all those people watching—"

She didn't let him finish.

"You were in a situation with no good options, and you chose one. That's all." Her warm, moist breath puffed into his ear, and he shivered. "You said you trusted me. Is that true?"

He nodded against her neck.

"If that's true," she told him, "if you truly trust me, then you're morally and legally obligated to believe me when I say you're a good man. You have no choice. I'm sorry, I don't make the rules."

He didn't believe her, of course. But Lauren was generally right about everything, and he did trust her. Totally and without reservation. So . . . he didn't *not* believe her either.

"Come on." She tugged his arm, and he followed her back onto the couch. "Let's stretch out and rest for a minute. I think we could both use a nap."

He eyed her consideringly. "Only if I get to be the little spoon."

"Whatever," she said with a sigh.

They sprawled sideways on the generous couch, and she obligingly squeezed herself behind him. Before dozing off, he blearily noted the absolute perfection of her soft belly against his back, her round arm circling his ribs, and her strong hand clasped in his.

And then, absolutely safe at last, he let go and slept.

24

ALEX WOKE HARD AND WANTING.

His mind had been wiped clean of grief and guilt, at least for the moment, and his rested body responded to Wren's proximity the exact same way it had been doing for weeks now.

When he twisted his neck just right, he caught a glimpse of the bedside clock. The two of them had only taken an hour's nap, and he had plans for their second night together. Plans involving that spacious whirlpool tub on the balcony.

Now to find out if Wren still wanted him, even after his umpteenth emotional upheaval of their limited acquaintance.

Only—shit. As gently as possible, he slipped out of her arms and went to find his wallet. Because if he didn't have a condom there . . .

"Alex?" Her voice was sleepy. "What are you doing?"

Better to know her intentions now, he supposed. "Checking for condoms. In case that's something we might need."

She rose up on one elbow. "I don't have any. I'm sorry."

The good news: Wren apparently didn't find emotional breakdowns a turnoff. That should serve them both well in the future, because he was who he was.

The bad news: When he checked his wallet one last time, its contents hadn't altered.

"I don't have any either," he told her. "Dammit."

"We can ask the front desk for help, I suppose." Her forehead creased as she considered the situation. "Or try to find a nearby convenience store that's still open."

Both valid options, but there was at least one other possibility. A good one.

"Or we can do things that don't require a condom." He arched a brow. "Fun things. Things involving that tub out on the balcony and its various jets."

"Oh." Her eyes went big. "I haven't done . . . things . . . quite like that before."

"Do you want to?"

Her legs pressed together as she shifted, and he knew her answer even before she spoke.

"Yes." Pink-cheeked but proud, she tipped up her chin. "I do."

"Whatever you want. Nothing more, nothing less," he reminded her.

She inclined her head, solemn. "The same goes for you."

Foolish woman. As if he didn't want anything and everything she might be willing to give him.

He let out a slow breath, offering one final warning. "We'll be outside, so you'll have to stay quiet."

She erupted in sudden laughter, covering her face and making those cute little snorty sounds as he stared at her in utter confusion.

"You're worried about *me* keeping quiet?" She raised her head, still grinning. "Unless you're asleep, you're talking, Alex. Between the two of us, who do you think is more likely to get loud?"

Oh, that was a *challenge*, and he was more than happy to meet it.

"With what I plan to do?" He raked his gaze up and down her round, lush body. "You."

All lingering amusement in her expression vanished. "Is that so?"

"Yes," he said. "That's so."

Reaching for the hem of his T-shirt, he stripped it off in one swift movement, then pushed down his jeans and kicked them aside. Neighbors might be able to hear them, but no one could see them on the balcony. He had no intention of wearing his swim trunks. Or anything else, for that matter.

Her face turned rosy, but she didn't back down. She gave his body her own leisurely once-over, and his erection strained against the fabric of his boxer briefs.

She rose to her feet and stood toe to toe with him.

In the blink of an eye, her BHE tee whooshed to the floor. Underneath, she wore a thin, white cotton bra, one without apparent underwire. Given her modest breasts, she didn't need more.

He didn't need more either. She was enough. She was everything, exactly as she was.

The darker hue and pebbled tips of her nipples showed through the fabric.

"Cold?" he asked. "Uncomfortable?"

She smiled at him slowly. "Not at all."

Her leggings clung to her thighs faithfully, and she peeled them down inch by inch, either because she was congenitally fucking slow or because she was taunting him. Probably the latter.

When she stood again, he kept his eyes on hers. "You don't have to get completely naked, Wren."

"Yes, I do," she said, and then her bra was on the couch, and her cotton panties were on the floor, and she was standing there completely naked as he choked on his own tongue and began coughing.

She was the Venus of Willendorf, only with smaller, lovely breasts.

She was unabashedly round everywhere else. Her belly especially, but her arms and legs too, and her wonderful, flagrantly large ass. She was composed of curves. She was glorious.

And she was laughing at him. Loudly.

She didn't bother hiding her face, and it was even better than her usual laugh, because he got to see her joy. Her pride in his reaction.

Her flush had spread down to her breasts, and although her hands twitched when his eyes ventured there, she didn't cover herself.

"I thought—" He coughed again, attempting to recover his stolen breath. "I thought you were *shy,* you infernal woman."

A dismissive flick of her wrist. "Cautious isn't the same thing as shy."

"No." He huffed out a laugh. "Evidently not."

Her tone was matter-of-fact. "Even though I don't have a ton of sexual experience, I'm not ashamed of my body. It may not be conventionally beautiful, but it's strong. It's mine. And it's obvious you want it"—she directed her gaze at his rampant cock, still pushing futilely at the material of his boxer briefs—"so what would be the point of hiding?"

"I love your body." He couldn't put it more plainly than that. "I'm fucking *obsessed* with it."

His poor, beleaguered brain couldn't determine his favorite view. That bountiful ass, or the tempting puff of brown curls atop her sex, or the subtle curves of her breasts, or—

"In that case . . ." She held out her hand, her eyes warm and happy. "Let's see who makes the most noise."

He held up a finger. "One last thing."

Stripping off his boxer briefs without ceremony, he straightened for her perusal. Turnabout, etc., etc.

Her harsh intake of breath was pure flattery. He drew his shoulders back and preened. And she'd said she wasn't shy, so he slid a hand down his belly and gave his poor, aching cock the firm stroke it needed.

When she bit her lip, he grinned. "Now I'm ready."

He intertwined his fingers with hers, and together they ventured out onto the balcony, removed the tub's cover, and began filling it with water. The night had turned invitingly cool, and he tugged her against him while they waited, naked body to naked body at last, and ran his hands over her back and down her pliant arms.

It was like hugging the softest, warmest, most erection-inducing pillow ever. But Jesus, she was so *short*. The curls between her thighs tickled his leg, and her breasts nudged against his belly, and there was no way they'd ever have upright sex.

There were benefits to her lack of height, though, as he discovered almost immediately.

When she spoke, her breath wafted over his nipple, and he shuddered. "If I pull you down to kiss you, are you going to bitch about your neck and back?"

"Yes," he said. "Do it anyway."

He obligingly bent low, and unlike their first, desperate kiss the previous night, this one was unhurried. A kiss to court her pleasure, rather than stake a claim.

Her lips weren't especially plump, but they were so very sensitive. When he took the lower one between his and sucked lightly, she swayed against him, her thighs parting against his leg. When he gently nipped, she made a rough sound in her throat and arched her back against his hand. When he flicked his tongue against the seam of her mouth, she gasped, and he took advantage.

Her mouth was slick and hot, her own tongue a sliding tease, and he skimmed his hands down—and down farther, because holy shit, she was a goddamn shrimp-woman—to her ass. The skin there was satiny and giving, cool until his palms warmed her.

At his silent urging, the press of his hands, she was almost straddling his leg, and there—oh, there, she wasn't cool at all. The heat fucking *seared* him.

She wrenched her mouth away, breathing hard. "The tub."

Oh. He'd forgotten about that, what with his whole Wren-is-naked-and-hot-and-kissing-me-thank-fucking-Christ preoccupation.

The tub was more than halfway full, and comfortably sized for three or four people. Perfect. With a flick of his wrist, the gush of water ceased, and the night went silent. He stepped inside the tub first and held her hand as she swung one leg over the high lip, then the other. The water was the perfect temperature, warm but not scorching.

As he sank down, he eyed the placement of the jets and grinned.

If he wasn't mistaken, Wren looked at them too, then glanced away, her color high.

Once they were seated, a gentle tug persuaded her onto his lap, straddling him. And oh, fuck, her pussy slid against his cock, and they both groaned, and he couldn't fucking *breathe*.

But if she didn't come first, he'd never forgive himself.

He clamped his hands on her hips. "Just . . . just stay still for a minute. Please."

When she nodded, he slicked his hands up her sides. He wouldn't rush this, not when he'd never touched her breasts before. Never held them or kissed them or—

He stroked his knuckles along the modest swells. Her nipples furled tighter, and he swept the pad of his thumb lightly over one peak. She shivered, her eyes closed.

He nuzzled against her ear.

"Watch me," he whispered, then licked her earlobe. "Watch us."

Her throat bobbed in a hard swallow, but she did it. Her

gorgeous, dazed eyes heavy-lidded, she tipped her chin down and watched as he cupped her breasts, flicked and plucked her hard nipples until she was squirming in his lap—a violation of her agreement, which he'd complain about later, much later—and ducked his head to rub his beard against her pale curves.

"Alex," she breathed, and he took one of those flushed, swollen peaks in his mouth. Sucked until she gave a thin, high cry, pressed down firmly against his dick, and rocked.

"This is another of my favorite tropes, Wren." He nuzzled her breast. "Fuck or die. Here we are, directly atop the San Andreas Fault, and if you don't come, an earthquake will end us all."

He took her nipple carefully between his teeth, and her hips jerked.

"That's—that's nonsense," she managed to get out.

"Just doing my part to save humanity," he said against her damp skin. "You're welcome."

His tongue playing with the hard tip of her nipple, he slid a hand between her thighs and parted her curls. The soft, hot folds of her pussy quivered against his fingers, and her legs shook as he circled her entrance, circled her clit, without ever giving her what she needed to come.

The angle of his neck was painful. Impossible to hold. So he dragged his open mouth over her chest and up her neck, nipping her soft flesh, and her moan vibrated against his tongue.

"I can't wait to fuck you," he said, licking the shadowed curve beneath her jaw, then a spot beneath her ear. "But tonight, I want to make you come with my fingers and my tongue, because, Wren—" He finally stroked over her clit with a fingertip, and she whimpered into the still night. "I'm really fucking good with my tongue."

"You should be." Somehow, even as her legs tensed and her

breath hitched with every brush of his finger over her clit, she was laughing. They both were. "It certainly gets enough use."

"You have no idea," he told her.

She clenched around the two fingers he slipped inside her, and he explored until she threw her head back and whimpered again.

There. When he went down on her later, he'd remember that spot.

Back to her swollen little clit. A tight, light circle. Another. Another.

"You're so responsive." He sucked at her neck, using his teeth, and flicked her nipple with his free hand. "Christ, you're going to feel good on my dick, Wren."

She came crying out, her back arched, her thighs shaking and tight around his hips, her pussy pulsing against his stroking fingers. He slipped his thumb inside to feel it, to feel what he'd done to her, and she squeezed hard with each spasm.

She was still clenching, still coming, when she grasped his cock in one small, strong hand and stroked up and down, and his brain shorted out. He could only see white, only feel her hot breath on his nipple, the wetness of her mouth as she sucked, the tug of her fist in his hair, only fuck into her tight grip until the burgeoning need of weeks and months exploded into orgasm.

He *roared*, bucking and lost, pouring everything he had, everything he was, into the slickness of her hand and the water and her round belly.

And as soon as he could see again, as soon as he could feel anything other than her hand on his twitching dick, he slapped a palm on the jet controls, and they thundered to life. His chest heaving, his lungs burning for air, he turned Wren in his lap to face those jets and spread her legs with his own.

She squirmed at the sudden stimulation, and he held her still and tight against his wet chest, one hand on her breast, the other sliding down between her legs again.

His voice was shredded, a rough, low taunt. "I thought you were going to be quiet."

"I was quieter than you," she panted.

The jets could take care of her clit. He wanted inside.

When he sank two fingers into her pussy, then three, she spread her legs wider and moaned loudly enough to wake their neighbors, and he didn't give a fuck.

"Maybe," he said, "but I'm not done yet."

He rubbed in just the right place, and after that, the argument was won. At least, until they tumbled into bed together and she got her mouth on him.

Once he'd sucked her clit until she screamed, sweaty and trembling, she offered a draw.

He took it. And then took her again.

25

"THREE PEOPLE, WREN," ALEX REMINDED HER FOR THE umpteenth time as they squatted and sifted through handfuls of sand and sea glass. "*Three separate people* called the front desk, concerned about a woman who sounded like she was in terrible pain. No one called about a man. Not one person."

He'd surpassed smugness somewhere around Mendocino, where they'd stopped for lunch, and now approached outright gloating.

And goodness help her, he'd earned that unbearable self-satisfaction. Every bit of it.

Nonstop talking had apparently made his tongue agile over the years. Very, very agile. As he'd demonstrated once more before they'd checked out that morning.

"No one mentioned a man, true." A pretty green circle peeked from the sand, next to a cloudy blue rectangle. She transferred both into his back jeans pocket for safekeeping, then patted him on the ass for good measure. "But you keep omitting the four people who reported agitated coyotes in the area overnight. Not to mention the hotel guest who insisted a lion had escaped from a nearby zoo."

The staff member maintaining the breakfast buffet had proven very chatty that morning. So chatty Lauren's face had nearly combusted from embarrassed heat, and she'd had to pretend great interest in the bagel selection lest the innocent employee unravel the Mystery of the Wounded Woman.

"Oh, my." Alex had frowned, brow creased in faux solemnity. "Did anyone note which was louder, the woman or the agitated—"

When Lauren had elbowed his side, he'd yelped and quit taunting her. Until they checked out and got back into the car, at least. After that, the only thing that stopped his ceaseless chatter was her tongue in his mouth, and she therefore employed said tongue whenever they were stopped in traffic or parked beside a scenic vista.

At some point, she'd realized he was *training* her, as if she were a seal clapping for fish. If she wanted quiet, she had to french him.

It was utterly ridiculous and utterly Alex, and she should be indignant.

She would be, any moment now. Once the memory of his tongue sliding against hers stopped sending spears of heat between her legs.

Sea glass really shouldn't turn her on like this.

"I have no idea what you mean. I don't remember hearing anything about coyotes or lions," Alex said, making no attempt to sound sincere. He straightened and stretched, both hands pressed to the graceful arch of his spine. "Shit, I'm sore today. Is this what the kids call blowing someone's back out?"

The sky had clouded over that morning, and a blustery wind swept his hair back from his face and plastered his clothing against his hard, honed body. He smiled down at her, bearded cheeks creased with happiness, gray eyes bright, and held out his hand for more of her sea glass mementos.

Too awed by him to speak—although she would never, ever admit that—she passed over an amber, rounded square.

He was magnificent. Unbelievably beautiful.

And not long from now, he'd be hers. Above her. Inside her.

Immediately after checking out that morning, they'd hit the nearest CVS and purchased a good chunk of the prophylactics aisle. Between that pharmacy run and all their kissing-related stops, the day's drive had taken longer than planned, but they'd finally made it most of the way to their destination, the Benbow area. His ex's wedding amongst the redwoods was tomorrow, and the reception would be held at the same hotel where they were staying that night.

This leg of the trip was almost done, and her decision to shorten their time on the road now seemed foolish. More than foolish. Near-tragic.

The route that day had been spectacular. After going inland a bit, the PCH had returned to the gorgeous, rugged coast. Far below sharp cliffs, waves had pounded the rocky shoreline as Alex drove and drove some more. And on this very special stretch of beach—Glass Beach, near Fort Bragg—that ceaseless churn had turned years of dumped garbage into . . . magic. Sand scattered with a rainbow of sea glass.

She'd rarely seen anything more gorgeous.

How many other magical spots had they rushed past in their haste, all because she hadn't wanted to leave on Saturday? They could have spent three more nights in each other's arms. Three more days bickering and kissing and exploring.

Three more days having *fun*.

When was the last time she'd simply had fun?

When she got back to her feet, he entwined their fingers, his smile fading.

"You look . . ." He frowned. "I don't know. Is something wrong?"

"I was thinking about how much fun I've had with you." Getting on her tiptoes, she pressed a kiss to the scoop of bare skin at his neck, above his tee. He was warm there. Salty. "Thank you for suggesting a road trip together."

That gray gaze sharpened on her, and his hands tangled in her hair, keeping her head tipped back to see his face.

"Let's extend the trip." The words were abrupt. Intense. "After the wedding, let's just keep going. I've always wanted to drive across the country, and neither one of us is working right now. We could stretch it out over three or four months, easily."

Oh, that was tempting. Much, much too tempting.

But his financial situation wasn't hers, unfortunately. "Alex, the production isn't covering my rent anymore. I can't afford to take an indefinite amount of time off."

He opened his mouth, and she held up a hand. "If you offer me money, I will turn around and climb back in that car and ask for a separate room tonight. If I'm sleeping with you, you're not paying me."

His lower lip poked out, and it shouldn't be attractive. It wasn't.

Okay, it was, but she was resisting its pouty allure.

"You'd be worth the money." He waggled his brows. "Just saying."

She set her fists on her hips and scowled at him. "Once again, please let me remind you that this is not—I repeat, *not*—*Pretty Woman*."

"Fine." He glowered down at her, still sulking, but he didn't argue. "When do you need to start work again?"

"I'd rather not drain my savings, so . . ." Her sigh was so deep, it hurt her chest, and she rubbed a hand over her sternum. "Six weeks after we get back, maybe? And no matter which job I choose, I'll need time to prepare."

Heaving his own sigh, he reached out and folded her into his arms, hugging her close. "You're the worst, Wren. The absolute *worst*. Good thing you're so cute."

Literally no one else in her life had ever called her cute. Not one.

And now her chest was hurting even more. Dammit.

"Tell me about your work options." He was bending low again, despite his poor back, his lips against her hair. "Knowing you, I'm sure they're all miserable."

Well, he wasn't entirely wrong. But he wasn't entirely right either.

"I could join a university friend's group practice." His palm was sliding soothingly up and down her back, and she leaned her forehead against his chest. "I like her, but I'm iffy about a couple of the other therapists in the group."

At her friend's urging, Lauren had met her potential coworkers soon after leaving the ER. Only to find that two of the guys, both younger psychoanalytic therapists, were condescending as hell and shared way too much information about their clients to a near-stranger.

Later that night, she and Sionna had coined the term *therapy bros,* and it fit the men all too well.

"That said, I don't know how much contact I'd actually have with them on a daily basis." She lifted a shoulder. "My work there would be different than what I'm used to. The people I'd see would need help, obviously, but typically wouldn't arrive in the middle of a life-threatening, acute crisis. And I'd meet with clients over the course of months or years, rather than evaluating them once and sending them somewhere else."

That part of things appealed to her. The ability to help a client over a stretch of time, to see any progress made . . . it sounded fulfilling, at least in theory.

He cupped the nape of her neck, kneading the taut muscles there, and she dissolved into him. "Okay. So what are your other options?"

"There's only one other choice, really." She rubbed her cheek against his tee. "I could go back to the ER."

His body tensed, turning to stone against hers, and he straightened abruptly. "Why—"

He sputtered for a few seconds, then found the words. The furious, furious words.

"Why the *fuck* would you go back there, Wren?" His voice was loud with outrage. "That fucking place burned you out. Worse, that fucking place broke your goddamn *heart*. And don't bother denying it, because that would be a lie, and you don't lie to me."

She didn't. Even when she probably should.

It would be extremely convenient to lie to him now, for instance, and tell him how excited she'd be to return to the hospital.

For literal decades, she'd made certain no one except Sionna worried about her, not even her parents. From almost the beginning, though, Alex had refused to be fobbed off. Refused to be assuaged. Refused to accept anything but what she—in his eyes—deserved, from others and from herself.

His anger on her behalf was a comfort, but also a burden. Because of it, she now needed to defend her thought processes to him *and* herself, when she'd never had to bother before, and it was . . . uncomfortable.

"I'm mostly better now, I think." The truth, although that wasn't her main reason for considering a return. "And I feel like . . ."

How could she explain it in a way he'd accept?

Still fumbling for words, she tried again. "I feel like, if I'm physically and emotionally capable of it, I should go wherever I can do the most good. Wherever my particular skills are most urgently needed. And that would be the ER."

"Even though working there makes you unhappy." His tone was hard. Inexorable. "Even though it hurts you."

Surely she could come up with a rebuttal to that statement.

She would, any time now.

"But you'd go back anyway." He was nearly vibrating with emotion, his huge heart thudding against her cheek. "Because how you feel isn't important. Because *you're* not important."

She jerked her head back to glare up at him. "That's not true!"

It was an automatic, angry denial. And if some small part of her brain slotted his words away, saving them for future contemplation, he didn't need to know.

"I don't think I'm unimportant. I just . . . I just want to do the right thing. The same as you, Alex." Her hands fisted against his back, her short nails stinging her palms. "Please try and understand."

"Oh, I understand, Wren." His jaw was a stony jut. "Trust me."

Time for a subject change. Stat.

Luckily, Alex could rarely resist talking about himself. "You said you wanted to think through your own work options on this trip. Have you come to any conclusions?"

The duo of deep, vertical creases between his brows didn't smooth.

"I know what you're doing." He gave her neck a squeeze. "Don't think I don't realize."

She raised her own brows. "It's a genuine question."

Fortunately, genuine questions and attempts at distraction weren't mutually exclusive.

"Fine. But our conversation about your job choices isn't over. On our way back down the coast, expect some hard questions, Wren." His lips quirked. "Among other hard items you might encounter."

She waited for it.

"Specifically, my penis," he clarified.

And there it was.

Even knowing what he'd say didn't stop her from snickering.

"It must have killed you to bite back your double entendres all those months."

His usual brilliant, beaming grin returned, and her shoulders relaxed.

"That wasn't a double entendre. Once you use the actual word *penis,* I feel certain you've reached single entendre territory." His laugh was a deep rumble, shaking through her. "Anyway, yes, you have no idea how hard it was."

Before she could respond, he raised a lofty finger. "And *that,* my dear Wren, is a double entendre."

She laughed along with him, and they were in accord once more.

"I still don't know what's going to happen next as far as work." His fingertips slid slowly up and down her spine, and she sucked in a hard breath at the teasing contact. "My agent will be at the wedding, since he represents my ex too. I'm meeting with him first thing tomorrow morning, and we'll probably go over our options then. Last I heard, there were a couple of upcoming projects that hadn't fired me yet. Then again, I blocked his number a few days ago and haven't checked my emails, so . . ."

He shrugged, and she stared at him in disbelief.

"You blocked his number," she said slowly. "Your *agent's* number. At a time when your career is possibly imploding."

"I told you. I needed time to think." His teeth sank into his lower lip, and she couldn't drag her eyes away. "Even if someone would cast me, I don't know that I want to do another big-budget series. Now or ever. Not after my experience with *Gates.*"

What other options did he have? "What about movies?"

He lifted a shoulder again. "Maybe? I don't know. I love being on camera, and I'd miss the camaraderie of working with a cast and crew, but I couldn't handle a repeat of the Bruno Keene situation. And again, that's assuming anyone would even hire me."

Don't feel guilty, she ordered herself. *He told you not to feel guilty*.

She drummed her fingers against his back, thinking. "Have you considered directing or producing something yourself?"

"Nah." He shook his head. "Too much organizational responsibility. My poor brain would explode. That said, it's probably what Marcus will do. Maybe I can beg him to cast me." His grin lit the cloudy afternoon. "At least he'll know what to expect, right?"

If Marcus didn't know by now, he never would. Alex sent his BFF a million complaining, all-caps, ridiculous texts per day.

"New topic," Alex announced decisively, maneuvering them so they could both watch the gentle surf's endless rush and retreat along the beach. "I love the ocean. And I love selkie AUs, so maybe we should act out that trope sometime. What do you think, Wren? You'll be the fisherwoman, and I'll be the naked seal-man lapping at your personal seashore?"

She had to laugh, even as a rush of lust weakened her knees.

No one else was within sight, so she employed her one sure means of shutting Alex up: her tongue in his mouth, her fingers fisted in the hair at his nape.

When she broke the kiss, they were both panting. And when he pinned her with his frank, hot stare, she deliberately licked her lips, leaving them obscenely wet.

"You're the *worst*," he told her again, rough and low, and she didn't argue.

She just laughed again.

26

"IF YOU'RE NOT INTO THE SELKIE IDEA, WE CAN PRETEND I'm a werewolf instead." Alex smirked at Lauren from across the table. "Clearly, I'm quite talented at making animal noises."

When properly inspired, anyway. Or, rather, *im*properly inspired.

If Alex hadn't already agreed to attend Stacia's wedding, he wouldn't have let Lauren out of that bed in Olema for days, because holy *fuck*, she was a goddamn *goddess*. An improbably short Venus, ripe and round and responsive, and luckily, much less prone to slapping him than his on-screen mother.

Huh. That was an idea.

He dug his phone from an inner pocket in his suit jacket and tapped out an addition to his ever-growing FIC TROPES TO MAKE DIRTY AF WITH WREN list. *Ancient god falls in love with human. Preferably a sex god of some sort.*

"On the contrary." As he tucked away his phone, she pointed at him with her fork from across the table. "People weren't certain whether you were a coyote or a lion, so I'd argue your skills are sorely lacking."

A small, self-satisfied smile curving her wide mouth, she finished the last bite of her blueberry mousse cake.

They'd driven through the forests that afternoon to reach the luxury resort, which nestled amongst the redwoods and beside a lovely river, and had arrived in plenty of time for dinner at the elegant on-site restaurant.

The lighting there was dim and romantic, the tablecloths pristine, the seating generously sized and plushly upholstered in velvet. The forest-green-and-navy-blue color scheme highlighted her extraordinary eyes, and he couldn't stop looking at her.

He leaned forward, elbows on the table, and enjoyed the way candlelight gilded the soft curve of her jaw. "You didn't complain about my skills last night."

Her cheeks went rosy, and she glanced around the room.

As far as he could tell, there were no cameras pointed in their direction, and he didn't recognize any of the other diners. Even if a dozen cell phones had been trained on them, though, wielded by a platoon of producers, he wouldn't have cared.

Let a hundred people see how much he wanted and adored her. Let a million.

"*Alex.*" Despite that familiar chiding tone, she tangled their feet together beneath the table. "So help me, you have the biggest mouth of anyone I've ever met."

He opened that big mouth.

She held up a hand. "And before you say it, I will: It's also the most skillful mouth I've ever encountered. By far."

Her voice was husky and hot, and her bare foot—when had she slipped off her wedges?—stroked under the hem of his pants, and he nearly passed out from the surge of blood evacuating his brain to parts farther south.

He sucked in a breath of too-thin air. "Expect another encounter tonight. Soon."

He nudged his own feet into the space between hers, hooking her ankles with his. Then he widened those ankles slowly. So slowly. And although he couldn't watch her knees part and her thighs spread through the damn tablecloth, he could trace the flush moving down her neck and over the pale expanse of flesh exposed by the low, round neckline of the swing dress. He could see her lips part, and her tongue dart out to wet that wide mouth.

Which was, to be fair, also quite talented. He planned to tell her so. In detail. In private.

He really should have insisted on sitting right next to her, instead of across the table. That thick, opaque tablecloth could have been a boon, rather than a hindrance. A barrier between prying eyes and where exactly his hand had gone.

"Alex . . ." The word was a thread of sound, cautious and brave. "For our first time, I just want it to be us. You and me, without role-playing. But . . . I read some of your bookmarked fics, and maybe, for our second or third time, you could, uh . . ."

"I could what?"

A more patient man would have waited instead of prompting her, but a more patient man would have been alone in his L.A. mini-castle, waiting for Wren to contact him, rather than on a road trip and sharing a bed with her, so fuck patience, really.

Her mouth worked, and then she made herself say it. "Maybe . . . you could be a god? Or a demigod, like Cupid? And I'd be your helpless mortal? Until I turned the tables and took control?"

His eyebrows flew upward as his brain short-circuited once more.

As soon as he could string two synapses together, he raised his hand, gesturing to the nearest server for their check, because they were clearly done with dinner and onto the next part of their evening together, and thank fucking Christ for that.

As she watched his reaction, her caution turned to smugness and a wide, wicked grin.

It looked damn good on her.

"Wren," he said, and he meant it with every atom in his reckless, needy heart, "you may be the worst, but you're also the absolute *best*."

LAUREN WASN'T A virgin, and as she'd told him the previous night, she wasn't particularly shy. Just cautious.

But this meant something to her. He meant something to her.

To be honest, he meant *everything* to her, and she didn't want to disappoint him. Even though she knew—she *knew*—if she spoke that concern aloud, he would look at her in absolute befuddlement, because he seemed to think she was . . .

Well, the worst, obviously. But perfect too.

Maybe that seemed like a contradiction, but it wasn't. Alex liked friction. He adored arguing. Breaking through barriers amused him. So if she was a wall, as he'd once accused, he enjoyed bouncing against her and testing her strength.

And he'd definitely loved toppling her. His coyote sounds were proof enough of that.

The bathroom door opened, and he padded out on long, bare feet.

His suit jacket had disappeared at some point. He now wore only dark, slim-fitting pants and a crisp white button-down. His sleeves had been rolled up to his elbows, exposing those thick, strong forearms, and a vee of golden flesh peeked from his throat, where he'd undone two buttons.

He tossed a box of condoms onto the nightstand and stalked toward the bed.

That graceful, determined prowl was for her, to her. The high color glazing his perfect cheekbones and the incinerating heat in his gaze were because of her.

So was the erection pushing insistently against the front of those obscenely flattering pants, and the sight of it might as well have been a finger on her clit.

Her breath hitched, and then he was there. Directly in front of her.

"Need your mouth, Wren," he rasped. "Need you."

Bending low, he cupped her face and wound his fingers in her hair and yanked her mouth to his in open, unapologetic demand, and that naked want seduced her more thoroughly than restraint ever could.

His tongue didn't tease this time. He forged inside her mouth and took possession.

She was moving somehow, they were moving, and she was too dizzy to understand how it happened, but he was sitting on the mattress now while she stood between his legs. The bed wasn't overly high, and their faces were almost the same height. But his arms were much longer than hers, so he could easily reach the hem of her dress.

Yes. No more clothing between them.

She tore her mouth free. "You can take it—"

"I will," he told her.

His mouth open and hot against her throat, he didn't strip off her dress. Instead, he jerked down her panties and unerringly stroked her clit. Again. Again.

"Already so wet for me." He sucked along her collarbone. "Can you take two fingers, Wren? Can I fuck you with them?"

Her legs shook, and she clutched his hard shoulders, the muscles moving beneath her hands as he circled her slit, spreading her slickness all over her pussy.

Before she'd even finished saying *yes, please,* his fingers were inside her, rubbing and twisting, his knuckles hitting somewhere she—

Oh, *God*.

His thumb pressed her clit hard, and she whimpered and tee-tered. He braced her with an unyielding arm along her back, lick-ing a spot beneath her jaw that made her gasp.

She was beyond words, but Alex had enough for them both, murmurs as hot as the July sun, rough as boulders breaking waves on the shore.

"I wanted to do this at dinner." His thumb flicked her clit, circled it, pressed again. "I wanted to put my hand up your skirt and finger-fuck you beneath that tablecloth and make you scream and come in full view of everyone in that goddamn room, helpless to stop yourself."

She knew he'd never do anything she didn't want, but—

Her body bucked at the image he'd painted, and she pushed frantically against his hand, spearing herself with those agile, twisting fingers, shoving his thumb harder against her clit, need-ing just a little bit—

His hand slipped out from under her skirt, and she was empty and shaking in near-orgasm, too weak to do anything but fall on the bed when he rose to his feet and pushed her onto the mattress.

"*No*," she whined, and wasn't even ashamed. "I was so *close*."

"I know." He didn't sound apologetic. "Farther up the bed."

It was an order, and she automatically obeyed, hitching herself higher as he tugged her panties down and threw them across the room.

In one fluid motion, he flipped her skirt up to her waist. His hot, hard palms pushed her knees high and spread her thighs wide, and he dove between them.

He was fucking her with his fingers again, rubbing insis-tently against what must be her G-spot, because *holy shit*, but she couldn't even focus on that, because his tongue. His *tongue*.

She fisted his hair. Clawed at his shoulders. Spread her legs as far as they'd go.

Last night, he'd learned what she liked, and he used all of that knowledge to break her. His tongue swirled around and over her clit, and then he sucked *and* swirled, even as his fingers rotated and rubbed her mercilessly, and—

"Alex, I'm—" Her head tossed frantically. *"Alex."*

She came with a loud cry, arching up and grinding against his face, against his tongue, against his fingers, taking what she needed from him. Her body disintegrated, shook, the spasms so hard they almost hurt.

"Good," he said, kissing her inner thigh. "One more, and then you're coming on my dick."

That time, he slung her thighs over his shoulders and fucked her with his tongue before he returned his full attention to her clit, her legs jerking with every flick, every suck.

It took longer than the first orgasm, but when she came, she was moaning and tugging his hair, pressing his face into her spasming pussy.

Once she'd collapsed onto the mattress, he wiped his mouth and beard with the back of his hand and knelt between her limp, spread legs, his stare hot with lust and self-satisfaction.

Holy crap. He was still fully dressed.

For that matter, if she flipped her skirt back down, so was she. But doing so would take energy she didn't currently possess, and since he'd just had that entire handsome face buried in her pussy, covering herself seemed somewhat pointless.

He stroked a possessive palm up one thigh. "Still up for more?"

She was sweaty and spent, but she wanted his cock inside her. The one straining at the placket of those fancy pants, the one she'd had stretching her mouth last night.

It was as hard and hot and perfect as he was.

Earlier, she'd imagined him above her for their first time. But that was before he'd taken her apart twice in the space of half an hour, and she intended to return the favor.

"I want on top." She lifted herself up on one shaky elbow. "If that's fine with you."

He grinned wickedly, giving himself a firm stroke through his pants. "If you want to ride my cock, rest assured, Wren: You never have to ask."

His smugness would cease once he was inside her. That was a vow.

"Take off your clothes, then." Her fine motor skills weren't the best right now, so she merely nodded in the direction of the nightstand. "And put on one of those condoms."

He undressed slowly, tauntingly, one button at a time, his heavy-lidded gaze on her body.

Since she'd already come twice, she'd need some help getting there again, and he appeared entirely too calm. Raising her left knee and sliding her right leg to the side, she reached over the mound of her belly and stroked herself with two fingers.

She knew her body, what rhythm and pressure worked for her. Within a minute, she was panting a little, rocking against her own fingers.

In response, he wrenched his shirt over his head before it was fully unbuttoned, his chest heaving, and smacked himself with the end of his belt when he whipped it out of the loops too fast.

"Fuck," he groaned, rubbing the reddening spot on his shoulder, but he didn't look away from her fingers between her legs, and he didn't stop unfastening his pants with his other hand. "That was your fault, Wren. You and those filthy, filthy, amazing fingers on your clit."

She shrugged, pitiless. "That's what you get for being a tease."

He tugged down his pants and boxer briefs in one movement, and she stopped touching herself to watch him kick away the garments.

She'd seen him naked yesterday, but she still couldn't get over it. Those gleaming swaths of golden skin. That lean frame punctuated by his broad, muscled shoulders, and round, taut ass. That thick cock, ruddy and twitching against his flat belly as he smoothed a condom over it.

With one agile leap, he was on the bed and crawling toward her. Then he pressed her into the mattress, his body heavy and hot atop hers, his tongue slick and sliding against her own.

He didn't taste like mint anymore. He tasted like her.

His palms slid along her hips, over her belly, until he was cupping her breasts, pinching her nipples lightly. He bent his head and took one in his mouth, flicking his tongue until she was gasping and aching again. His roaming hands cupped her ass and squeezed, and she squirmed against him.

Enough foreplay. She wanted him inside her.

At the slightest pressure of her hand, he rolled off her and sprawled on his back. She straddled his hips, and he held his cock ready.

He was too thick to simply slide down in one movement, so she sank down an inch at a time, his dick stretching her wide.

His fingers were hard on her hips, and he pressed his head into the pillow, flushed, his jaw jutting with strain. But he didn't thrust upward, and he didn't try to control her pace. He panted instead, rasping out *fuck, holy fuck, Wren, fuck,* while she took him.

Then he was seated fully inside her, so deep she had to rock her hips a little, just to know how it would feel, and—oh. Oh, yes.

He purred out one of those sinuous *ahhhhhhhh*s and reached

for her breasts, cupping them, plucking her nipples, flicking them until the sensation bolted straight to her clit.

Maybe he'd prefer if she rose and fell on him, but that gentle rock of her hips, that little surge back and forth, felt so good. She did it again and again, her hands braced on his shoulders, until her eyes closed at the way he pressed and slid inside and against her.

"Shit, Wren." He pinched her nipple harder, and she jerked against him. "Your pussy is so hot, and the way you're squeezing my dick—"

When she involuntarily clenched around him, he gasped and clamped his hands on her waist, pressing down and grinding her against him.

With the added pressure, he sank even deeper inside her, and she moaned loudly.

His voice was shredded when he spoke again. "Can I fuck you from below?"

She wasn't a small woman, so that seemed optimistic. It also seemed like something she desperately wanted to try.

Bending low, she took his nipple in her mouth and closed her teeth around it with the careful pressure he preferred, and a raw sound wrenched from his throat and vibrated through his chest. Then she lifted her head and smiled down at him. He was flushed and sweaty now too, his pupils blown, his eyes only for her and on her.

"Please," she said, knowing how much he loved that, and how much he was going to love what she'd say next. "Please fuck me."

He exploded into movement beneath her, big hands gripping her hips with bruising force, feet braced on the mattress as he bucked into her. Even with all his strength, he couldn't move her much, but it was . . . astounding.

So much friction. So much pleasure.

She moaned again, long and low, unable to look away from his commanding stare.

"Bouncing you . . . on my . . . dick, Wren." He was grinning, his chest a bellows as he gasped for air and fucked her. "Want to . . . bet whether—"

When she tweaked his nipples, his mouth dropped open, and he licked his lips.

She could barely form words, but she managed to come up with two. "Go on."

His hips stilled beneath her, and she cried out an incoherent protest.

"Want—" He licked his lips again, trying to catch his breath. "Want to bet whether I can make you come this way sometime? Hands-free?"

That was a sucker bet. She'd been grinding her clit against him with every rock of her hips, and she was already on the verge again. Hands-free.

Which he evidently knew, because he looked smug once more, and screw that.

She deliberately squeezed his dick inside her, as hard as she could, and he made that deep, raw sound again and held her down as he shoved his hips upward.

Her legs spread even wider, without her permission.

"Won't be long, Wren." His jaw worked, the veins in his neck bulging. "Need my fingers?"

That might mean him not—oh, why not say it?—bouncing her on his dick anymore, so no. She wanted to feel that power between her thighs, now and forever.

"Mine instead," she breathed, and slid her hand between his sweaty body and hers.

When she accidentally brushed his pumping cock, he cried out and gritted his teeth. "*Wren*. I can't—"

She rubbed hard, and he fucked her relentlessly, and then she was coming, clenching around him and ecstatic and crying out as he slammed her down on his dick one last time and went rigid. He shook beneath her, a roar ripped from his throat and echoing in the room.

Then they were both limp and panting, and she slid off to the side, gasping a little as he left her body. Once he'd taken care of the condom, his fingers laced through hers immediately. Other than that, though, neither of them moved for a long, long time.

Finally, he cleared his throat, and she turned her head in his direction.

"Let's do that a million more times," he told her. "Like, right now."

Bracing herself on an elbow, she glanced down at his penis, softening against his thigh.

"Fair point." He snickered. "The spirit is eager, but the flesh has a refractory period."

"Mine doesn't." It had to be said.

"Show-off," he complained, but he was grinning as he levered himself up enough to kiss her again, his extremely talented hand sliding slowly up her thigh. "Such a demanding harpy."

From that gleam in his eye, she knew what was happening next, and a million times didn't sound ridiculous anymore.

It sounded like just enough.

27

WHEN HIS CELL'S ALARM CHIMED FOR THE THIRD TIME, Alex groaned, reluctantly lifted his arm from around Wren's round, warm belly, and rolled over to tap the screen. The hush of the dim bedroom returned, and he pushed himself up to check whether she'd awakened too.

She was still curled on her side, facing away from him, her breathing steady and slow. Carefully, he smoothed some of her soft, fine hair away from her face, and nope. Not a flicker of consciousness. Her eyes were closed, her face relaxed, her body still.

He'd worn her out. Wren, who normally woke at the first alarm and tolerated his snooze-function habit with exasperated bafflement.

He felt like a goddamn king. No, a *god*.

This occasion called for a T-shirt.

I FUCKED THE WOMAN I LOVE INTO EXTENDED UNCONSCIOUS-NESS, AND ALL I GOT WAS THIS LOUSY T-SHIRT AND THREE OUT-STANDING ORGASMS.

Or A BOX OF CONDOMS: $9.99. WEARING WREN OUT WITH MY DICK: PRICELESS.

He'd arrange that ASAP, as soon as they were back home. In the meantime, he could and would gloat verbally. But not right now, because she needed her sleep, and he had an appointment to keep. Unfortunately.

He got dressed in silence and scrawled a quick note, leaving it on the nightstand. Unable to resist, he pressed a light kiss to her forehead before closing the door so carefully, it barely made a click.

Zach's text last night—fresh from being unblocked—had specified a secluded spot outdoors, one on the other side of the expansive hotel grounds from the wedding ceremony later that day. Nestled between a garden and the surrounding redwoods, the seating area should be far enough away from everyone and everything else to discourage eavesdroppers.

When Alex arrived, Zach was already there, sunglasses on and blond hair slicked back, tapping away at his phone.

At his client's approach, he held up a finger. "One minute."

No breakfast meant no medication, so Alex paced the little clearing while he waited. Probably he should have woken up even earlier to eat, but it wouldn't take his agent long to say *no one wants to work with you, have a nice life, or don't for that matter, byeeeeee.*

With one last swipe of his finger, Zach finished his task, then set his phone on the little wooden table between the two Adirondack chairs and gestured for Alex to sit.

Alex shook his head. "No meds yet. I need to move."

Zach rolled his eyes, and—that. *That* was why Alex would have severed ties long ago, if he hadn't felt guilty and responsible for his onetime friend and longtime business partner.

If Zach had rolled his eyes at Lauren, he'd have been out on his ass in a heartbeat. So why had Alex let his agent disrespect him for so long? Why so much guilt, when Zach had made plenty of money through their partnership and built a very healthy, very successful client roster?

"I'm delighted that you're willing to take my calls now." The sourness in Zach's voice puckered his mouth. "But since the only unexpected news came in overnight, so be it. Before then, it was only more people withdrawing your name for consideration in various roles."

Unexpected news?

Alex halted in front of Zach, idly rocking back and forth on his heels. "What's up?"

Zach took off his sunglasses and laid them on the table too. "To keep up with its streaming-service competitors, StreamUs is rapidly expanding its original programming, both scripted and reality based. They're willing to spend big to acquire unique talent and build buzz. Right now, between your Con of the Gates debacle and recent videos, very few people in Hollywood have as much buzz as you. For good or ill."

"They want—" Alex frowned, utterly taken aback. "They want to cast me in something?"

Well, he was certainly available. His willingness, however, depended on the project.

"In case you haven't noticed, your travel videos have gone viral, Alex. As of this moment"—Zach checked his phone—"they have over twenty million views each, and StreamUs paid attention. They want to build a reality travel show around you. Film your adventures on the road."

Twenty *million*? Holy shit.

Zach's lips curved into a small, pleased smile, the first Alex had seen from him in months. "The hook is that it's uncensored and unpredictable. Your raw reactions. No bleeping, no telling you to tone yourself down. It'll be targeted toward adults. Your inability to stop running your mouth or control what comes out of it will actually be an asset for once."

Fuck, that actually sounded—fun?

"I hope you're interested, because I don't think other offers are coming." Zach leaned forward, all the anger that had accompanied their recent interactions abruptly gone. "If you want a career in Hollywood, this is your way back in. The only way."

Work. Work he'd actually enjoy. Work that would allow him to continue supporting his mother, his charity, and Dina, and maybe even offer a comfortable life to—

His belly dropped, and he sat with a thump on the remaining Adirondack chair.

If he was out on the road all the time, where would Wren be?

His agent was still laying out the details. "They want you to have a partner, like in your videos. They're looking for banter. A bit of flirty tension. That sort of thing."

Oh, thank Christ.

"Then we're set. Lauren can be my partner." Alex grinned at his agent, renewed excitement kindling in his veins. "They can have the exact chemistry they loved from the videos, and I can have her with me. Win-win."

She wouldn't even need to pick between her two shitty job options. No ER, no therapy bros. Win-win-*win*.

Zach's mouth opened, then closed.

When he spoke again, each word emerged slowly, tentatively, as if he were sounding it out in his head first before saying it aloud. Alex had no idea what that process must feel like, but from Zach's furrowed brow and pinched expression, it wasn't enjoyable.

"I . . . don't think they'll agree to Ms. Clegg," he said.

"Is that so?" Alex folded his arms across his chest. "Have you asked them?"

"As a matter of fact, yes." His agent sighed. "Alex, I know you.

I've known you for roughly two decades now. I realize you care about her, but—"

"It's Lauren or no one."

His pinwheeling thoughts wouldn't be corralled, couldn't be, but that much he knew.

Zach's jaw worked. "I'll ask again, if you want me to, but . . ."

"What?" He leaped to his feet and resumed pacing.

"When I mentioned the possibility earlier, they . . ." Zach traced the grain of the wood on the chair arm with his forefinger. "There were concerns about her . . . audience appeal."

Alex would never understand.

After what Wren had shared of her past, after their encounter with his asshole fan, after what her own cousin had written, he knew many people—maybe even most people—considered her compelling, asymmetrical features and her charmingly round, short body ugly. He also knew the meanest among those people would use that as an excuse to dismiss her as unimportant or abuse her in some way.

He knew it. He still didn't get it.

Symmetry was boring as shit, and they lived in fucking *L.A.* Tall women with slim bodies weren't precisely an endangered species.

Wren was not only the cutest, hottest goddamn bird-woman on the face of the earth, but also unique and funny and smart and charming and kind and the perfect cohost of a travel show, and he'd fucking fight anyone who tried to argue otherwise.

"I suggested that perhaps she could stay behind the camera, as she's been doing up until now." Upon seeing Alex's expression, Zach rushed to add, "I got the sense she was uncomfortable being filmed, since we've only seen her arm."

Okay, fair. Alex's fists unclenched at his sides, and he continued pacing.

"But they want an on-camera companion, and they won't accept her in that role. And if you insist, I suspect they'll withdraw the offer." Zach scrubbed his hands over his face. "Help me out here, Alex. Tell me how we can make this offer work for both you and StreamUs."

There had to be a solution, but his head was all over the goddamn place.

Dammit, he needed to be able to concentrate for such a crucial discussion, which meant taking his meds, which meant breakfast. So much for getting back to the room quickly.

"Lauren and I are a package deal." That was the one thing he knew for certain. "So let's order some food, and I'll take my medicine. Then we can talk through negotiation strategies. If we figure out the right approach, we can convince them to bend on this. I know it."

"That makes one of us," Zach muttered, but he stood and slipped his phone in his pocket. "Okay. Let's take the morning and try to come up with something."

If Alex had his way, by the time the wedding ceremony began, Zach would be ready to make their case to StreamUs. And if all went well, Wren would never need to know her appearance had been a topic of discussion.

She'd said that kind of scorn didn't hurt her, but it had to, at least a little. He also didn't want to give her a bad impression of her future employer, because he intended to make this deal work. For her. For them.

Even if he had to take on an entire fucking streaming service and his own agent to do it.

LAUREN DIDN'T WAKE up worried.

Not with the memory of a long night's intimacy, Alex's unmistakable ardor and affection, so fresh. Not after he'd suggested a trip down the Florida coast someday, including a stop for her to meet his mother in person. Not given the way he'd slept cuddled around her.

And especially not when he'd left her a note on the nightstand. *Meeting with agent. I'll be back soon, so you might as well stay in bed, Wren.*

He'd signed it with a heart and a bold capital *A*.

No, she wasn't worried.

Only . . . he didn't come back soon. He didn't even come back that morning. After she finally left their bed and showered, she sent a worried text. To his credit, he responded right away with an apology, but not much of an explanation.

Things taking longer than expected was all he wrote. I'm sorry.

By the time he returned, the wedding was happening in half an hour, and she was pulling her black lace dress over her head. His eyes cloudy and distant, he dropped a kiss on her mouth, apologized again, said her dress was pretty, and hustled to the bathroom for his own shower.

They half jogged to the ceremony—held in a lovely riverside clearing, with the redwoods soaring overhead and an aisle lined with flowers—and made it just in time, with no opportunity to do anything but get themselves settled in their last-row seats before the music began.

He put his arm around her shoulders and played with the ends of her hair, but his eyes were on the ceremony, his jaw was tight with tension, and his attention was . . .

She didn't know. She honestly didn't.

What in the world had his agent said to him?

When the wedding ended and all the guests began heading for the expansive hotel ballroom, the site of the reception, he still didn't offer much information.

"We have a possible offer, but there are things to negotiate." He was holding her hand and walking slowly for her sake, but he didn't look at her. "I hope to hear more soon."

She would have asked for details, but the other wedding guests had finally noticed his presence, and a steady stream of fans and friends and Hollywood power brokers descended on him. Some offering seemingly sincere good wishes, others obviously looking for gossip.

He greeted them with a charming smile and kept her by his side in the ballroom, his thumb sweeping over her knuckles. But after all their time together, she recognized signs of his distraction.

His usual knife-edged humor had blunted, and he didn't seem to notice the incredulous looks she received, or the way a handful of his admirers simply ignored her, even after he introduced her to them.

Normally, he'd make them pay for that. Which would cause a scene, so this was good.

Wasn't it?

Another hour of schmoozing and occasional slights she swallowed in silence, and then the happy couple arrived, and everyone found their seats at the lavishly decorated tables. That was when the gorgeous bride—Stacia, apparently an award-winning actor on a sitcom Lauren had never seen—appeared nearby and tugged at Alex's arm. He twisted toward her, startled.

"There's room at the table next to mine for my favorite ex." She offered a cheerful but unapologetic smile to the rest of the table. "Come up front, Alex."

His face creased in a grin, he stood to gather her into an enthusiastic hug. "Congratulations, Stace. I couldn't be happier for you."

She hugged him back fiercely, then raised her brows in faux

hauteur. "So are you going to rescue me from boring small talk or not?"

"Only if there's a spot for Lauren too." Alex slid a hand down Lauren's lace-covered upper arm. "If not, I'll keep enjoying the good company at this table."

Stacia's smile didn't falter. "Lovely to meet you, Lauren. Of course there's room for you both."

No. No, that wasn't happening. Not when that other table, given its prime position, would probably be full of Hollywood's most beautiful and powerful people. If someone insulted her, Alex might emerge from his abstraction and ignite, and then they'd be positioned next to the head table, where everyone of importance could see and hear.

Whatever possible offer he'd received might be withdrawn.

It wasn't happening again. Not if she could help it.

"You go on without me," she told Alex, keeping her face placid. "My head is hurting a bit, and this area of the room is quieter."

Probably. She had no idea, but it sounded plausible.

His brows slammed together, and he gently brushed his fingertips over her temple. "Wren—"

She edged away. "Go ahead. I could use some alone time for my headache."

Poor Alex. He wasn't happy about leaving her. But he didn't want to disrupt a wedding by arguing in front of the bride, so he was stuck. Outmaneuvered, for once.

"Take some medicine." He allowed himself to be guided across the room, but he was still staring at her over his shoulder. "I'll be back to check on you, Lauren."

She imagined he would.

Dinner arrived, and she quietly observed everyone in that old, familiar way as she ate. From a neutral distance. No longer part of the proceedings.

Once Alex had settled across the room, a few whispers from nearby tables reached her ears. *I don't understand how they're connected* and *no way they're actually dating* and *what do you think happened to her face?*

When she was alone with Alex, she fit. They fit together. But his world wasn't hers, and that obvious disconnection—in looks, in wealth, in personality—was always going to draw attention and elicit commentary. As a lifetime of experience had taught her, such commentary would often prove unflattering. And that—

That was going to cause problems for Alex. *She* was going to cause problems for Alex.

Maybe not tonight, given his distraction, but soon. Often. Inevitably.

"Excuse me." A blond man with slicked-back hair bent low to speak to her, his voice quiet enough not to carry. "Lauren Clegg, correct?"

"Yes." Folding her napkin neatly, she laid it next to her plate. "How may I help you?"

He offered his hand, and she shook it. "Nice to meet you, Lauren. I'm Zach Derning, Alex's agent. I was hoping we could talk somewhere privately for a few minutes."

What on earth could he possibly need to say to her that would require privacy?

Nothing. Absolutely nothing.

"You work for Alex," she said. "I'm happy to speak with you, but not without him present."

"I'm concerned about him. I thought you'd want to know why." Zach tilted his head toward his client's table. "It's a matter of some urgency, and I don't think he'll share the problem with you until it's too late."

Alex's abstraction. The tension he'd carried in his creased brow all afternoon. His uncharacteristic secrecy.

Given Zach's appearance at her table, the situation might either involve her or require her assistance. And maybe she should go get Alex before speaking with his agent, but she didn't want to interrupt the wedding party's dinner, and it couldn't hurt to simply listen. Then she'd report back to Alex later, in their hotel room.

There. Decision made.

With a nod toward her oblivious tablemates, she gathered her purse and followed Zach through the ballroom's side exit, down a long hallway, and toward an elegant seating area in the hotel lobby, positioned discreetly behind some flourishing plants.

Once they were seated, Zach didn't waste any time.

"Overnight, Alex received an offer from StreamUs for a travel reality show. Good money. No restrictions on what he can say or where he goes." His blue eyes pinned her in place. "Did he tell you?"

She shook her head, caught between exultation—because holy crap, that job offer sounded custom-made for Alex—and confusion.

Why was Zach telling her this? And why hadn't Alex?

Zach leaned in closer, his voice barely above a whisper. "They want him to have a companion. A cohost. Someone to bounce off of and banter with."

She closed her eyes for a moment.

Oh. Oh, no. He wouldn't. He couldn't possibly have—

"He said he wanted you or no one," Zach told her. "And the offer requires a cohost with a preexisting fanbase, so StreamUs won't accept you in that role. If he digs in his heels, they'll rescind the offer, and he doesn't have any others. I don't know if he'll *get* any others, to be frank. So I decided to talk with you privately and ask whether this is something you truly want too, or whether it's Alex making assumptions and getting tunnel vision."

She figured Zach's explanation was eliding certain other truths—notably, how the service had probably reacted to her appearance—but it sounded honest enough.

It sounded exactly like Alex. The best of him, and also the worst.

Because yes, of course she was touched that he wanted her by his side. Of course his consistent advocacy for her, his belief in her, warmed her to her bones.

But what the hell was he thinking?

He might deny it, but he certainly wasn't thinking about *her*.

She wasn't an actor. She wasn't a reality television star.

More important, she didn't *want* to be either. She wanted to be a damn *therapist*. Where and how, she hadn't yet determined, but a brush with fame hadn't changed her training or her calling. And if he'd bothered to *ask* her, if he'd bothered to *explain*, she would have told him exactly that.

They would definitely be talking tonight. Her end of the conversation might involve a little yelling, but holy crap. He needed to quit being so damn presumptuous.

The good news: This problem had a simple solution.

"I absolutely, positively don't want to be on the show, as I'll inform him as soon as the reception ends. I'm sure you can easily find someone else." She stood, teetering momentarily on her wedge heels. "I wish you both successful negotiations."

If Alex hadn't already gone searching for her, he would soon, and he'd be alarmed to find her gone. She needed to get back before her absence caused any disruption.

Zach held up a hand. "Wait. Lauren, there's more."

Well, shit.

She dropped back into her chair. "What?"

"If you refuse, he will too." The agent's blue eyes were solemn. "He doesn't want to travel the country without you."

No. *No.*

She stared at Zach, aghast. "He didn't. Please tell me he didn't say that."

Her stomach twisted in revolt at the very thought, because she *couldn't.* She couldn't be responsible for Alex losing his career a second time.

The guilt would destroy her. Destroy them.

"He did." Zach met her gaze directly, without any signs of prevarication. "Lauren, from everything Alex has said and everything I've seen, you care about him. You want what's best for him, and I genuinely believe this is his last chance. If he doesn't take this job, his career is over. And StreamUs wants a decision soon. Tonight, if possible."

Oh, *shit.*

At the realization of what this conversation was really about, what Alex's agent was really asking her, she hunched over on herself and tried to keep breathing through the nausea.

Zach spoke carefully. Clearly. "The role is perfect for him, and with the way he spends, he doesn't have a ton of savings. He needs the money. For himself, but also his mom and his charity and all the other people he helps."

I imagine Alex's agent needs the money too, a spiteful, petty part of her brain added, but she ignored it, because Zach was right. Not being able to support everyone would gut Alex.

It would, in fact, leave him feeling the same way she did right now, as she waited for the inevitable.

Zach didn't make her wait long.

"If you're in his life, he won't take this role." The agent didn't sound happy about it, but he didn't flinch or sugarcoat the issue. "Is what you have with him worth his career?"

The hurt pierced through all those layers of composure, all that calm she'd painstakingly acquired and used to shield her heart for decades, and she couldn't muffle her sob.

The agent reached out to her, and she flinched back.

He withdrew his hand. "I'm sorry. But I had to say it, because Alex never would."

Zach had known his client for almost the entirety of their careers, and it showed. He understood Alex, and she did too.

He was all or nothing, always. He wouldn't accept another cohost while she was theoretically available. And even if she could somehow convince him she had no interest in that role, he wouldn't tolerate her staying in L.A. while he traveled the country. He'd turn down the deal without a second thought, or even much of a *first* thought, and there simply wasn't enough time to make him understand the truth: She wasn't worth that kind of sacrifice.

If they stayed together, he'd willingly cast aside everything for her. Again.

The only way to save him was to leave him.

Her joints ached as if she were febrile, and her chest hitched uncontrollably, but Zach was waiting, so she tried to speak. "I'll t-talk to Alex before the end of the reception."

She'd be tearing out her own heart, but she'd do it, because there was no choice.

If his world fell apart again, it wouldn't be because of her. She refused to be the means of his destruction a second time. Especially since his feelings for her—whatever they were—might not last long outside their little bubble of privacy and constant contact. They'd been friends for months, but lovers for less than a week. A blink of time.

Even if that fleeting moment had felt like an entire life stretched out before her, sunlit and horizonless and *hers*.

Zach's head was bowed, his voice thick. "For what it's worth, I really am sorry, Lauren."

She nodded, and a tear dripped from her chin to her belly, then another and another. The next time she raised her head, eyes blurry and stinging, nose running, he was gone, and she knew what she needed to do.

She couldn't tell Alex that Zach had spoken to her, or he'd fire his agent on the spot. But he didn't deserve lies, and she wouldn't give him any. Telling him she'd changed her mind about being together was true enough. And if he demanded further explanation, her anger at his unilateral decision-making was genuine, and she could play it up as necessary. Use it to cover the real reason she was leaving him.

She'd selectively tell him the truth and . . . go away inside. She'd draw down over herself all those layers of remove he'd stripped away and make herself inviolate once again. Impenetrable. Distant emotionally, and then distant physically, once she fled the wedding.

If she left him any hope of a future together, he'd hold out for her. He'd turn down or wait to sign the StreamUs deal in case she might come back.

So she wouldn't allow any hope.

Not even for herself.

28

AFTER FINDING LAUREN'S SEAT EMPTY AND HER TABLE-
mates uncertain as to when and why she'd left, Alex strode for
the nearest exit, thumbing out a text as he went: Where are you?
Are you okay?

When she didn't respond immediately, he headed for their room,
and thank goodness, there she was.

Only . . . what the ever-loving *fuck*?

Her skin wasn't just pale anymore, but pallid. Those beautiful
eyes had turned red-rimmed, and her eyelids and nose were both
puffy and pink.

Worst of all, she had that expression again. The one he hated
and hadn't seen in months. Neutral. Removed, despite all the evidence of emotional turmoil.

He now recognized it for what it was: protection. But protection from what, he couldn't say.

"What the fuck happened, Wren?" It was a snarl as much as a
question, because whoever had upset her this much was going to
fucking *pay*. "Tell me."

As soon as she was within touching distance, he reached for
her hand. After a single weak squeeze, she let him go and backed
away a step, and . . . something had gone wrong. Very, very
wrong.

Her lips tipped in a small smile that didn't reach her blank eyes. "I need to go."

Go where? To another hotel? Back home?

"What the—"

"Alex." Her throat worked, but she sounded entirely unbothered. "Let me explain."

Dread continued to unfurl in his belly, and he dropped abruptly onto the low couch, his legs unsteady. "Did someone say something? Because I swear to God, I'll—"

"I have to cut our trip short." Her wide mouth was white around the edges, but she was still smiling, still so calm he wanted to shake her. "I'm flying back home tonight."

It was a punch to his chest, so brutal he couldn't breathe, couldn't speak. All he could do was stare, dazed, his gut roiling.

"I'm so . . ." She paused, swallowing. "I'm so grateful for your company over the past few months. You've been . . . such a good friend. When we met, I was burned out, and now I'm better. Because of you. Better enough to work again. So thank you."

Another blow. Another *whoosh* of air from his laboring lungs.

A good friend. A good fucking *friend*.

No, he was more than that. After these past three days together—

"Wren." He clasped his hands between his knees, hard enough that his knuckles cracked and his joints ached. "You've been crying. Tell me what fucking *happened*."

"Sometimes when I don't feel well, my eyes get bloodshot." She hitched her shoulder, the movement jerky. "Anyway, before I left, I wanted to tell you how much I appreciated all your kindness. I'll, um—I'll miss you."

He huddled in on himself, shoulders hunched, shaking, because— she'd *miss* him? As in, she didn't even want to see him anymore?

Swiftly, she turned away from him and headed for her closet. Her suitcase.

Maybe she hadn't been crying, but he was, openly, because fuck pride. Fuck anything that didn't bring her back to him somehow.

"What about—" He dragged in a hitching breath. "What about us, Lauren?"

She stilled, her back to him. "I—I care about you. You know that."

"Yeah." He laughed, and it was loud and ugly and bitter enough to hurt his ringing ears. "I thought I did. I thought I knew that."

Her head bowed, but her words were uninflected. Emotionless. "This—what we had . . ." Another pause. "It was an interlude. A vacation from reality. But vacations end, and we have to return to our real lives. Yours is in Hollywood. Mine is in the ER."

From everything she'd told him, her lengthy stint in the ER hadn't been a *life*. It'd been an *existence*. Self-abnegation for a paycheck, and the thought of her returning was like having his heart gripped in a vicious fist.

"It doesn't have to be just a goddamn *interlude*." He surged to his feet and paced in front of the sofa, his pulse hammering at his temples. "I got an offer for a travel show today, and I want you to be my cohost. We could explore the world together, Wren. That could be your real life. *I* could be your real life."

She was still bent over her suitcase, unmoving, and he rushed on before she could respond. Before she could refuse him and cast him aside.

"Or if you'd rather be my PA, if you don't want to be on camera, we can make that work instead. I don't care. As long as you're with me." He raked his fingers through his hair and fisted a handful hard enough that several strands ripped free. "I need you, Wren. Please."

Her chest expanded with a deep inhalation. Then, finally, she turned to face him again, and her features might have been carved from stone. Those round cheeks were bloodless but dry. Her gaze landed somewhere over his shoulder, off in the distance, where she evidently saw something more important than him.

"This vision you have for our future," she said slowly, deliberately, "what made you think it would be something I'd want? Something I could live with?"

What—what did that mean?

"I thought—" He threw his hands in the air, panicky, his scalp afire. "I thought you *liked* traveling with me and filming our videos."

Her fingers clutched the handle of her suitcase, and the plastic creaked under the pressure. "I do. I did. But that doesn't mean I want to travel with you indefinitely, as my job."

"We can make it work, Lauren. Just tell me what you need." The plea was raw enough to scour his throat. "You could set our itinerary, or have your own trailer. Hell, if you wanted to specify a maximum number of days per month we could spend on the—"

"Alex." She closed her eyes for the length of a slow breath, then opened them and pinned him with that clear stare. "Haven't you thought at all about who I am? Haven't you noticed how important my work as a therapist is to me?"

He stopped dead.

"You haven't listened." Her lips pressed tight. "You haven't listened to me."

All his impassioned protests withered on his tongue.

The shame descended on him, so heavy his legs locked beneath him. He trembled beneath its weight, its inexorable press downward and downward again.

Selfish. He'd been unforgivably selfish *again*.

She was right. He hadn't listened. Hadn't paid attention.

Instead, he'd fucking *assumed*. That what she wanted was the same as what he wanted. That his work would make her happy too. That she loved him—or could grow to love him—the same way he loved her.

He'd failed to hear her, and he'd misunderstood. He'd misinterpreted her affection as something more than a friendship and some casual sex.

Only sex wasn't casual for him. It never had been.

But that wasn't her problem. He wasn't her responsibility anymore.

Soon, she'd be burdened and staggering under the mental, physical, and emotional weight of her work once again, and he wouldn't make her life harder with his neediness. His self-centered demands for her time and energy, when soon she wouldn't have either to spare.

I'll miss you, she'd said, and now he understood.

Soon, she'd have no space in her life for him anymore. Which was as it should be.

He'd long thought she was too good for him. This conversation only proved it, and good for her, really. Good for her for realizing it.

"Alex?" She'd moved a step closer, and was studying him now, her brow furrowed.

He wasn't her patient, though, or her lover. He was just a friend she'd fucked, and she didn't need to waste her concern on the likes of him.

"I didn't listen. I didn't think. I didn't notice." He laughed, and it didn't contain bitterness this time. Only defeat. "Then again, when do I ever?"

She bit her lip, and he couldn't bear her scrutiny a moment longer. His eyes dry through sheer force of will, he tried to smile at her.

"Why don't you pack while I give your best wishes to Stacia and her husband?" Turning away, he reached for the door handle. "I'll be back in thirty minutes to help you carry your bags down to the entrance."

He was out in the hall before she could respond.

Downstairs, in the lobby, he heaved open the door to a single-stall bathroom and locked himself inside. He sent a text to Zach with unsteady fingers: I need a few days to think. Stall them if you can. I'm sorry. Swallowing hard, he tucked his phone back in his pocket.

The marble floor stung his knees when he crumpled, but it was just another pinwheel of pain in a body already racked with agony. He couldn't contain it all a moment longer.

There, where no one could see, he cried so hard he threw up.

TUESDAY MORNING FOUND Alex back in his home.

Marcus had arrived at the hotel very late Saturday night, carrying both his duffel and a bag full of weird pastries he called *cocroffinuts*. He'd slept a few hours on the pullout couch, while Alex had spent the night miserably sniffing the bed's pillowcases, hunting for a whiff of coconut. And early the next morning, they'd begun their two-day, caffeinated-pastry-fueled trip back down the coast.

Because of Alex's shaky grasp on—well, everything, Marcus had done all the driving, and he'd done it without complaint. Even when Alex kept choosing playlists full of brokenhearted '80s power ballads. Including, notably, "Broken Wings" by Mr. Mister, which he played six times in a row before Marcus's increasingly visible misery finally prompted him to switch to Poison's "Every Rose Has Its Thorn," followed by Heart's "What About Love?"

"You know," Marcus finally said after the fourth repetition of Cheap Trick's "The Flame," his voice strained but patient, "music was still made after the turn of the century. Even sad music with electric guitars."

Alex stared out the window, where a cliff tumbled down to pounding waves far below. "The synth speaks to my soul."

Marcus raised a hand in surrender, then went back to driving.

When they'd finally reached Marcus's L.A. home, he'd emerged from the driver's seat with a groan, stretching his back. "Want to stay here for a while?"

They both knew Marcus would rather be back in San Francisco with April, and Alex might not prefer solitude, but maybe it was what he needed. It was certainly what he deserved.

"Nah." He slammed the passenger door behind him and circled to the other side of the car. "But thanks for the offer, dude."

Marcus's brow furrowed. "You'll be okay to drive home?"

"I'll be fine. Because of you." Before getting behind the wheel, he'd given his best friend a quick, hard hug. "See you on Friday."

Marcus and April were visiting Malibu that weekend, and they'd persuaded Alex to come along. Until then, he planned to stay offline and out of sight. Maybe by Friday, he'd have his shit together, although he doubted it.

Last night, back in his own bed once more, he'd barely slept. Even a long hike along the unlit, technically closed trail nearest his house hadn't helped clear his jumbled thoughts or ease the continual ache in his chest.

And now here he was, hiding in his own fucking backyard to avoid Dina's concerned scrutiny, picking at her excellent apple–sour cream pancakes and trying not to think about Wren.

Trying and failing.

Finally, he set aside his plate and downed his ADHD medication with coffee. If his stomach hurt later, so be it. Pain south of his heart might prove refreshing.

When he checked his phone, there were three new messages from Zach. StreamUs was pushing for a decision about the show, and so was his agent. *I don't know how much longer they'll give you,* Zach's last email read. *C'mon, man, isn't this exactly the sort of opportunity you wanted?*

It was. Zach was entirely right.

Only . . .

He sat back in his chair and stared at his property. His view. His home.

When he was very little, sometimes he and his mom had been forced to stay at cheap motels for a month or two, ones with cigarette burns and broken security chains and fleas, because she didn't have enough money for a security deposit.

Now, if he wanted, he could drive around the country—maybe even explore the world—in style, and he could get paid for it. Handsomely. All he had to do was make stupid jokes and grin rakishly and keep his constant stream of bullshit running freely. And when he was done, he could come back home to a fucking mini-castle, complete with a terrifyingly efficient housekeeper and a guesthouse.

A goddamn *guesthouse.*

All while Lauren was busting her ass in the ER, dodging punches and insults as she saved lives and broke her own heart, only to return home to an aging duplex with a turret and zero other amenities. All while his mother sat alone in her Florida house and reported to work and shelved books and continued getting older with her only child across the entire fucking continent.

His life was fundamentally selfish. *He* was fundamentally selfish.

Maybe he should just move back to Florida, near his mother, and find real work. Even though, in his experience, real work tended to absolutely blow.

But no matter what he decided, he was free until Friday, and his mother deserved a visit. It had been months since his last trip to the Gold Coast. And if he was desperate for his mom to hold him, if he wanted her to make him cinnamon toast for breakfast—his absolute favorite comfort food, bar none—and tell him everything would be all right . . .

Well, maybe that was selfish too. Whatever.

He was who he was.

So he sent Zach a text. Visiting Mom in Florida until Friday. We'll talk when I'm back. If they withdraw the offer in the meantime, fine.

Then he blocked his agent's number again, booked his flights, and did his best not to wonder where Wren was. What she was doing. Whether she was watching the same sunrise, and whether it banished her shadows and warmed her.

Sunrise or no sunrise, his world was so cold and dark, it might as well have been night.

Gods of the Gates Cast Chat: Tuesday Night

Carah: Hey, Alex, WTF is going on?

Carah: It's been days since your last text, asshole, and you haven't answered any of mine

Carah: No new posts or videos, no messages or emails or voicemails

Carah: Did you fall off the face of the fucking earth, or what?

Carah: Figured I'd ask here, since you're not responding anywhere else, and Marcus has been offline too

Maria: I haven't heard from either of them in a while

Peter: Same 🙁

Summer: Every Sunday, Alex sends me a link to his favorite music reaction video that week

Summer: It's usually the same Phil Collins song each time

Carah: In the Air Tonight? OH LOOOOOOOOOOORD

Summer: That's the one

Summer: It's like being rickrolled, only with an unexpected beat drop three minutes into the song

Summer: Philrolled, I suppose

Summer: Alex's knowledge of music seems to have stopped somewhere in the eighties or early nineties

Summer: Anyway, my point is, he didn't send me a link on Sunday

Summer: I wrote him because I was worried

Summer: I haven't heard back, and now I'm even MORE worried

Maria: Want me to stop by his house? I can do it tomorrow.

Carah: I'll come with you

Marcus: Hey everyone

Marcus: Alex is going through a rough patch right now

Marcus: He appreciates your concern and sends his love, but no house visits

Marcus: Give him a little time, and he'll be fine and back online

Carah: If someone hurt Alex, I will fucking GUT them

Maria: Get in line, my good bitch

Mackenzie: Whiskers's claws are very sharp and could probably disembowel someone

Mackenzie: Couldn't they, Whiskers, couldn't they

Peter: Damn

Peter: Whiskers goes HARD

Peter: Marcus: whatever Alex needs, we're there

Peter: Apparently that includes Whiskers and his Claws of Death

Marcus: Alex knows

Marcus: He knows, and he will fucking love you for it forever.

29

BATHED IN WARM, EARLY-MORNING SUNLIGHT, LINDA SANG along to her playlist as she spread butter over Alex's toast and sprinkled sugar and cinnamon on top.

"Home sweet home!" she howled, in her best imitation of Vince Neil. "Tonight, *toniiiiiiight!*"

Alex joined her, and the kitchen rang with their high-volume, off-key rendition of one of her favorite songs. In that moment, he could have been a kid again, riding along in the backseat as he and his mom rocked out to hair-metal bands.

Music purists *hated* that shit, and he didn't give a fuck. With each ripping guitar riff, each dated synth solo, he thought of his mother. He thought of their road trips together, and their school-day breakfasts together, and their matching feathered mullets inside her locket, and he settled more comfortably into his own skin for a fleeting moment.

He missed his mom. He'd been missing her for over a decade. And from now on, they'd be spending more time together. The shame of his failure to help her might never leave him, but she deserved better than a son she saw once a year.

If he stayed in L.A., he'd try to visit every other month. And if he moved near her . . . well, they could see each other as often as they wanted. Every week, or even every day.

It was Friday morning. His flight back to L.A. left in a matter of hours, and they still hadn't talked about his possible future in Florida. He couldn't delay any longer.

As she slid the plate of cinnamon toast in front of him, he set his elbows on the round kitchen table and looked up at her. "Thanks, Mom."

"It's your last day here, and it's your favorite." She ruffled his hair, exactly the same way she had for almost forty years. "If you wanted, I'd make you an entire loaf of cinnamon toast."

He'd felt like an exhausted old man since Lauren left him, his entire body stiff and aching. In contrast, his mom had been energetic and cheery during his visit, her movements easy, her black eye fading. Bike accident or no bike accident, she was in better shape than him at the moment, and he was glad for it.

Sitting in the chair beside his, she dug into her oatmeal, still humming between bites.

"Listen," he began, picking at the crust of the nearest toast slice. "I was thinking."

"That spells trouble." Her standard response, offered with her usual grin.

He tried to return her smile, but couldn't. At which point, she set down her spoon and studied him with disconcertingly sharp gray eyes.

"Sweetheart . . ." Her hand covered his. Squeezed. "I know you're hurting. I don't know why, and I didn't want to press, but I'm here if you want to talk about it."

He stared down at his plate until his blurry vision cleared. Then he laid his free hand over top of hers to make a hand sandwich, as they'd always called it.

"I'm considering moving back home," he said. "Near you."

Her graying brows drew together, and she clicked the remote to turn off the music. "What about your career?"

"I've played pretend long enough, don't you think?" He tried to laugh. "Besides, I don't have many job offers right now."

She was still watching him very, very carefully. "Do you have any?"

"One. A reality travel show for a streaming service." His shoulders twinged as he tried to lift them in a shrug. "It's a good opportunity, but I don't know."

"What don't you know?" Her head tilted, and her ponytail followed. "Why are you unsure?"

His jaw worked, but he made himself say it. "Maybe it's time for me to be less selfish."

"Alex . . ." Her chair screeched against the floor as she abruptly turned it in his direction. "What does *that* mean?"

He'd been avoiding the subject for over eleven years. Because he hadn't wanted to discuss anything that might cause her pain, and because he was ashamed. But he owed her an apology, at long last. He owed her amends.

He bowed his head and bit his lip until he tasted copper. "I'm so sorry, Mom."

"I don't—" Her hand turned, and suddenly she was holding his, squeezing as he trembled. "I don't understand, sweetheart."

His breath shuddered in his lungs. "I should have realized what he was doing to you. I should have stopped it."

No need to specify the *he* in question. They both understood.

"But . . ." Her hold on him tightened to the point of pain. "Alex, there's no way—"

"I introduced you, and I pressured you to stay with him when you had doubts," he interrupted, because no, he wouldn't let her absolve him, not when his neglect had hurt her so badly. "And then I left and didn't bother looking back. If I'd visited more often, I'd have known what was happening. If I'd called and asked questions, I'd have known what was happening. If I'd been a decent son, instead of a selfish asshole, I'd have fucking *known what was happening*."

She was shaking her head near-violently, those familiar eyes tear-filled and horrified, but he barreled on before she could interject.

"And even after I knew, I didn't do the right thing. I didn't come back home to support you." After so many years, the shame of it still burned, still turned his face tight and hot. "Instead, I stayed across the fucking country and avoided visits, because I couldn't handle all the guilt, even though I fucking deserved every bit of it."

Her mouth had closed, and she was waiting patiently for him to finish. But her knee nudged against his leg, and she was warm and soft, and oh, fuck, he fucking *missed* her, and he fucking missed Wren, and he hurt so badly. So, so badly.

Even though his voice hitched, he powered through the rest of it. "B-But at long last, I finally want to do the right thing. And maybe that's moving here, where you are, so y-you're not alone anymore."

When he bent his head, his tears dripped onto a slice of toast she'd lovingly made for him, ruining it.

"I'm so sorry, Mom." His chest heaved as he fought for air. "I'm so, so sorry."

Then he couldn't speak anymore, and somehow he was crying in his mother's cradling arms for the first time in decades, his face pressed against her neck. Even after all these years, she still smelled like baby powder. Baby powder and comfort and *Mom*, and he *needed* her.

After several minutes, when he was sniffling instead of sobbing, her shoulders rose and fell in a deep breath. Two. Three.

Then she spoke quietly against the crown of his head. "Are you done, sweetheart?"

He nodded, eyes squeezed shut against her shoulder.

"Okay, then. My turn to talk, and please let me finish without interruption." It was a request she'd made countless times during his childhood, because she knew him. She knew he'd want to interject, to argue, no matter what she said. "First of all, I'm not alone. I have coworkers and neighbors and friends, and when I spend time by myself, it's because I want a little peace. I'm not like you, Alex. I sometimes need breaks from other people."

All those people weren't *family*, though. "But—"

"What did I say about interruptions?" The familiar, fond-but-stern tone snapped his mouth shut. "You haven't abandoned me, sweetheart. We talk several times a week, and we have ever since Jimmy died. Yes, I'd prefer more frequent visits, but that doesn't require moving here, and it doesn't mean I'm lonely. I'm not. I just love my son and want to see him more often."

It was an interruption, but it had to be said. "I want to see you more often too."

"Then get out your calendar once you're home, and we'll schedule some visits." With a tender hand against his cheek, she urged his head from her shoulder. "Now let's talk about Jimmy."

At the sound of that monster's name, Alex flinched.

But his mother's eyes met his directly. Her brow was clear, her body relaxed. She didn't look scared or ashamed. Just . . . sad. For *him*, which was so like her he could have cried again.

"If I'd known how you felt, I'd have said this years ago. But I'm saying it now, and I want you to listen closely, Alexander Bernard Woodroe." Her palms cupping his face, she enunciated each word distinctly. "You are not and have never been *selfish*. You didn't notice his abuse because we *kept* it from you, baby. I was too scared and ashamed to say anything, and Jimmy wanted to isolate me, so he encouraged more distance between us."

When he tried to protest, she spoke over him. "You weren't my keeper, and you weren't an expert on domestic violence. You were a young man with a life of his own and goals of his own, and I *wanted* that for you. I *wanted* you to have your own life."

Lauren had said almost the exact same thing to him, only days before.

The two women he loved most in the world, the two women he trusted most in the world, the two women who never, ever lied to him, were telling him *the exact same thing*.

He exhaled shakily, his heart uncramping just a little in his aching chest.

His mother swept a thumb over his cheek, wiping away a stray tear.

"I didn't work so damn hard all those years to keep you by my side forever. I did it so you'd grow up strong and smart. So you'd have the chance to elbow your way into the world and make it yours." Her lips tipped up in a smile, even though her eyes were wet again. "Which is exactly what you did, Alex, and it makes me so freaking proud. Of you, but of me too. I'm your mom, and I raised you to be a hard worker and a good man, and that's *precisely* what you are."

It didn't sound like a platitude or false comfort.

It sounded like truth, as his mom saw it.

"So let me be clear." She shook his face a little in emphasis. "It would break my heart to watch you give up your life and career for me. It's not what I want, and it's not necessary. I'm an adult and perfectly able to care for myself and ask for help if I need it."

He pinched his mouth tight, loath to speak the words that sprang to mind.

Even without those words, his mother correctly read his expression. "Yes, I know. I didn't ask for help when I needed it before. But it's been eleven years, Alex, and I'm not the same person I was then."

For the first time, he could clearly see that.

Still, he hesitated. "If you need help, you'll tell me?"

"Yes." Her gaze was direct, her voice confident and sure. "I promise."

His head suddenly lighter on his shoulders, he found himself able to smile at her. "Pinkie swear?"

She laughed, and he did too, and they clasped pinkies, as they'd done to seal vows all through his childhood.

After one last kiss on his forehead, his mother sat back in her chair and picked up her spoon again. "I'm going to eat my oatmeal, then make you some new toast. While I do all that, you can tell me what happened with Lauren."

His smile died, and he slumped over the table.

Dammit, his mother had always, always been too smart for him. He hadn't successfully snuck out of their apartment *once*.

"I watched you two together when I called the other night." Her spoon clacked against the bowl as she scooped up a bite. "From what I saw, she cares for you very much, and you obviously love her. So why are you here, heartbroken and alone?"

She chewed her breakfast, the silver streaks in her hair glinting in the sun, utterly patient. Utterly relentless.

He might as well answer. She'd browbeat it out of him at some point anyway.

"I have no goddamn idea what happened." He couldn't help the bitterness in his tone. "In the middle of the wedding reception, Lauren said she had to return to her real life and her real job, thanked me for my kindness and *friendship*, and caught a cab for the airport. I haven't heard from her since."

Of course, he hadn't contacted her either, but she was the one who'd left, not him.

"That's odd." Lines scored across his mother's forehead, and she tapped her spoon against the surface of her oatmeal. "Did something happen at the wedding?"

He spread his hands, renewed frustration pounding at his temples. "Not as far as I know."

She thought for a moment. "What about the rest of the day? Did anything else happen that might have upset her?"

"Again, nothing I know about." Jumping to his feet, he began pacing. "I told her about the job offer, but she'd already decided to leave before that."

"Out of curiosity," his mother said slowly, "if Lauren had stayed and you'd accepted the offer, how did you intend to deal with the separation from her?"

He winced and paced faster. "I kind of, uh . . . assumed she'd want to come with me. As my cohost. Zach and I were negotiating with StreamUs about that when she left."

Her mouth dropped open.

"You *assumed* that?" Her low whistle hurt his ears. "*Wow*. Alex—"

"Lauren already tackled that part of things, believe me." He swallowed hard, his throat burning with yet more tears. "It wasn't smart, and it wasn't right, but I can't go back and change what I did, Mom."

Her little hum was starting to annoy the hell out of him. How had he forgotten that telltale noise? That unmistakable sign his mom smelled bullshit and intended to track down its source?

"And what if StreamUs said no? For that matter, what if StreamUs said yes and Lauren turned down the opportunity?" Her eyes narrowed on him. "What would you have done then?"

She knew. He knew she knew.

But she was forcing him to say it anyway, because his mom was *the worst*.

"I wouldn't choose a paycheck over Lauren." He scowled at her. "I'd have rejected the offer."

"Alex . . ." Her eyes shut tight, she seemed to shrink into her seat. "God, Alex."

Did she expect him to cast Lauren aside for a goddamn job? What the hell kind of man did she think he was?

Another lap of the island. Another. "What? Is it a crime to stay in the same damn state as the woman you love?"

"Of course not." She opened her eyes, and they were red-rimmed. Tired. "But sweetheart, I don't think you realize what you're doing to the people who care about you."

He threw his hands in the air, hurting and beyond frustrated. "Then *tell* me."

His mother's clear gaze speared through him, and she didn't hesitate.

"You're impulsive, Alex. Impulsive and generous and fiercely protective. You've been that way since you were little, and I love that about you. Always have, always will."

There was a *but* ahead, and he suspected he didn't want to hear the rest.

For her, though, he'd listen. For her, he'd do anything.

"But after the funeral, after Jimmy . . ." A single tear traced down her cheek, and she knuckled it away. "All that got so much more intense, sweetheart. Especially this last year, for reasons I don't understand, and it's *terrifying*."

"What—" His heartbeat was pounding against his skull, and he couldn't fucking *think*. "What does that even mean?"

"Suddenly, you're willing to give up everything you have, everything you've worked for, without a second thought. Not just material possessions. Your career. Your entire future. Your happiness. And you're willing to do it without looking for other options." Her words shook, but she didn't break eye contact. "Think about how that feels, for me and everyone else who loves you."

He tore a hand through his hair. "I'm just trying to do the right thing."

His mother pushed to her feet, walked over, and stood toe to toe with him.

"Sometimes doing the right thing requires sacrificing everything else, and sometimes it doesn't," she told him. "You've always been impulsive, but you used to try to make that distinction. You used to look for alternatives. Not anymore."

His mother swallowed so hard, he could hear it.

"If you've been atoning for what Jimmy did, it's time to stop. It wasn't your fault. And whatever happened this last year, find a way to move past that too." Her face bruised and tearstained, she raised her chin and stared him down. "You don't need to sacrifice your future to prove your love or become a good man. You're already a good man, sweetheart, and you always were."

Wren had said almost exactly the same thing. Again.

You're morally and legally obligated to believe me when I say you're a good man. You have no choice. I'm sorry, I don't make the rules.

He'd like to believe both of them. The two women he loved most.

Had he terrified Wren like he'd terrified his mother? Was that why she'd left?

His legs were unsteady beneath him as he staggered to the living room and collapsed onto his mother's couch. He buried his face in his hands and tried to think.

"Lauren worried about my future more than I ever did." God, his eyes stung. "Do you think—do you think I scared her too, and she was trying to save me from trouble by breaking up with me?

Before I could blow up at the next asshole who insulted her and wreck my career for good?"

His mother sat beside him on the sofa, and repositioned him with gentle insistence until he was resting his head on her shoulder again. "I don't know, baby. But for what it's worth, I saw genuine affection between the two of you. On both sides."

That night in Olema had felt like more than affection. It'd felt like love.

On both sides.

"Maybe give her a little time and space to miss you." She squeezed him. "And then, if she truly doesn't want you or won't let herself have you, let her go, sweetheart. You deserve someone who'll fight to keep you in her life, because you're a catch. And that has nothing to do with your money or fame or the volume of thirst tweets directed your way, and everything to do with your enormous heart."

Her palm patted that general region of his chest.

He sighed and held his mom tighter. "I wish you didn't know the phrase *thirst tweets*. Especially in reference to me. Especially *especially* since I'll be posting more shirtless pics soon." He paused. "I really enjoy all the attention and retweets and flame emojis."

"I know that too, sweetheart." Snorting softly, she kissed the crown of his head. "Believe me, I know."

THE AIRLINE AGENT at the check-in counter cringed when she processed Alex's ID and saw which flight he was on. Or, rather, which flight he would *not* be on.

"I'm so sorry, sir." She handed back his driver's license. "Passengers have to check in at least thirty minutes before departure."

He sighed. "Then I'll take a first-class ticket on the next available flight to LAX, if there's still an open seat."

Between his tear-choked, long-overdue conversation with his mom and his impulsive plans later that morning, he'd run absurdly late the entire day. Which wasn't a huge surprise, since time management had always been difficult for him, but he normally had his virtual PA to keep him on schedule. Or, in recent months, Wren.

Where was she? What was she doing?

Did she miss him?

Fuck, he hurt. His heart and his arm and his bloodshot eyes and *everywhere*.

Still, he offered the check-in agent a tired smile when she found him a ticket, and one relatively enormous credit card purchase later, he was going through security and walking to the business lounge. Along the way, his carry-on rolling smoothly at his side, he checked his phone.

His mother had sent a new text. Great visit, sweetheart. Love you. Don't forget what we talked about, or else I'll have to ground you.☺ Safe travels. Then, minutes later: Thanks for letting me be your mom again. I missed that. ♥

His lips tilted, and he blinked against the prickle in his sinuses.

Love you too, Mom, he wrote back, pausing at the side of the concourse. I won't forget. Less atoning, more thinking. ♥♥♥

He'd been thinking all afternoon, as a matter of fact.

Instead of scattering his thoughts, the pain had focused them.

If he wasn't irredeemably selfish, if he didn't need to atone, if he didn't have to prove his love through heedless self-sacrifice, then his path forward was clear. Finally, finally clear. No matter what did or didn't happen with Lauren.

He unblocked his agent and sent another text before he could change his mind.

Zach: I'm accepting the StreamUs offer, albeit with certain demands we can discuss tomorrow. He hesitated, but kept thumbing. That said, this is our last deal together. Although I appreciate all you've done for me, it's time for us both to move on. Thanks.

Because if he wasn't a terrible person, if he could believe both his mother and Wren when they said he was a good man, he deserved an agent who respected him, even when he was annoying. Which he would be. Often.

Maybe Francine, Marcus's agent, wouldn't mind that so much.

After another few gates, the business lounge entrance came into view. As he entered the quiet, expansive space, he began a text asking his best friend for Francine's contact information, and his phone's battery died three words into the message.

He dropped his bag onto the first available seat and rifled through its contents, but where the hell his charger had gone, he couldn't say. He could buy or borrow another, of course, but . . . he could handle being offline for a few hours. It might even do him some good.

Leaving his bag in the chair, he slid his cell into his pocket and claimed a plate at the end of the buffet. Then another, when he couldn't fit everything he wanted on the first. After a moment's thought, he ladled out a bowlful of yogurt too, because he was hungry and his stomach hurt.

He hadn't been eating enough at breakfast. Not for a long time, except with Wren.

His ADHD sometimes made remembering things like that difficult, but he'd had years of targeted therapy to help him deal with similar issues. The disorder might have been a contributing factor in his negligence, but it wasn't the root cause.

He understood that now.

Wren or no Wren, he would take more care in the future, because he hadn't earned that pain. He hadn't. No matter what had happened to his mother. No matter what had happened on the show.

Wren had told him that. His mom had told him that.

And he was finally ready to believe them.

30

MUCH TOO EARLY IN THE MORNING, LAUREN WOKE TO
someone leaning on her doorbell.

Alex, she thought wildly, the relief hitting her brain like a nar-
cotic. *Alex is here to*—

But no. He'd let her go almost a week ago, and there had been
no texts or phone calls or visits from him since. Not one.

Throwing back the covers, she knuckled away her tears and sum-
moned her new mantra.

"I did the right thing," she repeated for the millionth time, then
forced herself to shuffle to the apartment's entrance. "I did the
right thing."

She didn't even bother to check the peephole before flipping
the deadbolt and opening the door, because it wasn't him, and if
it wasn't him, she didn't care. Whoever it was, she'd send them
away so she could be alone in her misery once more. Even if it was
Sionna, whom she'd somehow managed to successfully avoid for
six entire days now.

Only that was a lie, because as soon as she actually saw her
best friend on her doorstep, she bent at the waist and burst into
uncontrollable sobs and stumbled into Sionna's arms.

An indeterminate amount of time later, she surfaced enough
from her haze of desolation to notice they were sitting on the couch

now. Lauren hiccupped and blew her nose with tissues that had miraculously appeared in her lap, Sionna's hand gentle on her back.

"I saw your car in the garage this morning and decided I was tired of you dodging me, so I called in sick." Her friend's voice was quiet. Soothing. "What happened, babe?"

Between sobs, Lauren told her. All of it.

Sionna listened patiently, as she always did. Then, after one last rub of Lauren's back, she settled against the couch cushions and looked thoughtful.

"That's it?" she asked. "You've told me everything now?"

At Lauren's nod, Sionna continued, her voice dry but not unsympathetic. "Allow me to summarize, then: After noisily fucking Alex, the man you clearly adore and who seems to adore you in return, you got a little angry at him for making unilateral decisions and a lot scared he'd destroy his professional future, so you made a unilateral decision to leave him, called him inconsiderate, and dumped his ass without warning in the middle of his ex's wedding reception, thus destroying any possibility of a romantic future with you."

The words dropped into Lauren's belly like a lead weight, and her stupid eyes prickled again. Fuck, that dispassionate summary made her sound like a monster. A hypocritical one too.

She tore her tissue in half. "I didn't call him inconsiderate."

The rest she couldn't deny, much as she wanted to.

"You questioned whether he took you and your preferences into account when making all his grandiose plans." Sionna's mouth quirked. "Which was an absolutely fair point, because he clearly didn't. But it's still an accusation of selfishness, or at least self-absorption."

Lauren froze.

That accusation . . . he'd leveled it against himself before. Spat it out like dirt in his mouth.

He'd called himself selfish. An asshole. A self-absorbed Holly-wood brat.

Because he'd failed to notice his stepfather's abuse. Because he'd acted in his show's final season.

For those self-proclaimed sins, he'd damned himself and scram-bled to make amends. But for him, it wasn't enough. Might never be enough. His continued self-loathing had been heartbreakingly clear that evening in Olema, when he'd nearly collapsed at the sight of his injured mother.

And then, at the wedding, overwrought and grief-stricken and desperate to drive him away, she'd confronted him without even a sliver of her usual caution. Without thinking about his history. The same way—as she'd informed him—he hadn't thought about hers.

The irony strangled the breath in her throat.

What she'd said, however true, however necessary, had to have confirmed his worst fears. And she'd wielded the accusation with-out care, after implying they were friends and nothing more, their time together a mere *interlude*.

Fuck. Oh, *fuck*.

She hunched in on herself. "God. No wonder he didn't argue after I said that."

"Ren . . ." Sionna was rubbing her back again. "Do you love him?"

She hiccupped again, the sound loud and ugly. "Yes."

There was no point prevaricating. Her best friend already knew, or at least suspected. Otherwise, she wouldn't have asked the question. And Lauren wasn't ashamed of loving him.

Alex deserved love. Enough to fill that huge, loyal, lonely heart of his.

And she'd beg, she'd *bleed*, to give it to him, but—

She was sobbing once more, her body bucking with it. "I can't—I c-can't let him d-destroy his career over m-me *again*. I *c-can't*."

"I understand that." Sionna's arms were soft and warm, and they drew Lauren close. "But, babe, I just . . ." She sighed. "I'm not sure that was a decision to make on your own. Especially without telling him everything and explaining how you feel. Without asking him whether he'd rather have a career or you, if he had to choose."

Lauren took a dozen deep breaths, until her chest no longer hitched so hard. Then she shook her head against her friend's shoulder, exhausted and so fucking sad, she wanted to sleep for a million years.

"But I knew what he'd say." She bit her lip against more tears. "I knew what he'd do."

He'd fire his agent.

He'd turn down StreamUs's offer.

He'd choose her. Every time.

And then he'd find himself without money or prospects, unable to keep supporting his mother, Dina, and the charity, and he'd hate himself for it. He'd fight everyone who insulted and abused Lauren, and his foes would be legion. Endless.

He'd choose her, and then he'd lose everything *but* her.

"He deserves more," she whispered, the words muffled against Sionna's tee.

At that, her friend went still.

"Ren . . ." Sionna's own chest hitched. "Sometimes I want to burn down the fucking world for what it's done to you."

After that, she didn't say anything else. She just passed out tissues and rubbed circles over Lauren's back until both of them had stopped crying.

LATER THAT DAY, Lauren attempted to stop missing Alex and distract herself from her doubts by searching for recent photos of him online.

If her logic was suspect, her fingers didn't care. They were already clicking to open a new browser window and typing in his name and limiting the results to the past twenty-four hours, because she had to see him. She had to see his face and his expression and know he was fine. She had to know he was better off without her.

Surely he'd realized that too, by now.

Because if he hadn't—

Firmly quashing that line of thought, she scrolled through the pics, none of which seemed to be from the past day, despite her search specifications.

Alex on a dais at Con of the Gates, his grin bright and savage as he detonated his career. Alex posing for a selfie while washing a car in only a pair of track pants, gleaming with water in the sun. Alex in his Cupid costume, laughing with one of the camera operators on set.

She'd studied all those photos before. Recently. Repeatedly.

God, she'd never spent so much time on social media in her entire damn *life*. But she couldn't seem to stop cyberstalking him. Or crying.

She also couldn't seem to find news of his deal with StreamUs, despite all the rumors still swirling. Worse, he hadn't posted a damn thing anywhere since she'd abandoned him in the middle of his ex's wedding reception. Not on YouTube or Instagram, where viewers were clamoring for more travel videos. Not on Twitter, where his followers mourned a sudden lack of shirtless thirst-tweet inspiration. Not on Facebook or—

Wait.

That was new. In a grainy, crooked photo, he was walking along a sidewalk outside a tidy strip mall, palm trees in the background. The shot could have been taken in any California suburb.

According to the provided information, though, the picture originated from late that morning in . . . Florida?

If he'd visited his mom, she was glad. Linda had seemed lovely and loving, and he deserved a vacation. That said, the photo truly was terrible. If she didn't know better, she'd have said Alex looked *not good* in it, which would be the only example of that particular phenomenon in human history.

She zoomed in, then zoomed in again.

Up close, the image was more than a little out of focus, but *shit*. Shit, he *did* look bad. Terrible, actually. Disheveled and haggard, with dark shadows under his eyes. A hobo rather than a Viking, caught in some awkward moment where he appeared stiff and miserable.

If he'd realized he was better off without her, that certainly wasn't apparent in the photo.

Ever since her conversation with Sionna, she'd been trying not to listen to the doubts that clamored louder minute by minute. But they wouldn't be denied now. They were all she could focus on, other than his bookmarked fics and his beloved face.

Maybe a bystander had taken an unlucky, unflattering shot. Or maybe Lauren had grievously injured them both by leaving him so abruptly, by refusing to discuss her concerns or how she felt about him before sacrificing her happiness for his career.

Her happiness, and maybe his too.

In that hotel room, she'd acted unilaterally, just as Sionna had accused. Ostensibly, Lauren had done it for his own good. But even in her own head, that was patronizing as hell, and he'd never wanted her to make those sorts of decisions for him. In fact, he'd lost his shit at the very idea only two weeks ago, after his fan insulted her.

I am the only fucking person in this car and on this planet *who can decide what my career is worth,* he'd raged, offended fury in every syllable, *and it's not worth my fucking soul.*

She had to assume he would say the same thing about his heart.

That is not your fucking decision, Lauren, he'd told her, but she hadn't really listened. She hadn't remembered. Not when confronted with his agent's story, not when wrestling with her own fear and guilt.

Unable to bear the sight of his possible misery any longer, she clicked over to YouTube. To the video they'd taken on Glass Beach, only minutes before debating their relative loudness during orgasm.

Alex stood grinning at someone the audience couldn't see. Her, behind the camera, rolling her eyes at him as he stripped off his shirt and preened despite the cloudy, blustery day.

He ran a caressing palm down his hair-dusted, broad chest. "Some say going topless on this beach is like finding a four-leaf clover. Guaranteed good luck."

"Literally no one says that," her voice informed the audience.

He raised a dark brow. "I said that. Just now, as a matter of fact."

She snorted, and the image bobbed slightly. "I stand corrected. Literally one person in the world says that."

When he shook his head chidingly, a lock of hair fell over his forehead.

"You don't know all the people in the world, Wren." His wink flustered her even now, a week later. "Besides, it's already working, ye of little faith. We've been here five minutes at most, and I feel really lucky. I can only hope to get even *more* lucky soon."

He meant they were going to have sex that night, of course.

But she knew his voice. Even amid all the innuendo and cocky posturing, she could hear the sincerity and affection. The blossoming of . . . wonder, almost. As if he meant it. He considered himself lucky to have her in his bed. In his life.

She paused the film on his bright smile and ran her forefinger over the roundish, green bit of sea glass he'd carried in his pocket for her, then the cloudy blue rectangle and the amber square. The three pieces she'd plucked from the shore that day and tucked carefully inside her toiletries bag. The three pieces that now lay on her nightstand, within easy reach, for when she needed comforting.

She hadn't been able to stop herself from taking those souvenirs. Even then, she'd known the day was special. Suffused with warmth and beauty and easy affection and laughter. She hadn't anticipated another day like it, possibly in her entire life.

So she'd gathered mementos for mourning while she could.

How many other wonderful places could they have explored together if she'd allowed them to leave over the weekend, as he'd originally planned? If she hadn't delayed their trip because she didn't want him to spend money on her?

Even though he'd told her he had plenty of savings. Even though he'd *wanted* to spend that money on her, *wanted* that extra time with her.

Why did she assume she wasn't worth a few extra hotel bills?

She'd been absolutely determined not to let him give up his career for her. On that awful evening at the hotel, stopping him—saving him, whether he'd asked to be saved or not—had seemed like an imperative, its importance clear and unquestionable.

But why did she assume she wasn't worth his career?

Alex always had a comeback for everything, and he'd had an answer for that question too. He'd shared it with her before, multiple times. Sorrow and rage in every syllable, he'd tried to tell her what she believed, how she saw herself.

You're not important enough to defend, even when someone insults you to your fucking face. He'd phrased it as a question, but it was more an angry lament. A condemnation of how little she valued herself. *How you feel isn't important. You're not important.*

She'd told him that wasn't true.

But even then, part of her knew he was right.

The best thing the world offered an ugly little girl was indifference. Pity stung exactly as much as insults, if not more, so she tried to avoid either. She tried to avoid notice. Even as a child, she'd understood it was important to stay quiet. Unobtrusive. And above all, undemanding.

Fortunately, adults were generally happy to ignore a short, fat kid with a bird's face, and she was generally happy to encourage their lack of attention.

Other kids, though . . . they couldn't be avoided, and they wouldn't be deterred.

But crying over the cruelty of others to her parents only upset them, and nothing her mom and dad did blunted the relentless tide of abuse, so she eventually stopped coming to them. And they never questioned whether that cruelty had actually ceased, probably because they didn't really want to know. Especially when her tormentor was also her cousin.

They loved her. She knew that.

But they'd taught her that family peace was more important than her feelings.

And since then, she'd spent decades giving away pieces of herself, because she didn't matter. Not as much as everyone else.

She'd given herself away at work, with every overtime shift she took, every holiday she worked in place of a colleague, every time she chose to ignore her increasing misery and work harder. She'd given herself away to her parents, who'd learned she would drop everything to help them at any time, no matter what they wanted.

At their urging, she'd given herself away to her asshole cousin too, even though she hated him—shit, she really did *hate* him—and she'd desperately needed a real vacation, not a job babysitting a man who required love rather than supervision.

Eventually, she'd given so much of herself away, there'd been almost nothing left by the time she boarded that flight to Spain.

Sionna had tried to tell her, tried to help her, but Lauren hadn't listened.

And then Alex had given her back. Piece by piece.

By prodding her to *speak*, to respond and make her voice heard. By encouraging her—as Sionna had—to be a shrew, to demand her due and act in her own best interests. By paying constant attention to her. By offering gifts. By defending her with all the love and rage and loyalty in his enormous, reckless heart. By glorying in her pleasure fully as much as his own. By insisting that her feelings and her safety and her happiness and her presence in his life *mattered*, always.

More than a random fan. More than even his career.

She hadn't asked for anything from anyone in years. Hell, she'd *volunteered* to give away more of herself and *rejected* receiving anything in return.

Alex had forced her to *take*. For her sake, and for his too, because he was a generous soul, and her happiness made him happy in return.

But even he couldn't make her take that goddamn hotel money. Even he couldn't make her accept the most loyal heart she'd ever known, despite how desperately she wanted it. Even he couldn't make her believe she was important and worth all his sacrifices.

In the end, there was only one person who could do that.

And she was terrified out of her fucking mind that she'd ruined everything.

From atop the nightstand, her cell rang.

The number on the screen baffled her. She'd broken his best friend's heart, so why in the world was *Marcus* calling her?

Well, if he wanted to yell at her, she deserved it. And maybe once he was done and she'd groveled a bit, he would tell her when Alex planned to return from Florida.

Or . . . had something gone wrong during Alex's vacation? Had there been some sort of accident?

She snatched up the phone and stabbed at the screen. "Marcus? Is Alex okay?"

He paused before answering, and the thud of her heart filled her skull, the room, the entire world.

"I don't know." When he finally spoke, he sounded troubled. "I was hoping you did."

Shit. *Shit.* "Where is he?"

"I don't know," he said again. "He'd planned to fly into LAX this afternoon, stop home for a few minutes, then drive to meet April and me in Malibu. His flight landed safely, according to the airport website. But he was supposed to arrive at the hotel a couple of hours ago, and we haven't seen him."

That . . . wasn't great. "Could he have missed his flight?"

"Maybe." Marcus's voice was tight with worry. "But no one's heard from him since the plane took off. He's not answering his phone or responding to texts and emails."

Alex would typically send his best friend a billion bored texts during a transcontinental plane ride. No wonder Marcus was anxious. She was too, and becoming more so by the second.

"He probably just forgot about our plans, but I want to make sure he's not sick or hurt." After the click of a door closing, the quiet buzz of background noise went silent. "Normally, he always responds to my messages. Even when he ignores everyone else."

In the ER, countless scared, sad families had shared some tear-choked version of this story. Nevertheless, she genuinely didn't think Alex would harm himself. Not directly.

But he was so *reckless* sometimes, and if he was hurting as much as she was—

She squeezed her eyes shut and tried to think. "Have you called his mom?"

"She's the last person he contacted before the flight. As far as she knows, he's not in Florida anymore, but she honestly has no clue." He made a frustrated noise. "I was hoping he'd reconciled with you and lost track of time and space and human existence, which was the best possible scenario under the circumstances."

God, if only. She'd give anything. *Anything.*

More important, she'd *take* anything.

"Um, no. I haven't heard from him since . . ." When she swallowed, she tasted bile. "Since the wedding."

"Fuck," Marcus muttered. "I'd check with Dina, but I don't have her number. Do you?"

"I don't. I'm so sorry," she said helplessly.

Another frustrated sound. "Then I should probably drive to his house tonight to make sure he's there and okay."

She didn't hesitate. "Let me do it. I can leave right now, and I'm much closer than you are."

Once more, Marcus went silent for a disconcerting amount of time.

"Thank you for the offer, but I don't know if that's such a great idea." He sighed. "He wouldn't thank me for telling you this, but he misses you terribly. If he's already in a bad emotional state to start with, seeing you . . ."

Although he trailed off, she understood precisely what he meant. Now he needed to understand *her*.

"I love him, and if he'll have me back, I'll never leave him again." Her face went hot, but she spoke the sentence like the simple truth it was. "So if that's your main concern, I'll go. I still have the keys to his house, and I can check inside and around the grounds."

Alex had insisted she keep the keys when she moved out of the stables, and she couldn't seem to mail them back after the wedding, no matter how many times she told herself to do it.

"Oh, thank fuck." Marcus let out a slow breath. "Whether he's there or not, please call to let me know. As soon as you can."

"I will." She hit the floor running. "I'm on my way."

As soon as they exchanged brief goodbyes, she yanked on her leggings and thrust her sockless feet into sneakers.

In less than a minute, she was out the door and on her way to Alex.

She hoped.

Please, let him be there.

AS SOON AS Lauren saw Alex's mini-castle lit from the inside, she called Marcus.

"The interior lights are on." She parked in the circular drive, right next to the entrance. "Dina turns them off when she leaves, so unless there's been an intruder, he's here."

She didn't want her reunion with Alex to occur while his best friend listened, but so be it. Heart pounding, she jogged up the front steps, rang the bell, and pounded on the door.

Nothing. Not a sound.

"He's not answering." Dammit. "Do you think I should let myself in? Normally, I wouldn't invade his privacy like that, but . . ."

"Desperate times," Marcus said. "Besides, he's given a good portion of L.A. his keys and security codes and told them to come by whenever. Consider this the very definition of *whenever*."

When she tried her key, however, she discovered it wasn't needed.

"The door's unlocked." She scowled. "I've told him and told him to lock up, but he never listens."

"An unlocked door could indicate an intruder, like you said." Marcus now sounded worried for her *and* Alex. "Lauren, I've changed my mind. Maybe you should wait for—"

"I'm going in."

Despite his voluble protests, she flung open the door and strode inside.

"You two belong together," he muttered. "Jesus Christ."

"His carry-on is in the hallway," she told Marcus, then screeched into the depths of the mini-castle. *"Alex! Where are you?"*

Marcus squawked. "Holy shit, my ear."

"Alex!" No answer, which was starting to make her nervous. *More* nervous. "Okay, let me look around."

Thank goodness, he wasn't lying injured anywhere in the house or on the grounds. And wherever he'd ventured, he hadn't been gone long. When she touched the hood of his car, parked neatly in the garage, the metal was still warm.

So where in the world—

Oh. Oh, she knew exactly where he was. Or at least, she knew what he was doing.

"He's walking somewhere nearby." Closing the front door behind her, she squinted into the night. "Either on one of the trails or the secret stairs."

She hoped the latter, because she didn't particularly want to trespass onto closed, dark, unfamiliar trails, especially given the panoply of local wildlife Alex had noted.

"Okay." Marcus let out a slow breath. "Why don't you wait inside, or by the front—"

"I'll go find him and call you once I do." With a swipe and a tap, she activated her cell's flashlight function. "Don't worry. I've got this handled."

A very loud groan emitted from the phone's loudspeakers. "If you get hurt searching for him, Alex will fucking *murder* me."

"I'll protect you," she promised, then promptly hung up on Marcus's objections.

The motion-sensor lights illuminated overhead as she half walked, half ran to the side gate, which was—

Unlocked and wide open.

Well, he obviously *had* taken the secret stairs. He was also due for another lecture about his personal safety, and once she was done begging his forgiveness and throwing herself at his feet, she'd be giving it to him.

Along with her heart, hopefully.

The night was cool, but the steps were numerous and her pace rapid, and she was sweating by the time she reached the top of the Saroyan Stairs. His favorite spot on the mountain, with stars twinkling above, the lights of downtown Hollywood sparkling below, and greenery all around.

At the first sight of him, her knees almost dissolved beneath her.

He was alive and upright, at least, and that was two prayers to the universe answered.

Halfway down the stairs, he sat on one of the benches, arms looped around knees tucked tight to his chest, staring intently up at the velvety, dark sky. As far as she could tell, he hadn't heard her approach. He certainly didn't acknowledge her presence.

He was still. A man constantly in motion finally at rest.

Whether that was good or bad, she didn't know.

When she took the first step down to him, another set of lights illuminated, puncturing his absorption. His head jerked in her direction.

At the sight of her, his lips parted, his eyes going wide.

She kept moving, step by step, allowing the rail to bolster her shaky legs. "Please tell me you're not injured in any way. Marcus has been frantic, and so have I."

"I don't . . ." His brow creased. "What?"

"You didn't show up in Malibu, and no one has been able to get in touch with you." A dozen more steps, and she'd be at his side again. Where she belonged. "Marcus called me. We were worried you were sick or injured."

"Shit." His eyes squeezed shut for a moment, his jaw working. "I missed my damn flight, my phone died, and I completely forgot about Malibu."

Four steps. Three. Two. One.

There he was, within her reach again. She sagged against the rail in bone-deep relief.

Slowly, his body uncurled, and his feet lowered to rest on the stairs. The unflattering light emphasized the shadows beneath his eyes, the shagginess of his hair and beard, the rumpled fabric of that long-sleeved, slate-blue Henley she loved.

She could ask him why he hadn't bought or borrowed a charger. She could find out why he'd missed his flight. She could scold him for worrying the people who loved him.

Or she could ask the only important question. "Are you ill or hurt in any way?"

"I'm not sick." His pause discomfited her. "And if I'm in pain, I brought it on myself."

Oh, shit. "Alex—"

He mustered a pale shadow of his usual grin. "Don't worry, Wr—Lauren. You won't be seeing me in your emergency room. It's not that kind of self-harm. I promise."

What that meant, she wasn't certain. But she didn't see any

obvious signs of illness or injury, and he didn't appear to be in acute distress.

"In that case . . ." She lifted the phone clenched in her sweaty hand. "I need to text Marcus and let him know you're okay."

Once she'd sent the message and confirmed its *delivered* status, she looked up to find his tired eyes trained on her, his lips tight.

"Sorry you came all this way for no reason, but thank you for caring about my well-being." His knuckles shone white as he gripped the bench on either side of his hips. "May I escort you back to your car?"

Now. She would do this now.

"No," she said.

"But—okay." His shoulders rounded, and he studied the stairs under his feet. "Okay. I understand."

She shook her head. "I don't think you do."

Courage, Lauren.

She was important. To him, and to herself, which meant this was the right thing. Finally, *finally*, she was doing the right thing.

"I would have come to see you anyway. If not tonight, then to-morrow." Sucking in a deep breath, she set her fists on her hips. "I have things I need to say, and it's going to be hard for me, so can you please let me speak until I'm done?"

He inclined his head, now watching her carefully once more, his entire body tense.

"I owe you an apology." When she focused on the wrong she'd done him, the words came more easily. "Not only for the way I left, but why I left. I shouldn't have abandoned you in the middle of a wedding reception, regardless of my reasons, but I *definitely* shouldn't have abandoned you without telling you what had hap-pened."

Those tired eyes had turned sharp as flint once more, his haze of exhaustion gone in a heartbeat. But he didn't say a word.

"I was already worried someone would say something terrible to me in front of you, because I knew how you'd react, and I just—" She blew out a breath. "I didn't want you to get in trouble over me. Again. So I sent you up to the front table, figuring that would keep you safe."

He opened his mouth, paused, then clamped it shut again. Which she appreciated, but this next part was going to be the true test of his self-control.

Her short nails biting into her palms, she braced herself and told him. "Then your agent tracked me down and asked to speak with me privately."

A low, muffled, furious sound erupted from his chest, and he jerked violently, his brows slamming together. His expression hardened to stone, but he grimly kept his mouth closed.

"I refused at first, but he said he was concerned about you, and you'd seemed . . ." Restless and ashamed, she tugged at the end of her ponytail. "You'd seemed *not yourself* since your meeting with him, and I didn't want to disrupt the reception by bothering you. So I went with him. Which I shouldn't have done, and I'm sorry about that too. I promise never to speak to one of your business partners without you present ever again."

At that, some of the fury faded from his grimace, and he blinked at her once. Twice.

"He told me about the StreamUs offer." Another tug at her hair. "He said it was your last shot in Hollywood, and if they wouldn't agree to have me as your cohost, you'd turn down the offer. He said even if they *did* agree, if I refused, you'd still turn them down."

She frowned at him, because she'd been wondering—"Was that true? Did you tell him that?"

Exhaling loudly through flared nostrils, he nodded.

Well, at least she hadn't bought an outright lie. There was that.

"I thought so. It sounded like something you'd say." She pursed her mouth. "For what it's worth, he seemed sincerely concerned for your future, Alex. And we both agreed the job was perfect for you. But we shouldn't have had a conversation about your life and career without you, and I want you to know I realize that."

Another tight-jawed nod.

"Finally, he asked whether what we had was worth your career." Now they were getting to the hardest part, and she shut her eyes, allowing the darkness to ease the confession. "And I thought of your mom and your charity and Dina. All the people you support, and how important that support is to you, and how devastated you'd be when you had to stop paying them because you had no work and your money was gone. I thought of all the people who insult me, and how inevitable it was that they'd do it in front of you again. I thought about how you'd react to that and whether your career could survive yet another blowup in my defense."

The memory of that moment left her dizzy and sick, and she blindly reached out for a rail or anything that could steady her on those steep, steep stairs—only to feel a broad, strong hand gripping hers tightly and another spread wide on her hip, bracing her against her own disorientation.

He wouldn't let her fall. Even now, after what she'd done, he wouldn't let her fall, and she had to swallow back a sob at the devastating sweetness of that.

"The thought of leaving you gutted me, Alex. *G-gutted* me." Despite her best efforts, her voice broke, and tears slipped out from under her eyelids. "But I told myself I needed to be selfless, because your career was more important than my heart. More important than me."

Another muffled roar rumbled through the night, and she bit her lip.

"So I decided your future for you. I left so you'd accept the job offer." When she bowed her head, more tears dripped to the stairs below, unseen. "That wasn't my right, and I'm so sorry."

Her chest was hitching hard, and she tried to calm her breathing. Calm herself.

He finally spoke, his voice choked and rough, his hand still firm in hers. "You've explained and apologized. If you want my forgiveness, you have it. But if that's the only reason you're here—"

"It's not. Maybe it should be, but it's not." She opened her eyes to meet his, allowing her tears to fall freely as she pled for her own future. Her own desires. Her own happiness. "I'm miserable without you, Alex. Absolutely desolate. And I can't keep giving away pieces of myself, or there won't be anything left. Not even my heart, because it's yours now. All of it."

His fingers clenched against her hip, his hold almost painful, and she welcomed it. Welcomed how his gaze turned open and bright with tears, welcomed the labored way he swallowed.

He was watching her with something like—wonder.

Like he'd wished on all those stars above and below them, and he'd wished for *her*.

"I love you. I *love* you." Through a thick throat, she forced out what they both needed to hear. "And I'm important, which means what I want is important, and so is my love. If you choose me over your career and the future you could have had without me, so be it. That's your decision, and if that's the only way I can have you, it's what I want too."

From the dazed disbelief and affection in his expression, the softness of his mouth as he gazed at her, she knew the answer to her next question. But she had to ask anyway, because he deserved a voice, and she deserved the words.

"I've told you what happened that night and why. I've apologized. I've told you how I feel and what I want for myself." She was clutching his hand so tightly, her fingers were going numb, but she didn't care. If it were up to her, she'd never let him go again. "Now I need to know what you want."

He licked his lips, and the sheen gleamed for only a moment before the overhead lights flickered out, leaving them in moonlit darkness.

Didn't matter. She wasn't moving anywhere anytime soon, unless he made her.

"I visited my mom this week," he said slowly, his brow furrowed once more. "She told me exactly the same thing you did, that what happened to her wasn't my fault. She also told me to stop sabotaging myself out of guilt. Which I hadn't—I hadn't realized I was doing. Not consciously."

His hand trembled slightly, and she held it even harder.

"But she was right." His lips quirked. "She's always right. Much like you. It's all extremely irritating and highly unfair."

At that spark of quintessential *Alex-ness*, she had to smile.

"So now I'm trying to think things through a bit more carefully. With a future in mind. Because maybe I don't deserve so much success, but I don't *not* deserve it either. I work hard, and I haven't done anything unforgivable. Which means . . ." He lifted a shoulder. "I'm going to attempt to get out of my own fucking way. Unless something is a matter of conscience and there's no other way to deal with whatever the problem is, I'll try not to blow up my life. For the sake of my mom and the charity and Dina, but also for me."

Oh, thank goodness. Thank *goodness*.

Or, rather, thank his mom, who'd been able to get through to him when no one else could. If he still wanted Lauren in his life after tonight, she was putting Linda on speed dial. Immediately.

"I like what I do. I like my career." He huffed out a half laugh. "I'd like to keep having one."

She laughed too, giddy with relief.

"This is all a long-winded, roundabout way of saying I accepted the StreamUs offer, although it'll be my last deal with Zach as my agent. I already fired him, earlier today. And now I want to go back and fire him again, only with my fists." The force of his sudden glower should have set the nearby succulents afire. When Lauren opened her mouth, though, he raised a staying hand. "But I won't. Again, in deference to my long-neglected self-preservation instincts."

His thumb on her hip moved in a small arc. A subtle caress, potent enough to make her shiver despite her lingering flush of exertion.

"I'd still prefer to have you on the road with me. But I won't make it a condition of my acceptance unless you want me to, because that's not fair to you, and I'm sorry." His eyes met hers directly, lines carved deep between his brows. "You should be able to freely decide whether to accompany me or not, and you can't do that if my answer depends on yours. I also shouldn't have made such a huge decision about our future without talking to you first or asking what you actually *wanted*. Which is a failing you and I evidently have in common, Wren"—he snorted softly—"and I'm sorry for that too."

He still wanted her. *He still wanted her.*

New tears spangled her vision, but she blinked them back and kept listening.

"Mom says I've always been all or nothing, and she's right." His chin tipped upward, and his tone was entirely unapologetic now.

"I'm greedy. I want it all. The job *and* you by my side every day. But no matter what you decide, we'll make it work. To echo an annoyingly wise woman: If that's the only way I can have you, it's what I want too."

On the car ride to his house, unsure whether she might find him deathly ill or bleeding from some horrible accident, she'd found herself envisioning what their future could have held, if she hadn't left. What it could still hold, if he was okay.

Panic, as it turned out, had made her priorities crystalline. It also spurred her willingness to think through all her options, not just the ones that came easily to mind. And when she considered her own happiness, not only the needs of others, what she should do had suddenly snapped into focus.

Maybe it wasn't exactly what he'd wanted, but he'd get past that. Quickly, unless she missed her guess.

"I'll come with you." When he actually gasped, his mouth dropping open in shock before splitting into the biggest grin she'd ever seen, she smiled back at him. "Not just because you want me there, but because I want to be there. I want to be with you, and I want to explore the country and the world."

"Wren!" he crowed, half rising to his feet and thrusting their joined hands into the air. "We're going to make the most awesome team anyone has ever—"

"I'm not coming as your cohost or PA," she interrupted, and he flopped back onto the bench and pouted at her. "I'll do teletherapy while you work."

Some patients couldn't come to an office or didn't want to, and she'd serve them. She'd help them, and be able to trace their progress, and hopefully emerge each day with her heart intact. She'd still do good in the world, but she wouldn't sacrifice her own happiness anymore.

"I have one more demand." When she poked his sulky lower lip with her fingertip, he kissed it. "You're not going to like it, but you're going to listen, and you're going to agree to it."

This time, his snort was loud and lusty. "Shrew."

He was grinning again, though, and his hand on her hip was exploring now. Gliding over her belly, along her thigh.

"When you look like I do, cruelty is unavoidable." His hand stilled on her leg, and she covered it with her own. "People will say terrible things. And when that happens, I want you to let me deal with it. You won't need to defend me, because I'll defend myself."

Because she was important. Too important to let herself be abused without consequence.

It was killing him not to interject. She could feel it in the twitch of his fingers, see it in the agitated rock of his body. But he let her speak without interruption, and she loved him for that too.

"I still won't give the unkindness of others unnecessary space in my life. If I got angry every time someone insulted me, I'd spend my life that way, and I don't want that for myself." The pain and rage in his eyes were for her, she knew. All for her, and she stroked his cheek in thanks. "But I also don't want to act as if cruelty toward me is acceptable and doesn't merit pushback. So I'll set boundaries and consequences, and we can talk those through ahead of time. Maybe if a fan is rude, we walk away immediately. If someone in the press says something offensive, we refuse to cooperate with their outlet in the future."

Some of the vibrating tension in his frame eased, and his shoulders dropped.

But his lips were still pursed tight as he looked up at her, his disapproval more than evident. "Wren—"

"Alex." She cupped his bristly cheek in her palm, the searing heat against her fingers mute evidence of his outrage. "Honey, please trust that I'll advocate for myself. Please trust *me*, even though I know I've given you good reason not to."

He closed his eyes and let out a shuddering breath. "You are the absolute *worst*."

Suddenly he was tugging her closer, until she stood between his knees, their faces almost level. And she would have kissed him—she desperately *wanted* to kiss him—but he was still grumbling, in typical Alex Woodroe fashion.

"You complete, raging *harpy*." His caressing fingers somewhat undercut the impact of his aggrieved glare, but only partially. "When you put it that way, there's nothing I can do but agree, right? Because if I don't, I'm saying I don't trust you. And we both know I do, and always have. I mean, for fuck's sake, I trust you so much, I tattooed your first words to me on my fucking *forearm*—"

She gasped, jerking in his grasp. *"What?"*

"—even though you dumped my ass in a goddamn *hotel room*. Which, to be fair, I maybe kinda deserved, but—"

She clapped a hand over his mouth. "Go back to the tattoo part, Woodroe."

This time, she knew to expect it. His tongue swirled over her palm, and although the wet heat and sinuous motion arrowed straight between her legs, she only raised a brow.

"So demanding," he complained when she removed her hand, but his mouth had curved into a smug, self-satisfied grin. "I stole that note you wrote to the B and B housekeeper and kept all the sticky notes you left for me at the house, so I had all the necessary words in your handwriting. And this morning, before I left for the airport, I had them tattooed on my forearm as a reminder."

Try as she might to follow him, she was lost. "I don't—I don't understand."

"I know who you are. The first thing you said to me." His smile

faded into solemnity, and his eyes were bright and earnest in the moonlight. "And you do. You know who I am, and you told me I was a good man. Since I trust you, that means it must be true. And now, if I doubt myself, I only have to look at my arm. For the rest of my life."

Carefully, he pushed up the sleeve of his Henley and exposed his left inner forearm, now covered by some sort of clear, shiny bandage.

Beneath that protection lay her words. In her writing. Tattooed onto his body in what appeared to be green ink with a hint of blue, although it was hard to tell in the darkness.

She kicked out a leg, then waved an arm, and the lights illuminated overhead, and yes.

His tattoo was the exact color of her eyes.

She covered her own mouth with the back of her hand, but only managed to half stifle her sob.

He'd essentially branded her words on his skin. And he'd done it that morning, before she'd appeared at his door, even though she'd left him so abruptly and with no good explanation. He'd done it with no expectation of her ever seeing it. He'd done it because he believed in her more than she'd ever believed in herself.

The profound sweetness of his gesture racked through her in another sob, and he gathered her close with his right arm, until his shoulder absorbed her tears.

She sniffled. "Is—is that a soul mark?"

With a gentle hand against her wet cheek, he raised her face to his. Then he kissed her, trembling mouth to trembling mouth. She tasted saline and sweetness, saw entire beaches of rainbow glass behind her closed eyes, felt the warmth of her silk blanket in the curve of his lips against her own.

"I fucking love you, Wren, and you're obviously my soulmate."

He leaned his forehead against hers. "Of course it's a goddamn soul mark. Have I taught you nothing, you obtuse harpy?"

Delightful. Asshole.

If she didn't love him so damn much, she'd wash his mouth out with soap, just like the killjoy nanny he'd once accused her of being. But his name was irrevocably embedded in each insistent *thump-thump* of her now-full heart, so instead she simply kissed him back.

And truly, it was the only reliable way to shut him up.

Rating: Teen And Up Audiences

Fandoms: Gods of the Gates – E. Wade, Gods of the Gates (TV)

Relationships: Cupid/Original Character

Additional Tags: Alternate Universe – Soulmates, Soulmate-Identifying Marks, Tooth-Rotting Fluff, Cupid Is Extra, Happy Ending

Stats: Words: 509 Chapters: 1/1 Comments: 8 Kudos: 54 Bookmarks: 9

Rainbow
RobinUnleashed

Summary:

Robin has lived in black-and-white so long, she's forgotten color even exists for others, people who've found their soulmates. Then she meets Cupid, and everything changes.

Notes:

You said you didn't need a present, but I disagreed.

Thank you to AeneasLovesLavinia for the beta read.

———————————————

The man is ludicrously handsome. She might even say he's *offensively* handsome. He's smug too, with a sly grin and a wicked twinkle in his eyes. She can't determine the color of those eyes, but whatever the color is, it's surely beautiful, like the rest of him.

No doubt *he* can see the many shades comprising his agile body and perfect features, because a man like him has to have a soulmate. A man like him has surely met that soulmate and caused her a great deal of bother, despite the happy future awaiting them.

He settles in the seat designated for patients in the triage room, one ankle crossed over his opposite knee, as if he came to the ER for an idle chat.

"What seems to be the problem?" she asks in her normal unflappable-nurse voice.

"I'm researching for a role. I need to speak with hospital employees, and I didn't want to wait until Monday to get permission from the administrators." He leans in close, as if sharing a secret. "I'm not always the most patient of men, Nurse . . ." He glances at her name badge. "Robin."

Now she recognizes him. The man in front of her is Cupid, an award-winning actor who's famously talented, famously gorgeous, famously wealthy, and simply . . . famous.

But in her ER, that doesn't matter.

She stares at him stonily. "If you're not injured or ill, I'll have to ask you to leave."

"Killjoy." He sighs and rolls his eyes at her. "Fine, then. My heart is hurting. Do something about it, Nurse Wretched."

She fights the urge to roll her own eyes. "I believe that's Nurse Ratched."

"I said what I said." That obnoxious grin is back.

So she asks him to roll up his crisp white shirtsleeve, and she prepares to take his blood pressure. Only—

The standard, rote procedure has never felt like this before. The contact with his arm zings through her with surprising heat. *Alarming* heat.

"Oh, my goodness," she whispers.

Cupid jerks away and stares at his arm as if it betrayed him.

"Ridiculous," he says, and then it happens.

He gives a choked-off exclamation and flaps his arm, as if in pain, but she can't pay him the attention a nurse should right now. She can only feel what's happening on her own arm.

Robin gasps at the sensation she's been waiting for her whole life, the sensation she never actually *expected* to feel.

The letters appear one by one on her forearm in an unfamiliar, messy scrawl.

As a child, she imagined those letters might itch and burn, might feel foreign on the skin, but they don't.

They're a caress instead, a tender stroke of her flesh. They're as ridiculously beautiful as him, each one a rainbow of jewel tones frosted like sea glass.

Ridiculous. It's a lamentable soul mark, to be sure, but it's hers.

When she looks up, his gray eyes are wide, his cheeks flushed a vivid pink.

He's her soulmate. *Her soulmate.*

It's a shame he's such a pain in the ass.

EPILOGUE

VIKA ANDRICH GLANCED AT HER NOTES FOR THE NEXT question, and Lauren braced herself.

"Tell me about the experience of filming with Carah Brown, Alex." The blogger leaned toward the couch where Alex and Lauren were seated thigh to thigh. "You two had a few key scenes together in *Gods of the Gates*, but now you're on the road in each other's company for weeks at a time. How has that been?"

Lauren's heart rate slowed once more.

Marcus had encouraged Alex and Lauren to accept Vika's invitation for a New Year's Day interview, and Francine—now Alex's agent too—had concurred. *She's sharp but not unkind*, Francine said. *She'll do right by you both, and a joint interview is a good way to appease your audience's curiosity on your own terms and help guide coverage of your relationship.*

So they'd said yes, but Lauren was still watchful. So was Alex, especially since they hadn't been given the interview questions ahead of time.

If something went awry, though, Lauren could handle it, and she intended to prove that. To herself and Alex both.

But this was another question that didn't require her input. Even better, it was one Alex could answer without hesitation and with total honesty. Unlike, say, Vika's queries about the final season of *Gods of the Gates*—which had just finished airing and been shredded by fans and critics alike—and whether he still wrote fanfic. Which he did, under the anonymous handle Pegosaurus, as part of the Cupid's Cuties community. But he couldn't tell Vika that.

He could, however, rave about Carah.

"She's fucking awesome," he declared with a grin, one Lauren knew was heartfelt.

On and off camera, the two former *Gates* costars bounced off each other like the good friends they were. Together, they'd made the show exactly what they wanted it to be.

Each episode took place in a new town or city. They explored its sights together, driving everywhere in one of Carah's many sports cars, bickering amiably the entire time. In each location, she tried a trademark regional food on camera while he highlighted a local charity. The production donated to that charity, and so did he. So did Carah. So did plenty of their viewers.

"We have a great time, and I think that's obvious to our audience," he summed up after a characteristically long-winded discussion of Carah's greatness. "I've never had more fun filming. Ever."

Vika smiled at them. "As cohosts, you and Carah are there for every episode. But other people often join your expeditions as well. Including you, Lauren. Can you tell me more about how that decision was made?"

Lauren's turn had finally arrived.

Alex squeezed her hand in mute encouragement, which she appreciated but didn't need. After a few months on the road with the television crew, she'd become largely accustomed to having cameras pointed in her direction and large chunks of her life available for public perusal. And after a few more months with her therapist, she had tactics for dealing with these sorts of situations and a good grip on what truly mattered to her.

She might be nervous, her fingers trembling, but she was also ready.

No matter how this interview went, she wouldn't read the response on social media. No matter how this interview went, Alex wouldn't detonate, because he too had been working with a therapist and learning to—as he'd put it—get out of his own fucking way.

No matter how this interview went, he'd still love her, and she'd still love herself.

That was enough. That was everything.

"Well, most of Alex's best friends are famous, so having them show up on camera isn't precisely a hardship for the production." She smiled slightly, using what Alex called her *Santa Ana voice*. "But I'm not famous, of course, at least not in my own right, and that's true for others who've joined us too."

The rotating cast of friends and family who accompanied them on the road had been an unexpected joy, piercing in its sweetness. Some shoots, depending on scheduling needs, Marcus and April or other former costars might come along. Dina. His mother. Sionna, who now rented Alex's guesthouse for the same price as the turreted duplex she and Lauren had once shared.

Even, occasionally, Lauren's parents, once they'd all gotten over the awkwardness of discussing why she wouldn't apologize to Ron and didn't intend to have any contact with him in the future. Aunt Kathleen hadn't spoken to her in over two months, and her mom and Aunt Kathleen still hadn't entirely reconciled, but so be it. If Lauren's parents chose to put her comfort before their own, she had to believe—she *did* believe—she was worth that sacrifice.

After that fraught conversation with her mom and dad, they'd started making an effort to see her, rather than assuming she'd always come to them. So whenever the show stopped relatively near California, her parents were likely to appear on camera.

And at some point during most episodes, so was she. Generally she stayed in the background, just another visitor on a tour, just another tourist taking photos. Just another explorer discovering the world and finding magic wherever she roamed, in between teletherapy appointments conducted in comfortable hotel suites.

Seeing clients long-term suited her, as she'd discovered. Tracing their progress and helping them surmount obstacles in their lives and minds week by week . . . it was hard but satisfying work, and it didn't leave her scraped empty at the end of each day.

In fact, her life overflowed with so much friendship and love and warmth and adventure, she could afford to share some of it with an unseen audience.

Normally, she didn't let herself be dragged directly in front of the cameras, but sometimes she did. By Sionna, or Carah, or— most often—Alex.

At their urgings, she'd take a deep breath, tilt her chin high, and describe what she'd seen that day, and she'd do so with absolutely no neutral remove. As a participant in her own life, rather than a spectator. Then Alex and Carah would tease her until she scowled at them and snorted with laughter.

In the third episode, Lauren had even kissed him on camera. Caught up in their usual banter, she'd forgotten their audience. But when she remembered, she didn't shy away from his arms clasping her tight, because she wasn't ashamed of herself or of him, and she refused to act as if she were.

"Here's how Alex and I think about it." Lauren took a sip of water, still smiling at Vika. "*Unleashed* isn't just a show. It's our lives on camera. And we want to share our lives with the people who matter to us, so we'll always welcome our friends and family on set. We'll always encourage them to come as often as they can and stay as long as they can, because their presence is a joy. We're also grateful for StreamUs's support of that decision and their help coordinating everyone's schedules."

There. She'd answered the question without fumbling her words, and her hands weren't shaking anymore.

She could do this. With Alex at her side, she could do anything at all.

FOR A MOMENT, Alex could only stare at her beloved face, awash with pride.

Her answer had been confident and clear. More than that, though, it was diplomatic and thoughtful and sincere and kind.

It was Wren, laid bare to the world.

He pressed a kiss to her cheek, then forced himself to turn back to Vika. "Yeah, filming with our friends and family is great. Especially when a bunch of them can visit at the same time, like in Vegas."

Vika leaned forward. "Speaking of Las Vegas . . ."

Well, they'd both known *this* was coming.

"So far, your Gold Coast visit with your mother is your most-viewed episode." She was nearly vibrating with eagerness, her expression avid and delighted. "But I suspect the upcoming Sin City episode will surpass those numbers. Care to tell our viewers why?"

The Gold Coast trip remained special to him for so many reasons. The pleasure of revisiting treasured sights from his childhood. The extended time he got to spend with his mom, all without a decade of grief and guilt tainting their love for one another. The way she'd adored Wren. The moment she'd told the camera, tears pooling in her gray eyes, that she was so proud of him it hurt sometimes, and he'd cried a little too.

But even with all those amazing memories, yes, Vegas was better. Not just the highlight of the show, the highlight of his fucking *life*.

"*Ahhhhhhh.* Good question." Grinning like the fool he was, he kissed the top of Wren's head and breathed in the familiar scent of coconut. "During our trip to Las Vegas, after countless weeks of pleading and lamenting my lost virtue, I finally got Lauren here to make an honest man out of me. On Christmas Day, because I'm clearly the most enticing present imaginable."

You're my wish come true, Wren, he'd told her in their blackout-curtained suite on the Strip, resting naked in her warm arms after one of their very frequent and delightful pegging interludes. *Please be mine forever. Please make me yours.*

They'd called everyone the next morning, and three days later, he became Mr. Wren Clegg. Or, rather, still Alex Woodroe, but they both knew that was just a formality.

"The hundredth time he complained about how cheap he felt, I couldn't take anymore, Vika," Lauren said, completely deadpan. "It was either a ring or a muzzle."

The frown was hard to muster, but he tried anyway. "Why was I not told about the muzzle option? We both know I enjoy—"

Her hand covered his mouth, and she spoke over him. "It was a lovely ceremony, and we're delighted so many of our friends and family could come on such short notice."

His mom and her parents. All his *Gates* castmates, other than Ian. Sionna. Dina.

Everyone had gathered in the small, lovely hotel chapel and watched Alex and Wren walk down the aisle arm in arm, because fuck tradition. They'd begin as they meant to go on. Together.

When he licked her palm, her thighs pressed together, but her face remained placid as she added, "Just think of how much money we saved on videography services, Vika."

Very dry. Very practical. Very Wren.

But he'd seen her blink back tears as they'd exchanged vows, just like him.

"My heartfelt congratulations to you both, and best wishes for a lifetime of happiness together." Vika's smile was soft. "Lauren, I noticed your necklace, and I wondered whether it was a wedding gift. It's quite unusual, isn't it?"

"One of a kind." Wren smiled back at her. "Just like my husband."

Since she wasn't a tattoo person, and he wouldn't pressure her to do anything that made her uncomfortable, he'd given her a necklace to wear over her heart. A platinum chain with a feather pendant, which he'd had inscribed with the word RIDICULOUS and studded with aquamarines the color of her eyes.

"You're not ridiculous," he'd told her when she opened the velvet box. "But I am. Ridiculously in love with you."

Except in the shower, she never took it off, to his continued smug delight.

Still, he'd itched to give her something else too, something she chose for herself, so right before their wedding, he'd begged her to name something—anything—she wanted. And to his absolute bewilderment, she'd promptly requested a bathrobe made from the same cotton fabric he used for his towels.

"One that fits me right," she'd specified. "I eyed that robe in the guesthouse for months, wishing it came in my size."

He'd stared at her, entirely nonplussed. "It *is* in your size, Wren. I called Dina while we were in Spain and had it made before your arrival. Why the fuck would I give you a robe that didn't fit you?"

"Oh." Her face had turned delectably pink. "I guess I shouldn't have assumed."

When he'd demanded an apology in nonverbal, naked form, she'd happily obliged.

"And what did you give *him* as a wedding gift?" Vika asked.

Once more, Wren smiled. "I wrote him a love letter."

"Oh, how sweet." Vika pressed a hand to her heart, beaming.

Since his reunion with Wren, the two of them had acted out so many of his favorite fics. They'd kissed for science. Banged once, to get it out of their systems. Pretended their marriage was arranged, then accidental. Last week, they'd even acted out the body-swap trope, with surprisingly hilarious results.

Wren had strutted around their fucking house like a goddamn peacock, spouting absolute bullshit the whole time and tearing off her shirt at every conceivable opportunity.

He'd never admit it, but *damn*. She could have won a fucking *award* for that portrayal.

She understood him. And because she did, for his wedding gift, she'd written him a story on AO3, featuring the two of them as her OTP.

Well, officially Cupid and Robin, but they both knew better.

The story was perfect. Better than anything she could have bought, because really, what the fuck did he need other than her love?

Nothing. Absolutely nothing.

"One more question, and then we'll get to the reader's poll, which ends . . ." Vika nodded to her assistant, who tapped her cell screen. "Now. They've chosen the final topic of the interview, and even I haven't seen the results. It'll be a surprise to all of us."

Huh. That seemed . . . potentially problematic, since some people were total assholes.

"Alex . . ." Vika's brow furrowed. "You've had a tumultuous past year."

If she hadn't asked a question like this, he would have been surprised. Happy, but surprised. He had his answer ready, once she was done talking.

She ticked off the events on her fingers. "There was an arrest. An attempted attack on the red carpet. An altercation with a fan. Professional censure and lost roles. A hit new show. A surprise wedding."

"There was also love." He stroked Lauren's tensing neck. "You left that out."

"I did." The blogger inclined her head. "That said, given some of the less-positive events that occurred, do you have any regrets?"

Of course he did. Over the last year, he'd inconvenienced and scared and hurt so many people he loved. And although he'd forgiven himself for not walking away, he couldn't exactly applaud his decision to keep playing Cupid in that terrible final season.

But his regrets were his own, and they were his to keep. And if they'd brought him to Wren, he'd bear their weight gladly.

So he told his first lie of the entire interview. "Nope. No regrets."

Vika's sharp glance revealed her skepticism, but she didn't push. She likely knew there was no point, not unless she wanted the interview to end prematurely.

And it wasn't a *total* falsehood, really. When it came to his arrest, he still had zero regrets. None. The people who mattered either knew exactly what had happened or understood he wouldn't have thrown punches without a damn good reason.

Everyone else could go fuck themselves.

"Okay." Vika gave a tiny shrug and let it go. "Time for our final question, formulated and selected by my readers."

Her assistant handed over the cell phone. Vika's lips moved slightly as she read the poll results, and she frowned.

There was a long pause.

"I'll be honest." The blogger sighed. "I don't love the question."

Wren's thigh against his didn't twitch. Her shoulder under his palm remained loose. Her eyes were clear and curious and unafraid.

"Whatever your readers asked will be fine." The steady confidence in Wren's voice couldn't be faked, and he decided to trust it. To trust her ability to weather whatever was about to happen. "Go ahead, Vika."

"What would you say to people who believe there's no way a marriage like yours, between two such different people, can possibly last?" Vika pinched the bridge of her nose and shook her head. "I'm sorry. Please feel free not to answer."

His skull began pounding.

He and Wren had different personalities and came from different backgrounds. Fair enough. But this question wasn't about that, really, and everyone in the room understood its unspoken, unkind implications.

The question was a veiled swipe at how she looked. It was a prediction that their marriage would fail because the public considered him—and not her—attractive.

His face was turning hot, his breathing fast, but he bit his tongue. Hard.

Wren laid a cool, steady hand over his. "I'll take this one, Alex."

Please trust that I'll advocate for myself, she'd said on those stairs months ago, his cheek cradled in her palm. *Please trust* me.

He took a deep breath. Another.

Then he nodded, a mute invitation for her to handle it.

After that, she didn't hesitate.

"Please excuse my profanity, Vika," she said calmly, "but in the immortal words of my husband: Those people can go fuck themselves."

Vika gasped, and his mouth dropped open for a moment too, because—*Wren*, of all people? *Wren* had invited untold thousands of people to fuck themselves?

And then, jubilant, he tugged his wife into his arms and squeezed her tight and laughed in her ear. Loudly. Unkind observers might even have called it a *cackle*.

When he pulled back and raised his hand for a high five, she returned it.

"Big Harpy Energy!" he shouted, and it echoed through their home. "Big Harpy Goddamn Energy, Wren!"

She inclined her head. "The Crone Arts student has become the Crone Arts master."

Her smile was serene and proud, and he loved her so fucking much, the sheer volume and force of it should have split him wide open.

THE NEXT DAY, despite Vika's doubts, Alex convinced her not to edit out the final question.

Three days later, her audience saw the interview in its entirety.

And ten minutes after that, the first new fan account— @LaurenCleggFTW—went live.

ACKNOWLEDGMENTS

THE FACT THAT I EMERGED FROM 2020—AKA THE CURSÈD Year of Doom—somewhat intact is entirely due to my friends and family. Those friends consistently emailed, DMed, FaceTimed, and wrote letters and postcards to remind me I was loved and never as isolated as I sometimes felt, and their efforts meant everything to me. I owe special thanks to Therese Beharrie, Emma Barry, and Mia Sosa, who kept me tethered to the world outside my Swedish apartment and who always, always cared about my well-being. You are so dear to me. Thank you.

My husband, as always, accepted me precisely as I am and did his damnedest to support me however he could. My daughter's pride and faith in me, her unstinting affection and joy and humor, lit the dark Swedish winter. My mom devoted so much time and effort to sending care packages of potato buns, Utz pretzels, and rocks (of course) across the Atlantic. She knew my long absence from the U.S. hurt me, so she cushioned the blow with each over-stuffed box, and I'm so grateful. I love you all.

I'm also very, very thankful to Elle Keck, Kayleigh Webb, and everyone else at Avon who worked so hard to make this book shine. Poor Elle had to accomplish some brilliant feats of editing with this manuscript, and I'm still not entirely sure how she managed to wrestle it down to a reasonable length while keeping everything I love about the story intact. Witchcraft, maybe?

As always, my amazing agent Sarah Younger has been indefatigable in her support. It means the world to me to have her in my corner, always.

Leni Kauffman created the most beautiful cover imaginable. I can't stop staring at it. It's not only gorgeous, but also perfect for and specific to the story, and I can't thank her enough.

I couldn't have written this story without a great deal of help. Susannah Erwin spent untold hours talking to me about California in general and L.A. in particular, and her incredible patience and generosity shaped *All the Feels* in countless ways. Erin generously shared her experiences as an emergency services clinician with me, and those experiences helped ground Lauren's character in reality. Shannon Bothwell planned one hell of a kick-ass road trip for Alex and Lauren, and I'm so grateful for her guidance. Once the story was written, Susannah, Therese, and Emma all tackled my 126,000-word behemoth of a draft and offered such insightful feedback—and Emma even read the book a second time once it was edited down to a manageable length, because she is one of the most giving people I've ever met.

Melissa Vera, Meryl Wilsner, and Brina Starler were kind enough to read the story and make sure Alex's character and experiences rang true to them, and I'm beyond thankful for their time and thoughtfulness.

Finally, I want to thank all my readers, and especially those who tweeted to me or emailed me about *Spoiler Alert*. Your kindness helped me through a tough, tough year, and I hope my stories provide you with joy and distraction when you need both. Hugs and love to you. ♥

Don't miss Olivia Dade's
delightfully fun romcom ...

'An absolute joy from the first page to the last'
Jen DeLuca

'*Spoiler Alert* is a delight. April and Marcus will melt your heart'
Jenny Holiday

Available from

PIATKUS

Praise for *Spoiler Alert*

"Dade delivers and then some. This book frolics through fields of fannish allusion and metatext. . . . It takes a skillful writer to juggle so many elements, yet the emotional through-line shines clear and strong at every point."

—*New York Times Book Review*

"With richly drawn characters you'll love to root for, Olivia Dade's books are a gem of the genre—full of humor, heart, and heat."

—Kate Clayborn, author of *Love Lettering*

"Olivia Dade is consistently one of my favorite authors. Her writing is warm and witty, frequently funny and often achingly poignant. She has a knack for creating sympathetic characters who leap off the page, with their vulnerable hearts and relatable struggles."

—Lucy Parker, author of *Battle Royal*

"Olivia Dade writes with such compassion and kindness for her characters, and, in the process, makes you want to live in the world she creates."

—Jenny Holiday, *USA Today* bestselling author

Praise for *All the Feels*

"An absolutely witty, swoon-worthy behind-the-scenes romp! Delightful from beginning to end!"

—Julie Murphy,
#1 *New York Times* bestselling author of *Dumplin'*

"*All the Feels* leaves you swooning and eager for more!"
—Denise Williams, author of *How to Fail at Flirting*

"Joyful, clever, and full of heart, with two irresistible characters whose connection is both gorgeously sweet and wildly hot. Mixing riotous humor and aching tenderness, *All the Feels* is all the things I love about romance. Olivia Dade has jumped to the top of my auto-buy list!"

—Rachel Lynn Solomon,
nationally bestselling author of *The Ex Talk*

"If you're a fan of romances that feature nuanced protagonists, whip-smart dialogue, scorching chemistry, and sidesplitting humor, look no further than Olivia Dade's books. This author is an absolute gem!"

—Mia Sosa,
USA Today bestselling author of *The Worst Best Man*

"Olivia Dade is so gentle with her characters, giving them each the space to become their best selves while also being loved for all their flaws. *All the Feels* is hilarious and poignant at the same time."
—Cat Sebastian, author of *The Queer Principles of Kit Webb*

"I adore *All the Feels*. This slow-burn romance had me falling in love every step of the way."
—Meryl Wilsner, author of *Something to Talk About*

"Olivia Dade once again delivers a book as sexy and charming as it is cathartic. Her books speak to my soul as she deftly tackles complicated subjects with humor, heart, and infinite kindness. I adored *All the Feels* and can't wait to see what she writes next. Olivia Dade is an auto-buy author!"

—Jessie Mihalik, author of *Chaos Reigning*